POSEIDON'S CHILDREN

Cover art and illustrations: Matthew Perry
Cover art (inspired by *The Evil Dead* movie poster)
and illustrations in this book
Copyright © 2012 Matthew Perry & Seventh Star Press, LLC.

Editor: Amanda DeBord

Published by Seventh Star Press, LLC.

ISBN Number 9781937929954

Library of Congress Control Number: 2012933493

Seventh Star Press
www.seventhstarpress.com
info@seventhstarpress.com

Publisher's Note:
Poseidon's Children is a work of fiction. All names, characters, and
places are the product of the author's imagination, used in fictitious
manner. Any resemblances to actual persons, places, locales, events, etc.
are purely coincidental.

Printed in the United States of America

First Edition

To Sara Larson, one of my best and dearest friends,
who was my guiding star on this long and turbulent voyage,
and to whom I am forever indebted.

And dedicated to the memory of Stan Winston,
who understood that creatures could be characters
rather than monsters.

The sea has never been friendly to man.
-Joseph Conrad

and the chill of the ocean on her back. "I'm sorry."

"For what?"

She lifted her head, raked a dripping curtain of bangs to one side so she could look into his eyes. "For being so neurotic."

"You're fine."

Susan smiled at him. "You're sweet."

David smiled back, grew quiet for a moment, hesitant, and then he said, "Move in with me."

She giggled. "Yeah, right."

"I'm serious."

And he was; Susan saw it in his eyes. "What about your father?"

"I'd rather sleep with you."

She smirked and touched her forehead to his. "What would your father say about you shackin' up with a girl you've only known for two seconds?"

David shrugged and his breath warmed her face. "As long as Dad gets decent grades in the mail instead of arrest reports, he just signs the checks. He's only come to see me once in the last three years, and even then he acted like I should've been honored because he took a couple of hours off from trying to rule the world."

"So he doesn't care...or you're not gonna tell him?"

"I'm one of his stocks. As long as I'm not costing him too much money or reputation, he doesn't give a shit."

"I'm sorry."

"Don't be." Below the waves, his hidden fingers stroked her hips. "Just tell me you'll do it."

Susan chewed her lower lip. The answer was there, begging to be spoken, and yet part of her mind wanted to quash it.

He hasn't even said that he loves you.

True, he'd never said the words, but he'd made it known in so many other ways. As soon as the semester ended, he whisked her away from Stanley University, flew her to this island resort where he catered to her every need, and —

And you love it.

Yes, she did, every minute of it. She only wished this fairytale didn't have to end. Maybe it didn't.

Susan allowed herself to say, "Yes."

He smiled. "Really?"

"Yes."

They kissed. It started out tender, but it didn't take long for it to turn passionate, ravenous — David's tongue dancing with hers. Susan felt his fingers leave her hips, felt them slide across her bikini briefs; they pushed the fabric aside, probed her most sensitive anatomy. David then pulled at his own swim trunks, yanked them down to free his burgeoning erection. She gasped and closed her eyes as he moved inside her. Their coupling mirrored their kiss; the rhythm was slow at first, gentle, building until they were splashing about in the tide.

Even if he never said it, no one had ever loved her more.

Susan gripped David's shoulders, screamed at the stars, and, when she opened her eyes, she saw that the voyeur moon held them in its spotlight. She glanced around, embarrassed, but saw no one. Over at the pier, even the seagulls were gone.

I must've scared them off.

She giggled and sighed. "My God, babe...that was amazing."

He kissed her chin. "*You're* amazing."

Susan looked back down at him. For a moment, she saw great tenderness, then his eyes flared with panic. His mouth opened in a primal scream as something wrenched him from Susan's embrace. She grabbed hold of his hands, tried to keep him afloat, and a dark shape broke the surf — a jagged dorsal fin that cut through the tide like a saw blade.

Shark, her brain shrieked. *A shark's got him!*

The sea around her warmed with blood. David's blood. His hands went limp, slipped from her grasp. She watched her lover disappear beneath the waves, watched the fin behind him thrash as its owner fed, then she turned and swam away, swam for her own life, her head above water, crying out again and again.

In the shadow buildings that lined distant sands, a window ignited.

Someone heard me!

She slogged toward shore, toward light and its promise of security, but the water fought her, strapped heavy weights across her thighs. "Help me! Please, help me!"

A hand.

It grabbed her by the ankle, so forceful, so *strong*. *David? No. It can't be him. He's* gone.

It pulled her under.

Susan fell forward, did a belly flop into the surf. She clawed at the sand, but found nothing to hold on to. She kicked, writhed and twisted as she tried to squirm free, and instead came face to face with her attacker. Light swept over it — moonbeam or searchlight, she didn't know which — and bubbles exploded from her mouth and nostrils in a muffled scream.

Susan Rogers had been right to fear the water. There *were* monsters lurking just below its churning surface. Now, they pulled her down into the dark depths; things with black and orange stripes, things with claws, with fangs like sharpened steak knives, and, unfortunately for her, they were not inclined to swallow her whole.

TWO

From his balcony, Larry Neuhaus aimed a flashlight down into the tide. He saw a woman there, near the beach, her hands clawing at the sand, and, when he jerked the light back a bit more, saw the shadowy form of her attacker.

A man?

No. Not a man. A large fin broke the surface, submerging as quickly as it appeared.

Jesus!

Larry ran back into his room. Peggy stood beside their bed, covering her nakedness with a robe. He almost hurried past her without saying a word, but she stopped him. "Where are you going?"

"She needs help." Larry unlocked the door and threw it open; a DO NOT DISTURB sign swung from the knob. "Call the police."

Peggy reached for the phone. "What's happening?"

"Shark attack!" He bolted for the staircase; three flights, the lobby and main entrance all went by in a blur. He heard the sound of distant sirens as he sprinted across the still-warm pavement, but he knew they would arrive too late.

He might already be too late.

Larry darted into the cold surf. His flashlight speared tiny fish, reflected off shells and flecks of debris swirling in the turbulence, but he couldn't find the girl he'd seen from his window. He moved further out, breathing hard and trying to ignore the frantic rhythm of his heart as he paced back and forth. He clutched at his own terrycloth robe, telling himself that he was insane for doing this.

The flashlight grew dim. He shook it; its innards rattled. And then something clamped down on Larry's shoulder.

Behind him, a figure stood waist-deep in the tide, silhouetted by a flashing red and blue aura. "What's the problem, sir?"

The light re-ignited in Larry's hand and he caught sight of a silver badge pinned to the stranger's jacket.

A policeman.

Larry exhaled in relief. "There's a girl and...and a shark!"

"Sir, get out of the water."

The man's tone was so cool, and his words so calm, that Larry's panic increased. "Don't you understand? I can't find her!"

"If you keep splashing around out here, all you'll find is the shark. We need to get out of the water *now*."

Larry looked back over his shoulder at the sea, smooth as glass, endless, and the light died once more in his grasp.

•••

Peggy Hern pulled a lacy, tasseled bedspread back into place, hiding the rumpled, sweat-dampened sheets beneath, then sat on the mattress edge and covered her bony knees with her robe. Wooden posts rose from each of the bed's four corners, suspending an ornate hardwood canopy overhead. Like everything else in the Sea Mist Inn, it reminded her of a romance novel, and, as she peered through a veil of curtains to the outside balcony, her heart ached for Larry, her Romeo.

Yesterday, they'd left their New York loft and all their troubles behind...or so she thought. She should've known better. You can't run away from your problems. Wherever you go, you bring them with you.

Larry stood flanked by two officers, explaining what he'd seen and heard. One — the young, skinny policeman who'd escorted Larry back upstairs — listened and took careful notes while his companion — older and grossly overweight — studied Larry's every move. Finally, after what the clock proclaimed to be twenty minutes, and what Peggy's mind swore was an eternity, the group came in from the terrace.

The big man shook his head. "This kinda thing's rare, Mr. Neuhaus, but it happens. Whole mess o' things can go wrong in the ocean at night; 'course, there's the undertow, jellyfish too, but we ain't had a shark attack in..."

"Six years, Chief," the thinner officer said, still writing in that notebook of his.

"Been that long, has it? Point is, don't go feelin' guilty 'bout not gettin' down there sooner. There's not a damn thing you coulda done. In fact, if you hadn't been up takin' a leak —"

"Getting a drink." Larry looked past the policemen, through the French doors and into the night.

Peggy wished for the ability to read minds, to hear the thoughts and fears that Larry kept locked away from her. Was he thinking of the poor girl who died tonight? Or were his thoughts of another time, of another girl he'd been unable to save? She started to ask him if he wanted one of his pills, then thought better of it.

The chief nodded. "Right, gettin' a drink. Point is, if you hadn't been awake to hear that poor girl screamin', I s'pose we'd all got up this mornin' and been none the wiser. 'Til her family or friends reported her missin', that is."

Larry rubbed his eyes and moved to Peggy's side. "Chief Canon, this is my girlfriend, Peggy."

The chief took off his large Smoky the Bear hat. "Ma'am."

Peggy offered him a nod and tightened the belt of her robe. The hallway door opened, startling her. Their elderly innkeeper entered the room. In his hands, he held a large silver tray supporting two ceramic mugs. Peggy saw the tea within them reflected in his eyeglasses as he approached.

"This will settle your nerves," he told them.

Peggy took a mug from his shaking hand. "Thank you, Mr. DeParle."

"Oh now, you don't have to call me 'Mr. DeParle.' Sounds so damn formal. Call me Ed." He offered the second mug to Larry, then sat down on a nearby chair.

Peggy took a sip, filled with welcomed warmth, then looked up at Canon. "So what happens now?"

The chief shrugged. "Well, ma'am, the way your man tells it, we're not gonna find this little lady alive. Just a matter now of closin' down this section of beach for the next day or so and draggin' the bottom. With any luck, she wasn't carried too far out to sea and we'll find the remains.

Or, God forbid, she'll wash in with the tide."

"Nasty business," Ed declared. "I got a daughter myself. If anything happened to her..." A tear formed, and he wiped it away with a trembling finger. Canon opened his mouth to say something, but then Ed changed the subject before the chief could speak. "Anyhow, I remember some three years ago, New Year's Eve, couple o' kids got to celebratin' a bit much and decided to join that...whatcha call it — Polar Bear Club?"

Canon fired a nervous glance in Ed's direction, but the innkeeper appeared not to notice.

"It was the coldest winter even I could remember," Ed continued. "Two of the kids were islanders and they got back to shore, but the other one drowned." He looked to the Chief of Police. "Where was he from?"

Canon put his hat back on, as if to signal that it was time to leave. "Somewhere in Vermont."

Ed nodded. "Vermont. Anyhow, it was nasty business, but I guess each town's got to have its share of nastiness."

"You're probably right," Larry agreed, his voice hoarse. He took a sip of tea.

Peggy could not help but wonder if he were wishing he'd been here to rush to the rescue of those drunken kids as well. What had his therapist called it — his "Savior Complex"? At times, Larry seemed to carry the burden of the whole world's problems squarely on his shoulders. Then again, his willingness to be there for others, to be there for *her*, was what Peggy so loved about him.

Canon moved toward the door. "I hope you folks can enjoy the rest of your stay. I know this was a helluva way to start it off, but Ed'll take good care of you. He's been runnin' this inn since before I was born." He opened the door, standing off to the side so that his deputy could exit first. "You comin', Old Man?"

Ed rose to his feet. "Right behind ya."

"'Night, folks," Canon told them, then left the doorway for the darkness of the hall beyond.

The innkeeper clamped his hospitality tray in his armpit. "Just bring the cups down tomorrow and I'll take care of 'em."

Peggy offered him a smile. "Thanks, Ed."

"You folks rest comfortable now."

"I don't think sleep will be all that possible tonight." Larry's voice was a distant whisper. He must have seen the worry in Peggy's eyes, because he offered her his best attempt at a smile.

"No, I s'pose not. You folks take care."

The old man closed the door. Outside, Peggy heard his footfalls grow distant and sighed with relief that the ordeal was over. When she looked up, Larry stared at her with the same unreadable expression his face had held since his return.

"I'm beginning to feel like one of your paintings." She set her mug down and rose to her feet. "Talk to me. Tell me what you're feeling." She felt his ex-girlfriend's name building momentum behind her lips, and before she could stop herself, it was out. "Are you thinking about Natalie?"

His watery eyes sparkled in the lamplight. "I heard that girl screaming and I...I thought I was still asleep, you know? I looked up at the mirror in the bathroom and...for just a second...it was smashed."

Peggy's breath caught in her throat. She looked at his hand to make certain he hadn't put it through the glass again. No open wounds. No fresh blood. White ridges of scarring were just where they should have been after months of healing. She quietly exhaled.

Larry went on, "I just stood there...staring at a damn mirror while she was out there being eaten alive."

"Hey, it's all right." Peggy ran her fingers down his cheeks, tracing the path she thought tears might travel.

"If I'd only *moved*..." He shook his head. "I just wanted to help her."

"I know. But there wasn't anything you could have done, here or back in New York." She wrapped her arms around his waist, kissed the nape of his neck. He raised a hand to her arm, rubbed it as she spoke into his ear. "I love you. If you want to go back home, I —"

"Can't do it." His eyes still managed to restrain their tears. "Chief Canon might need to talk to me again. Besides, the room's paid for, and I'd like to do a painting of the local lighthouse."

"You're sure?" Larry seemed to be handling things well, but after his recent emotional breakdown, Peggy was unsure about staying. "I'm sure that nice innkeeper would give us a refund under the circumstances, and if Canon really needs you, we can give him our phone number. I mean, how much more can you do for him?"

"I'm positive. You heard the deputy. It was the first attack in six years. Normally, this is a quiet place."

•••

DeParle was not at all surprised to see Chief Canon waiting at the bottom of the stairs.

Canon lit the cigarette that jutted from his lips. "This is damn serious shit here, Ed."

"You don't think it was Chrissy do you?" Ed asked, and with the words came a sudden prickle of gooseflesh on his arms. Christine DeParle, his only child, had been missing for several days.

Canon was quick to respond. "No. No, I don't."

Ed still felt chilled. "Was it really a shark?"

"All I know is that girl's dead, sure as shit. Somebody from somewhere is dead." He took a drag, the tip of his cigarette glowing brightly, then exhaled.

"Whatcha gonna do, John?"

The chief glared at him. "Shit if I know, Ed. Like I said, for all we know, it might have really been a shark that got ahold o' that girl tonight."

"You don't believe that any more than I do."

Canon pointed at Ed with his cigarette, his head shrouded by a cloud of smoke. "I'll tell you what I believe, Ed. I believe, since Karl Tellstrom moved out to that shack o' his, he's been plantin' some scary seeds in folks' heads, startin' with your little girl, and somethin's gotta be done about it. I'll be damned if I know what that is, though. What kinda god puts somethin' like him on this world anyhow?"

"I've asked you before not to say things like that, John." Ed wiped the sweat from his weathered face, then licked his lips; he wished desperately that the night's events were just a nightmare. "He can hear."

Canon threw the smoldering butt of his Camel on the floor, ground it to ash with the tip of his boot. "Don't give me that religious crap. I get enough of that from your ex-wife."

"You gonna talk to Tellstrom?"

"Yeah, I'll talk to the bastard, find out what he knows about Chrissy goin' missin'."

"Thank you."

"Don't thank me 'til I bring her home." Canon scratched his belly through the khaki fabric of his shirt, then turned away and merged with the shadows. Halfway to the Inn's main entrance, he stopped and craned his head to look at the innkeeper. "They found Atlantis the other day."

Ed snorted. "Been readin' that *Weekly World News* again?"

"Nope, it's been on the TV," Canon informed him. "Unless Katie Couric got it outta *The Weekly World News*. Happened about the time Chrissy up and left."

"You think Tellstrom saw the news — told her it was a sign or somethin'? You think that's why she ran off?"

"Can't say for sure."

"But you've got your suspicions."

"I'll talk to him," the chief said. And then he continued his walk toward the entrance of the inn and the waiting darkness beyond.

Three

Few people knew true darkness like Carol Miyagi. After all, the dark of night had its stars and moon to provide faint illumination. And, even when she closed her eyes for sleep, she found her own darkness lit by dreams and the memory of light. But here, in the endless depths of the ocean, there was no dawn, no knowledge of brightness, and therefore no recollection of it.

Beyond the sun's reach, the sea had hidden away secrets — evidence of crimes it had committed against the frail craft and ancient civilizations of Man. Over time, the floor of the abyss had become a museum filled with corroding exhibits shrouded by perpetual night, a private reliquary for the ocean's inhabitants and a few daring, uninvited guests...like Carol.

She'd spent much of her life swimming through shadow — hoping, searching, and waiting...for Atlantis. And now, her search had come to a dramatic end. The sounds of the surface faded, leaving only the hiss of her regulator and the resulting gurgle of bubbles to break the silence. She aimed the wide beam of her dive light to reveal huge, long-forgotten megaliths. Remnants of the once-great city stood silently in the dim nothingness that surrounded her, patiently abiding the empty centuries.

The marine archeologist paused for a moment to check the levels in her tanks. If her mixture were low, she would need to return to the bright world above, and she hated to leave this shadowy city. Part of her was still afraid it might disappear, like Brigadoon before the dawn.

Carol had discovered the first evidence of Atlantis, a cobblestone road paved across the floor of the Mediterranean Sea, in 2004, but it had taken a little over a year for her to publish her findings. Although she held a doctorate in archeology and a master's degree in history, she did not fit comfortably into the mold of an academic. She preferred working beneath the waves to working at the keyboard. Still, the paper she wrote, claiming that this had been a trade road to a lost civilization, had made her somewhat of a celebrity, albeit a controversial one, overnight. Her continued assertion that Atlantis was more than myth, however, soon led the scientific community to dismiss her as a lunatic whose work was unworthy of serious consideration. Everyone accepted that she'd found proof of *something*, but no one knew what. Many believed Greeks or Romans had constructed the road. Others doubted it was a road at all. It didn't matter. Her newfound fame allowed her to obtain a sizable grant from the Hays Foundation, and her search continued.

Last month, she found another section of road off the coast of the Azores and followed it, finding the ancient city at a depth of just 300 feet. Rapidly cooling lava had formed a bubble around it, encapsulating the ruins in a vast underwater cavern. It might have remained there, undiscovered for another millennium, if not for a recent quake. The rocky eggshell had cracked and crumbled, revealing the object of Carol's long quest hidden within.

At first, she knew her nay-saying peers would not admit this was Atlantis, as if the mere utterance of the word would cause them physical pain, but that would change after she completed her initial survey. The archeological community would embrace her and all would be forgiven. As if she needed forgiveness. Carol did not care about fame or adulation. What she wanted was respect. She wanted the old men who dominated her field to admit that she was not a crackpot. She wanted them to say that she was right and they had always been wrong. Carol had the feeling that she would need to find frozen shards of Hell before that would happen. She swam on.

Although several of the structures had toppled, the city remained in excellent condition, showing a lack of coral growth and barnacle infestation. The ruins also exhibited a magnetic anomaly that rendered the team's compasses and some electronic equipment useless, including their dive computers. When they entered the boundaries of the city, their display screens went berserk and their digital readouts flashed 88,888 — denying any further computation of the mixture within their tanks. Luckily, they had stocked their vessel — the *Ambrosia* — with old-fashioned air gauges whose needles fell as the air supply dwindled. They were crude, and did not offer any decompression information, but at least they worked.

No big conundrum. You're floating in the middle of Atlantis, she considered, and then scolded herself for such nonsense.

There were so many myths and theories surrounding the lost continent. She'd never seen a portal to another dimension, however, and while she believed in the existence of extraterrestrials, Carol thought they had better things to do than play with compass needles. Based on the water temperature, the change in local currents, and recent seismic disturbances, she knew the same volcanic activity that had claimed the city so long ago was still at work. Undersea volcanoes were notorious for creating electromagnetic surges and wreaking havoc on equipment.

Her team of ten archeologists and graduate students were busying themselves with the preliminaries of the expedition, chief among their tasks being to map the overall city. It appeared that only two-thirds of the city had been sealed within the cavern. The missing portion was probably rubble strewn across the floor of the Atlantic, at a depth beyond the capacity of their current equipment.

Concentrate on what we have, she told herself. *Chase the rest when the next check from the Hays Foundation hits the bank.*

She'd already spent the money in her mind. Atlantis was an immense archaeological vault that contained far too many relics for her meager crew to excavate on its own. Without more manpower, it would take decades. With new financing, Carol would hire a much larger staff, purchase a mini-sub, more underwater cameras, and so on.

The city appeared to be comprised of a series of rings orbiting a large Greco-Roman temple. The "rings" contained walkways, dwellings, and monolithic obelisks made of black and red stone. Bridges connected these sections to one another and, in turn, to the central plaza. It was safe to assume that the circlets once rose above the surface, the sea filling the areas in between to form canals. Many of the stone surfaces were rich with exciting glyphs. Carol had done her best to translate them, poring over pictures of the etchings in her cabin at night and writing what she could decipher in her journal. The language of Atlantis was oddly familiar and yet quite alien. It seemed to borrow in equal measure from Egyptian,

Greek, and Mayan — or, as a more logical and exciting prospect, *they* had stolen from *it*.

She swam deeper into the city, mindful of the short time allowed to her at this depth. The area teemed with mystery, and she knew there were treasures waiting for her in the dark.

•••

Petty Officer Earl L. Preston Jr. looked out at the ocean off the shores of New Hampshire, his white Coast Guard uniform contrasting handsomely with his ebony skin. The sun shone down on his cap, making his shaved head bead with sweat beneath. He removed his hat and wiped the perspiration away with his sleeve.

He'd joined the Coast Guard the day after his eighteenth birthday for reasons of which even he was not fully aware. His love of the ocean had surely been a contributing factor, but his love for his father, a father he'd never really known, had been the greater push. Earl Senior — everyone called him by his middle name of Lincoln, Link for short — had been a marine, a decorated hero. The man died in Desert Storm and was awarded the Medal of Honor, posthumously. Earl had been all of six at the time. What he remembered of the man was that Link had the largest hands. Those hands could pick up a basketball in one palm, the fingers draping over it like the legs of a powerful, oversized spider. Earl recalled how his own tiny hand, when slipped into his father's, had become lost and yet also felt so secure. Those were the only real memories Earl had of the man. Still, there were some days, when the ocean was calm and the air quiet, that Earl could sense his father's presence. And it was then that he hoped he'd made the right choices, choices that had made Link Preston a happy soul.

The wind blew harder against his face. Earl glanced down to check the boat's tachometer needle. It had risen from 1,200 to 2,200 rpms. He glared at his partner, a young man fresh out of the academy. "Goin' a little fast, aren'tcha, seaman? It's a patrol, not a race."

Seaman Peck nodded and eased up on the throttle.

Earl saw a lot of his younger self in this skinny white kid from

Chicago. There was the same hunger for adventure in this boy's eyes that had been vanquished from his own some time ago. When he received his first assignment, Earl thought every day would bring the search of vessels for drugs, the rescue of drowning women, the kind of excitement he'd seen on television. What he quickly discovered was that for every hour of thrills there were countless days of nothing but the endless stretch of the open sea. Peck would learn this, too.

A crackling voice, almost lost to the sound of the wind, came over the boat's radio. "Coast Guard 38942... Coast Guard 38942... This is Huey Four."

Preston picked up the microphone. "Huey Four...This is Coast Guard 38942. Go ahead."

"We just passed over a yacht drifting about four miles southeast from your position. It matches the description of the *FantaSea*, the Hoff's boat."

The news had been abuzz with two major stories over the last week. Earl had paid attention to both only because they had some connection to the sea. One was about an archeological find in the middle of the Atlantic...

"Is this Atlantis?" 20/20 *asked.*

...the other was the disappearance of Jerry Hoff and his wife, Karen. Mr. Hoff was an entrepreneur with his hands in everything from the sale of speedboats in Durham to the partial ownership of the Patriots. They had taken their yacht, a Hatteras sailboat, down the coast to a vacation home in Florida. Now they were several days overdue and their daughter, Virginia Hoff, a spoiled rich girl if he'd ever seen one, was making the rounds of all the television stations and crying for the cameras.

Earl thought the couple had taken off for an extended cruise. He assumed they would return red-faced at all the attention, smacking themselves for not calling their daughter about the change of plans.

Mama says, "You know what happens when you assume?"

"Roger that. Four miles southeast."

"I'd check it out myself, but I've got to get back to Portsmouth. I'm flying on vapor as it is."

"Understood...Coast Guard 38924 out." He put the microphone

back into its cradle and looked at Peck, noticing that the boy's hand was already on the throttle. "Now you can open her up."

A moment later, the fifty-foot yacht came into view.

Its sail was down and neatly secured to the boom with bungee cord. No billowing smoke. No sign of damage to its exterior. No one visible on deck, but the owners could've been below, sleeping or having breakfast in the cabin. As they pulled alongside, however, Earl found the yacht unanchored, its diesel engine quiet, at the mercy of the tide.

Peck maneuvered their patrol boat around to the ship's stern, and they saw *FantaSea* stenciled across its transom. Earl grabbed the coil of neon-yellow nylon rope at his feet. He tied one end to the metal cleat beside him before turning to Peck. "Get us closer, and I'll tie us up."

The seaman nodded and turned his wheel, bringing the Coast Guard cruiser within inches of the yacht.

Earl reached over to the *FantaSea*'s guardrail, tied the rope securely around the aluminum support, and pulled himself onto its deck. Peck began to walk toward the railing, but Earl waved him off. "Stay there. I may need you to radio for help."

"Sure."

He could see the look of disappointment on Peck's face. Earl hated to deprive the boy of his first real adventure, but experience had taught him that you did not blindly leap into the unknown. He had no idea what he was going to find, and if things went bad, the last thing he wanted was a still-wet-behind-the-ears kid getting himself killed.

Earl looked down into the *FantaSea*'s cockpit. The area was lined with shiny red cushions, reflecting the glare of the sun. The steering wheel turned slightly to the right, then back to the left, as if waving for someone to take hold and give it guidance. Earl scanned the remainder of the deck, saw nothing out of the ordinary, then ducked down beneath the boom, moving toward the hatch that led below.

His stomach rolled.

•••

POSEIDON'S CHILDREN

Carol Miyagi felt her stomach flutter with anticipation. She swam inside the cavernous temple, the centerpiece of these ruins. Liquid shadows shied away from her dive light; they raced across stone walls, across marbled floors and a domed ceiling, ancient surfaces immune to the march of centuries.

As she studied the interior, trying to imagine what it must have been like in life, Carol was reminded a shrine just outside Tokyo — monks clad in saffron robes, sitting at the feet of a large, golden statue in silent meditation and prayer. She was not Buddhist, but she still felt a sense of reverence as she entered and looked up into the peaceful face of the Buddha. Now, as she swam deeper into this vast sunken tabernacle, she had the same feeling.

Extensive pictographs had been etched into the surrounding stone. They displayed their arcane messages, taunting Carol, remaining just beyond her understanding. She was learning quickly, however. Words and phrases now jumped at her from the rock. In time, she would comprehend the glyphs' full meaning, and with any luck, would answer the questions she'd been asking her entire life: who were the Atlanteans? And even more important: what happened to them?

Her light found the gargantuan statue at the center of the flooded chamber and she stood in awe of its intricate detail. It was a larger version of a sculpted chimera she'd found in the sediment days before — a man, dressed in a toga, with the head of a toothy fish. It stared at the temple floor, arms beckoning to her, and, from its sides and shoulders, large tentacles stretched outward in striking poses. Some of these stone tendrils had not survived the centuries intact. They lay like decapitated serpents at Carol's feet.

Unhooking the digital camera from her dive belt, she snapped photos of hieroglyphics etched in the base of the form. Perhaps after she learned the language, they would offer some insight into Atlantean mythology. In the center of the rocky foundation, a large, raised circle of stone contained a familiar design. It was a three-pointed fork stabbing upward, the center prong longer than the ones on either side. A trident. Neptune's spear.

Neptune?

Her gaze rose to the fierce face of the statue. Surely this creature was not meant to be Neptune, the bearded old man of familiar sculpture and art. Or perhaps this representation was the god's root, his image altered by the other societies who had adopted him. She snapped off a few more shots of the ancient writings; the flash illuminated them like drowned lightning.

Carol froze.

She lowered the camera and aimed her light at a section of the hieroglyphs, confirming what she'd seen on the camera screen. Carved into this rock was the glyph for "flesh."

•••

The smell from the cabin was the reek of rotting flesh.

Earl Preston looked inside and saw that the gimbaled table was covered in streaks and splashes of blood, dried to the reddish-brown color of rust. The petty officer reached into his hip pocket and produced a handkerchief, which he placed over his mouth and nose in an attempt to filter out the stench of death that hung in the humid compartment. Part of him said that he should get the fuck out of there and have Peck radio the base, but the part of him that was bound by duty urged him to continue onward.

The creaking of the hull did nothing to alleviate his sense of dread. He drew his service pistol from its holster and proceeded toward the bow. The bed looked as though it had seen the business end of a weed whacker. Its sheets were stained in gore and sliced into ribbons, mattress stuffing peeking through the rips. Earl moved past a tiny bathroom, where a single rusty handprint blemished the wooden floor, and continued into the forward compartment. There, he found two bunks, both empty and untouched by the violence of the after cabin. For all the blood that desecrated the interior, there was no sign of the Hoffs, alive or dead.

He turned around, moved back quickly in the direction of the hatch and the fresh air beyond, and saw the drawing on the wall. It was a crude scribble done in blood, but he knew instantly it was a pitchfork. Was this some kind of occult slaying? A Satanic ritual performed at sea? He stopped, coughed from the stench that seeped through the handkerchief, and looked at the drawing more closely. It was not a pitchfork, not really. The prongs of a pitchfork were all the same length. This one had a long center point with shorter ones on either side. To Earl, it looked more like a three-pointed spear, the one carried by ancient sea gods.

He climbed back on deck, coughing uncontrollably.

"Are you all right?" Peck called.

"Get the base on the horn. Tell them we need someone to tow this back."

"What is it? Are they dead?"

He didn't know how to answer the question. "Tell them this is a crime scene and they need to get their asses over here A.S.A.F.P."

Peck gave him a strange look, then grabbed the microphone as Earl looked out at the open water, his mind drowning in questions.

FOUR

Larry awoke to find the curtains drawn. Peggy stood beside him, rummaging through dresser drawers; a long, tie-dyed beach towel wrapped around her body like a psychedelic toga, and her reddish-brown hair cascading over her bare shoulders in dripping spirals. Larry looked at her face. Free from the artificial colors of makeup, it seemed to glow.

"Morning, beautiful." He rubbed the sandman's dust from his eyes.

Peggy stopped searching long enough to flash him a smile. "You okay, Rembrandt?"

He gave a frustrated snort, wishing she would stop asking him how he felt all the time, then said what she wanted to hear, "I'd say I'm just fine with a dash of dandy."

"Well, here's a little bit of sugar to go with that." She kissed him, her lips and tongue tasting of mint.

"Mmmm. Well, I'm excited." Larry's hand moved beneath her towel, teasing her. "How 'bout you?"

She giggled and slapped at his forearm. "Get dressed before we end up spending the whole day in bed."

"I'm comfortable with that."

"I thought you wanted to make with the painting?"

"I do." His lips curled into a sly grin. "Maybe I should do a nude?"

Her eyes skirted his. "Come on, Larry."

He'd repeatedly asked to do a portrait of her, but she always declined. Seeing photographs others had taken of her through the years was bad enough, she'd told him, but everyone has their picture taken at one time or another. To be *drawn* implied that your form was worthy of admiration, like Venus or Helen of Troy, and, in Peggy's opinion, hers was not.

Larry wondered how such an attractive woman could have so little appreciation for her own form.

He tossed the covers off his body and rose reluctantly from bed. The hardwood floor on the way to the bathroom was cold, but the steamy spray of the shower promised warmth. As he was about to step into the tub, Larry's eye fell to the vial of prescription pills on the counter. The sight brought it all back again; that translucent red bottle still clutched in her dead fingers, the bedcovers tangled around her legs, the silence that swallowed her name and offered no reply.

The bottle on the counter mocked him. Paxil. An SSRI anti-depressant. Happy pills. There to help him "manage" the fallout from what the emptied bottle of pills had done to her.

Her choice, he reminded himself for the thousandth time. *I didn't shove the fucking pills down her throat.*

The voice on his answering machine when he'd come home that night had been hard, cold. Natalie's voice, the way it was when she was in that lost, desperate place from which he'd tried so many times to save her. So many times before he'd finally, to save himself, given it up.

Before he knew what he was doing, Larry swept up the medicine bottle, dumped its contents into the toilet, then flung it into the wastebasket. The shower was too hot but he lifted his face to it anyway. The sound of the spray filled his ears. Even so, he still heard the voice.

You asshole, it accused. *You never cared for me. You never cared for anyone but yourself. You fake* asshole!

The hot spray hurt his face. He held his head under it, clenching his teeth.

You were never there for me.

He held his breath against the pain, pain in his face, in his chest. *When you get this I'll be dead.*

He covered his face with his hands and sank down on his knees with the scalding water beating down on him.

You murderer!

"Hey! You go back to sleep in there?" Peggy pounded on the bathroom door.

Larry scrambled up, horrified that she might discover him this way. "No, sorry...I'm almost out."

Hastily, almost savagely, he washed himself, then turned off the water.

This has got to stop.

Remembering his Paxil, he flushed the toilet to make sure Peggy wouldn't see them floating there. When he went back into the room, she was dressed in a T-shirt and blue jean shorts, rummaging once again through her things.

"Have you seen my camera?" she asked him. "I've looked everywhere."

"Nope, haven't seen it."

"Larry, are you sure? I really wanted to take it with me today. You sure you didn't move it somewhere, or see where I stashed it?"

"How in the hell can you expect me to know what you did with it?" he roared at her.

Peggy stared back at him; the hurt in her eyes froze him with shame.

"I'm sorry, honey. I didn't mean to —"

"I know you...I understand you're..." She scooped up her purse, her hurt turning to frustrated anger. "Tell you what. I'll just meet you downstairs in the lobby when you're ready."

She stormed into the hall, slamming the door.

"Damn," Larry muttered. *Asshole.*

He got dressed, but hesitated before going down to meet Peggy. He didn't want to blow this. He had to pull himself together. He opened the French doors to clear his mind for a moment, the wind toying with his loose-fitting shirt and damp hair as he moved onto the balcony.

Below, the shore was nearly void of activity. A square of neon tape, marked "POLICE LINE — DO NOT CROSS," divided a stretch of sand from the rest of the beach. A few scattered groups of onlookers had gathered, but the tape held them back as if it were a wall of stone. A single police cruiser sat on the street. In the light of day, its blue and red strobes looked dim and insignificant. Out on the water, a police boat slowly moved across the waves. Larry watched as several thick cables descended from its stern, disappearing into the depths.

They're dragging the bottom for her. I wonder how long it will take them to find her.

He wished he had one of those pills to take.

FIVE

The Chief of Police smoked a cigarette, listened to the local oldies station, and wished he was somewhere else. His black-and-white police cruiser had been parked on the shoulder of this dusty side road for nearly an hour. A few yards ahead, a wooden shack stood on a foundation of stilts erected in the tidal waters. To Canon, it looked as if it were ready to collapse into the abiding sea, but some curse kept it standing.

He glanced at his watch; it was just past eleven. "Shit."

As he stared at the shack, Canon felt sweat bead up on his belly, moistening his uniform. If there was one thing in this world John Canon hated, it was heat. He wondered why he didn't just go on down there and get it over with.

You're afraid of the bastard, that's why.

Damn straight. It was the smart way to be. Sure, there were islanders who didn't believe Karl Tellstrom was dangerous, but those idiots would probably let the Reverend Jim Jones tend bar.

Canon looked once more at the worn shanty, sighed, then opened the car door. He hadn't observed anyone coming or going from the shack all morning. With any luck at all, Tellstrom was asleep or, better still, wasn't even home. The ocean's cool breeze blew across Canon's damp skin and he fanned himself for a moment with his large-rimmed hat.

I sit here any longer, I'll get heat stroke for sure.

He slammed the car door and plodded toward the shack; loose gravel crunched beneath his feet like layers of eggshell.

So much for sneakin' up.

A few feet ahead, a rabbit ran across the road without stopping. Canon pondered the sight for a moment, then continued his march. "It's a black cat that's bad luck," he muttered to himself. "Scared rabbits don't count for shit."

The shack drew nearer with each step. Its boards were faded and full of holes, as if a thousand species of insect had feasted upon it over the years. Spider web formed a lace curtain across its porch, and its support stilts were all but hidden beneath a lumpy crust of barnacles.

The road was deserted in both directions. Visitors normally stuck to the town proper and rarely ventured to this side of the island. Occasionally you'd find a group of hikers or a lone sightseeing vehicle, but for the most part, this shore went unseen by tourists.

Canon closed his eyes, took a deep breath, and thumbed the strap off his revolver. He'd never drawn his weapon on another living soul, and he didn't intend to make history today, but...

He stepped slowly onto the wooden deck; his heart skipped a beat when the boards creaked. Rusted hinges hung from the doorframe; a torn blanket dangled in place of the missing door.

"Karl?" Canon pushed the drape aside and peered into the dimness. The stench of rot and excrement made his lips curl in disgust. He pressed the back of his left hand to his mouth and nose and coughed. "You here, Karl?"

Light streamed through the shack's Swiss cheese roof, revealing the potbellied stove that stood in the middle of the room. Tattered throw rugs attempted to conceal the decaying floor with little success. In the corner, a mildewed mattress bled stuffing across the floor, exposing skeletal springs. Half-eaten fish were strewn about, rotting in the heat and crawling with flies. And, on the far wall, someone had painted a trident, the emblem of the Old Ones. Canon's suspicions were confirmed. Anybody that would make this rancid hut their home was not playing with a full deck.

He felt something sticky on the inside of the doorframe and quickly pulled his hand away. The pads of his fingertips were red, a crimson syrup flowing sluggishly down his digits into the palm of his hand.

Canon swallowed. He stepped cautiously inside Tellstrom's den and turned around, knowing what he would find, yet still unprepared for the sight that greeted him. It was the wall of an abattoir; rust-colored handprints and streaks of arterial spray darkened the wood around the door in all directions.

His gaze drifted from the evidence of past slaughter to the drawing of the trident on opposite wall. He thought it had been sketched with paint. Now knew better. It was drawn in blood.

"Holy shit. Holy fucking shit."

Pandora's box was open.

Under his breath, John Canon muttered an old prayer, a prayer he hadn't said in years. He unclipped the walkie-talkie from his belt to call it in.

SIX

When she saw the "Gifts From The Sea" sign careening in the wind like a square pendulum, Peggy went inside and Larry followed.

Shopping usually helped to lighten her mood, but every store in town seemed to be a Xerox clone of its predecessor. What she wanted was something unique to Colonial Bay, something that couldn't be found around the corner from her apartment back home.

"Help you?"

Peggy turned to see an older woman dressed in a dark blouse and a long black skirt. The corners of her mouth were turned up in a smile, and her silver hair was tied into a bun that rested on the back of her head like a cap.

"Just looking, thanks," Larry said, walking past Peggy to a display of driftwood sculptures. She thought of telling him that this woman had been talking to her and not him, but she didn't want to re-start their argument. She hated to fight in public.

"Well, be my guest," the shopkeeper urged. "If you need anything, let me know."

Peggy moved to a bin of brightly colored shells and saw a large, polished conch. She put it to her ear, hearing the sounds that, as a child, she believed came from a little world within the shell, a world that sang just for her. She smiled, thinking how silly the notion now seemed, then put the shell carefully back onto the pile.

I wonder what used to live in these, she thought as she rubbed the rippled surface, *and I wonder if they know the going rate for their vacant homes is a buck fifty.*

"Hey, Peggy, take a look at this." Larry held up a statue for her inspection, a driftwood figure sitting on a rock.

At first glance, Peggy thought it was a mermaid, but then she got a closer look. While the sculpted torso was clearly that of an attractive female, its head and tail were those of a fish. She ran her hand along the figurine's spine, felt the smoothness of the wood. It was a hideous thing, and yet she could see it was beautifully rendered. "Nice."

"Isn't it great?" Larry had recently celebrated his thirtieth birthday, but his voice was that of a ten-year-old in Toys-R-Us. "It's a siren or something."

What does he see in that thing? Peggy wondered. *Better yet, what does he see in* me?

She'd seen pictures of Natalie. Heroin chic or no heroin chic, the woman could've been a model. And even if he wouldn't admit it, Larry still had feelings for her. Why else would he have erupted with such anger and frustration at her death?

The memory of Larry smashing his hand through the mirror gave Peggy a chill.

She continued to study the carving, monstrous face stuck onto a nymph's comely form, looking as if two statues had been broken and spliced together by mistake. Could a vacation really fix what was wrong with him? With *them*?

"What's the matter?"

"Nothing," she said absently.

"No, really. You hate it, don't you? If you don't want me to buy it —"

"How much is it?"

"I don't know." He looked around and caught a glimpse of the older woman as she walked by. "Excuse me, Miss..."

"DeParle," the older woman told him. "What can I help you with?"

"We were wondering how much this was."

DeParle stepped over to them, looking down at the carving Larry held in his hands. She grabbed hold of the glasses that hung around her neck. "Ayuh. That one'll cost you ten dollars. The larger ones'll run ya twenty-five."

"We'll take it," he told her, then asked: "Did you say your name was DeParle?"

"Ayuh."

Peggy smiled. "Any relation to the DeParle that runs the Sea Mist Inn? That's where we're staying."

"We were married."

"Oh." Peggy changed the subject. "I'm curious, do you know what this statue is, outside of ugly?"

"Oh, I wouldn't say it was ugly," the woman told her, taking the driftwood piece up to the register. "It's one of Poseidon's children."

"I told you it was mythological," Larry said, opening his wallet.

Peggy thought it strange that Mrs. DeParle looked up as if he'd just uttered something offensive.

•••

"You're sure she got weirded out by what I said about this?" Larry gave the driftwood monster a pat on the head. It sat on the restaurant table, taking up the space between them as they waited for their lunch.

"What else would it have been?"

He shrugged. "Maybe you asking about her ex-husband?"

"You brought the name thing up," she snapped.

For a moment they were silent. In New York, such a gap would have been filled by the cacophony of traffic noise, or by muffled voices from a neighboring loft, but this unfamiliar New Hampshire shore was eerily void of such distractions. They sat looking at one another. It was as if they were sitting on opposite sides of a valley rather than a table, and neither wanted to be first to cross the divide.

"I miss you," Larry finally ventured. "I'm sorry I've been —"
An asshole. "— such a jerk. It's just that, after last night I...I took my frustration out on you and I'm sorry."

She pushed the driftwood aside, reaching over to take his hand in hers.

"I love you, Peggy," he said apprehensively, the words coaxing a smile from her, "and I don't wanna screw this up."

"Rembrandt..." She brought his fingers up, grazed them with her lips, the whisper of a kiss, then said, "I love you too, and we won't screw this up."

SEVEN

Carol Miyagi walked across the *Ambrosia*'s deck. She'd paid the price for her stay in the sunken Atlantean temple with a long decompression, and now her mind entertained thoughts of a hot shower.

Alan, her assistant, called out, "Childs was on *Dateline* last night, part of the so-called panel of experts that evaluated our segment on the ruins."

Dr. Edmund Childs, archeologist extraordinaire, was the closest thing to a nemesis Carol had. She sighed. "Did he congratulate us?"

"He said you're full of shit."

Carol leaned against a bulkhead. "He told Stone Phillips I'm full of shit?"

"Ann Curry," Alan corrected. "He said all the evidence points to the Mediterranean Sea and Thera as the locale of Atlantis, not the Azores."

"*Gejashiku!*" she spat, calling Childs an asshole. Carol started cursing in Japanese while still in grade school. To her, it sounded more elegant, less crude than the English — and her teachers and other authority figures had no idea what she was saying. Her cursing had become so much of a habit that, when she visited Japan, it was now embarrassing. How had her grandmother put it? Why does such a beautiful and intelligent girl talk like a gutter whore? "*Aitsu wa dotokushin no kakera mo ne!*"

Her partner held up his hand. "In English, please."

"Plato said Atlantis was outside the Pillars of Hercules. *Outside*. Meaning past the Straight of Gibraltar and in the Atlantic Ocean."

"Plato also said it was larger than Asia and Libya combined. What we've found isn't anywhere near that size." He saw that she was ready to protest and held up a precluding hand. "I'm not saying Childs is right, Carol. I'm just pointing that out."

"What we've found is only a fragment of the entire city. The rest is just beyond the reach of scuba."

Alan nodded.

She looked out at the restless sea and the horizon beyond. "Did we get the new grant money?"

"Nothing from the old gangster yet."

"He's not a gangster, Alan," she said. *Not this conversation again.* "He's a Republican."

"His money's dirty."

"Money isn't dirty. *People* are dirty. And dirty or not, Roger Hays is our only source of funding."

"Fine. But one day, when you piss him off, he'll stick your feet in cement and plant you in that city of yours."

She laughed. "Okay, Jiminy Cricket, your objections have been duly noted. Now, about the funds —"

He sighed. "Acting under duress, I'll call Tom Kravitz in New York to see if Hays has signed the check."

"*Domo.*"

"Now *that* I understood." He moved closer to her. "You're welcome."

Carol jerked back a bit at his advance. They'd been friends for years, but the physical aspect of their relationship was still new to her. The idea that a man would show her any kind of affection and warmth was a far stranger thing for her to grasp than Atlantean theories, not a bad thing, mind you...merely odd. It had taken a while to get used to. In fact, although they'd slept together on several previous voyages, this is the first time they had actually shared a cabin.

Alan pressed his mouth to hers, the motion of his tongue coaxing, but not forceful, against her lips.

She responded in kind, permitting her own tongue to meet his, taking the kiss further. The sweet sensation of taste and touch mingled with the smell of his cologne, awakening a tingle of excitement deep within her. Before someone walked by, or the kiss could take them into a frenzy of mad groping, she pulled away.

"See you later," he said.

Carol nodded, wiping her lips, feeling them curl into a grin beneath her fingers. It was probably a form of indecency to watch him as he walked away, seeing his butt under his shorts as it moved and flexed, but she did it anyway. When he was gone from sight, she closed her eyes and decided to change the temperature of her shower.

EIGHT

Tom Savini, the make-up effects man behind the gore of *Friday the 13th*, once said that he felt like a hitman, that he was being paid to kill people. What Savini had done was all movie trickery. What Dante "The Horror Show" Vianello did was the real McCoy, and strangely enough, Dante wagered it all paid about the same.

Horror Show slapped his copy of the New York Times on the table in the center of the room and wrapped duct tape around Sam's torso, around his arms and legs, confining him to the rickety old chair. Duct tape. Like the force in *Star Wars*: it had a dark side, a light side, and it bound the universe together. At the moment, it bound the unconscious man very nicely indeed.

After taking a few backward steps to observe his handiwork, Dante took off his jacket, folded it, and placed it on the far side of the table. He pulled a cigarette from his breast pocket, sat down, and looked at his Rolex. It would be dark soon, and body disposal was a task best accomplished under cloak of night. Deciding that he needed to wait a bit, he took a moment to reach the proper mindset, like an actor finding his character.

Over the years, the role of a killer had become a comfortable shoe Dante could slip in and out of easily. Outwardly, he looked the part. He stood just over six feet tall, and his hair, dyed jet black to remove a skunk streak of gray, was combed back and plastered to his head. A failed attempt on his life had left him with a huge scar around his neck. The fan of horror films that he was, Dante liked to call it his "Frankenstein line." And behind this walking stereotype of Versace suits, slicked-back hair, and Brooklyn accent was a gifted, savagely alert mind, a mind that kept him at the top of this sordid profession, a mind that now grew restless.

He looked at his watch again.

Time to go to work.

Horror Show rose from his chair, walked over and gave his captive a rough slap across the face.

Sam opened his eyes and looked around, dazed and struggling against the tape that imprisoned him. "Where am I?" he asked, then recognition took hold. "Horror Show? What the fuck?"

Horror Show removed the unlit cigarette from his lips and sat down on the edge of the table. His voice was low and raspy, another gift from piano wire to his throat. "A little shitheel punk like you stealin' from one of the richest sons o' bitches on the fuckin' planet. What the hell were you thinkin', Sammy?"

The thief looked as if he were about to speak. Horror Show placed an index finger across his lips, shaking his head back and forth. Sam closed his mouth and turned on the waterworks, letting a flood of tears run down his ruddy cheeks.

Until tonight, Sam Cox had been a courier, a gopher, a small-time hood. He ran money back and forth between numbers rackets for Roger Hays' organization. Over the past six months, the accountants noticed some discrepancies. At first, it was a dollar here and a dollar there, nothing big. Most had been chalked up to miscounting and nothing was said. Then Sam got stupid and greedy, two characteristics someone in the business *cannot* afford if they want to keep breathing. The thief knew this, which is why he blubbered wildly now.

Horror Show grinned, displayed gleaming white teeth. There was a rumor on the street that he filed them down to points, like a shark, but they were wide and even. "Mr. Ludwig doesn't want any excuses, Sammy. *He* knows you did it, *I* know you did it, *you* know you fuckin' did it." Horror Show removed something shiny from his pocket; a pearl-handled straight razor. "Bein' around all that money day in and day out. I bet that was tough, am I right, Sammy?"

With of flick of the wrist, the blade unfolded. The thief's eyes caught the reflected light and ignited with fear. Just the response Horror Show was looking for.

"For Christsakes, Horror Show, put that thing away! You and I both know that Ludwig just wants Hays to get his money back. If I could just talk with Mr. Hays I could —"

"You think Hays cares about *you*? You think he would come down off his throne and get his hands dirty with this penny ante shit? He doesn't even know you *exist*. Besides..." Horror Show grinned and produced a small object from the same pocket that housed his straight razor. He held it out for Cox to examine. The man's face fell. It was the key to a storage locker, locker 927 to be exact. "He's already got the money back, what you didn't piss away on ten dollar whores anyway. A locker at the bus station, Sammy? Just a few blocks away from your own apartment? Pretty fuckin' sloppy."

Cox didn't speak.

Horror Show put the key back in his pocket and produced a small chunk of granite, which he began to rub. "Know what this is Sammy? It's a chip off of John Dillinger's tombstone. Some guys have rabbits' feet." He tossed the shard into the air and caught it in his palm. "I got this.

"See, Dillinger was the most wanted son of a bitch in America. I mean every beat cop and G-Man in the whole fuckin' country was gunnin' for his ass. So what does he do? He buys a ticket to a fuckin' movie and gets that ass blown clean off."

Cox didn't laugh.

Horror Show laughed for him, then slid the stone back into his pocket. "So I keep this to remind me that actin' stupid will getcha killed."

The hitman rose to his feet. He walked around to the back of the chair and placed his hands on Sam's shoulders, his right hand still holding the gleaming blade.

"And stealin' from Hays was stupid, Sammy."

Cox shook his head.

Horror Show couldn't see the man's face, but he could hear him sob. He grabbed Cox by the hair, pulled his head back to bare the skin of his neck, then leaned down so that his lips were at the man's ear. "You should be glad Ludwig didn't bring this to Mr. Hays' attention, Sammy. See, Hays...he would've ordered some real medieval shit. Slow..*painful*. As it is —"

He opened Cox's throat with a single swipe; hot, arterial blood leapt freely from the gash.

"— you just get to die."

Horror Show watched the light fade from Sam's eyes, then

strolled over to a sink in the corner. He washed the blood from his hands and razor with water and bleach, folded the now clean blade into its carrying position, and slid it back into his pocket. He then dried his hands, put on a clear plastic face shield and pair of Rubbermaid kitchen gloves, and switched on the large portable stereo he kept on the shelf to his right.

Frank Sinatra crooned *In the Wee Small Hours of the Morning*.

Horror Show grabbed his New York Times off the table, and took a Hefty Lawn and Garden trash bag from beneath the sink. He threw the supplies onto the floor, then lifted his electric chainsaw — a Craftsman model that had been plugged into the wall behind the chair the entire time. This was the most important portion of his trade. It was also the element he enjoyed least.

Clean up.

He undressed the scrawny man and threw the bloodied clothing in the Hefty bag. Next, Horror Show carved up the corpse, broke the body down into its component pieces, creating a puzzle he would never reassemble. He cleared the dew of blood from his face shield, wrapped each limb and pound of flesh in newspaper as carefully as a butcher might jacket hamburger, then tossed the remains onto the bed of clothes in the trash bag. He would put the Hefty bag into a suitcase weighted with bricks and wheel it out through the tunnels, surfacing in the alley behind Antonio's Italian Deli. There, he would place the body in the trunk of Sam's own car for deposit in the East River — the Gangster's Graveyard, as he liked to call it.

As the hit man wrapped Cox's head, he noticed the newspaper's headline and laughed.

It said that someone had discovered Atlantis.

NINE

John Canon stood in the shadow of Colonial Bay's lighthouse. He cleared away the last grains of sand, looked down upon what was left of the man; the throat had been torn out, and the lower jawbone was missing. The arm that still sported a watch was more or less intact, but a crushed stump of bone and mangled flesh hung from the opposite shoulder. A colony of ants had claimed the lifeless flesh as their prize; they scurried in and out of an empty eye socket, some getting stuck in globs of congealing plasma and sand, writhing and twitching their countless legs as if dancing.

"Fuck." Canon turned away, looked out at the waves, half expecting to see something emerge from them. "Who found him?"

Deputy Ray stood beside the shallow grave, spade in hand. "A teenage girl. Her metal detector picked up his watch. She's with Doc Northcutt now, still pretty freaked out."

Canon pinched his eyes closed, wishing it would all go away.

"Chief?"

"What?"

"Should we stop dragging the bottom now?"

Canon's eyes snapped open, and he pointed to the ravaged body still partially entombed in the beach. "You see any tits on that corpse, son?"

"No, sir."

"Then keep draggin' 'til ya either find me a girl's body or I tell ya to stop. That clear?"

"Sure, Chief."

"You know who Roger Hays is, don'tcha, Ray?"

Everyone knew who Roger Hays was. He was on Forbes's top ten list five years in a row. He owned casinos, skyscrapers, even islands in the

Caribbean, and was rumored to be involved in organized crime.

Ray said nothing.

"Roger Hays," the chief continued, "called to report his son missing. Seems he was here with a girlfriend. Nobody's seen or heard from 'em since yesterday. I think you know where I'm goin' with this, Ray."

Canon unfolded the sheet of paper he held in his hands, the grainy black and white image of a young, smiling man in his early twenties. He stared at it a moment, glanced down at the remains, then shook his head. "Hays faxed me this picture of his son, David. No way to tell just by lookin' at him, so get this body to the medical center at Black Harbor. Have 'em get the Hays boy's dentals and see if it's him."

Ray nodded. Canon thought he could see a light-green tint seeping into the boy's complexion. "What now, Chief?"

"Now I wantcha to go raise the red flag at the pier." The flags signaled swimming conditions for the day, mainly undertow. Blue meant the water was fine, enjoy! Yellow urged caution. Red meant keep your ass dry if you want to keep it. "Last thing we need is another *accident*."

The deputy obliged, trotting across the beach until he disappeared behind an outcropping of rock.

Canon gave his attention back to the open grave. He hoped the corpse was not the Hays boy. At that moment, Canon would have wished it be his own son, if he had one, rather than the offspring of one of the most powerful men in the world.

He wadded the fax in his hand and watched waves make kamikaze runs on the rocks. He wanted the blood he'd found spattered on the walls of that shack to be Karl Tellstrom's. He really did.

TEN

Very much alive, Karl Tellstrom strode confidently down the sidewalk toward The Shirt Shack, arms swinging at his sides. He was a few inches on the short side of six feet and his skin had been tanned to a deep bronze. Tourists from the mainland, *Landers*, he called them, paid little or no attention to him as they passed him by. Why should they? Karl was just another twenty-something in Hawaiian shorts. He was one of them.

He ground his teeth, sickened by the thought, wishing he could take all of them back to his shack and paint the walls with them.

The townspeople, on the other hand, knew him all too well. Whenever he passed a pair of islanders, the sight of him killed their conversation. They never looked him in the face, perhaps afraid that his cold, distant eyes might somehow hold a kind of power over them (at least, that's what Karl believed), but he could hear their exchanges in his head as clearly as if they had been telegraphed to him.

"There goes the Tellstrom boy, Charlie. Shame 'bout his father last summer. He was a good man. Died almost ten years to the day of his wife's —"

"Worst boating accident I can remember, Sarah. Bunch o' drunken tourists hit her with their outboard while she was swimmin' past the reef. Karl was —"

"Ayuh, boy never got over it. You heard he moved out to that old fishin' shack —"

"Been meetin' with a bunch o' kids out there. Barbara DeParle says —"

"Some kind o' cult he's formin' out there. Don't like it. Don't much like it at all —"

"— what he's doin' with the DeParles' little girl. She's gone missin', you know. Right before those kids got attacked on the beach. Horrible mess that was..."

Karl walked on at a steady clip, a smile spreading across his face. Let them talk. It was flattering to be the subject of so much gossip and heated debate. A week ago, he'd been the crazy Tellstrom boy, on his way to oblivion. Today, his message was ringing in much more receptive ears, ears that now understood what he'd known his whole life: The people of Colonial Bay were meant to be something far better than what they had become.

He reached his destination and stopped, watched as a woman locked the door to The Shirt Shack. Sue O'Conner. On her T-shirt, the town's tiresome motto was printed in big, bold lettering: COLONIAL BAY: AMERICA'S HOME BY THE SEA. Tellstrom had the sudden urge to voice his disdain of those words, but instead he smiled.

"I don't understand you," he said, his voice mild.

Sue jumped; she dropped her keys onto the hot pavement. Karl bent down to pick them up, held them out for her. "I know what some people are saying about me."

"Never been one to listen to gossip." Her gaze alternated between his tanned face and her keys. "I ain't scared o' you, you know."

Tellstrom smiled; the ocean breeze moved through his short-cropped raven hair. "Of course not. Why should you be?"

After a tense moment, she took back her keys. "Anyway, what's not to understand?"

Streetlights bathed the storefront in their orange glow. Sounds of swooping gulls and crashing waves provided subtle background. And Karl could feel that his time was coming like the evening tide. Destiny, long kept at bay by his father, was now free to call to him, but he knew the change that he sought would not happen overnight. Karl would now awaken Sue to the calling within her own veins, the call that would, he hoped, lead him to greatness and her to follow him.

"Every day," he began, "you open up your store, listen to men and women bitch at you, and sweat to death over your hot presses."

Her mouth opened to speak, but instead she lowered her eyes and stared at her sandal straps.

"Look at me, Sue."

"I don't think so," she whispered, still focused on her feet.

Karl felt the urge to grab her by the chin and force her to look into his dark eyes.

Hey, his mind called out. *Don't get carried away now. Not when you're so close. Look at all you've been able to do already...*

Easier thought than done. Karl's temper had a habit of...getting away from him sometimes.

But not tonight, he vowed. *Not tonight.*

Karl took a breath. He had to keep his anger in check now. This was too important. If he could make Sue, a pillar of the community, understand him, could make her *join* him, then others from her clan would follow.

"Sue...I promise I won't bite...unless you ask me to."

She snickered in spite of herself and turned her eyes up to meet his.

"Do you like who you are?" he asked.

"Karl, it's gettin' late and I'd like to get a swim in —"

"While it's dark?"

She nodded her head.

"Answer my question," he whispered.

"I'm makin' good money."

"But you're not happy, are you? You can't be *happy* pressing shirts for *Landers*. You can't *like* being the lapdog of rich shits from the Hamptons who think you owe them something. You feel trapped, don't you? You feel you were made for something more, something bigger and better than this."

Sue said nothing but her eyes spoke volumes.

He went on, "You say to yourself: 'If only I could cast away this lie and live like my ancestors, then...then I'd be happy.'"

She shook her head. "Fantasy."

"*Your* fantasy. Have you read the Bible, Sue? — I mean, *really* read it?"

She shrugged. "I've read it, talked about it with the Teacher."

Karl's smile faltered a bit. "Mrs. DeParle?"

"Yeah. She says Jesus appeared as a man to make human beings understand the Word."

"And they killed Him," Karl told her. "They nailed Him to a tree because the Pharisees thought He was a threat to their power. DeParle is just like them. She wants to be the one who gives the message. Anyone who preaches something different is speaking nonsense, a heretic. But if it's the truth, how can it be blasphemy?"

Sue nodded.

Good.

"In the Bible," Karl went on, his smile returning, "Jesus goes to the Sea of Galilee and tells the people, 'The right time has come. Turn away from your life of sin and believe the Good News.'"

And then Tellstrom reached into the pocket of his Hawaiian shorts. He didn't want to wear them, but saw no way around it if he was to be seen on the street. It would not do him any good if Joe Tourist saw a naked man walking through town. Karl produced a folded sheet of newsprint and spread it open so that the headline was clear: LOST CITY FOUND NEAR AZORES.

Sue's eyes widened, and she took the paper from his grasp hesitantly, as if it might not be real. "Is this...?"

"Poseidon," he said with a grin. "This *USA Today* calls it Atlantis, but yes...it is."

The look of astonishment on her face gave way to an ecstatic glee.

Karl Tellstrom placed his hand on her shoulder and she did not shrink from his touch. In fact, she raised her hand to his and squeezed his fingers as if to show her gratitude. "Come with me," he told her, still quoting scripture, "and I will make you fishers of men."

ELEVEN

Larry bolted into the night surf, clad only in his robe. A powerful wave slapped him across the face, nearly knocked him off his feet. The salt water burned his eyes, and, for a moment, he could not breathe, but he had to keep going.

Someone was drowning out here, a girl; she needed him.

A hand shot up from the tide, waved for help. Larry took it, pulled, and a familiar face broke the surface. Natalie. What the fuck was she doing here?

Then she threw her arms around his neck, brought her face closer to his, and he saw that he'd been mistaken. This wasn't Natalie.

This was a corpse.

As Larry stared into the dead girl's filmy eyes, his hands ran up the length of her back, his fingers skidding over the jagged vertebrae of a naked spine. He shoved the thing away, looked through a gaping hole in its right cheek — a window to the glistening jawbone within. Its torso was just as ragged, with whole sections of flesh torn away. An eel slithered out from between two exposed ribs, fell back into the tide, and swam away.

The dead thing spoke; water cascaded over bloated, wrinkled lips with every word. "You tried to help me, Larry. Now I need to help you."

Larry whirled around, moved back toward the deserted shore, and the horror followed.

It held out its hands as if to embrace him. "Larry, stop! Listen!"

He scanned the beach in every direction, searching for the Sea Mist Inn, and was met instead by the rocky face of tall cliffs. Concrete steps; they snaked their way up the side of the rock wall. Larry stumbled through loose sand, wrapped his hand around a cold metal guardrail, and climbed.

When he glanced back over his shoulder, he found the dead girl still in pursuit.

"You're in danger," she called after him.

Oh, yes. Of that much, he was certain.

Light swept the top of the stairs, and Larry saw Colonial Bay's lighthouse silhouetted against moonlit clouds. A small yellow bulb glowed above the door. He slipped, regained his footing, and, when he chanced another downward glance, he saw that the dead woman had gained on him.

Larry bolted for the entrance; the knob turned easily in his grasp, and he pushed his way inside. He slammed the door closed, slid the heavy metal deadbolt into place, then hunched over, hands on his knees as he panted and tried to catch his breath.

"The flesh is the clay of the gods," came from behind him.

Larry spun around.

The dead girl sat on a spiral staircase at the center of the cylindrical room, her pale eyes shimmering in the dimness. "Only the chosen can be sculptors."

He backed up against the curved wall; his outstretched hand knocked an old-fashioned lantern off a nearby shelf and it shattered against the concrete floor.

Light bled down through metal grates, bathing the revenant in bands of light and shadow, revealing far more than Larry cared to see. She turned her head away and coughed, spilling seawater. Through the opening in her cheek, Larry spied movement. A small crab; it scurried from her mouth, moved down her neck to perch on her moldering left breast. She brushed it away, and the crustacean landed on its back near the smashed lantern, its tiny legs writhing madly as it tried to right itself.

Larry groaned.

"Leave Colonial Bay," the corpse warned. "If you don't, Chief Canon will be dragging the bottom for you." And then it stood; its bloated fingers made a sickening *squish* as they grabbed the cast-iron stair rail. "Natalie was wrong about you, Larry. You're not a murderer, at least...not yet."

Before he could ask her what she meant by that, the dead girl climbed up toward the light. Larry pursued her, stunned, emerging in a glass-walled chamber at the top of the lighthouse. Huge warning lamps spun in the center of the room, blinding him.

Larry lowered his head, blinked, and, when he looked up again, he found the girl. She stood on the metal ledge that encircled the turret. From the base of her neck to the small of her back, not one inch of flesh remained. Her spine had been washed clean by the tide; the polished bone gleamed in the spotlight.

Larry stepped through an open doorway and felt the chill of the ocean breeze. "Who are you?"

She turned to face him, her bloated lips curved into a grotesque smile. "Susan Rogers."

"How do you know Natalie?"

She raised one distended leg, straddled the guardrail. When she spoke, there was compassion in her voice, "There wasn't anything you could've done for her, or for me. It was fate. It was what the gods had intended."

Larry wanted to moan. Instead, he found himself asking, "What's *my* fate?"

The dead girl's smile widened. "That's up to you."

With that, she let go of the guardrail and fell over the side.

Larry sprinted to the railing. He looked over the edge, but saw nothing. Her body wasn't smashed on the rocks below, nor was it lying in a heap on the sands of the beach. She'd vanished.

He sat up in bed, panting, covered in sweat. The clock on the side table said three in the morning. Beside him, Peggy was a comfortable-looking contour beneath the lace blanket, facing him as she slept. Larry could not help but stare into her gaping mouth, the vision of the corpse still fresh his mind.

He shivered.

Larry threw the covers aside and slid from their bed. He needed a drink. Without even bothering to switch on the bathroom light, he removed the cellophane wrapper from a plastic cup and filled it with tap water. He put the cup to his lips, gulped it. His reflection studied him from the gloom of the darkened — *unbroken, thank God* — mirror.

Crazy fuckin' dream.

On his way back to bed, Larry brushed against something wet.

He turned on the light and stared at the bathroom door. There, his Sea Mist Inn robe hung from a small hook. He reached out and felt the terrycloth fabric.

It was soaked, drenched up to the waist.

TWELVE

The thunder of waves smacking rocks filled the air. Barbara DeParle cherished the taste of salt on her lips, the smell of the night surf on the wind, the squawking of gulls that shattered the silence of these early morning hours. She loved the sea. It was the only place she felt truly at home.

She slipped into her heavy blue robe, then gazed at the withered flesh of her hands. They were covered in misshapen splotches; blue veins, once invisible, could now be seen clearly, and her arteries stood out like thick ropes beneath tissue-paper skin. She sighed, then turned her attention seaward, wishing that she could dive into the water once more and knowing there was no time for it.

A paranoid feeling prompted her to scan the beach in all directions. *How long have they been there?* she wondered. *What have they seen?*

Ed's voice rose above the surf. "Thought I'd find you here."

Her ex-husband walked toward her from the shadow of the rocks. Part of her still wanted to see Ed as he once was, as the man who proposed to her the night of their high school graduation, but that was sixty years ago. That man was long gone. There was no going back. His eyes were now dull and submissive, like those of a puppy begging for forgiveness, forgiveness that Barbara was unwilling to offer.

"The Inn's been quiet since Chrissy left," he told her. "Even full o' tourists, it seems empty. Today I go to her door and start knockin'. I says, 'You gonna sleep the whole day away?' It didn't hit me that she was gone until I opened the door and saw her bed was made. She never made her bed. I told her to, but she never did."

Barbara tightened the belt on her robe. "She's lost to us."

"You don't believe that." Ed reached out, but she pulled away.

He'd been unwilling to be her husband; she was not about to let him be her solace.

"I do believe it." Barbara's face twisted in disgust. "She's with *him* now."

The innkeeper looked away again, as if ashamed of what he was about to ask. "Barb, this awful business with the Hays boy and that girl, it was just a shark attack, wasn't it? I mean, you don't think Chrissy had nothin' to do with it, do you?"

She shook her head, unwilling to even consider the possibility. "I thought I might read about the attack in the *Herald.*" She paused to look at Ed, reading his face. "But there wasn't a paper today."

Erik and Melody Jones were the editors of Colonial Bay's newspaper. They hadn't missed a day of work in five years.

Barbara went on, "Mike Richards didn't open his bait shop on the docks, neither."

"Really? Maybe they went on vacation."

His tone further goaded her. Their world was falling down around them, and Ed damn well knew it. "Maybe they did. Maybe the whole damn town will just up an' go on vacation." She stared out at the waves. "I remember teachin' the Tellstrom boy the Book after church on Sundays. I taught him right from wrong. I taught him...I..." A lump rose to block her throat. She swallowed, and the pain of it brought tears to her eyes, tears she was too old to hide.

"Hey, none o' that now." Ed reached out to comfort her. "Don't think about it, Barb. If you keep thinkin' about it, you'll crack up. An' you're much too pretty to fall all to pieces."

She shrank from him, wiped the tears away with the back of her hand. "Tellstrom's right, you know. This town is like a prison."

"Don't talk like that, hear? This town's our home, our sanctuary."

"There's a whole world out there, Ed. A whole world we've never even seen."

"The only world I wanna see is right here."

Barbara's eyes narrowed, her face as red as her hair had once been. "And that's all you ever want to see."

She walked past him and down the beach without looking back, fresh tears streaming down her cheeks.

Ed remained there on the shore, gazing out at the tide without seeing it.

•••

Unseen eyes watched Barbara and Ed as they stood talking on the deserted strand. Their daughter, Christine, stood behind a rocky outcropping, water dripping from her naked body onto the beach like rain, creating pits in the sand where it landed. She watched and waited, muttering silent prayers for her parents to leave.

Karl was expecting her.

Christine's back began to itch and she reached her arm around to scratch it. Her tattoo. She could not feel the drawing, of course, but she knew it was there. The mark itself was nothing special, just a plain black figure, no more than an inch in length, but what it symbolized was far more dramatic.

Her mother had put the brand there after the bloody show of her first period. She'd asked for neither, but she had no voice in it. The gods, and her parents, had decided her fate long ago.

She hated them.

Time passed like a meandering slug. How long had it been? Ten minutes? An hour? To Christine, it seemed an eternity. Her eyes climbed the side of the escarpment, saw the lighthouse lamps ignite clouds overhead.

Karl.

Karl waited for her.

At last, her mother walked away. Her father stayed behind, looking out at the sea, but after a minute or so, he too left. Christine gave a sigh of relief, and, when she thought it was safe, she moved from her hiding place.

The lighthouse rose like a flaming dagger into the heart of the night sky. *My love is there,* Christine thought, taking concrete steps two at a time. *He's waiting for me.* She ran to the small wooden entrance and pushed it open.

"Karl?"

No answer.

"Karl, you here?"

Silence.

Christine ran for the spiral staircase and pain stabbed through her left foot. She screamed, her cry echoing up the spire, and when she looked down, she saw a smashed lantern, glass shards littering her path like a thousand crystal knives.

"Karl?" Tears of agony welled in her eyes. She hobbled up the stairs, her lacerated foot leaving blood on every step. When she reached the glass-walled room at the summit, she could not see him, but she knew he was there. "Karl?"

"Over here." His voice was faint, almost lost to the whistle of the wind. She turned to find him standing naked at the guardrail, looking down on Colonial Bay the way a king might survey his kingdom from atop the highest minaret of his castle. His jet-black hair tossed in the ocean breeze and the searchlamps struck his face at an angle, giving it an unearthly glow.

"They're sleeping now," he told her, his lips curled into the cruel smirk she'd seen so many times. "The wolves of the sea lying caged, with their prey as their jailers."

Christine limped over to the open doorway, leaving a rosy trail on the floor behind her. "I'm bleeding."

Tellstrom turned to her; shadow swallowed his face whole. He placed a hand on her cheek, his sun-kissed skin warm as a bonfire. She liked it. He moved his hand down her face and neck until it cupped her left breast.

"Alone at last, my love." His cheek slid across hers; his lips pressed against her ear. "My queen."

She felt faint and reached out to the railing for support. "I'm hurt."

Karl glanced down at her bleeding foot, then smiled into her eyes. His own eyes were distant, cold, and unreadable. Christine knew some people in town thought Karl was crazy, but they didn't understand him the way she did. On another night such as this, she'd come to him with an obscene longing, she'd given herself and her precious virginity over to him so willingly, and she'd asked him...no, *begged* him to take her away from Colonial Bay. But Karl told her that he could not leave, not as long as his mother was buried here. And then he cried. Until her parents, and everyone else in this damned town, saw the depths of his emotion, they could not know him as she did.

And they could never love him.

"I can take away your pain." He laid her down on the metal grating. "Will you let me?"

Christine nodded.

Karl teased her with soft kisses, then squeezed down on her breast with all his strength. She cried out through clenched teeth, wrapped her free hands around his brawny wrist. May the gods help her; she *liked* it. All her life, her parents had told her she was special, but she'd never believed it until Karl came to her. Any girl in Colonial Bay could've been his, yet he'd chosen her. For once in her life, she had something of her own, something her parents would never approve of, something that hadn't been planned. This was *bad*, and she loved it.

After a moment, he released his death grip on her breast and lowered his head to suckle at her bruised nipple, rousing it with the slow stroking of his tongue. She felt the moist warmth as he worked against her flesh, licking clean the bloodied claw marks he'd made.

Karl then turned his attention to her mangled foot; he pulled a glass scalpel from her heel and another jagged shard from between her toes. She bit down on her bottom lip, wanting to scream but fearing what he would do if she did. Karl dropped his mouth to her sole, wiped away the grime with the fondle of his tongue, and, when he'd finished washing her clean, he took a rag from a discarded toolbox nearby and wrapped it snugly around her wounds.

He wiped her blood from his lips and chin, smeared it across his face. "Soon, we'll remind them how we were meant to live."

Christine moved against him, the hollow between her legs aching for him to fill it, to replace the pain with the pleasure only he could give to her. She could sense his greatness, could *feel* his power. His vision of the world would become reality. She believed that.

"Thou shalt be lord of it, and I'll serve thee," she quoted from Shakespeare's *The Tempest*, then kissed him, tasting the warm, salty copper of her own fluids on his lips and tongue.

He slipped into her, and in a few moments, her pain was forgotten.

THIRTEEN

A sense of dread curled up in Alan Everson's gut and made itself at home. In the weeks since their discovery of the lost city, they'd made incredible strides. Despite what they had to work with, their motley crew of archeologists had managed to map and take extensive photographs of the ruins. Carol Miyagi worked day and night on the translation of Atlantean glyphs, and was now able to grasp the language — a hybrid of Egyptian, Greek, and Mayan pictographs. But with each passing day, their cash reserve dwindled. They'd been waiting for new funding from the Hays Foundation to arrive and save them from their money problems, but now...

He entered the cabin they shared and found Carol taking notes, one hand pressed to a large glossy photograph of stone etchings, the other speeding a pen across paper in her journal. Her reading glasses caught the light of a desk lamp, reflected hieroglyphics hiding her exquisite eyes.

Alan forgot his worries for a moment as he drank in the sight of this striking woman. He hadn't told her he loved her, was not sure whether that was even the correct word for his feelings. At first, they'd just been two lonely best friends who happened to sleep together on these long expeditions (Once, Alan used the term "sex buddies" and Carol nearly fell out of the bunk laughing). Over the past year, however, he'd felt a shift in his feelings he was not quite sure how to interpret. They, like the glyphs Carol hovered over, were an alien language he could not decipher. The only thing Alan knew with any certainty was that he cared about her a great deal, and the news he bore would devastate her.

He knocked on the bulkhead, drew her attention away from her studies.

"Hey there." Carol smiled and tapped her finger on the glossy.

She'd once told him that she hadn't learned to speak English until she was seven. Whenever an American told her she had a lovely accent, she had to hide her laughter. When she visited Japan, they said the same thing. "I've got it, Alan. I've been able to decipher about half of these. I can't tell if it's a mythology or part of —"

"Roger Hays...his son was just killed."

"*Masaka.*" Her smile withered; she slumped in her chair and put down her pen. "*Oya, maa.*"

Alan didn't know what she was saying, but the look on her face whispered, "this can't be happening."

After a moment, she looked up at him and spoke English again, "How?"

"Shark attack. I just got off the phone with Kravitz in New York. He said Hays is leaving tomorrow night to claim the body and make all of the arrangements."

Carol nodded, still dazed. "Of course. Um...we should send some flowers. Did he say where the funeral would be?"

"No...he...he just said Hays wouldn't be back in the office until sometime next month..." Unable to gaze at her, he looked at the floor. "And that he hasn't signed the grant check yet. He won't be able to sign it until he gets back."

"Next month?" Her sympathy for their benefactor turned to frustration in an instant. "They can't just wire the funds?"

"You know Hays doesn't phone in his donations. He likes to make a big show of his philanthropy."

"I can't believe...who's running all of his businesses while he's away? He doesn't have some underling who can sign *a check*?"

"The foundation is separate from his companies, Carol. He decides how the funds are distributed, and he's the only one authorized to sign the checks." Each endowment came by mail, accompanied by a press release showing Hays signing the check; the smile on the gangster's face said, "See, I'm a good guy. Nothing bad going on here." Alan shook his head. "Kravitz assured me that we will get continued funding, but he can't go to Hays about this right now."

She took off her glasses and flung them onto the desk. "What are we supposed to do in the meantime? We need supplies. We need more people... Christ, we still need *the basics*."

"We should be able to work here another week or so."

"And then what?"

Alan shrugged. "Then we dip into our savings..."

She looked at the ceiling and snorted.

"...Or we fold up and take a few weeks off."

Carol stood so fast that her chair shot across the cabin floor. "We've only laid some groundwork here. Everything is still preliminary. The second we raise anchor, some other *gejashiku* will come out here with a larger expedition, better funding, and some decent deep-sea equipment."

"Don't you think you're being a little paranoid? I mean we're only talking about a few weeks here."

She began to pace like a caged tiger. "And if someone else moves in? Do you think Hays is going to want to fund an expedition to go over territory somebody else has already covered? I know him. If he can't lay sole claim to something and stick his name on it, he doesn't want anything to do with it."

Alan thought for a moment. "Then we'll get funding from somewhere else."

"Who else will give it to us?" She pounded her temples with her index fingers. "I'm a kook, remember? They've made me a leper. Gangster or not, Hays was the only one who would even touch me. Without him, we'd be doing voiceovers for the Discovery Channel right now."

"Don't be ridiculous, Carol. There aren't any other expeditions circling like vultures, waiting for us to leave so they can swoop in."

She stared at him, stunned. "Now who's being ridiculous? This has been in *Time, Newsweek*..." She grabbed the printout he'd given her earlier in the day. "It's on the front page of this morning's *USA Today*! They're not going to just sit back and politely wait for us to get our act together."

It was true, of course. If this was Atlantis, and Alan had yet to see proof to the contrary, it was the greatest archeological discovery of all time. If they didn't continue here, others most certainly would.

"You're right," Alan said. "But, again, we're only talking about a few weeks. If we'd totally lost our funding and weren't coming back, I could see it. But no one is going to jump in here and steal this from us, from *you*, as soon as we sail away."

"How am I supposed to stop them? What do you expect me to do? Piss in the water and mark my territory?"

"I'm surprised you haven't already."

She glared at him. "*Chikusho!*"

Alan hated it when she cursed in Japanese. Rather than letting her bait him into an argument, however, he spoke calmly and offered her his most understanding face.

"Sorry. That was uncalled for. I know how important this is to you. But this is the hand we've been dealt here and I don't see any solution other than to wait for —"

"I need to get to New York." She moved away to her locker at the far end of the cabin, pulled out a knapsack, and threw it onto the bunk.

Alan blinked in disbelief. "You what?"

"I need to talk to Hays."

"Like hell you do. The man's son was just *killed*. Hays has lost a child, his *only* child. He's a mess. Even mobsters have feelings."

"I know that, all right...but I can't just sit here and watch everything I've worked for be pulled out from under me." Carol tossed some clothes onto the bunk. "I'll give him my sympathy...and...and I'll be a real *baita* and ask him to sign the check before he leaves."

"He's leaving tomorrow."

"I'll take the *Sea Wasp 2*. I'll catch a flight out of Horta to Lisbon, and then grab the first plane back to New York. I'll be back here the day after tomorrow at the latest."

The *Sea Wasp 2* was their twenty-five-foot outboard motorboat, a twin to the one they kept moored back in the States.

Alan opened his mouth to yell that she was crazy, but thought better of it. It was useless to argue with Carol when she was like this. Instead, he shook his head, speaking more to himself than to her, "Do you know how shitty this is? How inappropriate?"

"Yes," she snapped, confusion and aggravation moving across her face in waves. "I know. I also know that I don't have a choice. I have to go in person. A phone call would be too cold and inhuman. I'll offer our condolences, explain our situation, then leave."

"Fine. I'm going with you."

"No. I need you to stay here and handle the expedition." She chuckled, then added, "No sense in both of us looking callous."

"I don't want you driving a speeding boat in the middle of the Atlantic at night by yourself. And as your partner, I know you well enough to know that you're not a people person. You need help with this."

Carol said nothing. She produced a Harvard sweatsuit from the locker and stuffed it into her knapsack, not looking at him.

"Let me do the talking for you, handle this with the necessary tact." He pointed out the cabin door with his thumb. "Nielsen can take care of things here."

After a moment's contemplation, she conceded. "Go tell Nielsen he's in charge. He'll love that."

"He'll do fine."

Carol looked up from her packing. Her bottom lip trembled. She looked close to tears, but maintained her self-control except to mutter, "Thanks."

Alan gave her a quick salute and left her alone.

FOURTEEN

What did Man do before fire?

Cornelius Shiva — Neil to his friends, Corny to the kids who used to beat him, Shithead to his father — knew the answer, of course. Before fire, Man cowered in caves and prayed not to freeze or be eaten. Before fire, Man had no power on this earth at all.

Neil sat in the gloom of a deserted warehouse, his face awash in the red and orange light that danced on the end of his match. He watched the wood blacken as fire ate its way down, felt heat as it neared his thumb and forefinger, but he allowed the flame to kiss his skin before extinguishing it. He tossed the spent matchstick aside and lit another, creating new and even more exciting patterns of light.

A flame was like a snowflake; no two were ever the same.

Fire had been Neil's fascination most of his life, and he had the scar tissue to prove it. His right arm, shoulder, and chest were a mass of disfigurement that dated back to the night he burned his father alive.

They said murderers went to Hell.

Neil hoped that was true.

As he looked into the glow of his match, he dreamed of Hell's conflagration. But, with his luck, arsonists probably had their own special Hell; an abyss from which they could gaze in upon the glory of the holocaust, but could never touch it, or bathe in its warmth. An eternity without fire...now *that* would be a pyromaniac's Hell.

But what Neil did all those years ago...could it really be considered murder?

The police thought so. They'd called it cold-blooded and calculated. His shrinks, on the other hand, said he'd been acting out of fear for his own life, that the years of abuse he'd suffered at the hands of that man had somehow warranted the pyre.

Neil saw truth to both sides of the argument.

After all, Eric Shiva had been a drunken son-of-a-bitch, and a murderer in his own right. Neil watched through the crack in his bedroom door, watched his father beat his mother mercilessly, watched him rip at her clothes and mount her in the middle of the living room while *All in the Family* played on the television set. And, of course, Neil had been the sole witness when his father pushed her down the stairs and broke her neck.

His father had been arrested, but the death was soon ruled an accident. They'd found alcohol in his mother's blood; after years of taking the man's blows, she'd finally given in to his poison. And, just like that, Neil was sent back to live with her killer.

With his wife dead, Eric Shiva needed a new outlet for his rage. Neil's ten-year old face had provided such a release; but he'd endured the names...

"Hey, Shithead, *bring me my beer."*

"Come here, you little bastard, *and fix me a sandwich." "Clean this place up, you goddamn* moron."

...endured the bruises and black eyes in silence. He endured them because, late at night, in the privacy of his room, Neil Shiva would strike a match and burn his own flesh, would deaden his nerves to the sensation of pain. If he couldn't feel his father's cruelty, the man would have no power over him.

Then, two months to the day of his mother's death, Neil's bedroom door opened in the middle of the night. His father tore the pajamas from his body and pinned him to the floor like an animal. Agony stabbed through Neil as his father violated him, the smell of the man's breath like the sickening vapors from a whiskey still, and, when it was over, his father slapped him on the back of the skull and left him there to cry and bleed in the darkness.

Neil curled into a fetal position, episodes of violence replaying in his head, rage clouding his eyes in a crimson fog. And then, he saw it; his father's face engulfed in hot flames, a screaming skull, crying out in agony as the limitless pain it had inflicted on so many others returned home to consume it.

Neil went to the garage and picked up a gas can.

With great care, he slipped into his father's bedroom. He poured dark fuel over the area where Eric's heart should have been, watching the clothing drink. He splashed gasoline onto sheets, comforters, and hands — hands that had lashed out against his mother, hands that had pinned him to the floor — then moved the spout to the man's face and allowed it to hover there for a moment.

This man was not his father. This was just the bastard who happened to come inside his mother. This was the face of a murderer, a rapist.

This was a face he would burn.

Neil splashed amber fuel, watched as it ran into Eric Shiva's nostrils, eyes, and ears. The pain must have been excruciating, because, even in his drunken stupor, Eric shot straight up in the bed; his eyes burned, but that was nothing compared to the burning yet to come.

Neil struck a match and tossed it. Flames, blue and swift, spread up the boy's arm and engulfed his father in seconds. But Neil felt no pain; he was far too enthralled by the writhing torch that danced on the mattress before him, the burning mass that had once been a human being.

He heard screams, but they came to him as if from space, distant and removed from his reality.

They didn't last long.

As Neil watched the man die, his guilt turned to awe, his shame to power. He didn't have to cower in the dark like a caveman, afraid of the world. No. With the help of the flame, he could take control.

A thick blanket enveloped him, hid the bonfire from his eyes as it smothered his own flaming skin, and Neil was carried from the smoky room. There'd been a hearing, but Neil had little memory of it; what he remembered was the hospital that came after. He was at the mercy of others once more, separated from the flame. At first, he didn't think they would ever let him leave, but he learned quickly what to say to the doctors, knew just what they wanted to hear, and soon he was freed. Did the staff think he was cured? Neil didn't believe that for one second. The courts had only given them so much time, however, and New York was full of juveniles far crazier than he.

But there was no madness in the flame, only power.

Neil could harness it, could wield it; and, to his delight, he found this to be a sought-after skill in certain circles, one that paid quite handsomely. Tonight, for instance, Mr. Ludwig had ordered him to turn an old warehouse into ash. Ludwig never said why, and Neil knew better than to ask, but the reason was obvious: the big man, Roger Hays, wanted to build a skyscraper, and this old building alone stood in his way.

The flame danced on the head of Neil's matchstick. He brought it to his mouth, ignited the cigarette that hung from his lips, then took a nice, long drag. The tobacco fibers glowed in the dimness.

Neil leapt to his feet and moved to the center of the warehouse, a carpet of oily rags and old *New York Times*. He took the cigarette from his mouth and placed it in a fresh book of matches, creating a timer. The Camel would smolder until it reached the waiting heads of the matchsticks. They would ignite; spread the flame to oil-soaked rags. Dry, wooden skids would act as kindling — combusting easily, carrying the blaze toward the outer walls. At that point, the warehouse would become unstable, would disintegrate, and the roof would collapse in upon the holocaust below.

It was going to be a glorious achievement.

Rats — their bodies gaunt, their fur matted — scurried around him as if fascinated by his work. He offered them a smile before placing his timer. The white surface of the cigarette turned gray as it smoldered its way toward the matches. Neil stood, scanned the interior of the warehouse one last time, his mind coloring its surfaces with fire, then he sprinted to the safety of an alley across the street.

From the shadows, Neil watched flames lick the window glass of the warehouse, transfixed by their beauty. He wondered if the rats would ignite, would escape the building like fiery demons from the mouth of a volcano. That would be an interesting sight indeed.

Sirens. A neighbor must have called 911.

Fire broke through the walls, growing in strength and intensity, becoming more and more powerful. Firemen would be too late to stop the destruction. Yes. Even now, tongues of orange flame consumed the roof, rising up toward the moon as if trying to scorch it.

The arsonist grinned into the darkness, his eyes twinkling with reflected firelight. As the building died, there was no sense of guilt, only a warm feeling of supremacy and great satisfaction.

FIFTEEN

Kip Lunden leaned over the stern of the *Maggie May*, reaching for his buoy. He hoisted it from the surf, pulling up the nylon rope that tethered it to a wire cage below. He paused, searching the sea for Coast Guard patrols and conservation officers.

Trap fishing was not illegal, but you needed a permit, and Kip had no money to pay for one. Every cent he had seemed to be eaten by *Maggie May*, which was always hungry for repair to one part of her anatomy or another. And, if they caught him trapping without a license, evidence in hand, it would mean a two-thousand-dollar fine or a year in jail.

The fisherman could no more afford the penalty than he could the permit.

It was all just a big government scam. You paid to catch crabs and lobsters; if you wanted people to help you, you had to pay for each of them to be registered. You then had to pay more money if you were going to sell what you caught (a Trader of Lobster Meat and Crab Meat Fee, they called it). Some might say that these fees were small compared to the fines, but it was the principle of the thing. The government was worse than the fucking Mafia, and Kip would be damned if they'd get any more of his hard-earned money than they did every April.

The water lay still in all directions.

Kip continued pulling up rope, and, when his cage broke the inky surface, it was empty. While this was disappointing, it wasn't what angered him. No. What made him mad was the gaping hole in the side of his trap, wires pulled outward in all directions like the petals of a metallic flower.

Damned animal nuts.

Just another problem Kip had to deal with: environmental

activists. They went around with their wire snips, cut open his traps, robbed him of his income, and for what? For fear that, if a cage happened to break loose from its buoy and sink to the bottom, any fish or crab stuck inside would starve to death. Never mind that *he* might starve. No. These kooks just snipped away, freeing their crustacean pals and making Kip late on his dock payments.

Of course, tampering with traps was against the law, but therein lay a Catch 22. So Kip would curse these vandals, mend his traps, and the cycle would go on, and on, and on.

"They get another one?"

It was Ralphy, Kip's mate; he made his way down the ladder from the flying bridge, a freshly opened Sam Adams cradled in his hand. It was a good thing Kip wasn't licensed, because old Ralphy sure as hell wasn't worth the fees. The only help he provided on these nightly runs was to empty Kip's beer cooler.

"Yeah." Kip threw the ruined cage onto the deck where it landed with a clang. "Damn crab lovers."

Ralphy held his bottle up in a toast, "May they all get the itchy kind and be unable to scratch."

Kip scanned the horizon again. The surface of the water was smooth as silk. No sign of another ship anywhere. The damage had to have been done earlier in the evening. *Just once*, he thought, *I'd like to catch one of these pricks in the act.* It would almost be worth the loss of his trap if he could catch the culprit with wire snips in hand. Kip thought of a proper sentence to administer if such a meeting ever took place. Chopping the asshole up into chum and feeding him to the crabs sounded pretty appropriate.

Kip sighed; two more traps to bring up before they could head back into Exeter. He glared up at his shipmate, watched him down the last beer. "We'd get done a whole lot quicker if you'd help."

Ralphy gave a salute. "Aye, aye, Skipper."

He climbed down off the ladder, staggered toward the buoy at the *Maggie May*'s bow, the empty bottle still clutched in his hand.

If he throws that overboard, Kip thought, *I'll kill him.* The ocean was his living, and dumping trash where you fished was like pissing in your own drinking water.

Kip grabbed the next buoy and brought it on board, pulling rope. There seemed to be weight on the other end.

Good, the night won't be a total loss after all.

Sure enough, when his trap surfaced, it was teeming with lobster, all with carapace above the three and a quarter-inch legal limit.

Hot damn!

Kip smiled at the cage and set it down on the wooden deck at his feet. Inside, lobsters crawled over one another as if playing a slow-motion game of leapfrog.

A thunderous splash caused Kip to jump.

His eyes shot up to the horizon; light from the mainland sliced sky from sea with surgical precision. He found no Coast Guard cruisers, however, no conservation officials, not even a diver bobbing in the water with metal snips in hand. In every direction, the surface was obsidian glass.

Must've come from the bow.

"Ralphy?"

The idiot must've dropped the trap back in the water.

Then came another possibility: *Maybe he fell in.*

Kip frowned. Ralphy had downed a lot of beer. Kip dropped his line and looked toward the bow; the *Maggie May*'s cabin obstructed his view. "Ralphy?"

Something crawled over the railing; Kip heard water run off its body onto the deck in a hard rain.

The fool did *fall overboard.*

Kip shook his head. If it weren't for the fact that he'd known Ralphy since kindergarten, he'd throw the bastard off on the dock and find himself a new mate, one that actually knew what the hell he was doing. But, as things were, the man was down on his luck and had nowhere else to go.

Kip removed the rope from his trap and coiled it. The lobsters paid him no mind; they climbed over, under, and around in an orgy of motion. If there were more in Ralphy's trap, he might actually be able to buy a new fuel line for *Maggie*. The current one was buried beneath a layer of tape.

Another body climbed aboard. The sound of wet feet smacking

the wooden deck was unmistakable.

Kip's breath caught in his throat and he dropped the cord.

It's the crab lovers!

They'd grown tired of going after his traps; now, they wanted to take their wire snips to his belly. No trapper, no traps. It was some kind of Lobster Liberation Organization gone mad.

Kip ran to the cabin and grabbed a machete off the wall. He used the large blade to cut fish and heavy-duty lengths of rope. Now it was all that stood between him and this unknown boarding party.

He heard glass shatter and the deck lights flickered out, plunging the ship into darkness.

Kip thought of the radio in the cabin, then remembered it was broken, in need of a hundred and twenty dollars worth of repairs. A hundred and twenty dollars he'd been unwilling to spend. Kip might have felt differently if it had been his only source of communication, but there was —

The marine radio.

He had to get up to the flying bridge, had to call for help. Fuck the fines the Coast Guard would slap him with when they got here.

Kip held the machete out in front of him like a sword and stepped from the cabin; sweating, he raised his voice to the dark, "Whoever you are, I got a big fuckin' knife. You'd better haul ass off this boat before I gut you like tuna!"

Squishy sounds of wet movement near the bow were the only reply.

His eyes shot up the ladder to the flying bridge. He put the machete up to his mouth, bit down on the blade, and climbed hand over hand. Movement, swift and unnatural, registered in Kip's peripheral vision. He froze in mid-step and peered into the darkness.

An octopus.

Kip could make out the pulsating sac of its head, could see its tentacles writhing like black snakes in the moonlight. Then he saw the arch of a sinuous back, saw the spiked dorsal fins, and he realized what was on his boat was no octopus.

The creature snarled, leapt onto the cabin's roof, its legs bent like the hindquarters of a dog.

Kip reached for the next rung and pulled himself up.

It was on the ladder below him now. Its claws scratched at the aluminum. Its respiration warmed his heels. It grabbed Kip's exposed calf, its slimy touch like a branding iron pressed to his flesh. Once, as a teenager, he'd been stung by a jellyfish. That pain had been a pinprick by comparison.

Kip bit down on the blade and screamed, kicking until he was free.

The pain faded quickly; his leg went numb, became dead weight dangling from his hip, and he pulled himself onto the flying bridge. In the moonlight, he saw swelling, saw a seeping ulcer where the "sting" had pierced him. The loss of sensation spread, moved up into his torso, and Kip found himself struggling to breathe.

The creature clawed its way onto the bridge.

Kip crawled backward, hyperventilating, his heart slamming against the rear of his sternum. He grabbed the machete from his mouth and held it out against his attacker, but numbness devoured all feeling in his arm.

The blade fell to the floor with a loud clatter and the beast moved in; its head eclipsed the moon like a huge, blossoming flower.

Kip was poisoned, paralyzed. The marine radio hung just above his head, but it might as well have been a million miles away.

The platform shook beneath him. The creature closed in. Fluid dripped down from it, soaking his clothes.

But he couldn't move.

He couldn't feel *anything*.

And a moment later, he was grateful for it.

SIXTEEN

Ten o'clock in the morning.

Larry sat in his folding chair on a rocky plateau, his easel by his side. He looked up at Colonial Bay's lighthouse, trying to convince himself that Susan Rogers had been a dream and nothing more. It was the only sane explanation. Dead bodies didn't go out for midnight strolls.

His eyes focused on the round ledge near the top of the tower, the ledge where Susan had been standing before she jumped, then followed the arc of her fall. No body lay on the beach, nor the rocks that surrounded it.

There was no body, because it was all just some weird fantasy.

His mind kept throwing the image of Natalie's dead body over his eyes. She hadn't been like the rotting abomination he'd seen —

Dreamed!

— last night. She'd been lying on her bed, just as beautiful as ever, and then Larry had seen her eyes. They'd been open and glassy, lifeless. Her long, red hair lay in a puddle of her own vomit, the empty vial of pills still clutched in one rigid hand. The phone dangled off the hook by her side, the same phone she'd used to call his machine, to tell him that he'd brought her to this end.

Natalie was wrong about you.

Dream or no dream, Larry knew that was true. At least, he hoped he knew.

He returned his attention to the canvas; he'd drawn a rough outline and it craved paint. The wooden box in his lap held various tubes of color, twisted into a mélange of shapes through constant use. Many were covered in multi-colored fingerprints, others in a rubbery layer of dried acrylic.

As he scanned his collection, Larry's eyes kept drifting back up to the lighthouse. Was the entrance like the one in his dream? The thought munched on his brain until he felt he needed to have a look, just to get on with his life.

Larry put down his paints. He studied the cliff face until he found a path to climb, then grabbed hold of the rock. With some effort, he managed to pull his weight onto higher ground.

Just like the rock climbing wall back at the club, he thought, out of breath, then hoisted himself onto a grassy plateau.

In daylight, the lighthouse looked more like a huge barber's pole than the ominous spire of his dream. Its flaking paint and sparkling glass hardly instilled fear. It was just another historical landmark, a symbol of another time.

Larry should've been shocked to find a cement staircase that led down to the beach, but he wasn't, just as he wasn't surprised to see a wooden door at the base of the lighthouse. He moved to it, took the warm brass knob in his hand.

It's gonna be locked, Neuhaus. This place is a landmark. You don't think they'd just let you waltz —

Larry opened the door, looked in all directions, then entered. Sunlight filtered down from the grated ceiling, illuminating the interior. Large fishing nets hung from hooks in the wall, and intricately woven spiderwebs swayed in the breeze from the open door.

His heartbeat increased.

On the floor, at the foot of a wrought iron staircase, a lantern lay smashed in a pool of blood. Larry ran his fingers through his sweat-dampened hair, visually following a blood trail up the stairs, and a tiny crab scurried out from beneath the bottom step.

"Christ," he muttered.

It's a crab, his brain conceded, *but it needn't be* the *crab. It can't be.*

But, in his dream, he'd knocked a lantern off the shelf. It fell to the floor, shattered. And now, here it was, smashed at his feet.

You were sleepwalking, his mind reasoned. *You hit the shelf in your sleep and your subconscious incorporated the act into your dream. Ever hear the one about the guy who ate the world's largest marshmallow? He woke up and found his pillow was gone.*

"Okay," Larry murmured in agreement, anxious to prove that he was still in control. "Sleepwalking would explain the robe being wet."

Right, his mind consented. *Nothing insane about a little walk in your sleep. Hell, Jennifer Aniston does it all the time!*

But how did the girl know about Natalie's message on his machine — the one that began with "uncaring bastard" and ended with "murderer"?

She didn't know shit, you knew about it. It was your dream. You wanted to be told that it was all right, that the people you couldn't save couldn't be saved.

It all sounded logical enough. The blood, however, could not be so easily explained. He studied his hands, wondering if he'd smashed the lantern as he'd smashed the mirror, but his wounds hadn't reopened, and no new cuts appeared.

The flesh is the clay of the gods.

"Blow it out your ass."

Larry ascended the stairs; the glass-enclosed room was just as he remembered it. A gust of cool wind met him at the open doorway. He stepped onto the metal catwalk and strolled around.

The blood trail came to an end, as though the donor had spontaneously healed, or leapt over the side. Larry looked down.

Still no body. That's something at least.

From the lighthouse spire, visitors to Colonial Bay's streets appeared as multi-colored insects fleeing to and from an unseen nest. Larry found himself longing to be one of them, blissfully ignorant of what, if anything, was happening.

SEVENTEEN

Peggy paid a visit to Colonial Bay's Historical Society. She'd wanted Larry to join her, but he'd been anxious to paint, and she was happy to see him enthusiastic about his art again.

If you'd asked her a year ago, she would have said marriage was a certainty, that everlasting happiness was all but guaranteed. But who could predict the future? Nobody. At least, in a novel, you could look ahead if the suspense became too great.

Peggy had written a few romance novels over the years. She'd typed them up, printed them out, and sent the bulky manuscripts off to an array of publishers, only to receive a collection of rejection slips. Peggy read the letters — which all began with "Thank you for your interest in..." and ended with "We regret to inform you..."— and felt like crying, but Larry was quick to cheer her up. He reminded her that even Dr. Suess and Stephen King were turned down a hundred times before they made it big. And so Peggy kept at it, and, every time she mailed off her work, she held out hope that the next reply would be "the one."

The one.

She'd known Larry Neuhaus was the one the night they first met. He had an aura of strength and determination; he knew what he wanted to do with his life and knew he'd do it. Peggy liked that.

In the time that they'd been together, however, Larry had abandoned many of his dreams. Painting no longer held any enjoyment for him, and he made no attempt to hide it. She'd seen him punch a hole through a half-finished canvas more than once, scaring her, not because she thought he would turn his anger and frustration onto her, but because she knew they were killing him inside.

Wasn't that what the mirror was for? Slashing up his hand and wrist like that? Wasn't he trying to kill himself then, the way Natalie had?

Peggy shivered.

Another life, she thought. Although Larry's breakdown had been the most horrible experience she could remember, Peggy was glad for the changes it wrought in him. His enthusiasm was returning, a fact that made her happier than she'd been in a long while. His confidence and determination would soon follow, bringing back the man Peggy fell in love with, the man she knew he could still be.

She strolled over to a glass case, looked in on a miniature representation of the entire island. As she studied the model, her eyes fell upon a tiny metal plate:

Colonial Bay

Founded 1680

Even older than America.

Her gaze shifted to a single white steeple sitting high upon on a hill, wondering if everyone in town practiced the same faith.

It had probably been that way in the beginning, she thought. *Escape to The New World and Enjoy Religious Freedom.*

Peggy stepped away from the display and a row of portraits caught her eye. She moved down the gallery, looked at each face and name in turn.

If I did let Larry paint me, she wondered, *would I end up in some museum like this?*

She skimmed the texts mounted next to each frame, discovering that the church she'd seen in the model had in fact been Colonial Bay's first permanent structure; that it was not until 1758 that a shop was erected in the town. She also learned that the Pennacook and Massachuset tribes who lived on the mainland were afraid to visit this island.

Probably scared of seeing some of these faces.

Peggy suppressed the giggle she felt in her throat, wondering again how people might view her portrait in three hundred years. She shook her head.

At least I'd have better hair than these guys.

And then one of the canvases attracted her attention. The man reminded her of Mel Gibson in *Braveheart*. And, when Peggy looked over his accompanying text, she found a familiar name: Jonathan DeParle.

As in Ed "the innkeeper" DeParle? She studied the man's drawn features and smiled. *Well, Ed, your great-grandfather's worthy of a trip in the old Wayback machine. Hubba hubba.*

She pulled herself away from the picture, moved down a side hallway. The walls of the corridor were lined with muskets, bayonets, archaic bullets, and other relics. An accompanying plaque claimed they were from the Revolutionary War.

A mural depicting the construction of Colonial Bay's lighthouse covered the wall of the next room. In the center of the room, a display case held a patchwork quilt of flags that had flown over the town through the years. Peggy saw a British flag that was torn in one place and blackened in another, as if someone had rescued it from a fire. She found a "DON'T TREAD ON ME" banner...several versions of Old Glory... and one other flag, a flag she was unfamiliar with; a pure white banner, and, at its center, imprisoned by a hoop, was a large red trident.

EIGHTEEN

Howard Monroe grabbed his briefcase and made his way up the sidewalk to Colonial Bay's only school. Even after ten years of this routine, he still couldn't get used to the summer quiet. Classes had been over for two weeks, and no student would pass through these doors again until fall. He fumbled with his key ring, wondering why he always had trouble finding the right one, then stepped inside.

"It's the same shit every summer, buddy," the principal whispered, his footfalls echoing through the empty halls. "Everyone else is out there swimming and enjoying the day while you're stuck signing forms. You knew the job was dangerous when you took it."

When he turned a corner, Howard found the door to the pool propped open with a small wooden wedge. He looked into the chamber and saw the pool filled beyond capacity.

That's impossible, I saw them drain the thing myself.

A puddle slowly soaked its way through his shoes and socks. He lifted his foot and saw a trail of water that extended from the pool into the gloomy hall.

What the hell...?

The principal followed the trail and found the office door ajar.

Vandals. There are vandals in my office.

Howard stood motionless for a moment, unsure of what to do and cursing himself for not owning a cell phone. It would take a few minutes to get to the pay phone in the teacher's lounge, then another fifteen minutes for Chief Canon to get out to the school. Too long. The culprit, if he or she was still in the building, would be out the office window and gone by then.

Howard snuck down the hallway, his briefcase held tightly in his hands. He would walk into the office, come up behind the trespasser, and whack them over the head with ten pounds of paperwork. Once or twice, the squish of his wet shoes caused him to grimace, but no one came to the office doorway. He neared the door, eased it open with his sweaty palm.

The lobby was untouched, nothing out of place. Wet footprints on the light-brown carpet offered the only clue that something was wrong. He glanced over at his office. That door, too, stood ajar, painting a sliver of light across the lobby. He hesitated, took a deep breath, then made his approach.

It looked as if a hurricane had struck. Books, folders, and loose paper littered the floor. Pictures hung at odd angles or had been ripped from the wall. And, most distressing of all, a naked woman knelt on his freshly cleared desk, looking like a cat ready to pounce.

"Hello, Principal Monroe." Her voice sounded strangely familiar.

"Who the hell are you? What are you — ?"

"You mean you've forgotten me already?"

His eyes traveled down the length of her back; they came to rest on a small black tattoo at the base of her spine. "Christine?" He moved to the desk. "What...? Where are your clothes?"

"I don't wear clothes anymore. Why wear a mask on top of a mask? A little silly, don't you think?"

"Come on." He set his briefcase down. "I'll take you home. I hear you've got your parents nearly out of their minds with worry."

"They were always out of their minds," she said, her voice growing distant.

"Let me help you, Chrissy."

"Help me? You're the one who needs help. You, my parents...All of *you* need help, not me. Karl's already helped me."

Howard felt a stream of ice water run over him. "Chris, is Karl here?"

"Colonial Bay isn't our home, it's our prison. Did you know that?" As she spoke, she slid off the desktop and put her hand on his cheek.

His eyes drifted down to her breasts. They were badly bruised. "Oh, God," he muttered, and his gaze met hers. "Did Karl do this to you?"

She smiled over his shoulder. "Why don't you ask him?"

Howard's stomach sank.

"You surprised us, Principal." A voice came from behind him. "School's out for the summer...bastard."

Howard spun to see Karl Tellstrom. The boy leaned against a file cabinet on the opposite side of the room, naked as the day he was born. Sunlight streamed in through the blinds, painted him in yellow stripes.

The principal motioned to Christine. "What'd you do to this girl?"

Karl grinned. "What I've been doing for a lot of people. I've opened her eyes."

Howard took two steps toward the door, but Tellstrom gave the filing cabinet a push. It fell to the floor in front of the entrance, blocking Howard's retreat. Karl shoved the principal back into the center of the office.

Howard regarded Tellstrom without flinching; some people in Colonial Bay feared this little shit, but he was not among them. Karl had always been a bully, nothing more or less. "You listen to me, *boy* —"

"No, you listen to me, Howie!" Tellstrom pulled a filing drawer from the downed cabinet, dumped its contents onto the already littered floor. "You're weak, you and your whole fucking clan...and this island's long overdue for a change."

Christine stood behind Karl. She slipped her arms around him and ran her fingers through the thick, black curls of hair that grew from his chest. She looked at the principal, and, for the briefest of moments, he saw in her eyes the little girl he'd once known, the one who knew right from wrong, then she turned away and buried her face in Tellstrom's neck.

"You're crazy," Howard declared with conviction.

"Yeah, I probably am." Karl craned his neck to kiss Christine's forehead. "I'm in good company. Peter the Great was crazy. Columbus and Alexander were crazy."

"I'll go find some rope," Christine murmured. "We can tie him up and keep him in here...away from the pool."

Tellstrom nodded, then returned his attention to the principal. "You should've stayed home today, Howie."

"Karl, it's not too late to put a stop to this."

The boy shook his head. "Do you know how pathetic you sound?"

"I *sound* like a sane human being."

"*Exactly.*"

"If your mother were alive," Howard began, "she'd be sick to see what you've become."

Karl's sunburnt face grew even redder as the rage boiled behind his eyes. "My mother would be proud of what I've *become*!"

The principal heard the whoosh of air pushed into his ear, then felt a jolt of pain as the metal filing drawer collided with his skull and sent him to the floor. His eyes fluttered open, displayed double images to his reeling brain. The forms converged into focus, permitting him to see Karl Tellstrom's nude form standing over him, the filing drawer raised high above his head. Blood dripped from a sharp corner of the tray, and the principal's gut churned at the realization that it was his own.

"Karl, no!" Christine tried to grab his arm, but Tellstrom backhanded her, slammed her back against the desk.

The wounded principal propped himself up with his elbows.

Karl struck him hard across the face with the drawer, ripped another gash in his cheek and shattered his jaw.

Howard fell back against his desk. He coughed, spraying cherry droplets. His head spun, but he remained conscious, moaning and gargling as the pain blazed through his brain.

Tellstrom lifted the cabinet above his head. "What I've *become* is the savior of our fucking people!"

This time, the drawer came down with such force that Howard's face gave way with a loud *crack*. A crimson splash dotted the walls and surrounding clutter; the principal's arms and legs convulsed for a moment, then his body became inert. A dark spot appeared in the crotch of Howard's shorts as his bladder released its contents one final time.

"You should've stayed home," Karl repeated. He lifted the misshapen tray; saw the wreckage that had once been a face, and smiled uneasily at his own handiwork.

Christine rubbed her cheek. She stared up at her lover with shock-widened eyes, convinced this had to be a nightmare.

"It's begun," Tellstrom told her, the bloodied drawer still clutched in his hand.

Nineteen

New York rain pelted the glass. Below, the pavement was dark. Below, rivers formed and swept candy wrappers, bottles, and old condoms through grates into waiting sewers. Below, umbrellas passed one another in alternating bands as huddled masses moved uptown and downtown, moved in and out of cabs, subway stations, and doorways. In the distance, where twins of glass and steel once pierced low rain clouds on their way to Heaven, loomed an empty gray void.

Roger Hays gazed at the vacant New York skyline from his high-backed, leather chair. Once, the view made him smile at the glory of his successes; now, it only served to remind him of his losses. He remembered watching helplessly on a London hotel television as his lofty offices fell in a cloud of ash and rubble, remembered some of his employees diving from their windows to escape the coming flames. He recalled wives and husbands, daughters and sons, fathers and mothers, all weeping an endless shower of tears. While he was able to rent new spaces for furniture, to recover some of his files and to hire new staff and aides, his vast power could not resurrect his former headquarters and all the wealth in the world could not bring back the dead.

Tonight, he would see his son on a slab.

He took a sip of wine and watched the rain. Heaven's tears. Had he been thinking rationally, he might have wondered about his inability to shed even a single tear of his own, but his mind was occupied solely by rage.

They said a shark stole David's life, but Hays couldn't help feeling skeptical. The fact that his son's face had been mutilated made it feel like a hit, something Komarovsky, his chief rival, might have ordered.

Yes.

Hays leaned back in his chair, merciless thoughts playing in his head. The killer needed to be human so that he could have this person tortured for hours, perhaps days, and finally executed. Then he could feel some contentment, a sense of closure. He studied the drops of rain hitting his window, then lowered his eyes to the pool of red wine filling his glass. Blood for blood. He drank deeply, pledging that his son's killer would pay in full.

The intercom sounded on his desk. "Mr. Hays?"

He ignored it. He'd given orders not to be disturbed.

"Mr. Hays, a Dr. Miyagi here to see you. She says it's urgent."

Miyagi? What was *she* doing here? "It will have to wait."

He heard the door to his office open and gave a resigned sigh. Secretaries made poor bodyguards. Anyone who wanted to get to him could, which was why Hays kept a loaded .45 in his top desk drawer. Miyagi was quite benign, however, so he spun his chair around to face her unarmed.

She was not alone.

"Mr. Hays?" It was the archeologist's assistant, Alan...something; he walked cautiously into the office with Miyagi in tow. "We can't say how sorry we are, both for this intrusion and for your loss."

Roger looked past the man to Carol, biting his lip to contain his mounting fury. Everyone from the doorman to the mayor was sorry for him. He did not need, nor did he want their pity. "How good of you to pop in and pay your respects. I thought you were in Atlantis."

She moved toward his desk, her head bowed, her slight accent more noticeable than usual as she spoke, "That's where I'd like to be, sir, and I would never bother you, disturb you in this time of terrible tragedy —"

"What do you need, Carol?"

She raised her head, eyed him. His tone had surprised her. It was level and quite business-like.

Alan stepped forward to speak for her once more. "Mr. Kravitz told us that you have not yet signed the necessary paperwork for our continued funding."

Hays breathed, annoyed. He knew this Alan had never cared for him, nor for his money, and he doubted if the man truly cared anything for his pain. In fact, when the check failed to arrive, Hays wondered how upset the man really was. "I haven't *seen* the paperwork. As you know, I've had a bit of bad news and —"

Carol broke in, "Without your further support, we'll be forced to halt operations and this discovery, the return on your investment in this project, will be taken away." She was visibly nervous, but set in her convictions and straight to the point. Hays had always liked that about her. In fact, if he could be said to truly like *anyone*, it would be Miyagi. "I wish this could wait until your return, but, with the news coverage this discovery has generated, we wanted to protect your interests."

The businessman smirked. "You could have called me, you know."

"I was afraid your office wouldn't put me through."

"If they were worth a damn, they wouldn't have. But then if they were worth a damn, you two wouldn't be standing here now either." Hays reached over and pressed a button on his intercom. "Miss Shone?"

"Yes, Mr. Hays?" his secretary responded.

"Have Kravitz bring me the paperwork for Dr. Miyagi's continued funding."

"Yes, Mr. Hays."

The archeologist gave a slight bow of appreciation and respect. "Thank you. You don't know what your continued support means to me, especially in your time of grief."

"Oh, I think I do." He rose from his chair; his glass needed a refill, and his mind needed a distraction. "Would you care for some wine?"

"Yes, thank you." She looked to Alan and he nodded.

"It's Australian," Roger told them. Glasses hung from a rack above his wet bar like odd stalactites. He plucked two more free and poured. "I picked up a case when I was there on business last year, and I've become quite fond of it."

Hays extended a full glass for Miyagi. After a moment, he turned to see why she hadn't come for it. She stood at the other end of the room, staring at his bookshelf. "See something you like?"

She pointed to his shelving, her eyes wide with shock or amazement, Hays could not discern. "Where did you get this?"

Hays followed her finger to the driftwood sculpture sitting amid his other knick-knacks. He swallowed hard. "I picked it up in Colonial Bay."

The archeologist feverishly motioned for Alan to look at the statue.

When her assistant saw the figure, his face reflected hers. "What does it mean?"

"I don't know." Miyagi looked at Hays, still vacant. "*Where* is this from?"

"It's a small town, an island off the coast of New Hampshire. It's where my son David was killed. I'm going there this evening." They continued to stare at the carving. Hays saw nothing remarkable about the thing. He'd picked it up as a conversation piece. "What's so exciting?"

"This sculpture," Carol began, regaining some of her composure, "it's just like one I found last week in Atlantis."

Hays approached the carving, suddenly reminded of his trip to Australia. The stars had seemed somehow different there, and he realized they were upside down in the southern hemisphere. Something he saw every day transformed into something fascinating. The same was true now. This statue had sat on that shelf for years, just a piece of furniture, like his desk. Now, it was something mysterious.

Miyagi tore her eyes from the sculpture and looked at Roger, her face serious. "How can we get to Colonial Bay?"

TWENTY

Larry's head pounded, his brain practically screamed. He grabbed the suitcases from the closet and started to pack. They would take the next ferry off the island, drive back to New York. Peggy would understand. They were in danger.

His headache worsened until he found he couldn't think. Finally, he took some Advil and forced himself to lie down on the bed. He closed his eyes, listened to the music of his own pulse, and sleep somehow overtook him.

The projector in his mind showed the same clips again and again: the lantern...the crab...the warning...

Leave Colonial Bay.

...and his eyes sprang open to find that the room had grown dim. He looked at his watch. It was now 8:30.

Larry rubbed his temples, hearing a much calmer voice in his head, a voice all artists hear but seldom heed. It was the voice of logic, the voice of reason. It said, "Let's think rationally about this, Larry" and "Is this a wise thing to do, Larry?" Years ago, this same voice told him that he'd never make a living with his art. The voice had been wrong then, and he'd laughed at it, but now...now he desperately wanted that voice to be right.

You had a very vivid dream and went sleepwalking, reason maintained. *If you stop recognizing this for what it was, start believing that a dead woman did talk to you...well, old pal, then you're crossing over into the realm of the insane. Do you really want to put Peggy through all of that? Hasn't she been through enough because of you?*

The phone cried out. Larry jumped, then picked up the receiver with noticeable hesitation. "Hello?"

"Hi, Rembrandt."

He looked at the suitcases still littering the floor. "Peggy..."

"How's the painting coming?" Her voice sounded very distant.

"Fine. It's...um..." Larry looked at his watch again, then closed his eyes. "Where are you?"

"The book depository."

"Where?"

She giggled in his ear. "I'm at the library. I saw this flag at the museum and I wanted to do some snooping about the town history. Key West tried to become its own little country at one point. I think this island might have done the same thing and...and I know you're not into the whole history worship."

"Not so much, no."

"Well anyway, you know how you're always telling me I should keep writing my silly little bodice-rippers?"

Larry could see what was coming. "Yes."

"I think Colonial Bay would make a great setting for a new novel."

He swallowed. "Oh..."

"And I thought I should know a bit more about the place if I'm gonna write about it."

"Yeah, might help." His eyes opened and drifted back to the suitcases. "The thing is —"

"They're gonna close up soon. You ate dinner already, didn't you?"

"No...I...food?"

"Great. Too into your painting, huh?" He said nothing, and after a beat, she went on. "I've been so busy researching, I haven't stopped to grab anything either. Why don't I meet you at this place called The Wharf? It's open until eleven and I hear it's a really good buffet-style thing."

"Buffet?" The artist sighed. The voices were arguing for control again, but Reason was gaining ground over Let's-Get-the-Hell-Outta-Here. Why did he have to flush those pills? "Yeah, I'm good with that."

"You don't sound enthused."

Larry rubbed his eyes. "I'm just..." *Trying to hold it together?* "Just tired."

"Poor baby. Not *too* tired, I hope?" And then she purred.

Larry laughed. Coming from Peggy, a sexual overture struck him as being quite funny. "No. You know me. Never too tired for that."

"Good. See you around..." In his mind, he could see her looking at her watch. "Nine o'clock?"

"It's a date."

"I love you."

"I love you, too." He listened for the click at the other end of the line, set the receiver back down onto its cradle, then walked over to the suitcases and kicked one. He tossed the luggage back into the closet one piece at a time. "Logic and Reason score. And the crowd goes wild."

TWENTY ONE

Sunlight faded beneath the waves.

Jeff Wilson walked down a near-deserted stretch of sidewalk on the edge of town, briefcase in hand. He was a sales representative for national hotel chain, a job that required constant travel. This month, the hierarchy had seen fit to send him on a mission to Colonial Bay, one of the few "tourist traps" in this country that didn't boast one of their hotels.

"Excuse me, sir."

Wilson jumped. He whirled to his right, saw a shadowy figure standing in a narrow alley, and put a hand over his heart. He wasn't an old man by any means, but living on the road as he did, his steady diet of Big Macs and Whoppers had forced his doctor to voice concern. "Christ! What are you tryin' to do? Kill me?"

"Sorry, sir." A young man, no more than twenty, moved into the orange glow of freshly ignited street lamps, dressed only in his swim trunks. "Didn't mean to frighten you. My name's Jason."

"Well, Jason, you nearly gave me a heart attack."

"Sorry. It's just that I don't have any pockets." The boy tugged at his trunks to show that it was the truth. "I had my wallet tucked in the waistband, but it fell out when I cut through this alley. You got a flashlight in your car I could use for a sec?"

"Yeah, I got a light." Wilson reached into his pocket and pulled out his keys; a small flashlight dangled from the metal ring on a chain. He tested it to see if it still worked. It did. Removing it would take too long, but, if he handed the whole key ring over, the boy might take off and leave him stranded. He gave a frustrated sigh, then aimed his light into the alley. "Where'd you drop it?"

"Thanks, sir."

The salesman paused. "I want you to know, I got about three dollars in cash on me and some travelers' checks. No credit cards. I don't believe in credit cards. So, if this is some kinda mugging, you can just turn and walk the other way right now 'cause you won't get piss from me."

Jason snickered. "I don't want your money."

Wilson nodded and followed the young man in. The tiny spotlight moved along the alley floor, revealing dirt, a roach or two (big-city crickets, as Wilson called them), and some stray trash.

No wallet.

"Where exactly did you lose this thing?"

"'Bout half way," the young man said; his voice sounded somehow different.

A loud crackling sound filled the alley, like brittle branches being snapped in two.

Wilson stopped to listen. "You hear that?"

"Yeah." Jason rasped, his breathing labored, asthmatic.

Wilson turned his light in the young man's direction, and something clawed at his right hand. Pain burned across his knuckles, leaving a warm splash in its wake. Wilson dropped his keyring and covered the wound with his left palm. As it fell, the light streaked across his attacker. A pointed, gray snout lunged toward him, filled with row after row of glistening teeth.

Wilson opened his mouth to cry out, but a webbed talon rushed in to fill it. Sharpened claws punched their way through the soft tissue of his gullet, grabbed hold of his spine, and pulled it apart.

•••

Peggy hurried down the sidewalk.

Her trip to the library had been a total waste of time. The librarians told her that most of the records she needed had been lost in a hurricane, but Peggy knew it was a lie, could see it in their eyes. Larry would say that she was just being paranoid, but they *were* hiding something.

The question was what.

A sound found Peggy's ear, a muffled cry from the alley to her left. She stopped and peered into the darkness. "Hello?"

The darkness offered no reply.

Peggy shook her head.

Hearing things, she thought. *First conspiracies, now this.*

Before she could take another step, Peggy heard more sounds of distress; someone was having trouble breathing. "Is anybody there?"

More wheezing, gagging sounds, louder this time, more urgent. Peggy imagined an elderly woman lying on her back in the dark, trying to catch a breath and failing due to heart attack or respiratory disease. She scanned the area and saw no one else nearby; Colonial Bay's streets were nearly deserted.

What if it were you lying in there?

Peggy frowned. She checked her cell phone. Her reception had been spotty at best since leaving the mainland, and she currently had no bars.

What if you were dying and nobody stopped, nobody even bothered to try and help?

Peggy took a deep breath, then ventured into the alley. She took a dozen or so steps before calling out again, and the warm glow of street lamps faded quickly to absolute darkness. It was just as though she'd strolled into a cave. Back in New York, she would've said that only a crazy person walks into a dark alley. Yet, here she was. "Hello?"

The wheezing stopped.

"Do you need help?"

A sloshing sound, someone stepped in a puddle.

"If you can hear me, please answer."

A low growl filled her ears, a gargling snarl. It was the noise a drowning cat might utter as it went under for the final time.

Sudden terror made Peggy mute. She turned to run and her feet caught on something in her path. She fell to the ground, clawed at the cobblestone in a panic. Her fingers closed around a small plastic flashlight and she picked it up. The slender beam showed her what she'd tripped over. It was the fallen body of a dead man; his glazed eyes stared up at her with sleepy fascination.

A raven hulk rushed toward her.

Peggy rose to her feet again; the light caught only a glimpse of it, a webbed foot, a claw that scratched against the concrete as it ran. Wet talons gripped her arms, restrained her, pulled her back into shadow. Something like a bear trap closed around her shoulder and her body ignited with pain.

Peggy found she was finally able to scream.

PART TWO
POSEIDON'S CHILDREN

TWENTY TWO

A bright light waved and flickered in the distance.

Peggy drifted toward it. She felt numb, but numb was good, much better than the pain. There were voices all around her in the darkness, one of them Larry's.

"*Peggy*," he cried. "*Oh Christ, get an ambulance!*"

More voices, strangers; they worked to save her life.

"*I can't stop the bleeding!*"

"*Load her in the boat.* Careful!"

Her parents died five years before, a plane crash over South Dakota. She hadn't thought of them in months, and suddenly felt guilty for it.

"*Black Harbor, we have a young female, approximately thirty years of age, with...*"

I'm twenty-eight, *thank you very much.*

Then, strangest of all: "*Tellstrom's done it now.*"

Who's Tellstrom, and what has he done?

The moon. It was the moon Peggy was looking at, its light filtered through ocean depths. Was she drowning? No. Somehow, her consciousness had been uprooted, transplanted into the graceful flesh of a dolphin. After a moment of disorientation, she swam rapidly through the brine, feeling a sense of speed, of *power*. A single thrust of her tail propelled her up; she broke the surface of the waves and somersaulted into the night.

Her new body plunged back into the depths. She caught up with a school of Allison tuna, swam through the heart of the cluster in a corkscrew pattern. The fish scattered, then quickly regrouped. Peggy could almost hear them hurling obscenities her way.

A sea turtle swam by her, huge and ancient, and she gave chase.

Its immense front flippers moved like canoe paddles...back and forth, back and forth. Its shell showed signs of wear, as if it had survived countless battles. She glided alongside it for a moment, then let the creature lumber along its course alone.

Peggy had been swimming and diving before, but she'd always perceived the sea as a place of untold danger, filled with predators and risk. Now, she saw her new home as an astounding empire of beauty. She couldn't wait to see what adventures lurked around the next bend.

Another figure rose from the depths, a female silhouette. Long hair flowed out from her head like the petals of a black rose. Then she drifted into the moonlight, a corpse; bloated, skin darkened from exposure until it was gray with black splotches. Her lips had been stripped away, leaving an eternal smile, and her eyes had gone white as milk.

It spoke, and, despite the water, Peggy understood every word: "It's too late for you."

Peggy tried to swim away, but the drowned woman lurched forward and grabbed her.

"Don't let Larry share your fate," the carrion warned. Peggy saw parrotfish grazing within the confines of its ribcage. "Tell him to leave you. Let him go. *Make* him go."

Peggy's strength abandoned her, left her prisoner to the phantasm's grip.

"If Larry stays, they'll kill him. Or worse...he'll become like you."

Peggy wondered who the girl was, wondered why she was so concerned about Larry, then a horrid thought came to her: this was Natalie's corpse, come to drag Peggy down into some watery hell.

The corpse read her thoughts. "I'm not Natalie. I owe him."

Shadows rushed, plunged Peggy back into darkness. She felt a dull throb, as if the nerves of her body were being muffled under a thick blanket, as if her brain had been made deaf to their protests.

Peggy opened her eyes.

Slowly, things came into focus and she saw Larry standing over her, holding her hand, flashing a quivering grin.

"Hi, gorgeous," he told her.

She parted her lips to speak. "Dead...girl?"

"No, honey, you're fine. You're in a hospital."

Another man was there, older, late forties, perhaps fifty, dressed in blue scrubs. He pushed Larry aside with a polite "Excuse me" and proceeded to shine a penlight into Peggy's eyes. "Do you know your name?"

"Peggy," she croaked.

"Do you know what day it is?"

She thought for a moment. "The last I remember it was... Monday?"

The man in scrubs nodded. "Still is, just barely. Do you know where you are?"

"Larry said a hospital."

"What's the last thing you remember?"

"I heard some voices...I was in a lot of pain."

Scrub-Man nodded again, then moved over, allowed Larry access to her again.

Her lover reached out, took her hand in his own. Thankfully, whatever drugs they'd given her hadn't deadened her ability to feel the warmth and comfort of his touch.

"Let him go."

Not on your life.

Larry smiled down at her, and Peggy returned the best grin she could muster, holding too tightly to his hand.

"How am I doin'?" she asked.

"You're gonna be fine."

"But will I be able to dance again?"

Larry snickered. "You couldn't dance before."

"I could do the Cabbage Patch with the best of them." Peggy attempted to sit up and her head began to spin, a fireworks display flaring across her eyes. She fell back against the pillow. "Whoa...Won't be trying that again soon..."

"You need to take it easy, babe."

Her mouth was dry. "Could I get a glass of water?"

Scrub-Man poured her one, and Larry held it to her lips.

"Not too fast," Scrub-Man warned.

Larry pulled the glass away and she moistened her lips with her tongue. "Thanks," she told him.

Scrub-Man tapped Larry on the shoulder. "Could I see you for a moment?"

He nodded, then squeezed Peggy's hand. "I'll be right back."

"Promise?"

Larry kissed her lightly on the forehead. "Promise."

He released her, joined Scrub-Man at the door.

Peggy wondered how long she'd been out, then decided she would ask later. Her eyelids grew heavy from the medication. She resisted, afraid she would discover *this* had really been the dream, that her reality was the embrace of a corpse somewhere in the shadowy fathoms.

Finally, she could fight no more and rested.

•••

The man in scrubs, Dr. Brahm, followed Larry out into the hallway and closed the door to Peggy's room behind him. "I need to talk to you about your wife's condition."

"She's not my wife, not yet...we're engaged."

Brahm nodded. "Does she have any other family?"

"No. Her parents are both deceased." Larry wondered momentarily when it was that a person wasn't an orphan, but merely had dead parents. "I'm the only family she's got."

Satisfied that he'd fulfilled the needs of protocol, the doctor went on, "She's suffered a broken shoulderblade and she's lost a lot of blood, so she'll be very weak and need plenty of rest. We'll keep her for twenty-four hours for observation, and then, when she leaves, she'll need to have that arm in a sling to keep it immobilized.

"We've stitched up her wounds. The interior stitches will dissolve on their own, but the ones that are visible will have to be removed in ten days."

Larry nodded, then he asked the question that had been bothering him all night. "She was losing so much blood, doctor...why'd they have to ship her off to another town? Doesn't Colonial Bay have its own hospital?"

"They have a doctor — he has the same office the town doctor's had for more than a hundred years — but it's what we like to call a 'Band-Aid Station.' He can treat minor injuries and illnesses, administer first aid, but, if a tourist gets in a car crash or a boating accident, Black Harbor Medical Center is better equipped to handle such emergencies."

"What about the townspeople?"

"Excuse me?"

"Somebody needs an appendix out, they have to come out here for the surgery?"

Brahm blinked, then shrugged and said, "I suppose so."

Larry shook his head and looked through the small window in Peggy's door. She was sleeping. "What kind of animal could do that, Doc?"

"I can't be certain. We have several varieties of sharks in these waters that —"

"Sharks?" Larry's gaze snapped from the window. "What do sharks have to do with *this*?"

"I'm afraid I don't follow you?"

"Peggy was attacked in an alley. She was bitten on dry land."

Larry's confusion spread to the doctor. "Mr. Neuhaus, I've seen shark attack victims before, and this bite is characteristic of such an attack. The —"

"I don't care what it's characteristic of, she wasn't in the water. She was a hundred yards from the beach. I'd just talked to her on the phone at the library. Look at her hair, at the clothes she was wearing when they brought her in. They're bloody, but other than that, they're dry as a bone."

Brahm stared at him a moment, then scribbled something in Peggy's chart and said, "Shark or not, she *was* mauled. With that in mind, her wounds have been washed and thoroughly cleaned. I've already had some blood work ordered on her, a CBC and a tox screen —"

"Shouldn't you...I don't know...give her rabies shots, in case it was a pit bull or something?"

"We don't want to treat a condition she doesn't have, especially in her weakened state." Brahm capped his pen and slid it into the breast pocket of his dark-blue scrub jacket. "I treated a three-year-old a few years back who was mauled by a Dalmatian. She loved the Disney movie and the parents bought her the dog before checking into the facts about their nature. This just *isn't* a dog bite. These teeth were clearly serrated. And the size of the punctures, each was nearly an inch wide and deep...If it's not a shark, I honestly don't know what it could've been."

Larry frowned. The only thing he cared about now was getting Peggy well. He wanted to take her from this hospital as soon as possible and leave Colonial Bay.

Brahm put a hand on Larry's shoulder. "I know you're concerned about her. Hell, I'd be out of my mind too if it were my wife lying there, but it looks like she *is* out of the woods."

As he looked at Peggy, tethered to machines and an IV, Larry had a different feeling.

TWENTY THREE

Barbara DeParle sprinted for Colonial Bay's church. The building was centuries old, but showed no signs of its age. The other town elders had spared no expense to maintain it. All that work and expense always seemed silly to Barbara. After all, the church, with its ornate stained glass and solid oak pews, had never been used. Like a house built on a Hollywood back lot, it was real only for cameras and tourists.

What was the old saying? Religion has made an honest woman of the supernatural.

The large doors were made of thick, heavy wood, but the old woman pushed them open with ease. She rushed into the pitch-black interior, hurried past unlit candles surrounding the marble altar. Barbara didn't need them. She saw perfectly well in the dark.

To the right was a slender door. She pushed it open, descended stone steps two at a time, hoping she wouldn't slip and tumble the remainder of the way down. The cramped staircase gave way to a vast temple; flickering candlelight offered warm, reverent illumination denied to the altar above. Barbara ran to the mammoth statue at the center of the chamber and fell to her knees.

"Varuna," she cried, "hear my prayers!"

She babbled on in the ancient tongue, a dead language that was father to all others. She spoke of her missing Christine, confessed her fear of Tellstrom, and then she told her god of Peggy Hern.

Word spread quickly through Colonial Bay that a woman had been attacked, been *bitten*, and lived.

Barbara wished Peggy dead, then felt guilty for it. What was done was done. Varuna had a purpose for everything, even Karl Tellstrom; as priestess to the town, and to all of Poseidon's children, it was Barbara's job to divine what that purpose was and then act to further it.

She knelt beneath the effigy, peered into its sculpted eyes. Its face, the down-turned snout of a shark, normally provided her great solace, but there would be no consolation tonight.

Barbara felt her world coming apart.

As she continued her chant, she found a trident chiseled into the statue's pedestal. She traced it with her aged finger, coaxed a spectral light from the stone. The glow did nothing to quiet the commotion; a thousand thoughts buzzed around her brain, each coming to the same conclusion: Barbara had to see Peggy.

TWENTY FOUR

Roger Hays entered Black Harbor Medical Center's morgue. He noticed three things immediately; first, the room stank of disinfectant, as if someone had recently doused it in a valiant attempt to cover a much darker stench; second, a stainless-steel table adorned with gutters, and, resting on said table, the shrouded contour of a corpse; and the final point of interest, a lab-coated gentleman seated at a desk on the other side of the room. The man ate a sandwich as he watched an episode of *COPS* on a small television. How anyone could dine in the same room where autopsies were performed was beyond Roger's understanding.

Hays cleared his throat.

The lab-coated man looked up. "Can I help you?"

"I'm Roger Hays. I'm here for my son."

The man wiped his lips with a napkin, then shut off his TV and grabbed a clipboard from a nail above his desk. He met Hays at the edge of the table, scanning the paperwork. "I'm sorry for your loss. We just need you to fill out these forms. They have a place to list the mortuary where you'll be —"

"Is this him?" Roger indicated the sheeted cadaver on the table between them.

"N-No."

"May I see my son?" The young man regarded him as if he'd grown a third eye; Roger frowned. "Is there something unusual in the request?"

"No, it's just that I...I *really* don't think you want to do that."

"Yes, I *really* do."

"Sir, I don't mean to sound insensitive, but...half his face is gone. We had to identify him based solely on dental records. I don't think you want to remember him —"

"I appreciate your concern." This man was trying to dissuade

Hays because he did not want to see an outbreak of wailing grief, or to clean vomit off his floor. There was no danger of either. "Now, will you honor my request, or do I need to call the hospital administrator?"

After a moment's hesitation, the attendant crossed the room to a stainless-steel wall of drawers, each marked with a number, like lockers at a health club. He checked his clipboard, then opened the proper cabinet.

Number 20, Roger noticed, *same as David's age.*

A light fog drifted from the opening, lowering the temperature of the room. The attendant reached in and pulled out the long, metal shelf on which Hays' son lay. Like the body on the table in the center of the room, David had been tucked in snugly with a white sheet.

Roger surveyed the cloth, preparing his mind for what lay beneath. Where the hill of an arm ought to have been, the linen cascaded directly off the torso. Where David's washboard stomach and muscular chest should have pushed at the shroud, the fabric formed sinkholes. Roger felt numbness creep through his body.

"Have you ever seen a shark attack victim, Mr. Hays?" the lab-coated man asked.

Roger shook his head. He'd seen many gruesome sights in his time. People in organized crime get an education fairly quickly. But, to his recollection, he'd never seen a shark's leftovers.

The attendant cleared his throat. "You're going to see —"

Hays reached out and pulled back the sheet. His son stared up at him with a single glazed eye. Upper teeth attempted a smile, but their lower mates had been ripped away with the jawbone. It was hard to believe this thing had once been human.

Roger felt grief well up in him, but he kept it at bay. If Komarovsky had done this to his boy, Hays would pay him back with interest, but he had to be sure. He cleared his throat. "You're certain it was a shark?"

The man flashed Roger a questioning stare, then flipped through the pages on his clipboard and nodded. "Several sharks, actually."

"Several?"

"Yes. The M.E. states there are at least three distinct bite patterns."

"You didn't perform the autopsy?"

"No, sir."

"Are you the coroner, or the night watchman?"

The man straightened his posture. "I'm one of the Medical Examiners on staff, sir. I'm just not the one who examined your son."

"How much do you know about shark attacks? Have you *actually* seen one?"

"Yes, sir."

Roger looked the man squarely in the eye. "I take it you know who I am?"

"Of course."

"As you might imagine, men in my position receive death threats from time to time, threats that are also aimed at our families. I need you to look at my son and confirm what's in that report. I need you to tell me, without a doubt, that it was a shark."

The man said nothing. His gaze alternated between Roger and the clipboard in his hand, then, either to humor a grieving father, or because he feared Roger's reputation, he put down the report and studied David's remains. "That's odd."

"What?"

The man hesitated, but Roger's cold stare urged an answer. "The skin appears to have been gnawed off the bone. Sharks bite down with up to 900 pounds of pressure; think of a fully loaded pick-up pressing down on a row of steak knives. They can also swim at speeds of twenty-five miles an hour, which means they hit their prey like a freight train. The force of this impact and the pressure of the jaw will inflict what we call a crush injury, massive bruising and bone fractures. Once they have something in their mouths, they thrash their heads around in the water, tearing away entire sections of the carcass. The way the arm is torn away is totally consistent with this type of attack. But..."

"Yes?" Roger pressed.

"Your son's ribs are still intact." He pointed down at the gaping hole in David's abdomen, then to what was left of his face. "And, even though his jawbone is missing, the rest of the skull is undamaged."

"What about his missing eye?"

"A crab may have taken that."

"A crab?"

"There are marks in the remaining flesh around the socket that suggest it was clawed out."

"Clawed, or gouged?"

"Well, either way, it was done post-mortem. And, obviously, the sharks didn't do it."

No, but a man *might have.*

Hays allowed his eyes to fall back to David's savaged form, still searching for a whisper of Komarovsky. He saw long scratches on his son's shoulders and pointed them out to the examiner. "And these? Did a crab do these?"

The man gave these wounds a cursory study. "They're not deep enough to have been a contributing factor in his death. They could be anything. The body was probably raked across the reef by the tides."

"He wasn't scratched by whatever killed him?"

"Sharks don't have claws, Mr. Hays."

"And you're still certain sharks did this to him?"

The examiner regarded him evenly. "I'm no expert on sea life, but I'd be hard-pressed to think of another animal with a bite radius this large...and the wounds were made by flat teeth with serrated edges, like those of a shark.

"I'm sure you've seen news reports in recent years, sharks schooling off the coast. No one knows why. An area can go years and years with no activity, then things heat up again. In fact, we just had a woman brought into the hospital this evening after an attack."

Roger's head did a bird-like twitch. "Did she survive?"

"She was alive when they brought her in."

Hays needed to find this woman, needed to see if she had the same mysterious injuries. He had to know who or what had stolen his son from him. Roger concealed what was left of David with the sheet.

Good-bye.

He placed his hand on the body's veiled forehead, then his eyes rose to meet the examiner's. "Where did they take her?"

•••

Larry stood outside Peggy's room, watched her sleeping form

through the rectangular glass in her door. A nurse checked monitors and made notes, assuring him her condition remained unchanged. He took another drink of his coffee, surprised to find it tasted more like Starbucks than mud. Larry was afraid to sleep, afraid that something might change for the worse and he'd be caught unaware.

A somber figure approached, an older man, wearing what appeared to be an Armani suit.

At first, Larry thought it was an administrator, then he realized the time. It was now after midnight. The desk jockeys had more than likely gone home, leaving the work of medicine to the practitioners. There was anger in this man's face and...something else, something Larry couldn't put his finger on.

When the stranger noticed that he was being watched, his face lightened, banishing the dark trait before it could adequately be defined. "Excuse me." He pointed to Peggy's room. "Is this the shark attack victim from earlier this evening?"

Larry was unsure of how to reply, or even if he *should* reply. "She was attacked. The doctor said it was a shark, but it had to have been something else."

The man perked up. "Such as?"

"I'm sorry if this sounds rude, but...who the hell are you?"

The man extended his hand. "Roger Hays."

Larry reluctantly shook it, his face puzzled. The name was familiar, but he didn't know why.

"My son died in a shark attack two nights ago," Roger explained. "I just wanted to see if this young lady was all right."

The bewilderment left Larry's eyes. Perhaps that justified the dark expression he'd seen earlier. If he'd been told that Peggy had just been *killed*...well, he'd probably have had another seven years bad luck. "I'm sorry about your son."

"Yes." The man's tone turned interrogative. "I understand that you may have witnessed the attack."

Larry shook his head. "Sorry. I saw an attack on a woman."

"Could you describe her to me?"

"I don't see what this —"

Roger raised a hand to silence him. "Please."

Larry looked at the fluorescent fixture in the ceiling, trying to recall the screaming face he'd seen for but an instant, fighting to separate it from the nagging image of the rotting corpse in his dream. "She was young...long hair...I only saw her for a second."

Hays regarded him with great interest. "My son sent me a picture of himself and his girlfriend of the moment." He produced an iPhone, found the right picture, and handed it to the artist.

Larry had never seen the young man in the Stanley University sweatshirt, but the woman...he recognized her. She'd been a beautiful girl. He stared at the screen for a few moments, trying to burn the image into his mind's eye, to replace the dead woman with this living one.

Hays stood by silently, watching him, waiting impatiently for him to speak.

"That's her," Larry finally croaked.

Hays nodded as if he'd known the answer all along.

"I tried to..." Larry swallowed. "What was her name?"

"Susan. Susan Rogers."

Larry felt a sudden chill; he shuddered.

Hays appeared not to notice. "Did you see the shark?"

Larry shrugged. He'd aimed his flashlight into the water, saw a silhouette below the waves, but he hadn't known what it was until that dorsal fin broke the surface. "I saw a shape in the water...a fin...it —"

"Was it a shark, or was it something else?"

"I couldn't pick the thing out of a lineup for you, if that's what you're asking. I thought it was a shark, yes, but it could've been some other animal... Look, not to be rude again, but it might save us both some time if you told me what you're looking for."

"I'm trying to find out what killed my son. I assume you've seen pictures of a shark before. Did what you saw, this shape, did it look like one?"

"It looked like...wait..." Larry suddenly remembered his first opinion. "To tell you the truth, before I saw the fin, I thought it was a man down there with her."

"A man? Are you sure?"

"I thought so, but obviously it wasn't...I mean...no one came out of the water, and I saw the wounds —" Hays offered him an odd glance, and Larry realized he'd seen Susan's body only in a dream. He pointed to the door. "— Peggy's wounds. No *man* could do that."

Hays whispered something that sounded Russian; the darkness returned to his face, and he said, "You'd be surprised at what a man can do."

TWENTY FIVE

A perfect New England night; the air was cool and the sky clear, so clear in fact that every star seemed visible to the naked eye. A full moon hung over Colonial Bay's school, making it easy for the clans of Poseidon to find their way into the building.

Christine stood by the diving board, watching Karl Tellstrom smile and greet each member by name as they entered the pool chamber. Erik and Melody Jones, the editors of Colonial Bay's newspaper, were among them. So was Mike Richards, owner of the bait shop by the docks. Karl could not hide his surprise, his joy. A week ago, this was to have been a small group, but word seemed to have spread to half the town. The discovery of Atlantis was the key. Karl told them it was a sign, that it was time for them to stop living a lie. Some believed him immediately, others took longer to convince, still others would never believe.

Karl caught sight of her and flashed a seductive grin. Christine offered him a slight smile in reply, but she knew he sensed her uneasiness.

Her thoughts turned again to Principal Monroe. All they'd wanted was to keep him away from this business at the pool. But something had come over Karl, something dark. He'd crushed the man's skull and slapped Christine hard enough to leave a mark, and she didn't have a clue as to why.

Maybe father's right. Maybe he is *crazy.*

She shook her head. No. Insanity was a *human* quality, and Karl was not now, nor would he ever be human. Being human meant being weak, frail, and worse; it meant being one with the breed who murdered Karl's mother, who mowed her down with the spinning blades of their motorboat and left her bobbing in the surf like so much flotsam and jetsam. No. Karl had more in common with the insects that roamed the beach than with human beings.

Their people had been imprisoned for nearly three hundred years, waiting for someone like Karl to come along. A leader who had no fear of humankind. He'd told them it was finally time to put the Man in his place, to crush him the way —

The way Karl crushed poor Principal Monroe's skull?

Christine shuddered. *Yeah, just like that.*

The gathering now filled the entire chamber. Bleachers were crammed to capacity, and the tiled floor lay buried beneath countless feet. Out the door, the onlookers spilled into a connecting hallway, trying to observe Tellstrom through fogged glass walls. Karl moved through them, shaking hands, patting shoulders, embodying all their hopes and dreams.

If they'd seen what Karl had done to Mr. Monroe, would they be so willing to follow him?

After all, Monroe was no human murderer. He was a Paralicht, no different from Christine.

An accident.

What about that slap?

She unconsciously rubbed the tender flesh of her cheek.

Was that an accident?

Before Christine could think of a reply, Karl moved to her side. He spread his arms, as if trying to hug the entire congregation, then began to speak.

"Last night, I walked the streets of this town, and no human being looked twice at me. I stood inches away from them, and they just went on about their business without fear. Some have argued for centuries that this is how it has to be. In the light of day, they claim we must act like the humans, we must speak their language, and above all else, we have to *look* like them. I tell you now that it's a lie. I'm *not* human. I'm Charodon, one of the three clans of Poseidon...created by the gods as a race superior to all others. Bred to hunt, to kill.

"Charodon." He beat his muscular chest with his fist, then pointed to Christine. "Paralicht." And then he motioned to a man at the end of the bleachers. "Kraken.

"The humans have always known we were stronger, have always *feared* us. Their ancestors chased our people across the globe until they finally trapped us on this rock...and within our own flesh.

"We no longer need to be confined to these prisons."

Someone clapped, sparking a wildfire of applause that spread through the audience until the entire chamber resounded with a cacophony of echoing war cries.

Karl held up his hands to quiet them, smiling that darkly charming grin. "We've been hunting Landers as they trespass into our territory, the sea. And tonight...tonight we've shown that we can claim them on their terrain as well."

He motioned to the chamber door.

A figure entered, Jason Duke, and draped across his arms was the carcass of a man. The coppery smell of blood wafted through the humid room, adding to the restlessness of the audience. The crowd parted, and Jason laid the body at Karl's feet.

Christine stared at Jeff Wilson's lifeless form, her heart beating faster. She wished she could have met the man in that dark alley instead of Jason, could have tasted his flesh when it was still warm. She licked her lips, hoping she might get to dine when this meeting adjourned.

Karl looked out at the congregation, *his* congregation; his *army*. "You see! They're not the demons your parents scared you with as children. Perhaps, hundreds of years ago, they were stronger, but not anymore. They've forgotten us and denied their own past. They bleed, they *die*...and when enough of them are dead, *they* will fear *us* again."

The crowd erupted in fresh applause.

Karl smiled down at Christine; she knew it was meant to be affectionate, but tonight, it gave her chills. She took his hand just the same, rose to her feet to stand beside him, queen to his self-appointed king.

"Today," he announced, "is the dawn of a new age. Today, the children of Poseidon are free."

Members of all three clans joined together in chanting Karl's name. If they'd been Contras or Sandinistas, they might have thrust their rifles into the air. Instead, they held up their bare fists. They had no need of Man's weapons. They *were* weapons.

A single voice rose above the din; Sue O'Conner, the Shirt Shack owner, "I hear another woman got attacked tonight. I hear she lived."

A shocked silence settled over the congregation.

Karl's eyes dove to Jason. "Is this true?"

The boy lowered his head and fell to his knees. "Sorry, Karl. She started screaming, people heard her, and I didn't wanna be seen, so I took this first kill and ran."

Karl blinked; his ice-blue eyes became black, inhuman orbs. He reached down, grabbed Jason by the throat and lifted the boy off the tile. Karl's hand changed, shaped itself into a large, webbed claw. His features altered as well, as if an unseen seamstress were unraveling his tissues like yarn and then re-knitting them. "Do you know what you've done?" he asked, his teeth honed to jagged spikes. "If she lives, she'll be —"

"She's dead," Jason croaked, fighting against Karl's grip, trying to draw breath.

Christine spoke up, "Even if she lived, there's no guarantee she's infected."

Karl glared down at her with shark's eyes, dark and soulless. She felt her body tense, preparing for a slap. Instead, he thought for a moment, his skin becoming tiger-striped, orange and black; emerging gill flaps expanded and contracted from his neck and upper shoulders.

The audience stared at him in silence.

Karl let Jason go and stared right back at them, trying to regain his composure. "We'll find out if this woman's alive, and to what extent she's been influenced."

He glanced at the entrance; a lone silhouette nodded, then left the room.

"But now, Poseidon's children," Karl went on, "it's time to play."

The crowd cheered once more, a shifting sea of flesh, congealing into new and exotic contours.

Karl's gaze fell on Christine, and he mouthed, "I love you."

She smiled in spite of herself, banishing her doubts, if only for the moment. Karl bent down to kiss her, his lips now thin slivers, and, as they embraced, she began a metamorphosis of her own. Her skin turned semi-transparent, and her own lips inflated as if to fill a mold.

Together, they left the bright confines of the school for the dark freedom of the night.

TWENTY SIX

Bright mist swirled around white Greco-Roman columns. Peggy thought she'd stepped onto the porch of a plantation house from one of her novels. Past the pillars, however, she saw no fields or Spanish moss.

People moved by her, descended marble steps toward a cobblestone street below, their multicolored robes surfing the wind. A bridge stood directly across from her, red and black stone arched across a canal or river. The crowd converged on it, everyone going to the same event.

Peggy lifted her eyes to the horizon.

A pyramid of gold and sable glass towered high above the haze. She felt drawn to it, as if it were vital that she get inside. The strange compulsion took control of her, forced her down the steps. She became one with the moving mob, a fish caught in a current.

Darkness moved over the crowd, halting its march; each and every person turned their attention skyward.

Peggy awoke to the sound of her door opening.

Larry?

No. As she concentrated on this shadowy figure, Peggy noticed it was female.

Mom?

Peggy's mother always brought her chicken broth and Ritz crackers when she was sick. She was sick now, wasn't she? She was in bed and there was a dull ache, a pain crying out to be heard but lost somewhere in the fog that coated her eyes. And then her brain peered out from beneath the hazy blanket, reminding her that her mother was gone.

"Who's there?" Peggy muttered, and the words echoed in her ears.

The shadow was caught by the wall lamp beside her bed; the woman from the gift shop. "I don't know if you remember me."

Peggy blinked, fanning the mist. "Mrs. DeParle?"

The woman grinned as if flattered. "That's right."

"I —" Fog crept back in and she rubbed her eyes to try and clear it. "I sound dopey, don't I? They have me on this medication...Great stuff."

Barbara's tone was quite maternal. "No need to apologize, dear."

"Why are you..." Peggy yawned. "...you here?"

"Just wanted to make sure you were okay. Word spreads quick in a small town."

"I'm sorry." Peggy's voice turned childlike, her cheeks rosy with embarrassment. "Are you mad at me?"

"Mad?" The old woman's face...so much like Peggy's mother; the same light of concern in her eyes, the same caring warmth to her hand as she reached out to cover Peggy's fingers. "Why would I be mad?"

"I shouldn't have gone in that alley. I knew I shouldn't have..."

"No, child, I'm not mad at you. Just wanted to see how you were mending."

Peggy smiled and gave a sleepy nod. "They said I'm gonna be just fine."

Barbara's eyes roamed her injured shoulder.

Peggy turned her head. The room strobed and a semi-circle of gashes, tied closed with surgical thread, peeked into view. Self-conscious, Peggy reached up to cover the wounds; her blue hospital gown was flimsy, but it did the trick. She returned her cloudy eyes to Barbara, wondering briefly how bad the scars would be. "Looks worse than it really is."

DeParle nodded. "I'm sure. You were tossin' and turnin' when I walked in."

"Oh, that." Peggy's lids grew heavy. She felt her head drop and forced herself to snap back to attention. "I don't know...I've had the weirdest dreams. Maybe it's the...the stuff they gave me. Great stuff."

"Yes, you said. Weird how, dear?"

The surgical tape that held Peggy's IV in place was making her itch. She absently rubbed at her arm and slowly shook her head. "Oh... just strange, stupid stuff. I was...going to bore you to death."

She giggled nervously, but the look on the old woman's face was serious.

"My mother used to have these dreams that would come true," Barbara told her. "I don't think she was psychic or what have you, but sometimes they would. Since then, I've always been fascinated by the meaning behind them. What are the dreams about, if you don't mind me bein' nosey, that is?"

There was no mystery behind the first dream. Peggy was vacationing by the ocean, and every gift shop they'd visited, with the exception of this woman's, had been filled with dolphin images and nick-knacks. Add that to the fact that Natalie had been haunting Peggy almost as much as Larry and *bingo*. No need for psychoanalysis there. The second dream however...that one was just odd. "I was in this Roman city, and everyone was headed for a huge pyramid...Are you all right?"

DeParle swallowed. Was that a tear in the corner of her eye? "Fine, dear."

But Barbara wasn't fine. Something Peggy said had upset this woman, just as something Larry said when he purchased the siren figure had. Peggy was about to ask about it, but her eyelids slid closed again, and when they opened, the old woman was gone. She looked about the hazy room, feeling it spin around her. Finally, the medication pulled her deeper into the fog, and she gave in to its demand for sleep.

•••

Barbara paced across the living room so fast and furiously that she thought the carpet would begin to smoke beneath her feet. Ed brought her some tea, his attempt to calm her down. She took the cup in her trembling hands, drank quickly, and returned it to him empty.

"You even taste that?" he asked.

"She's Callisto, Ed!"

He viewed her with skepticism. "You know that for a fact?"

"She's been bitten and lived...she dreamed about the pyramid. What more proof do you need?"

"Barb, there hasn't been a Callisto since Roanoke."

"No attacks since then...least, none we know about." She caught sight of the framed photo that sat on a nearby end table; the smiling image of Christine. Happy. Innocent. A lump rose in Barbara's throat and she forced it down again. "I was hopin' Chrissy would've come to her senses by now...before it got this far."

Ed nodded. "You ever wonder if we weren't too old to start a family?"

"Never really gave it much thought." And then the night she gave birth was immediately in her mind, as vivid and as fresh as if it were yesterday. "I just remember how happy she made us when we had her."

As Ed walked to the window, Barbara saw joy overtake his face, as if he were sharing her memory. It didn't last. "I shoulda never let you talk me into that damned ritual."

Barbara shrugged, suddenly feeling an itch at the small of her back. "That's the way it's always been done."

"Still don't make it right." Ed watched the sun rise outside his window. "The look in my baby's eyes when I had to...had to hold her down so you could go an' draw on her."

Barbara thought back to her own marking ceremony, remembering the pain of it all. There had been the pain of the needle on her skin, creating the image of the trident for all to see, then came the pain of her responsibilities. The first was a sting that had faded with time, but the second never lessened.

"She never looked me in the eye after that. Never." Ed turned to Barbara, his face filled with a horrible blend of anger and disgust. "If we hadn't gone and done it, she wouldn't have —"

"Wouldn't have what, Ed? Run away?" It was Barbara's turn to vent. "Who wouldn't let her go swimmin' at night?"

"Someone might see her, or worse. You want her to end up like Tellstrom's mother?"

Barbara shook her head. "Tellstrom might be crazy, but he sure has one thing right. Our people can't go on hidin' forever."

Ed threw up his hands. "What else can we do, Barb?"

She had no answer for him, and so they stood and stared at one another, neither willing to give.

TWENTY SEVEN

The *Sea Wasp* raced toward New Hampshire coastline.

Carol Miyagi studied her map, tried to keep the wind from taking it prisoner. Beside her, Alan stood with his hand on the throttle. He'd spoken no more than five words since they'd left New York. She tossed him a glance. Normally, she could look into his eyes and tell what he was thinking, but his mirrored sunglasses showed her only a reflection of the sea ahead.

"Let's hear it." Carol folded the map and pushed the hair from her face; wind caught it, blew it from her scalp like a tattered black pennant.

"Hear what?"

"Hear what's on your mind."

"Just wondering what you're hoping to prove. You know there's no way that carving in Hays' office came from Atlantis. It's a driftwood sculpture like any number you'd find at seaside souvenir stands."

"But whoever carved it has to be using an Atlantean artifact as a model," Carol pointed out. "Someone has actually been to the city. Who knows how many valuable treasures they've robbed from the site, artifacts that could aid us in research."

Alan smiled. "Or maybe the sculptor is *from* Atlantis?"

Carol grinned back.

The notion of Atlantean descendants was nothing new. Spanish conquistadors encountered natives on the Canary Islands who claimed to be from the great city. These villagers presented stone tablets of alien writings, writings they could no longer read. But conquistadors cared little for history; they slaughtered these people and searched their villages for hidden gold. Though they found no precious metal, they kept the glyph-covered stones. Fresh out of Harvard, Carol spent more than a year studying the symbols, and, while they shared similarities with the markings of Atlantis, many looked more like crop circles than hieroglyphics.

"I don't think we'll find any Atlanteans," Carol sighed. "And I don't know *what* I hope to prove. I only know that I need to check this out."

"I love seeing you in Nancy Drew mode. Very sexy."

Carol giggled. "Glad to know I have your support." *Because I love you,* her mind added.

Love.

She loved her work, but interpersonal love...that was something of a mystery to her. Carol never had a boyfriend growing up, and in college, she'd even toyed with the idea that she might be a lesbian. Her flirtation with that notion was brief, however. She didn't love women, but she could at least *connect* with them. She'd never been able to do that with men. Not even her father.

Actually, he'd never connected with her.

He'd kept her at arm's length. Perhaps because he was old-school Japanese, believing that women should remain second-class citizens. Or possibly it was due to the fact that he'd lost his entire family at a young age, and, as a result, vowed never to grow close to anyone again. Carol was no shrink, but this second analysis had given her some comfort growing up. She'd rather see her father as a heartbroken man than as a chauvinist, a man who'd prefer his daughter grow up a proper geisha and not a scientist.

Then there was Alan. He'd never been afraid to care for her. When the rest of the world seemed to be against her, he was consistently there to cheer her on, to believe in her when no one else would. When she went off on her wild hunches, he was always with her, trying to hold the reigns as she fought to be free of them. And above all else, he was the only person on earth she trusted.

Whatever it was they shared, it was important to her.

He was important to her, as was his support.

Alan turned his head and Carol saw herself reflected in his shades. *God,* she thought, *I look like I haven't slept in days.*

"You always have my support," he told her, then leaned over to kiss her cheek.

"*Domo.*"

As he pulled away, Carol saw something in the periphery of his mirrored glasses: a ship, rolling on the waves. She looked over her shoulder and found a fishing trawler listing slightly to one side.

Alan turned the wheel in the ship's direction. "They look like they're in some trouble."

As they approached, Carol saw the trawler's name painted on its stern. "*Maggie May?* Wasn't that an Elton John song?"

"Rod Stewart." Alan picked up the microphone attached to their marine radio. "*Maggie May...Maggie May...*This is the *Sea Wasp*. Do you need assistance?"

A crackle of static came in reply.

"*Maggie May...Maggie May...*This is the *Sea Wasp*, I'm a hundred yards off your stern, do you require aid?"

Again, nothing but static. Alan tried several different frequencies, but the result was the same.

Carol stared at the seventy-five degree angle of the boat's flying bridge. "What do we do?"

"We can't leave her here. We'll check her out, and, if no one's on board, we'll call the authorities to tow 'er in. Take the wheel."

Carol nodded, grabbing the controls as he released them. Carefully, she piloted the boat toward the unnaturally high gunwale of the *Maggie May*, easing up on the throttle until the *Sea Wasp* matched the trawler's leisurely side-to-side sway. Carol then cut the engine, allowing the gentle motion of the billows to bring the ships together with a thud.

Alan found a length of rope; he lashed the two ships together and started to climb over, waving Carol off. "Stay here."

"I'm going."

"It could be sinking."

"If you go, I go. You always give me *unko* for going off on my own. I'm not letting you fly solo, either."

With a sigh, Alan boarded the trawler and she followed him over the railing. Wire traps piled in stagnant seawater on one side of the deck; they'd been ripped open, emptied of whatever catch they once held. Carol followed Alan into the ship's cabin, trying to maintain her balance on the fun house floor of the deck.

Alan flicked switches on the boat's radio. "Busted."

"That explains why no one answered your hails."

"I don't think there's anyone here *to* answer."

Carol was about to turn and leave the cabin when something else caught her eye.

Alan saw her puzzled expression. "What is it?"

The boat shifted slightly. Carol grabbed onto a shelf for support and pointed to the opposite wall. There, above an unmade bunk, drawn in blood, was the same symbol she'd seen in the Atlantean temple.

A trident held hostage within a hoop.

From the forward deck, the unmistakable noise of footsteps on wood.

They were not alone on the boat after all.

•••

"There she blows," Petty Officer Earl L. Preston Jr. said aloud.

The *Maggie May* tilted to one side as if it were a whale about to dive, a black-and-yellow speedboat lashed to its railing like an odd Siamese twin. Margaret Lunden reported both her husband Kip and his mate missing, was even able to relay the approximate location of their favorite fishing spot, but she didn't say anything about twenty-five-foot motorboat painted like a yellowjacket.

Smugglers? Drug smugglers?

How was Earl supposed to teach his apprentice seaman the drudgery and boredom of everyday Coast Guard life when this crap kept happening? He saw no movement on either ship, but he decided to approach with caution. "Bring us around and then cut the motor."

"Cut the motor?" Peck sounded confused. "Shouldn't we announce 'Coast Guard'?"

"Drug runners pack serious firepower. You wanna let 'em know where to shoot?"

"No."

Peck did as he was asked, the current allowing them to drift stealthily up to the two vessels.

Preston leapt onto the deck of the trawler and unholstered his weapon. Cautiously, he made his way along the outside of the cabin, the barrel of his gun casting a long shadow. Inside, he heard voices, a man and a woman.

The woman said, "That explains why no one answered your hails."

"I don't think there's anyone here *to* answer," the man replied. There was a pause and then he added: "What is it?"

They know I'm here.

Earl whirled around the corner. "Coast Guard! Get your hands in the air!"

The couple inside jumped at his command and thrust their hands toward the ceiling of the cabin. They appeared to be unarmed, but appearances were often deceiving.

The man spoke up happily, "Officer! You just saved us a call."

"Is that a fact?" Keeping his eyes on the couple, Earl pulled a walkie-talkie from his belt. "Peck... Peck...you read me?"

"Are you all right? Do you need help? Over."

"I'm fine. Get the base on the horn. Tell 'em we got the *Maggie May*, and have 'em run a check on the boat *Sea Wasp*."

"Copy that, sir. Consider it done. Over and out."

Earl clipped the radio back onto his belt, his eyes still glued to his prisoners. "You, Lucy Liu...mind tellin' me what you're doin' on this boat?"

Her eyes narrowed and her companion glanced at Earl, his smile evaporating. He placed a restraining hand on her arm, as if he thought she would say what he was obviously thinking. When she did speak, however, she only asked, "May we put our hands down, Lieutenant?"

"I'm a few stripes short of lieutenant, ma'am, but yeah...slowly."

They lowered their arms and the man offered an explanation, "We were on our way to Colonial Bay when we saw this trawler listing. It looked like she needed help, so we radioed her. We got no response, so we came on board to make sure everyone was all right, but they're not."

Earl lowered his weapon, but did not holster it. That story seemed to gel with what he'd heard from outside. He plucked the radio from his belt again. "Peck?"

"Still checkin' on that boat, sir. Over."

"That's fine. Run these names too."

"Sure thing. What are they? Over."

Earl pointed at the woman. "Name?"

"First...middle...last, or all of the above?"

"All of the above, if you please."

"Dr. Carol Toki Miyagi."

He relayed the information to the radio. "*Dr.* Carol — C or a K in Carol?"

"It's 'C'."

"Carol, with a C, Toe Key...spell that."

"T-O-K-I"

"T-O-K-I," Earl repeated.

"M-I-Y-A-G-I."

"M-I-Y-A-G-I, like the guy in *Karate Kid*."

Carol rolled her eyes. "*Dankon.*"

Earl shook his head. "Call me a dick again lady and your ass is in a cell."

She blushed and looked at the floor.

Earl turned his attention to her companion who was smiling for some reason. "Now you."

"Dr. Alan James Everson."

"Aren't you going to have him spell it for you?" Carol asked.

Earl glared at her, then asked Alan, "One 'L' or two?"

"One."

"'A' and an 'E,' or two 'A's?"

"Two 'A's."

Earl relayed the info to Peck; as he clipped the radio onto his belt, he saw the bloody trident. He took a step back and his revolver started to rise.

"Hold on!" Carol followed the guardsman's gaze, a mix of fear and fascination in her voice. "You've seen that symbol before?"

"What do you know about it?"

"I've seen it too."

"Where?"

Her eyes fell to the barrel of his gun. "Do you really need that?"

"You tell me, Doctor. What are you two doctors of, anyway?"

"We're archeologists," Alan told him.

"*Archeologists?*"

They nodded.

"You're one of *them*," Earl chuckled. "You think some sea creature attacked this boat, right? Somethin' everybody else thought was extinct, like a big-ass dinosaur or somethin', right?"

Reports of strange creatures off the coast of New England originated with the Massachuset and Pennacook tribes. Early sailors to the new world spoke of mermaids and sirens. And, every now and then, Earl still came across people out here looking for monsters.

While he did not share their belief in sea serpents, the idea of finding some unknown animal was not without merit. Earl read enough about the sea to know that there were 80 known species of whale and porpoise in the world's oceans. Of that number, 11 were not found until the last century, the most recent one having just been discovered in 1991.

Bits of dead animals continually washed in with the tide. And, sometimes, a beachcomber would find something odd. Scientists and the news media would look at the carcasses, try to place them into established niches, assign tentacles to squids and octopi, fins to sharks or marlin, translucent masses to portions of jelly fish, and so on, and so on. But once in a while, something would come ashore that defied categorization. These finds would make it into the papers, relegated to the back page almost as an afterthought, or perhaps to fill space on a slow news day, and a week or so later they were forgotten.

Now, Earl could almost hear the yarn these scientists were about to spin.

An ancient creature had managed to remain undetected by Man, and now it's begun to attack because...because pollution killed its favorite fish fillet or some such crap. People shouldn't fuck with Mother Nature. What was it his mother always said? *Whoever heard of a mouse making a nest in a cat's ear?*

"We don't work with dinosaurs," Alan told him, halting the run of his thoughts. "We deal with ancient civilizations."

Earl's eyes darted back and forth between his captives and the bloody sketch drying on the wood. "Like those dudes that found Atlantis a few weeks ago?"

"We," Carol told him, "*are* those dudes."

The officer's mouth and his gun dropped at the same time.

A crackle on the radio, "This is Peck. Over."

"What is it, Peck?"

"I got word back on those I.D.s. The *Sea Wasp* is Miyagi's boat. And I just figured out why those names sounded so familiar. They're in all the magazines right now because they found Atlantis. Over."

"Very thorough, Seaman." Earl holstered his weapon and radio, then leaned against the door frame. "So, Doctors Miyagi and Everson. You mind tellin' me where you saw that symbol before...and please don't say Atlantis."

Carol regarded him soberly. "Sorry."

Earl shook his head. *Oh shit.*

TWENTY EIGHT

Roger Hays couldn't believe the stupidity, the *ineptitude* of the fat bastard that sat across the desk from him. Even if he couldn't be sure Komarovsky murdered his son, Roger might make a call to have this idiot killed. He would be doing the human race a favor. "You said Miss Hern was the victim of a shark attack, like my son, but I know she was really mauled in an alley here in town."

"That woman...how's she doin', anyway?" Chief Canon's pudgy face became watchful, intent, his concern genuine, but also self-serving, as though Peggy Hern's wellbeing was important to his own. Had this been any other officer, in any other town, Hays would have chalked it up to legal worries, but he assumed nothing.

"They have her listed in stable condition."

The chief nodded, satisfied; his laced fingers rested comfortably on the crest of his gut. "You say you heard she got bit in some alley? Well, sir, it sounds like you've been talkin' to the wrong people. What'd her doctors say?"

"They said it looked like a shark attack."

"Ever seen sharks roamin' alleys?"

Roger tested the waters: "Ever seen sharks with arms and legs?"

The fat man's bloated face deflated. "What?"

"The coroner said the bites on my son were inconsistent with a shark attack. I saw his body; he was *clawed* at." Hays watched the color drain from the chief's face. *The lard-ass* does *know something.* "Mr. Neuhaus said, at first glance, the thing that attacked my son and his friend looked like a *man*, a man with fins."

"He never said anything like that to me."

"Probably because he thought it would sound too crazy."

The chief didn't miss a beat. "It does."

"Three attacks in three days doesn't seem a bit unusual to you?"

"I hear tell that before they invented swimmin' suits, there were *no* attacks. When people and sharks share the same water, it's usually not the shark that gets hurt."

Hays leaned over the desk and grabbed the man by his collar; it was moist with sweat. "You listen here, Chief. I *know* there's something going on in this town. I *know* you're connected to it. You'd just better pray —"

"Mr. Hays..." Canon's eyes narrowed. "...*I* know you've had an awful tragedy smack you square in the ass —"

"You don't know shit."

"— which is why I'm not gonna lock you up for attempted assault on an officer. But —"

"You fat fuck."

"*But*, if you don't get your friggin' hands offa me right this minute, it's *you* who'd better pray."

And then Hays saw something in Canon's eyes, something he didn't like; the glint of a caged tiger, all the power and hunger bottled up within, boiling just beneath the surface of that icy glare. Roger released the chief's collar and slowly backed away from the desk.

Canon rubbed his neck, regarded Hays with an even stare. "Now, take your son back to wherever it is you wanna bury him and get on with your life."

"Until I find the truth, Chief, this will be my life." And with that, Hays stormed out of the office. There was still time to catch the next ferry, to make the drive to Black Harbor before nightfall. He needed to speak with Larry Neuhaus one more time.

•••

As the sun dipped its toes into the sea, Ed went to his living room couch. His ex-wife slept there, still tucked into her afghan cocoon. He reached out and shook her shoulder. "Barb? John's comin'."

Her eyes popped open and she reached out to grab his wrist in a death grip.

"It's just me, Hon."

She let him go and rubbed her eyes. "What time is it?"

"A little after eight."

She stood and stretched. "I gotta get the shop open."

Ed gave a wag of his head. "Eight at night. You sat down this morning and drifted off to sleep, so I covered you up and left ya be."

Her mouth dropped. "Why the hell didn't you wake me?"

"I figured you needed your rest."

"I *needed* to open the store. How's it gonna look if —"

"Barb, half the stores in town never opened today. Yours wouldn't have made that much difference."

Barbara stared at him, slack-jawed.

Then John Canon and his young deputy, Ray, burst into the room, giving the couple a start.

"We got ourselves a big problem," Canon told them. "Roger Hays came into town and laid into me about Peggy Hern bein' attacked on dry land, starts goin' on about sharks with arms and legs."

Ed dropped the teacup he'd been holding.

"That Hern woman," Barbara blurted. "She's Callisto."

Canon's eyes widened, and Ray touched his forehead in the same way that a Christian might make the sign of a cross.

"You sure on this?" the chief asked.

Barbara nodded. "She dreamed of Poseidon."

Cannon rubbed his temples, then dragged his fingers down the length of his face. "Fuck me."

Poor Ray had gone white as a sheet; he was already making steps for the door. "Chief, it's gettin' dark and all. Mind if I —"

"Go," John told him, his eyes still on Barbara. "Get some sleep, though. Who knows what shit'll hit the fan tomorrow."

The deputy nodded, then tipped his policeman's hat toward Barbara as he left the room. "Teacher."

"Night, Ray."

Canon rubbed his chin with dismay. "What are we gonna do now?"

Barbara shrugged. "I gotta go to her."

"Whatcha gonna tell her?" the chief asked.

"I dunno."

"I say leave 'er be. The less she knows, the better."

"She's in a world o' hurt, John. Think Tellstrom wants a Callisto runnin' around? He'll kill her if he finds out."

"She might prefer death," Ed said somberly.

Barbara glared at him. "No. I'm gonna go to her...gonna make her understand."

Ed looked at his own feet. Things were getting out of hand too fast, like going downhill in a car with no brakes. *Varuna help us all.*

•••

Jason neared the pyramid, saw swift-moving clouds reflected in its raven glass, then the world went dark and he couldn't breathe. His eyes sprang open to find tiger-striped claws wrapped around his throat, pulling him up the tiled wall of the pool chamber.

Karl Tellstrom; the putrid ghost of last night's kill still haunted his breath. "She's alive! She's Callisto now!"

"I'm...sorry...I..." Jason gagged and tried to pry himself free of Karl's grip.

"Finish what you started," Tellstrom snarled, then he let go and stepped away, gillslits in his neck pulsating.

Jason slid down wet tile, gasping for air. Tellstrom's strength was incredible, even for a Charodon, but madness often granted surprising power, didn't it? And Jason had come to believe that Karl Tellstrom was quite mad indeed. Then again, sometimes it took a lunatic to get the job done. After all, a sane person might have been content to live out his days in the seclusion of Colonial Bay, never tasting freedom, never knowing what it was like to go out into the world and just...be. Jason longed for the day when he didn't have to stay in his human form for hour after endless hour. And, if Karl could get them their freedom, then, for better or worse, Jason would follow him.

"Both of you," Karl indicated another figure, a shadow undressing in the gloom, "go to Black Harbor. Bring the bitch here."

Jason rubbed his throat. "Alive?"

"I don't care if she dies there or dies in front of me. Just go, *now*. Do whatever you have to do, but I want her at my feet."

The shadow, now naked, stepped into the light. Canon's deputy, Ray; he knelt before Tellstrom and said, "It will be done."

•••

"What exactly am I looking at here?" Dr. Brahm removed his eyes from the microscope. He knew it was a blood sample, but the cells had an odd quality about them, a peculiarity he couldn't adequately define. "Is this supposed to be *human*?"

Sandra, the lab technician, took a drag from her cigarette, tried to calm herself. The entire hospital was a no smoking zone, but fuck it. "It *is* human, and it *isn't*. There are mutant cells running through it and they're...taking over the other cells."

Brahm took another look at the sample, fascinated. "Have you isolated the mutated cells?"

Sandra nodded excitedly. "Oh, yeah."

"And...?"

"See for yourself." She handed him the lab report, then watched him read it. "The mutation is carried using a retrovirus as its vector. It looks like a genetics experiment on speed. There's base substitution going on, with the existing nucleotide bases being...*replaced* by these new foreign ones. Plus, there's an alien amino acid being inserted into the poly-peptide chain."

"A mutation." Brahm swallowed. "Is it lethal?"

"You're the doctor. You tell me."

He knew his microbiology, knew that mutations like this, missense mutations, where amino acids were altered, could result in anything from the creation of an inactive enzyme, which was rarely fatal, to the production of chemical carcinogens. What most frightened him, however, were the mutations of entire pairs of nucleotide bases. Change even a single base and you can radically alter the genetic information of a cell. Change them all, and if the cell didn't die...well, it had never been done successfully to his knowledge.

"At this rate," Brahm began, his mouth the Sahara, "how long before every cell in the body's affected?"

"At that rate —" Sandra lit a new cigarette from the ashes of the first and pointed to the report. "— it's probably happened already."

The physician rubbed his face with his hand, unnerved. "Let me see the patient information."

Sandra grabbed a clipboard and handed it to him.

Patient 764. It didn't ring any bells. He read on. *Multiple shoulder lacerations...broken scapula...cracked clavicle...possible shark attack.*

Brahm felt suddenly ill.

TWENTY NINE

Peggy tucked her hair behind her ears. "You look like a million bucks."

Her room was dark, with only her various monitors and a small wall lamp to provide illumination. Against this murk, Larry's smile was indeed priceless.

"So do you. Well, half a million anyway." He kissed her deeply, rubbing her shrouded form with his hands.

"I see my untimely accident hasn't affected your sense of humor," she told him as their lips parted, then his hand slid up her hospital gown to her breast and she slapped it away. "Or your sex drive. What if someone walks in here?"

"The doctors will understand. See, it's a medical fact that all men are like Mr. Spock: they need sex every so often or they die."

Peggy giggled. "Nice try."

"Damn." Larry snapped his fingers and sat in a bedside chair. "Did you sleep well?"

"It was okay. *Lonely*. I missed you beside me." She smiled slightly, then said, "That DeParle woman came to say 'get well soon.' Guess I must've made the news."

"Someone paid me a visit, too."

Peggy turned on her side, mildly surprised her body permitted the move. Yesterday, such a motion would have made her wince with pain, but today...it was as if she'd never been hurt. The drugs they were giving her must really be wonderful. "Who?"

"He said his name was Roger Hays. His son was killed in that attack the other night."

She rose onto her elbows, quietly amazed she could do so. "His *son*? I thought you saw a woman?"

"I did. But they were together on the island, and they found the boy's body. Looks like he was killed in the same attack."

"Oh my God."

"What happened to you, Peggy?"

"What do you mean?"

"I mean Dr. Brahm thinks you were on the menu too."

"What?" She blinked, her hand drifting to her shoulder. "He thinks...a shark? Larry, I wasn't even in the —"

"I know. I pulled you out of that alley. But...I saw something weird the night of the attack, something I didn't want to tell the police."

Peggy nodded, *needing* him to explain.

Larry spoke quietly, in a tone just a notch above a whisper. "When I looked into the water that night, I thought I saw a person attacking that girl. It looked like there was a man under the waves with her."

"The Hays boy?"

Larry shook his head. "No. A man with fins."

"If you'd said that the night of the attack, I would've called your doctor."

"And that's why I didn't tell the police, but I told Hays. He looked at me like it was what he wanted to hear. I'm not sure what he knows, but he gave me the creeps." He remained silent for a moment, then asked, "Why did you go into that alley?"

Peggy felt the blood rush to her face. "I...heard a noise."

"So you walked *toward* it?"

"You're one to talk. It sounded like someone was having an asthma attack. You don't just *not* help someone if they're not breathing."

"Go on," he urged.

"I fell over the body and —"

Larry held up his hand to halt her. "What body?"

"The guy on the floor of the alley...the *dead* body."

"There wasn't any body. You were alone."

She swallowed. "It must've dragged him off."

"It?"

"What you said about a man with fins...it doesn't sound so crazy after what I saw. There was something in the alley with me. It was too dark to get a good look. I saw...I got a glimpse of its foot. It was webbed."

"As soon as the doctor says you're ready, we're getting out of here."

"She needs to leave now."

Their eyes shot to the doorway as Barbara DeParle entered the room and closed the door behind her.

"Right now."

"You came by earlier," Peggy said.

DeParle gripped the bedrail. "Do you think I'm a crazy old woman?"

Peggy's face reddened. "My inner voice used a little more tact."

Barbara's eyes ran from Peggy's face, to Larry's, to the door, then back again. "I promise...I'll give you all the answers you need, but you gotta believe me when I say we need to leave here."

Dr. Brahm opened the door and Barbara jumped at the sound of his voice. "Good evening."

"Hello, doctor," Peggy said, her eyes still focused on Barbara.

"Just need to take a quick look at you here." Brahm moved over to her bedside, inspected the wound in her shoulder. "I'm amazed at how quickly this is healing. Any dizziness or nausea?"

"No. I was tired earlier, but now I feel like I could run the Boston Marathon."

Barbara listened, nodding as if Peggy's answers were perfectly normal.

The look on Brahm's face, however, suggested they were anything but. "Any pain or discomfort?"

"Nope. Feel all stretchy-bendy again." Peggy shrugged her shoulders and tilted her head to demonstrate. "You've cured me."

Slowly, Brahm's eyes rose to meet Larry's. "Can I talk to you for a moment, Mr. Neuhaus?"

"What is it?" Peggy asked, now certain something was wrong.

The doctor tried to cover, "It's nothing, really. I just forgot to get some information from him earlier."

Larry gave the doctor a cold stare, then turned to Peggy. "Will you be all right?"

Peggy nodded, certain Larry would share the information with her anyway; she returned her gaze to Barbara, wondering what the old woman knew.

•••

Larry closed the door to Peggy's room and turned to face Brahm. "What?"

"Look, I could stand here and give you all the medical and scientific lingo, but *I* don't even completely understand it right now. Your fiancé has come into contact with some kind of retro-virus. It appears her entire cellular structure's...altering."

Larry swallowed; he searched for his voice and found a pale imitation, "What can you do?"

"There are literally millions of pieces to a DNA strand, and they're...they're all changing in some way. I've never seen anything like it. Nobody has."

"What do you mean 'nobody has'?"

Brahm hesitated. "This is a small hospital, Mr. Neuhaus, so today I've been in contact with several specialists. They're looking at what we have and I'm sure they'll want to run some tests of their own. We'll do everything we can to find out what this is and what we can do."

Larry didn't know what to believe; he looked through the window into Peggy's room and was shocked by what he saw there.

•••

"Ever hear the word 'Callisto'?" Barbara moved to Peggy's bedside. "The Greeks used it for one of their myths; a young, beautiful girl gets changed into a beast by the gods, but the word's much older than that. In a very ancient tongue, it means 'anointed.' My ancestors used the word to describe people like yourself, people who survive an attack and come away from it...transformed."

"Miss DeParle...Barbara...I don't —"

"Hold out your hand."

Peggy held her arm out in the air, feeling a little silly as she did so. "Now relax it."

Impatient, but wanting to see where this was leading, Peggy let it feel like dead weight at the end of her arm.

Barbara nodded. "Now concentrate on it."

Peggy frowned. "Concentrate how?"

"Focus on it...clear your head and focus on your fingers, your palm, your wrist."

Peggy did as the woman asked, relaxed and concentrated on her own hand. Suddenly, she became aware of tingling in her flesh, then tightness. It was as if her muscles were stretching and relaxing without conscious effort. Then, her fingers actually lengthened; there was no pain, just a slight pulling sensation, as if the hand were hyper-extending to touch something just out of range. Coloration drained from her skin, leaving it almost transparent. She could actually see the shadows of veins, arteries, and bone working within her. Tissue seemed to liquefy and congeal, filling in the spaces between phalanges to create webbing. Finally, her bones grew until they pierced the softened flesh at the ends of her fingers and formed sharpened claws. The entire metamorphosis took only a matter of seconds, but Peggy saw it all in slow motion.

She shook her head, denying the horror below her wrist. "No."

"Yes, child. You're Callisto now, but you're not alone." Barbara held out her own hand; aged flesh melted and was replaced by smooth, translucent pink webbing. The old woman smiled. "You're one of Poseidon's children."

The statement washed over Peggy as if she were a stone struck by a tremendous wave. She remembered the driftwood sculpture Larry bought at the shopkeeper's store, the half fish-half woman on a rock. She covered her mouth with her new hand, cringing at the feel of it against her lips.

When Peggy looked up, she saw Larry; he stared at her through the rectangle of wired glass in her door. His eyes were wide, and his mouth misshapen, his lips open and twisted in shocked disgust. Before Peggy could say a word, before she could even cry, the lights went out.

•••

Bob Jacobs had worked hospital security for nearly ten years. Power outages were rare, but they did happen. The key was to stay calm and do everything by the manual.

The emergency generator kicked on almost immediately, filled the hallways and corridors with a crimson glow.

Bob made his way toward the basement stairwell. First, he'd check the breakers to make sure nothing was tripped, then he'd call Black Harbor Power and Light. The hospital was a priority, so power should be restored long before the back-up generator failed.

The staircase was dark, except for the slight glow of an EXIT sign just above the door. Bob swept the steps with his flashlight, then made his way down. His nostrils filled with an acrid mixture of burning rubber and ammonia. The guard shined his light toward the cinderblock wall, revealing a mass of smoldering wire where the switches had been. On the concrete floor, he found a pile of scorched and dented metal boxes; it was as if they'd been blown from the wall by a tremendous surge of power, or ripped from their roosts and thrown down. The former sounded more logical.

Where's that ammonia stink coming from?

Bob stepped into the chamber with caution, and his light caught something of interest almost immediately. A metal grate; it sat next to the open manhole it was meant to conceal. Bob shook his head. Sewer gas. They were lucky the explosion didn't reduce the entire hospital to rubble.

Looks like we move to step two and call the power company.

Bob was halfway back to the stairs when he noticed a circle of light dancing in the darkness, not on the wall, like the spot of a flashlight, but in the air itself. It looked as if the world's largest firefly had been trapped down here in the basement.

"Who's there?"

No response. The light moved toward him, its motion fluid and organic.

Bob's hand went to his holster, caressed the metal butt of his sidearm. He was about to issue a warning when the light came within inches of his face.

It was the size of a baseball, covered in a latticework of tiny veins, but it wasn't floating; it seemed to be growing from a long, dark stalk.

And then Bob's flashlight found something else in the shadows, a gaping slit rimmed in long, crystalline thorns. As impossible as it was, Bob realized he was staring into a huge mouth. He drew his weapon, but, before he could fire a shot, something swiped toward him out of the gloom. He felt a cool breeze on his throat, felt a jab of pain as if he'd been punched, and then the room rushed by his eyes in a spinning blur.

Bob wondered why there was a decapitated body in the corner of the room, dousing the ruined fuse boxes in gore, a body dressed in a brown security guard's uniform.

•••

The power outage brought Larry's impromptu meeting with Brahm to an end. He rushed back into Peggy's room, his mind filled with so many different feelings and thoughts that it was difficult, if not impossible, to separate them. To be told that monstrous changes were going on within the woman he loved was horrifying enough, but to see them externalized...it had to be a trick of his mind, a mirage brought on by sudden worry, or the result of going days without his Paxil.

A small emergency light above Peggy's door cast a cherry tinge onto the scene. Peggy sat bolt upright in her bed, *The Creature from the Black Lagoon*'s talon where her hand had been. Larry opened his mouth, but could find no words to fill it.

Peggy lowered her eyes and turned away. "Oh, God...don't look at me."

"How...?" was all Larry could manage.

"We have to get her someplace safe."

At the sound of the voice, Larry jerked his head in Barbara's direction. He'd forgotten she was even in the room. He was about to accuse the old woman of something, of what he didn't know, but when he saw that she too had a webbed appendage, the sight robbed him of his imputations.

"This is serious," Barbara continued. "They'll kill her if she stays."

Larry shook his head, unable to comprehend.

Barbara grabbed him by the arm; her grip was *strong*. "There are creatures out there, more powerful than you'd be willing to believe right now, and their leader hates your kind with a passion. To him, Peggy is an abomination, and he'd just a'soon see her dead than leave her be."

It was as if Barbara were speaking to him in Chinese. He knew the words, but he could not understand the way in which she'd strung them together. He swallowed hard, forcing bile back down his throat. "You can help her?"

"I dunno...I..." Barbara cocked her head toward the door. "Someone's coming."

And then Larry heard it — footsteps in the hall, approaching fast.

•••

It was going to be one of those nights.

Being the charge nurse normally meant that Helen had a lighter patient load, but not tonight. Someone called in sick, forcing Helen to take on twice as many cases, one of which coded on her. And now the power was out.

Luckily, the generators came on-line and Helen was able to continue her charting and other paperwork. The new computer system was amazing; she could pull up the location of any patient in the hospital, see their meds listed, know their doctors' names and diagnoses, see when they were scheduled for surgery, and any number of other fun and useful tidbits.

Helen heard bare feet slap the linoleum, wayward patients coming down the rose-tinted hallway.

She leaned over her desk, ready to tell them to return to their beds before they fell and busted their heads open, but the charging shapes weren't patients; they weren't even human. Their movements were swift and predatory. Helen caught glimpses of anatomy that made no sense together: arms, legs, fins, tails, and teeth...far too many teeth. There was no time for Helen to run, or even to scream. The nurse waved her arms madly, as if the ferocity of the motion would frighten the beasts away and prevent the attack she knew was imminent. There was a tug at her abdomen, the burning pain of scalpels in her gut, and she was tossed against the back wall.

Helen's hands went to her stomach, felt the shredded fabric of her uniform and the sticky warmth beneath. When she looked up, she saw a dark mass slip off her desk, dragging bloodied paperwork onto the floor with a sick splat; she followed it down.

The beasts moved to her computer terminal and one of them started to type.

•••

Peggy's door creaked opened; a dark shape looked in.

Larry grabbed the shadow from behind, held it in a stranglehold and pulled it inside.

"Let go of *me!*" the intruder cried as it worked to free itself.

Larry tightened his grip and wrestled it to the ground. Barbara sat on the bed with her back toward the door, holding Peggy close to her, using her own body as a shield. She looked up, saw what was struggling in Larry's grasp, and sighed with relief. "Let go of him."

Larry glanced up at her, then at the thing in his arms. It was a man, but that fact meant nothing. His eyes returned to Barbara. "You sure?"

She nodded.

Larry let go and backed away.

Roger Hays staggered to his feet, smoothed his hair and adjusted his tie; his eyes darted around the room with contempt. "What the *hell* do you people think you're doing?"

Larry ignored him and motioned for the two women. They climbed down from the hospital bed, Peggy holding the spot on her arm where she'd removed the IV needle.

"What's going on here?" Hays demanded.

"We're leaving." Larry opened the door, peered down the hallway in either direction, then turned back to his companions. "All clear."

They stepped out into the rosy gloom; Roger was two steps

behind them, confusion and mistrust still swimming in his eyes. Why would Hays show up now? Did the man know more than he was letting on? Larry was certain of nothing but the fact that Peggy was in real danger.

"Follow me," Barbara directed.

The group hurried down the hallway, followed by the sound of screams.

•••

Brahm checked room after room, finding patient ventilators and other equipment still online. There was no reason why they shouldn't be; backup generators kicked on the instant power was interrupted. But, because he didn't know the cause of the outage, the doctor thought it wise to make sure.

He felt a tap on his shoulder and nearly leapt out of his skin.

"Sorry, Doc." It was just one of the orderlies. "Didn't mean to scare you."

"I'm fine," Brahm told him, still startled.

"Anything you need me to do?"

"Yes." Brahm pointed down the hall. "Why don't you check those rooms, let people know that everything's fine and the power should be back up soon."

And, with a quick nod, the orderly strutted off down the corridor.

Brahm hadn't taken more than a few steps into the next room when he heard the screams; they were loud, shrill, but definitely male. The doctor didn't know what he might find when turned around, but monsters weren't even in his realm of possibilities.

The first creature stood on two legs; a tall, muscular nightmare. It hunched over, its arched back outlined in a spiny dorsal ridge. Its shadowy tail swept the width of the hallway, ending in a wide fin like an oriental fan. And, most frightening of all, its face was the triangular snout of a great white shark.

A second animal stood over the fallen orderly, its hinged jaw filled with jutting fangs. A serpentine stem grew from its forehead, crowned by a glowing ball of blue-white light. This creature was shorter than the shark-thing, covered in shimmering scales, and it held the orderly's screaming face in webbed talons.

Brahm took a step from the doorway to attempt a rescue, but it was already too late. The beast clamped its enormous mouth around the orderly's skull and bit down with an audible wet snap.

The shark-thing caught sight of Brahm and rushed the doorway where he stood, accelerating with frightful agility; a beard of long, black filaments trailed from its chin like catfish whiskers.

Brahm slammed the door and the creature plowed into it, forced it open just a crack. Somehow, Brahm managed to push it closed again; he fumbled for the deadbolt and locked the monster outside. When he stood upright, a single black eye stared at him through the wired-glass in the door. It quickly disappeared, replaced by a scaly fist that turned the window into a sparkling explosion. The creature clawed the wire mesh from the opening and reached down for the lock.

Brahm scanned the room in a panic. His eyes drifted past the window on the opposite wall, then shot back to it. Five flights. Too high to jump.

Rabid growls came from behind him. Unable to reach the bolt, the shark-thing threw its weight against the door, cracking it.

Out of options, Brahm ran to the window. The latch slid easily, but the glass wouldn't budge. *Painted shut.* He pulled a pair of bandage scissors from his pocket, slashing and scraping at the seams.

Behind him, the door splintered. Brahm glanced across his shoulder and saw the shark-thing's snout punch through the wood; its serrated teeth formed a feral grin.

Brahm worked feverishly, chipped away paint until he could get the window open. Outside, there was no ledge to crawl across, no awning to break his fall, no tree to climb. He scanned the wall and found a drainpipe to his right. He took off his scrub jacket and climbed onto the windowsill.

The creature managed to reach the deadbolt; it rushed into the room, arms extended, jaws opened wide.

Brahm grabbed the pipe and swung over. He pinched it between his thighs, looped his scrub jacket around it, and, holding fast to both ends, started down.

The animal reached out and tugged viciously on the pipe. Brahm saw a support bracket pop loose from the wall and concrete dust rained into his eyes. He continued down the face of the hospital, reaching the second story windows before the vibration became too great. Metal brackets fell past him and his drainpipe pulled away from the building.

Brahm closed his eyes.

•••

"What was that?" Hays wanted to know.

Fear ignited in Barbara's eyes. "They're here."

Peggy paid little attention; she cringed against the wall, fiercely rubbing her now human hand. To a passer by, it would have appeared as if she were trying to wipe a mark from her skin, but it was the flesh itself she wished to be rid of.

"Where can she hide?" Larry asked.

Before Barbara could respond, the sound of heavy breathing drifted down the corridor, like overworked horses charging toward them. Larry knew there was no time for debate. Whatever these things were, they were coming to claim Peggy's life.

He pushed the women. "Get to the stairs."

Roger opened his suit jacket, produced a .45 pistol from a holster concealed within. Larry's stare froze on its barrel.

"For protection," Hays told him.

Larry wondered briefly what this man needed protection from, but it didn't really matter. As demonic sounds filled the hallway, Larry was just glad someone was armed. "How'd you get that past security?"

"I came in through the emergency room entrance. No metal detectors. They'd go off every time an EMT wheeled in a gurney."

A duty nurse sat behind a desk at the end of the hall; she caught sight of Hays' weapon and her eyes widened.

"Call security," Larry told her. "No, call the police. Tell them there's a dangerous animal loose in the hospital."

She nodded, picked up the phone to dial.

A pair of dark shapes entered the hallway behind them. One of the silhouettes Larry recognized from the night of Susan's attack, the same half shark-half man he'd seen in the waves. The other creature was different, more bizarre; a snake with a glowing head slithered from between its eyes.

"Is that what attacked my boy?" Roger asked.

Larry nodded. "Yes."

"Quit your jawjackin'," Barbara urged. "We gotta run!" They hastened down the hall, everyone but Roger. The man stood frozen, the red glow of emergency lights casting a sinister look across his face. The creatures were stopped at the far end of the passage, unsure of their target, but they weren't going to stand still for long.

"Come on, Hays," Larry called.

Roger turned to him, rage welling from somewhere within. He'd found his son's killer. Nothing else mattered. "You go on."

Peggy and Barbara were halfway to the stairs. Larry turned away; ran after them with a speed born of fear, not so much for his own life, but for the woman he loved. He heard the echo of gunfire as he reached the steps, but there was no time to stop and watch the action.

•••

Dr. Kyle Brahm landed on the canvas top of a Chevy Cavalier convertible; he bounced off the fabric like a trampoline, then laid there for a moment. The clanging drainpipe, and the throbbing of his own heartbeat, filled his ears. After a moment, when he realized he was still alive, he opened his eyes and laughed.

•••

Roger Hays stood his ground in the center of the corridor, blocking the creatures' charge. He raised his .45, held the butt in both hands as if he were home on his firing range, only now the targets had faces; grotesque, unnatural faces.

"You bastards killed my son!"

Roger took aim, centered his barrel on the shark-like head of the first creature. It came at him with remarkable speed. He squeezed the trigger, heard a resounding thunderclap, and saw a flash of light that burned the image of the hallway and the two beasts into his eye like the negative of a photograph. Petals of blood bloomed from the creature's shoulder. It staggered, then fell backward onto the linoleum, its tail flailing, digging craters in the plasterwork of the walls.

The other monster, the one with a light bulb jutting from its forehead, halted and turned its attention toward its injured comrade. The wounded animal made a gesture that suggested it was fine, then rolled over onto all fours, resembling one of the fin-backed dinosaurs Hays had seen in museums. A dark river flowed from the hole in its shoulder, but it was still alive, and like any wounded creature, it was angry. It charged, its sharpened claws clicking against the floor as it advanced, its jaws wide open.

Hays dove over the counter of the nurses' station; landed on a chair. The seat, upset by his weight, tipped off its rollers and the floor rushed up to meet his face. A thunderous crash rocked the desk as the creature smashed into the spot where he had been standing a moment before. Roger's body was flooded by pain, but he challenged its control. He was not going to be a meal for this freak of nature, this murdering evil that had claimed his only son.

Hays still held the gun in his hand. He heard the creature get to its feet, felt the warmth of its breath on the nape of his neck; he rolled onto his back and blindly fired off a shot. The beast moved from the line of fire with cat-like speed and was gone from view.

"Forget him!" The voice was deep and gurgling, an evil spirit from a cauldron. Roger realized it was the other creature, the one with the glow-tipped whip on its head; it wanted to continue after Neuhaus and the women.

On the floor beside Hays, a nurse sat on her knees, her ears covered to block out sounds from both animal and gunfire. Roger hoped she would have the sense to *stay* down. He, on the other hand, rose to his feet and fired off another round; it struck the wall just behind the now moving targets.

The demons bolted through the reddish gloom with great speed and determination.

Hays ran after them.

•••

Peggy glanced over her shoulder, more than a little surprised to see Larry still there. After all, she was a freak now, wasn't she? Peggy wished she had time to stop and talk to him, time to find out if his feelings toward her had changed. If he could no longer care for her, no longer *love* her as she still loved him, she would understand, but she would also stop running. Better to let the animals rip her heart out quickly than to die slowly from its empty ache.

Their footfalls echoed through the stairwell, sounding more like a stampede than three people. Barbara seemed so strong for her age. Peggy's condition was also surprisingly good. Despite the workout she'd given her shoulder, it caused her no pain at all; it was as if her body had gained strength and the ability to heal in addition to the power to transform into...into what she had yet to fully discover.

Above them, the door to the stairwell flew open. Peggy looked up; the face of her pursuer hung over the railing, eyes like two polished black marbles, a string of drool dangling from its saw-toothed jaws. It growled at her, then began its own descent.

Peggy studied her hand, saw it was normal and knew it was not.

Why couldn't they have just killed me? I wish I'd never screamed for help in that alley.

If she'd just let the creature have her then, this nightmare would be over and she'd be having a catfight with Natalie in Heaven right now.

And then Larry would've blamed himself for not being there a moment sooner, would've put his hand through another mirror, or worse.

Peggy's stomach sank and she turned her attention to the steps, suddenly aware of the fact that she had no idea where they were going. She supposed it didn't matter.

Barbara knew.

Peggy trusted this woman; she had a feeling that she *needed*

Barbara, a feeling that this woman was important to her in some way.

Maybe she has the cure. Maybe she's taking me to a place where she can make me normal again.

Peggy prayed that was the case.

They reached a metal landing; to the left, a door stenciled with a large "1," to the right, the stairs spiraled down into the basement. Barbara turned to Larry. "Leave us!"

"No way!"

"You can't go where we're goin', and they'll only kill you if you try."

Peggy let go of the railing and took his hand. "Larry, do what she says. *Please*."

He squeezed her fingers, then looked to the old woman. "You'll protect her?"

"With my life."

He nodded. "How will I find you?"

"Get to the church in Colonial Bay." Barbara's voice was nearly lost beneath the growls and clatter from above. "There's a door behind the altar."

Barbara tugged at Peggy's arm, pulled her toward the basement stairs. Peggy broke loose and ran to Larry; she kissed him deeply, passionately, then pushed him away and rejoined Barbara, a single tear racing down her cheek.

"Go," Peggy told him. "Just...just go."

Larry stared at her a moment, shot a glance up the stairway, then ran onto the first floor. When she was certain that he wouldn't follow, Peggy resumed her downward trek.

A large white "B" marked the door at the end of the staircase. Barbara pushed it open. What they saw was more maintenance closet than basement; mops and brooms hung from hooks on the wall, mop buckets sat filled with pungent water on the floor, and chemicals and cleaning solutions sat on shelves waiting to be used. On the other side of the room, two more doors, one was marked "Incinerator," the other "Laundry." Barbara led Peggy toward the Laundry.

Industrial washers, dryers, and rolling canvas hampers filled the room. Barbara paid attention to none of them. Instead, she ran to a large metal drain in the center of the concrete floor. The grate must have been heavy, but the old woman cast it aside as if it were made of cotton. "This storm drain runs about half a mile, then empties into the bay. In you go."

Peggy stared at the opening. "Half a mile through the sewer?"

Barbara nodded.

"No." Peggy back away from the drain, wanted it all over and done.

Barbara flashed a look of annoyance. "We don't have time for this. You need to do what I say when I say if you wanna live."

Reluctantly, Peggy moved to the edge and jumped in. The splash echoed in her ears as she surveyed her cramped surroundings. She was up to her waist in cold, glutinous water that stank of mold and excrement.

Barbara splashed into the tunnel beside Peggy; she took a moment to orient herself, then grabbed Peggy's hand. "This way."

Peggy let the old woman guide her into the foul darkness of the drainpipe. The concrete cavern filled with the faint echoes of gunshots and screeching behind them, and Peggy hoped that the creatures, whatever they were, had at last been slain. Their horrible mewling returned, however. They hadn't abandoned their chase; in fact, they were closing in.

Within minutes, Peggy could see moonlight dancing on swells in the bay. The drain's opening was like a cave in the cliff face. Fetid water rushed over their feet, an engineered waterfall that fell into the ocean below. Peggy scanned the rock around the opening. It wasn't smooth, but it couldn't be easily climbed, and the drop into the waves was at least fifty feet. She threw up her hands. "Great. What now?"

"Now, we swim."

Peggy looked down at the breakers and realized Barbara meant for them to jump. "I can't."

"Yes, you *can*."

"You mean change, don't you? Forget it. I'm not becoming one of those...those *things*."

Barbara placed a hand on the small of Peggy's back and pushed.

The tide flew toward Peggy at break-neck speed; it rushed into her mouth, silenced her screams. When her lungs shrieked that they would drown, her body instinctively transformed. First, her neck opened; slits became undulating flaps, pushing oxygen-saturated water through filters that allowed her to breath. Peggy reached up to touch her newly formed gills, amazed and terrified by them at the same time. As before, the process caused her little pain. Muscles expanded and tightened. Bones lengthened in her fingers and toes. Veins and arteries could now be seen, pumping fluid to and from her extremities like dark rivers. Her skin was not only transparent, but phosphorus as well, glowing with an inner system of illumination, as if strings of Christmas bulbs had somehow been implanted in her flesh. She'd seen nature programs about creatures that lived in endless night at great depths, alien things that appeared to be made of light; it seemed that Peggy had now joined their ranks. She longed for a mirror, so she might gaze upon her new face, then wondered if she would have the courage.

Peggy felt a change in the current as something swam up to tap her on the arm. It was dressed in Barbara's clothing, a being of light; eyes like islands in a phosphorous pool, and a flat, paddle-like tale. Unlike the things in the hospital, this was truly beautiful to behold. Barbara undressed, allowing the garments to float away. Following Barbara's lead, Peggy removed her hospital gown, and, together, they swam into the liquid night.

•••

Fueled by hate, Roger Hays made short work of the stairs. He was about to exit onto the first floor when a door swung closed below him.

Why would you come down there? Why not escape through the lobby?

Roger followed the noise down. He found two doors; both were closed, leaving no clue as to how he should proceed.

Sounds of movement from the Laundry.

Hays pressed against the doorframe; sweat beaded on his forehead and upper lip. *Heat from the incinerator*. He pushed the door open and leapt into the next room.

The creatures were there. The animal with the face of a shark, his son's murderer, climbed through an open drain in the floor. The second beast dove at Roger, the underbite of its huge mouth open and screeching, its webbed claws extended like knives, the same claws that had so easily taken David's eye and marred his body.

Hays squeezed the trigger. A bullet burrowed deep into the monster's maroon flesh, propelled it backward. Roger fired again and hit the beast in the chest for a second time. He continued firing until the clip was emptied and the blaring sound of gunshots replaced by impotent clicks.

Mortally wounded, the beast fell against one of the industrial dryers; fluid poured down the glass hatch, obscuring the tumbling linen within. As it slid to the floor, its shape changed wildly. It became a puzzle box of flesh, worked and reworked by phantom hands; at times, its anatomy twisted into that of a human being, a man.

Roger lowered his smoking gun and gaped at the creature, mystified. This was no horror film, no comic book. This was the real world. Animals could not become...

For a moment, the beast's face grew wholly human and Hays recognized the man from Chief Canon's office.

Holy shit, one of the fucking deputies!

A splash.

Roger jerked his head in the direction of the open drain. The real prize had escaped into the sewer below. Frustrated, Hays returned his attention to the still-shifting form on the floor. He knelt beside it, stared into its eyes, one human, the other more like that of a fish. "What the hell are you?"

Dark, arterial blood trickled from the corners of the creature's misshapen mouth. "Charodon."

Roger had no time for gibberish. "Where'd the other one go?" The animal was silent except for its labored breathing, so Hays shook it violently. *"Where did it go?"*

The monstrosity seemed to settle back into its original hideous incarnation. It actually smiled, its voice a raspy gargle as it spoke, "Colonial Bay."

"How many of you fucks are there?"

"We *are* Colonial Bay," it uttered proudly, then breathed its last.

Roger rose to his feet, scanned its horrific topography.

"My God."

The whole town? Was that possible? Shit, none of it was possible, but here it was lying dead at his feet. Colonial Bay was full of shape shifting killers.

"Jesus fucking Christ."

Hays paced back and forth for a moment, tried to clear his head to make room for rational thought. He wanted to go after these monsters, but first things first. There was a body on the floor, and bullets from his gun were lodged in its chest. Roger wiped sweat from his upper lip. It was so hot that he couldn't think of a proper —

The incinerator.

A canvas basket sat full of unwashed sheets; Roger ran to it, grabbed a sheet and spread the fabric across the cement floor. He slid his hands beneath the creature's armpits, clasped them together over its bloodied chest, and dragged it onto the sheet. Hastily, he wrapped it, took hold of the fabric, hauled it across the basement floor, out the door, and into the incineration chamber.

A large incinerator stood in the center of the room, firelight dancing through the metal grill across its opening. Hays pulled the shrouded beast over to the makeshift crematorium, burning his hands on the hot metal as he opened it up. Roger pushed the dead weight up the searing wall and into hungry flames. He stood there for a moment, sweat forging rivers down his face, watched as fire consumed his kill, wishing the animal were still alive to feel its skin char.

Roger Hays burned his hands a second time as he closed the grate and backed out of the incinerator room. He saw a container of bleach on the shelf, poured some over his hands, and washed them thoroughly in a mop sink, removing any trace of blood.

Hays stopped in mid step, wondered why he'd just gone to so much trouble, and could find no logical explanation. If the monster's carcass *had* been discovered, he wouldn't face prosecution; it was a rampaging animal, nothing more. The police, the National Guard, maybe even Homeland Security might have helped him with his vengeance, his *justice*. These murdering freaks had to be exterminated, and Hays couldn't do it alone, not the whole town.

He needed help.

Roger made his way up the stairs and walked across the dim lobby, adjusting his tie and smoothing his hair. He had a phone call to make. When he reached the exit, realization flashed across his mind and he knew why he'd disposed of the body so quickly and completely.

Habit.

THIRTY

Carol Miyagi found the room to be a sizable improvement over the cramped cabin she and Alan shared. It had everything; a king-sized bed, large oak dressers, even a brass make-up table with an oval mirror.

Make-up? Oh, Lord, when was the last time I put on make-up?

They'd spent forty-five minutes explaining everything to Officer Preston. *Everything*; the temple they'd discovered, the trident symbol etched into its stone, even Roger Hays' sculpture and its twin on the ocean floor. Then Preston asked how they were connected to Hays, and, apparently satisfied, allowed them to go their merry way.

When they reached the island town of Colonial Bay, however, they found it to be almost as deserted as the *Maggie May*. Many of the shops were closed, as if it were October or April rather than the busy summer vacation season. Unfortunately, the inns told a different story and they were lucky to find a vacancy here at the Sea Mist.

Beveled glass doors opened onto a balcony; Alan Everson stood at its railing and admired the view. Carol removed her hairclip, let the dark locks cascade over her shoulders, and walked out to stand beside him.

He stared out at the sea. It covered more than two thirds of the Earth, an alien empire on their own planet, teeming with exotic life and the secrets of dead civilizations. And yet, in the moonlight, it seemed for a moment that there was no Atlantis, no mysterious statues and symbols, no Coast Guard officers waving guns, no one else in the world. Carol put her arms around Alan, rested her head comfortably against his chest.

"Thank you," she told him.

"For what?"

"For being here with me. It almost feels like a vacation."

He snickered at that. "As long as I've known you, you've never taken a vacation."

"Vacations are for people who want to get away from their lives and the people they see every day. I don't."

Alan kissed the nape of her neck, and she wondered if this might not be the perfect moment for her to say that she loved him. "We should go inside," she told him instead.

"That's a good idea." His breath caused the fine hairs of her neck to stand on end. "The bed will probably be hard as a rock, though."

Carol grinned. "Compared to that bunk we've been rolling on, I think we'll be just fine. Now..." her voice lowered to a sensual whisper, "...*hamete chodai. Fukaku hamekonde chodai.*"

Alan hated to hear her Japanese when they fought, but he loved it during sex. He lifted her in his arms and she laughed as he rushed her back into the room.

It turned out the bed was quite comfortable.

THIRTY ONE

Dr. Kyle Brahm tried to get hold of himself, to allow rational thought a swift return to its nest and let logic sort through the night's happenings, but, so far, reason was still running scared.

Larry Neuhaus sprinted across the parking lot.

Brahm dove at the man, pressed him flat against a rusted Volkswagon van. "*What the hell?*"

"I don't know much more than you right now." Larry pushed him away. "They came for Peggy and I need to get to Colonial Bay."

"There aren't any more ferries tonight."

Neuhaus rubbed his hands through his hair in frustration. "Do *you* own a boat?"

Brahm blinked, then frowned. "I *live* on a boat."

"If you want answers," Larry told him, "I need your help."

•••

Black Harbor's sheriff had never liked hospitals; stepping into a building that housed so many diseases, you couldn't help but catch *something*.

The Sheriff walked through a fury of activity; investigators scurried from body to body, collecting stray fragments of corpse, swabbing each splatter of gore, photographing and numbering everything in between. There were so many pictures being taken that the entire corridor looked as though it were in the clutches of a furious electrical storm.

Judas Priest on a fucking crutch.

In all his years in law enforcement, he'd never seen such savagery. It never ceased to amaze him just how many ways there were to mutilate the human form. As soon as he thought he'd seen every possible desecration, someone came along and found a new one to add to the catalog.

The sheriff turned to two of his officers, Bowker and Eads. "Where's your witness?"

They led him to a door marked LOUNGE. It was no more than a glorified locker room; in the corner, a microwave sat atop a small refrigerator, and, in the center, folding chairs surrounded a card table. At the far end of this table, a woman in a nurse's uniform sat crying. The door swung closed, cutting them off from the symphony of discussions and movement in the outer hall.

Eads handed him a notebook that had two words written on the factory-lined page.

Emily Hunter.

"Morning, Ms. Hunter," the sheriff told her. He always used the term "Ms." when questioning a woman, unless he knew for a fact she was married. It saved him a shitload of lectures from the Femi-Nazis. "I'm Sheriff MacIsaac. I'd like to ask you a few questions about what happened here tonight."

"I didn't see anybody get killed," she burst out. "I didn't even know anyone was dead until one of the other nurses told me."

"But you did see *something*."

Emily looked at her hands, which were folded neatly on the table before her. "Can I please call my husband? If this makes the morning news, he'll be worried out of his mind."

"I'm sure we can arrange that, but first I'd like you to tell me what you saw."

She hesitated. "I was at the nurses' station when this group of people came running down the hallway. I noticed that one of 'em was waving a gun."

"What kind of gun?"

Nurse Emily shrugged. "A big one?"

MacIsaac nodded patiently. "Go on."

"This other man ran up and told me to call the police, said there was an animal loose in the hospital."

Now we're getting somewhere. "And did you?"

She nodded. "I picked up the phone straight away, dialed 911."

"Then what happened?"

"Then the fish-men came into the hall."

"The fish...men." His face tightened. Stories of sea monsters in the area were as old as New Hampshire itself, if not *more* ancient. His own grandfather used to warn him, *"If you don't wait half an hour after you eat before swimming, the sea monsters will get you."* MacIsaac's grandfather had been a real piece of work.

"The two women, and the guy that told me to call, they ran off, but the man in the suit —"

"It was a guy in a fish suit?"

"No, a regular suit. He was the one with the gun. He stood there in the hallway and just started shooting at 'em."

"At the...at the fish-men."

The nurse nodded.

"And did he kill 'em?" MacIsaac wanted to know.

She shook her head. "No. One of 'em came at him, and he dived over the counter. Nearly landed square on top of me."

"So you were still behind the desk at this point?"

Emily nodded. "I ducked down on the floor. Between the sound of the gun going off and the horrible sounds of those...those *things*...it's a wonder I'm not deaf."

Bowker motioned for the note pad and MacIsaac gave it to him. He scribbled something on it, then handed it back. The sheriff read what he'd written. It said, "Head Case". MacIsaac tossed the pad back to his officer, biting his own lip. Clearly this woman was terrified and the sheriff was not going to make light of it. "So the things just ran away then?"

Emily nodded, still studying her hands.

"And the man with the gun?"

"Ran after 'em. He seemed real angry with 'em."

Of course, who wouldn't *be angry with the* fish-men. "Well, thank you very much for all your help, Mrs. Hunter."

"I hope you catch those things."

MacIssac backed toward the door. "I'm sure we will. You just take a minute to compose yourself, then go ahead and make that call to your husband."

She smiled. "Thank you, Sheriff."

MacIsaac nodded and exited the room, his two officers right behind him. When the door was safely closed, Bowker and Eads began to laugh.

"People are dead here," the sheriff was quick to remind them. "This ain't a fuckin' joke."

The men forced themselves to stop their laughter.

"And parts of what she said make some sense. I want you guys to have the Crime Lab check all the hair samples they find and see if some belong to an animal." MacIsaac pointed to a camera mounted on the upper wall. "Then I want you to check the security tapes and see if we can find a usable shot of it, or at least the guy who was gun happy."

"Yes, sir," they said in unison.

As MacIsaac walked away, he felt the urge to sneeze into his handkerchief. He removed the cloth from his nostrils, checked its contents, and thought, *Great. This shithole's given me the damn swine flu.*

•••

Brahm's boat was not the yacht Larry had expected, with a wet bar and a hot tub on board for good measure, no, this...this was an oversized sailboat. "You live on this thing?"

The physician nodded. "I've got an apartment in town that I sublet for the summer."

As he climbed aboard, Larry stared at the sail wrapped neatly around its boom, then at the night sky. "Not very windy."

Brahm untied the moorings and pointed aft. "She's got a motor...if it works."

"What's *that* mean?"

"It means, I rarely have time to take her out anymore." Brahm moved to the cockpit. "It means she hasn't been serviced in over a year." He turned the key. "It means I hope you brought your chewing gum, just in case." He pressed the button that ignited the engine and the diesel fuel caught.

Larry gave a sigh of relief at the motor's enthusiastic humming.

Brahm placed his hands on the spoke of the wheel, guided the ship away from the dock. "Next stop, Colonial Bay."

And Peggy.

THIRTY TWO

Night dives were like walking in space; the feeling of near weightlessness, surrounded in all directions by cold darkness. The only way humans could visit this environment was either dressed in protective suits, or in the confines of specially built craft, bringing their own bottled atmosphere with them. Peggy Hern had been on night dives before, but her swim to Colonial Bay was an entirely different experience.

Tiny fish swam by them in rivers of confetti. They approached the reef separating the island from open water, and it was like flying over the surface of another world; coral stems grew as candy-colored grass, forming a living mound of activity. Next, Peggy saw huge tree trunks standing in her path and climbed them with her eyes, discovering that they were actually stilts, a foundation for the town's boat docks. She could clearly see the undersides of ships made shadow by the moon above.

Barbara led her through this forest of posts toward a rock wall. At first, Peggy didn't understand where the old woman was taking her, but then she saw an opening. They entered the fissure, swam through the tunnel beyond, and surfaced in a large cavern.

For a moment, Peggy could not breathe, then gills instinctively passed the baton of respiration to her lungs, allowing her to inhale and exhale normally. She didn't know if the lungs had suddenly reformed, or if they sat dormant within her chest while she swam. It didn't really matter.

Upon closer inspection, Peggy realized this was not a natural cavern, but a crafted one. The walls were covered in odd hieroglyphics, and candles sat on perches in the rock. At the center of the cove stood a huge statue, a stone monster; it resembled the creatures that hunted her, but this one wore a toga.

"Where are we?" Peggy asked, not recognizing her own gurgling voice.

"The temple of Varuna." Barbara lifted her arms as if to embrace the idol. "Below the church." Peggy nodded, looked at her hands and feet; they were still webbed. "How long can I stay...like *this*?"

Barbara shrugged. "As long as you want, child. You're one of Poseidon's children now."

"What's that mean?" Peggy demanded. "I don't even know what the hell that means!"

Barbara crawled from the lagoon and walked into the heart of the chamber, beckoning Peggy to follow. The air was cold against her nakedness, but the reverent flames of a hundred melting candles lent the altar some welcomed warmth. A book sat on the granite table, a volume so old that it looked as if it might crumble at the slightest touch. Barbara did touch it, however, and, as she opened it, its binding moaned. On the yellowed pages within, Peggy saw the same pictographic language that adorned the walls. Barbara translated the story, or perhaps it was a *Reader's Digest* synopsis from memory.

"A long, long time ago, the gods came upon the Earth and its riches. They descended from the heavens, and, from the world's creatures, created the clans of the earth, of the sky, and of the waters. But we angered the creators and they abandoned us." She swallowed, choked back rising tears. "Then came the slaughter. Hate, kept in check while the gods were here, came to a boil. The clans started killing each other, tried to wipe each other out. Humans weren't stronger than any other breed, but they had numbers on their side. The children of Poseidon were chased from their homes and hunted across the globe. We kept running, kept fighting, but after so long we just wanted all the killing and dying to stop. One day, the founders came to this island. They named it Croaton, which means 'new life,' and they said *enough*."

"Enough," Peggy echoed, bemused.

Barbara closed the book, sent a cloud of dust into the air. "They built Colonial Bay and started living like humans. They figured it was the only way to survive. And that's the way it's been...right up to now."

"So why the sudden public display of mayhem?"

The teacher curled her tail into a spiral, then sat upon it as if it were a cushion. "'Bout a year ago, a young man named Karl Tellstrom became a kind of prophet. He's been telling people just what they've been waiting to hear — that they don't have to be afraid anymore, that things can get back to the way they were before the gods left us."

Peggy looked into the grinning face of Varuna. "By killing us? Hunting us like animals?"

"By huntin' *them* the way *we've* always been hunted."

"Enough with the *we*! Until tonight, *I've* never been hunted." Horrified, Peggy stood up and paced like a caged zoo specimen, the black ovals of her eyes locked with Barbara's. "You didn't pop by the hospital tonight to say 'get well soon.' You got the news that I'm *not* a welcomed addition to the family. You know what, *fine by me*. You take it back."

DeParle eyed her. "Take it back?"

"Yeah!" Peggy's voice resonated in the hollow cavern. "Cure this!"

Barbara looked at her own webbed toes. "Child —"

"*Stop calling me 'child*,'" Peggy roared. "I'm *not* gonna live like this. You got that?"

"I understand what you're going through."

"Tell me. Tell me what I'm going through. I sure as hell don't know what it is."

Barbara's face was unreadable.

Peggy swept her claws down her new body. *"Look at me."*

"You've been given a gift, dear. A beautiful gift."

"You think Larry will think *this* is beautiful?"

"Does it matter what *he* thinks of you?"

"Are you profoundly stupid?"

"No," Barbara sighed. "And neither are you. You're a young woman in love. All you can think about, all you can see when you look into that crystal ball there in your mind is life with the man of your dreams. And sometimes..." A lump rose in her translucent throat and she forced it down again. "Sometimes you lose yourself to that love and you can't tell what's right and what's wrong. Whatever makes your man happy makes you happy. That's all that matters."

Peggy continued to pace.

Barbara went on, "I wish this hadn't happened to you. I truly do.

But, it *has* happened dear, and now you've got some hard choices ahead of you. You have to be strong enough to make 'em. You and Larry aren't part of the same world now. I know you love him. You have to love him enough to push him away."

Peggy stopped her pacing, remembering the warning from her dream, the dead thing telling her she was no longer human, that she had to make Larry leave her. As she looked at her claws, at the glowing rivers of phosphorous that gave them light, Peggy thought of Larry's face when he saw them in her hospital room. It was an expression of loathing. Her anger faded and genuine sadness filled the vacancy in her eyes.

"You can be strong, Peggy." Barbara was on her feet; her tail swung behind her, slapping the stone altar. "You may not believe it now, but you can be. Remember what I told you, you're not alone. I'll help you." The old woman took a step toward her, and Peggy backed away. "If you'll let me."

Barbara reached out to touch Peggy's transparent cheek, smoothed away a single tear.

Peggy trembled. She covered her mouth with her own hands, shocked by the feel of her thickened lips, and sobbed uncontrollably. This time, when Barbara went to embrace her, Peggy did not fight it.

"Tellstrom did this to me?" she asked, shaking. Tears streamed from her eyes onto DeParle's shoulder.

"Yes."

"God damn him."

Barbara looked to Varuna's downcast face. "Yes," she murmured, then shed tears of her own. "Damn him."

THIRTY THREE

"What did you say?" Karl's tiger-striped face clouded with rage and his teeth honed to daggers; at his clawed feet, several Kraken lay sleeping, beards of tentacles sliding lazily across their slimy chests.

"She got away," Jason repeated, blood flowing down his wet chest in threads. He transformed into his human form; the bullet pushed out of his shoulder and onto the tile, pain searing his nerve endings like a hot iron, making him feel as though he could pass out at any moment.

"You really fucked things up, *didn't you*," Karl growled. "Where's Ray?"

"Gone."

Karl growled. "*You shit!*"

"It's not my fault, Chrissy's mother —"

"*The Teacher?*"

Jason nodded, squeezed his eyes shut against the pain. "She was there...helped 'em escape."

Karl turned and threw his fists against the tiled wall, venting his rage; a child throwing a tantrum. He looked around the room as if searching for something to destroy, and his dark stare fixed on Jason. "*I'll tear you apart!*"

Tellstrom charged him, pushed him back with alarming swiftness. Jason's head collided with the tiled wall and birthed a shower of comets and stars that danced before his eyes.

"No, Karl!" Christine, her voice was stern, but more than a bit uncertain; she fixed her worried eyes on Jason.

Tellstrom threw her a forbidding glare.

"Please," she pleaded, returning his gaze. "You're better than this."

Karl frowned at her protest and proceeded to wrap his talons around Jason's neck.

Christine's eyes shot back to Jason and she blurted, "I'm pregnant."

Both men's jaws stood gaping at the announcement.

Karl released Jason and staggered back several steps, his eyes focused doubtfully upon Christine. "A child?"

She nodded.

Jason's stomach sank. *Chrissy...no... It's not true...*

When he dove from the drain, Jason considered swimming off into the ocean depths. He'd blundered his mission, and Varuna only knew what had happened to Ray. If the humans had killed him, they'd dissect his body as a natural oddity. If they'd merely wounded him, however... captured him *alive*...how long would it be before they forced a betrayal from him? How long before the hunters showed up at their doorstep, ready to destroy them?

Jason couldn't abandon Chrissy to the humans.

Then there was Karl. His behavior had become wild and senseless, and Jason feared what might happen to Christine in the arms of this madman. True, Karl needed her. She was royalty, after all, and her allegiance kept the more moderate clans allied to him. What Jason had never been able to understand was her attraction to Tellstrom. One day, he feared the man would go into an uncontrolled rage and kill her.

It was for her sake that Jason returned. And it was for her that he now faced Karl's wrath.

Please, don't let it be true, Chrissy. Tell me you said it just to make him leave me alone.

The engine of rage that drove Karl Tellstrom suddenly lost steam. "We have a child."

Jason wanted to change the subject, even if it meant suffering Karl's fury. "What do we do about the Callisto?"

"Tomorrow," Tellstrom's eyes were still firmly planted on Christine. "If the Teacher does have her, I know exactly where she'll be. Right now, I need to rest. Christine needs to rest. And you, you look like shit, *you* need to rest."

Jason cleared his throat. "The humans shot Ray."

"Not the first," Karl said with indifference, gently touching Christine's face with his talon. "Certainly not the last."

Christine chimed in: "But if the humans come to —"

Tellstrom shook his head. "It doesn't matter. The war needs to begin somewhere. Why not here?" Karl leaned in and kissed her with great enthusiasm, as if he would protect her. As if he *loved* her.

Jason thought he would be sick.

THIRTY FOUR

Dante "The Horror Show" Vianello sat in his loft, putting the finishing touches of paint on his new model, a Japanese garage kit of the battling creatures from *Alien Vs. Predator*. He told himself to stop and go to bed hours before, but the need to color the unfinished vinyl goaded him on. He stopped for a moment to rub his eyes, then admired the craftsmanship of the piece, both his and the sculptor's.

The collecting bug had bitten Dante long ago. While still a teenager, he'd stolen cars with Carlo Tosti, selling them for a few hundred dollars to spend at the local comic book store. Then, as he made his way through the ranks of Roger Hays' organization, his growing take had allowed him to buy bigger, better, and far more rare items until his apartment had become a museum of pop culture.

The other wiseguys thought he was nuts. Why blow hundreds of dollars on a set of *Star Wars* lobby cards? Why not a Lexus or a trip to the Bahamas? Fuck 'em. It was his money. Every man had his passion. For Carlo, it might be trips and cars, but for Dante, it was these bits of Hollywood.

The phone rang, shocking him from his trance.

Dante dropped his paintbrush and snatched up the receiver. "Do you know what fuckin' time it is?"

"Is that any way to say hello?"

Shit. It was Ludwig. *What the fuck's he doin' up?* "Hey, Boss."

"The man wants to see you."

Horror Show sat bolt upright. "What...? You mean face to face?"

"Yeah. His son was killed and he'd like you to handle some

of the arrangements."

Horror Show closed his eyes and nodded. He'd heard about Roger Hays' boy, David. However, he'd heard it was some kind of boating accident. It sounded strange to him at the time and it appeared his instincts were correct. Hays' son had been murdered, and now the man wanted blood. "When?"

"Tomorrow, what the fuck, *today*."

"Where?"

"A town called Colonial Bay."

"Colonial Bay?" Horror Show scanned the table, found a pen and paper to take notes with. "Where the fuck's that?"

"Take I-95. It's an island just off the coast, halfway between Hampton Beach and Little Boars Head."

The hitman frowned. "And where the fuck's *that*?"

"It's off New Hampshire," Ludwig huffed. "Buy a fucking map."

Fucking map, Horror Show scribbled, smiling to himself. *Check*.

"You'll want to take your boy Tosti...O'Shea...and Shiva."

Shiva? — The torch? What was he getting into? Horror Show put down his pen and reached into his pants' pocket; his fingers grasped the sliver of Dillinger's tombstone he kept there. "Where will we find the man once we get there?"

"Stop by the warehouse in the morning. I'll give you the details and a care package, so you can express our sympathies."

Weapons, and if Shiva was coming along, explosives. Horror Show feverishly rubbed the finished side of his granite shard, unaware that he was even doing so.

THIRTYFIVE

Carol Miyagi awoke from a wonderfully deep slumber, found herself still in Alan Everson's embrace; she smiled, the inner flesh beneath her pantyline still tingling at the memory of their coupling. Carol lifted Alan's arm and slid from between the sheets. She stretched, noticing how nice it felt not to have her fingertips brush against the metal bulkhead of the *Ambrosia*'s cabin, then she began her daily workout.

Tae-Bo; a mixture of martial arts, boxing, and dance. It increased her strength, toned her body, and helped her fit into her unforgiving wet suit.

Carol spun around, kicked out, and, when she turned again, she saw Alan watching her from the bed.

"I wish I had the video camera," he told her. "We could make a best-selling workout tape: Learn Nude Tae-Bo with Mistress Miyagi. Give Billy Blanks a run for his money."

"Very funny."

"I thought so."

"You would." Carol walked over to the knapsack that held her clothes, and her eyes caught sight of the compass packed within. "Oh, my God."

Alan sat up in the bed. "What's wrong?"

She ran the device over to him. The needle pointed to magnetic north, then jerked to the west before returning. It repeated the move at regular intervals, as if receiving a pulse.

He shrugged. "It's broken."

Carol gave his arm a slap. "It isn't. Remember what happened to our dive computers?"

"You think whatever affected our equipment — ?"

"Is here too?" She threw on a robe and snatched the compass from his hand. "Why not? The statue in Hays' office, the drawing on the *Maggie May*...this place *is* connected to our city."

Carol threw the French doors open and stepped onto the balcony. The compass needle was still being jerked toward the west; her eyes rose, searching for what it wanted her to see. There were many shops, some homes beyond those, and a church. The church sat high on a hill. Isolated. A signal from that location would be less likely to be blocked or absorbed. But a magnetic force strong enough to tug on a compass needle from that distance...

She shot a glance through the doorway toward Alan. He was still on the bed. "Get up. We're going to church."

THIRTY SIX

Larry and Brahm made their way from Colonial Bay's boat docks to the church. Half-way up the concrete ramp, Larry stopped. "Wait here."

The physician shook his head. "I want answers."

"It looks like there's only one way in or out of this place." Larry pointed to the heavy oak doors. "What if those creatures find out where she is and come for her again?"

"You think they'd be bold enough to walk up here in broad daylight?"

"They were bold enough to attack a hospital, weren't they?"

Brahm produced an iPhone.

"Who are you calling?" Larry asked.

"I'll use it to warn you." The physician unclipped a small black box from his belt. He tossed the object to Larry, who caught it before it hit the pavement. "I'll page that beeper. It'll vibrate, and you'll know someone's coming."

Pretty damn good thinkin' there, Doc.

Larry clipped the beeper to the waistband of his shorts. "If I'm not out in half an hour, make your way back to the boat and get the hell out of here."

"Don't worry."

Larry ran for the doors; stained glass windows painted the interior in rainbows. He felt his way along pews that lined the center aisle, moving toward the altar at the front of the church. This didn't feel like any house of God he'd ever been to. It had a creepy, hollow quality.

The door was right where Barbara said it would be. He opened it, heard the creak of unoiled hinges, and saw stone steps descend toward the faint glow of firelight below. Larry ran a hand over his mouth, unsure whether he should call out for Peggy or delay until he saw what awaited him. Deciding to wait, he closed the door and moved cautiously down the steps.

When Larry reached the rocky landing, his breath deserted him.

Alien writing covered the walls of the cavern, and a colossal statue filled its center. Larry scanned the chamber, anxiety crawling through him. He didn't see Barbara. Most important, he didn't see Peggy.

"Is anyone down here?" he asked the temple, his voice a booming echo. "Peggy?"

"Over here, Larry."

His heart beat wildly with relief as he ran across the tabernacle to meet her. She stood at the edge of a tidal pool, completely naked, her arms crossing her chest as if she were a virgin sacrifice, an offering to the pagan god this temple was built to honor. He took off his shirt and held it out to her.

"You must be freezing."

She made no attempt to reach for the clothing, did not even acknowledge his gesture. Instead, her eyes were transfixed on her feet. "I'm fine."

"Where's Barbara?" Larry asked, holding the shirt closer to her, trying to get her to see it.

"She had to leave."

"She left you *alone* down here."

Peggy shrugged, still not looking at him or his shirt. She swayed back and forth as if rocking herself to sleep. "This is the temple of their god. I have 'sanctuary.'"

"Here, put this on." He moved the T-shirt closer still.

She grabbed it blindly from his hand and held it at her side.

A tight expression of concern formed on Larry's face. "What's wrong?"

Her eyes remained downcast. "You need to go."

Larry shook his head. "I'm not leaving you again."

"It's not safe for you here, all right?" Peggy finally looked up, her eyes red and irritated by recent tears. Then, with great deliberation, she said, "I don't want you here."

"DeParle told you to say that."

"She just got me thinking about us...about our future. And the more I sit here and think about it, the more I know she's right. You deserve somebody better, somebody you can touch without making that curdle face you had last night when you saw my...my hand." She chuckled through fresh tears. "Someone who can give you children without flippers!"

"Stop it."

"I can't stop it!" She swiped a hand across her face, trying to halt the raging streams that flowed down her cheeks. It was a futile gesture. "There's nothing I want more than to leave with you, than to *be* with you, but I'm different now."

"I don't care about that."

"How can you *not* care about it? Have you given it any rational thought?"

Larry checked the silent beeper on his belt, shot a nervous glance toward the empty stairs; he would feel better when they were far from Colonial Bay. "We can talk about this later."

"*No*," she huffed. "What...later? We need to talk about this now. We've got plenty of time. 'Sanctuary,' remember?"

"This is insane. Brahm's outside. He's talked to some specialists. We can get you some help."

"You can't help me. Nothing can change me back to what I was. I'm not the girl you fell in love with anymore."

Larry looked straight into her eyes, his stare unwavering. "I don't accept that."

Peggy shook her head, her voice brimming with frustration. "You can't save everyone."

"You really believe I could just decide I don't want you anymore?" he asked, feeling like an idiot as he fought back tears of his own. "When I had my...when I broke that mirror, you didn't walk away from me."

"You were going to get better. At least, I hoped you would. I never will, Larry." She swallowed hard and turned away. "I wish I was dead."

"Don't say that! You're not like her!"

"Like Natalie?" Her despair flared into anger and she threw his shirt aside. "Do you know how *sick* I am of that bitch? — of what she's done to our lives? What about me, Larry? Did you think about me when you went running off to be *her* hero? — when you sliced your wrist open on that glass?"

"No," he confessed. His stomach sank; tears broke free and burned their way down his face. She was right, of course. Natalie could've killed herself at any time and left him in blissful ignorance. Instead, she called out to him and he ran to her, unthinking, as if he were Pavlov's dog. She'd sucked him into her downward spiral, and he'd dragged Peggy along for the ride. "I wasn't thinking about anything, least of all you. Now you're all I do think about."

Peggy looked away. "Too late."

He rushed her, grabbed her by the arms, felt them tremble within his grasp. "It's not too late, damn it! I'm going to take you out of here and —"

"Stop playing hero," she cried and her eyes snapped back to him. "I'm not your damsel in distress! I'm the fucking dragon! God, how can you even stand to look at me?"

"You're my life," he answered without hesitation. "Don't you know that? I'm always going to love you, to *want* you. What do I have to do to prove it?"

Peggy looked back to the cavern floor, as if trying to think of a proper test. When she found one, her eyes locked with his. "You want this freak show?" She wiped at her cheeks again, then pulled him to her in a close embrace. "Make love to me."

"*Now?*" he asked, stunned. "Brahm's waiting for —"

"Let him wait. What are you afraid of?"

Larry looked back at the stairs. "Those things could —"

Peggy pressed her fingers against his lips to hush him.

"Sanctuary," she whispered, tracing his mouth. "You say I don't disgust you, that you still love me...*Love* me."

And then she kissed him. Larry could not believe her enthusiasm. He returned her passion, his fears evaporating as he became lost in the moment. She was alive, they were together, and he wanted her as badly as she wanted him. If she needed proof of his devotion, he would gladly provide it.

Larry stirred to arousal. He grasped Peggy's head and pried her

from his lips, gazing deeply into her eyes. The pupils had widened until they were now black holes rimmed in yellow. They looked up at him with pure hunger, wanting his flesh. He found himself wondering if she sought to caress it or consume it, but quickly vanquished the idea.

"Show me," he told her, undaunted. "I want to see you."

In a single, violent motion, Peggy pulled off his shorts and underwear, nearly causing him to lose his balance. She knelt, clasped him in her hands, guided him between her lips and into her expectant mouth. This was not an act she'd been skilled at in the past. He would feel her teeth raking his sensorial flesh, filling him with far more pain than pleasure. Now, however, he felt nothing but her tongue tracing tingling shapes and figures on his receptive skin. She slid him in and out, her mouth and fingers working in perfect harmony. The sensation was incredible. He shut his eyes and braced himself against the etched stone of the temple wall. It was so good, in fact, that it took him a moment to realize her teeth were *gone*. They'd receded into her gums and been replaced by a soft pallet.

Larry uttered a low moan. He reached down to run his fingers through her long hair and felt the mane slide through his grasp. His eyes opened to see her reddish-brown crown shrinking into her scalp, pulled inward as if by some mechanism hidden within her bobbing skull. She took him deeper than ever before, drawing him into her soft, pulsating tissues. The sides of her neck opened like the flaps of a plane, showing off her surging gills. He felt as though he might come at any moment, but Peggy slowed her nod until his need lost its urgency, then stopped altogether.

He slid from her lips as she rose to kiss him, pressing her exposed vulva against his leg, slicking his thigh with her craving for him. "Lay down," she commanded, her voice raspy and alien to his ears.

Larry did as she instructed, feeling the chill of the stone against his back. She crawled onto him, her nipples poking at his chest, her skin throbbing as if it were the wall of an artery. She kissed his mouth, her lips fuller and wider now than they'd ever been, and then he felt her heat. As her body impaled itself upon him again and again, Larry felt the muscles within her work against his length, although whether it was a conscious effort on her part or merely an element of her transformation, he didn't know.

The artist watched in awe as Peggy shifted into her other self. She was one of his rough sketches, drawn, erased, and redrawn, constantly evolving into a finished masterpiece ready for paint. Her skin became transparent, glowing with an inner light that allowed him to view the pumping and fluttering of her anatomy. At one point, he thought that he could even see the shadow of his own erection rise and fall within her. Her arms and legs lengthened, the fingers and toes altering to become the webbed appendages he'd seen before. She bent her head, letting him witness a spiny dorsal fin unfurl from her naked scalp, protruding from the back of her skull like a flag, then tracing its way down her spine. As he lay there, bathing in the glow from Peggy's body, Larry felt something move against his scrotum and lowered his gaze, amazed to see a long, flat tail frolicking behind her.

He watched these radical modifications overtake her form, and what struck him most were the things that remained so familiar. Her warmth, the way she touched him, the sound of her breathing, the noises she made in ecstasy...if he closed his eyes...he kept them open, however, not wanting to miss an instant of her transformation.

Larry felt a spasm within her, unsure if it were the fine tuning of her form or a powerful orgasm, then he watched as she threw her head back to scream at the roof of the cavern, her ear-splitting cry echoing through the chamber. The sound of her climax, and the feel of her inner convulsions, brought Larry to conclusion as well. He slammed his eyes shut and grunted heavily, his body tensing, then relaxing as he sucked in the damp air of the cave.

When it was over, Larry began to laugh, the sound maturing to a hearty, boisterous cackle. He opened his eyes to look at the luminescent being that still straddled him. Her breasts, now transparent and laced with veins of rhythmic light, were her only familiar feature, and yet she was beautiful. He'd feared she would look like the things that had chased them the night before, but she was a completely different animal. Hers was the appearance of an angel, not a monster.

She looked down at him, puzzled. "Are you okay?"

Larry nodded, gasping. "Words cannot describe how I feel right now."

"Am I..." She lowered her head, "...hideous?"

"Oh, God, no." He rose up to kiss her new mouth and she wrapped her arms around him tightly, as if to keep him from running away. When their lips separated, he added, "You're incredible."

She closed her translucent lids, turning her black eyes gray. "If you want to leave me, I'll —"

"Peggy." He reached up to clasp her chin, pointing it toward him. "I've passed your test. I love you...I *need* you. If this is how I can have you, then so be it. You're beautiful."

She smiled, her mouth widening to an unimaginable expanse, then moved in to kiss him once more. He cocked his head, put a hand up to hush her.

"Quiet for a second."

Larry saw his shorts and underwear lying wrinkled on the ground and reached for them, digging through the fabric for Brahm's beeper. His hands felt around the waistband until they came to the small black box he'd clipped there.

It vibrated wildly.

A creaking sound in the distance. Someone just opened the door.

"What is it?" Peggy asked, her voice a gargled whisper.

Larry frowned. "Company."

THIRTY SEVEN

Dr. Kyle Brahm stood in the bushes; his gaze shifted from his watch, to the church doors, then back again. How long had it been? Twenty minutes? Twenty-five? What was taking Neuhaus so damn long?

At thirty minutes I should go back to the boat, he reasoned. *And then what? I still won't have any answers. Those things wouldn't show themselves in the light of day. Even when they attacked the hospital, they cut the power to the lights.*

Brahm was about to stand up and go to the church when he saw figures climb the footpath toward him, a white man and an Asian woman. What was that in her hand? Whatever it was, it appeared to lead her his way. Brahm glanced at his iPhone, wondered if they had somehow tapped into the GPS and were now able to pinpoint his exact location.

Instead, the couple passed him by and walked over to the church entrance, cautiously surveying the surrounding area as if looking for watchful eyes. Brahm lowered himself even further into the shrubbery to avoid detection, and, after a moment, the pair entered the building.

Oh, shit! Brahm dialed his pager.

•••

The sun filtered through stained glass prisms, bathing the church in a patchwork of colored streaks and shadow. Carol felt along the wall for a light switch and was suddenly blinded. Alan, ever the Boy Scout, had thought to bring a flashlight. He swung the beam away from her eyes, traced the doorframe with it, but found no button, knob, or toggle of any kind.

This is too weird, Carol thought.

Alan, as if reading her mind, had an answer. "This church probably dates back to before electricity."

"Yeah," she whispered. "But wouldn't they have it *installed?*"

He shook his head, searching the room with his light. "It might ruin the historical feel of the place. They're probably going for that 'colonial settlement' look."

Carol stepped into the structure; hollow was the only word she could find to describe it, but even that did not accurately convey the emptiness. She held the compass out into the gloom. "Shine that light down here, will you."

The beam revealed a mad tug-of-war still going on between true north and another magnetic influence: the pulpit.

Carol hurried down the aisle to the front of the church. The pull of true north became less and less insistent, yielding victory to the impostor hidden somewhere in this building. The archeologist searched the altar, lifting the cloth covering to admire the stone beneath.

"What are you looking for?" Alan asked.

"I haven't got a clue," she admitted. "Something odd. Something that looks as if it shouldn't be here."

He snickered. "That would be you and I, fearless leader."

Carol stood, irritated, and backed toward the wall to get a better view of the entire scene. Something was here. She could almost feel it in the air like static electricity, but what *it* was eluded her. She checked the compass once more for guidance. The needle faced the wall behind her, twitching as if it longed to spring forward and bury itself in the wood.

Carol whirled around. A door, hidden in the shadows; she pushed it open, heard hinges squeak in protest, and found a downward staircase made of stone. The object of their quest awaited them down there. She grinned at Alan. "The game is afoot, Watson."

He followed her down.

Carol turned the corner, and what she saw filled her with chills. "Oh, my God..."

It was an exact replica of the sunken Atlantean temple, except the statue (the glyphs dubbed it Varuna, not Neptune as she'd originally guessed) was completely intact. Even the carvings on the walls, so far as she could tell, were identical. They told the Atlantean version of Sodom and Gomorrah; a tale of gods who traveled in great boats across the heavens, and of the two cities that had angered them, cities destroyed by holy fire that rained down from the sky.

Carol glanced down at the compass needle, saw it aimed at the unbroken idol, and turned to Alan. He was still gazing around in awe, his eyes the size of saucers. She cleared her throat.

Alan blinked and his gaze met her own. "What's it doing here?"

"I don't know what's going on, but let's see where this thing —" she held up the compass, "— leads us, and maybe we'll find out."

They stepped into the tabernacle, the needle guiding their steps. Their footfalls joined the sound of dripping water, filling the vast cavity of the chamber with echoes, adding to the mysterious feel of the place. It truly felt as if they'd stumbled onto a lost world.

•••

From her hiding place behind a rocky outcropping, Peggy watched the two strangers approach the statue. She tried to stand, but Larry grabbed her and dragged her back down to her knees.

"What are you doing?" he whispered.

Her tail slapped at his back as she fought against his grip. "Can't let them near the altar."

"Why the hell not?"

She stopped fighting and shook her head; her new eyes were wide, coldly blank. "I...I don't know."

"Then I suggest we let them do their thing and leave."

Peggy gave a slow nod.

•••

When Alan stepped up to the stone altar, he felt the warmth of countless candles; their melted wax formed multicolored stalactites as it poured over the edge and dripped onto the temple floor below. Their light illuminated a very thick, very ancient book.

Carol opened the volume with great care and smiled at its contents.

"What is it?" Alan asked.

"I'll have to translate it. The language is the same as the glyphs. It's Atlantean."

She felt along the base of the statue, looking for possible openings, sealed compartments, but found none. "I don't understand what's creating the magnetic pull."

Alan looked into the grinning face of the stone god above. "It looks like ordinary stone." He returned his attention to the altar and frowned. "Someone's been here recently. Half of these candles are new."

"And you're worried they might come back, none too happy to find us in their temple?"

"The thought had occurred to me."

Carol picked up the book. "Okay, let's go."

Alan's eyes widened. "You're taking that?"

"We need some answers, don't we?"

"You don't think they'll *miss* it?"

"I won't tell them we took it if you won't."

A stern, gravelly echo, "Put down that book!"

Both archeologists whirled around; they scanned the chamber for the owner of the voice. Alan even shot a glance upward, fearing he might see the toothy face of the idol glaring down at him with burning eyes. The stone figure was still only that, and the chamber appeared to be theirs alone.

Not taking any chances, he gave Carol a gentle shove toward the staircase. "Go!"

She ran for the steps, Alan not far behind her. He noticed that she still held the book tightly against her chest.

Mistake, he thought, half expecting some trap to snare them for their desecration.

As they mounted the stairs, Alan saw something come into the periphery of his vision: a glowing shape that rose from the rocks like a ghost.

•••

Peggy didn't know why she wanted to stand up and cry out. But, when that woman lifted the aged book from the altar, it was as if someone else took control of her nerves, a puppet master manipulating a doll. She felt Larry's insistent hand on her arm, pulling her downward, but she didn't, she *couldn't* obey it.

"Put down that book!" she demanded, still fighting to break free of his grip.

"Peggy," Larry called, trying to keep it to a whisper. "What the hell are you doing?"

She smacked him hard across the back with her tail.

He fell forward and finally released her arm.

Peggy rose up; she saw the man, watched him run up the stairs, and, with a grace she had not previously possessed, she leapt over the rocks onto the stone floor. She was going to chase them, going to get that book.

Larry, still naked, was on her before she'd taken more than a few steps; he pushed her onto the rough floor of the temple. She clawed at him, her long nails dragging ribbons of skin from his shoulder. He cried out, but did not let go.

After a few moments, Peggy's compulsion became faint enough to suppress and her squirming stopped. She gently wrapped her tail around Larry, hugged him, told him she was fine again. The sensation of feeling she now received from her additional appendage was strangely wondrous. While her new form gave her heightened senses, it also seemed to spark flashes of insanity.

"Are you okay?" Larry's words were a Morse code of hot wind on her fluke.

"I'm fine," she told him, tasting the warm saline of her tears. The salty flavor made her long for another swim. "What was that all about?"

"You tell me." He let go, allowed her to roll onto her side.

"I don't know. I just had this feeling that I had to stop them. It was... pretty scary." She touched his shoulder and he drew in air through clenched teeth. When she took her fingers away, they were red. *"You're bleeding."*

Larry gave the furrows she'd tilled in his flesh an uncomprehending glance. "Looks like you...ah...you got me good."

"I don't know what happened...I..." There was terror in her guttural voice. "Larry, I could've killed you."

"No," he said with conviction. "You could never do that."

"I don't know *what* I might do now." The tears flowed more freely and her thickened lips quivered. "Oh God, what's happening to me?"

He reached out and took her in his arms, held her tightly to him.

"It'll be okay," he assured her, stroking her back, his fingers skidding across the ribs of her fin. "I'm gonna go back to the Inn and find you some clothes. Then I'll be right back here. We can get in the car and hop the next ferry over to the mainland. We'll be back in the apartment tonight."

Her voice was loud in his ear, "I can't go back there."

"Then we'll move," he told her, not understanding what she meant. "We'll get a cabin on a lake...or a beach house. I can work on my paintings and you can write...Look, I know this won't be easy for us. I do. But we can get through this."

When they made love, Peggy thought it would be for the last time. If Larry saw what she had become, she reasoned, he would push her off of him, run screaming from the temple, and she would never see him again. But that didn't happen. Instead, he'd looked up at her, concentrated on her new face. It was the look you gave someone who'd gained too much weight since you'd seen them last, the look that searched for the old, thin person within. Peggy couldn't tell what Larry saw, but he held her; he told her he still loved her. She didn't know if that was wonderful or just truly sick.

Her eyes moved between bloody claws and the marks in Larry's shoulder. When she spoke, her voice betrayed both exhaustion and dread, "DeParle was right. You should get out of Colonial Bay. Forget about me and just —"

Larry stopped her words with a kiss. In his arms, the horror plotline her mind was weaving came suddenly unraveled, yielding to the love story she desperately wanted. No matter what had happened to her, no matter what lurked in the unseen dimness ahead of them, Peggy knew her future was with Larry. Fresh tears came to her eyes, but they did not spring from a well of fright or self-pity; they were tears of joy.

"I'm not going anywhere without you," he whispered as they parted, then pointed at his nose. "See this face? This is my determined face."

She snickered, wiped her eyes. "I was wondering where that went."

He smiled. "There's no negotiation here, no backing down."

"Do you know how much I love you, Rembrandt?" She reached out to brush his face with her hand, the bunched webbing between her fingers tickling him.

"I love you, too." He took her talon from his cheek and kissed it. "We *are* going to get through this."

She breathed in deeply, believed he was right, and nodded.

"I *will* bring you some clothes and we *will* leave here together." His eyes roamed her new body. "You...uh...do know how to change back, don't you?"

Peggy nodded.

Satisfied, Larry ran to his clothes, his balls flapping madly. He dressed, then threw a glance around the temple. "Will you be all right here by yourself?"

"I'll be fine." She saw red stripes appear through the fabric of his shirt and her stomach fell. She closed her eyes. How could she have done that to him? "Just...hurry back, okay?"

"You bet." He pressed his lips to hers one more time, and she wondered if he was growing to like the new feel.

•••

When he climbed the stairs, Larry slammed into a shadow, a figure that ran down the chapel aisle from the opposite direction.

"Neuhaus?" Brahm; he still clutched his iPhone in one hand, its lit screen showing him the way. "You're alive. Those people ran out of here scared shitless, and I thought —"

He caught sight of Larry's bloodied shoulder in the faint light.

"Christ, what did they do to you?"

"They stole a book and Peggy went all 'kill...destroy.'"

"*She* did this to you?" The physician grabbed hold of Larry's shirt; he pushed it up, revealed the claw marks, and was unable to hide his shock. "These need stitches."

"Are they fatal?"

Brahm blinked. "Well...no, but —"

Larry pulled his top back down and winced. "Then they can wait. I need to go back to my hotel and get Peggy a change of clothes. Who were those two?"

The physician shrugged. "They ran off down the hill and I ran in here. We can still catch up to them. They were on foot. The book's that valuable?"

Larry didn't know what to believe anymore. Perhaps the book *was* important. It might tell him why this had happened to his love, and, of far more importance, why she'd reacted so strangely to its theft. "You go after them. Find out where they're going. I'll be at the Sea Mist Inn, room 201. Meet me there."

"Go to my boat first."

"Why?"

"There's a flare gun in the cabinet above the sink. We might need it, in case they're not willing to just give this book back."

"Have you done this before, Doc?"

Brahm grinned and shook his head. "No, but I could get to enjoy this cloak-and-dagger stuff pretty quickly."

He ran out the church doors and left Larry in the dark.

THIRTY EIGHT

Earl L. Preston, Jr. walked with his cap under his arm and his mind in overdrive.

Doctors Miyagi and Everson had revealed the involvement of Roger Hays. It was easy to tie the businessman to the *FantaSea* mystery. He had dealings with the missing Jerry Hoff. That was a matter of public record. And it wasn't a stretch to assume the captain of the *Maggie May*, Mr. Kip Lunden, now also missing, had been running drugs or weapons for Hays' organization. Lunden had been out there at night, without a license, and with the fishing trade going down the shitter, Earl had found more than a few captains hauling something other than tuna to make ends meet.

Earl drew a straight line on a map of the New Hampshire coastline, connecting the spots where the derelicts were found; Colonial Bay was almost exactly half way between them. And who was frequently photographed spending his summers in Colonial Bay?

Roger Hays.

Despite his discovery, Earl knew he had no business going to this island town. His job began and ended at sea. Any evidence he had, he should turn over to the mainland authorities and move on. The problem was, he had no real evidence. He needed to find something to tie it all together before another ghost ship crossed his path, and there was nothing more he could learn from his patrols with Peck.

Earl paused for a moment outside Lieutenant Soderbergh's office door, thinking up his story. In all his years as a seaman, he'd never lied to a superior officer, and the thought that he might need to start created a sick turning in his gut.

You're putting your commission on the line...for a hunch?

He took a deep breath and knocked on the door.

"Enter."

POSEIDON'S CHILDREN

Earl stepped into the office, stood at attention, and saluted the man who sat behind the desk.

Soderbergh looked up from his paperwork, peered at him over the rim of his eyeglasses. "At ease. What's on your mind, Preston?"

Earl relaxed. "Sir, I need to request a leave of absence."

"You know the drill. Fill out the proper forms with the dates you want, set them in my mailbox, and, if I can, I'll approve them."

"The dates would start today, sir."

The lieutenant flashed an annoyed expression, then put down his pen. "What's goin' on, Earl?"

"It's my brother, sir...I just got word he got himself hurt in a car accident. Looks bad, sir."

The annoyed look on Soderbergh's balding face melted from the heat of newfound sympathy. "Jesus, Preston, why didn't you come out and say that to begin with."

Earl shrugged. *Because I only just thought of it, sir.*

"How bad is he?"

"He's critical, sir. Momma, she's real upset." The guardsman's stomach was upset, the guilt of every false word gnawed through its lining like a parasite. "I really need to be there for her."

Soderberg stood; his naked scalp glowed in spilled light from the window. "Then go, son."

Earl pointed to the paperwork on the man's desk. "What about — ?"

"I'll take care of it. You go be with your mother. Just give me a call to let me know how things are going and when to expect you back for active duty."

"Thank you, sir. You don't know what this means to me."

The lieutenant held out his hand and the guardsman shook it. "Just go take care of your family, officer."

"Yes, sir." Earl saluted before leaving the room. As he moved off down the hallway, he felt his father with him; the spirit was not pleased.

I don't know why this is the right thing to do, Dad, but it is. You'll see.

Half an hour later, Earl was on the road.

THIRTY NINE

Cornelius Shiva sat in a diner on Mulberry Street, waiting. He lit another match, watched it wilt as the flame made its way to his fingertips, then tossed the blackened wood into the table's ashtray.

Mr. Ludwig called early this morning, awakened Neil from the usual nightmare.

He'd been digging up Eric Shiva's grave to make certain his father, his *rapist*, was dead. Every night, he'd open the coffin, and every night, his father's moldering skull would rush toward him, its eye sockets still blazing with the inferno that engulfed it years ago. And Neil would stand there, unable to talk, unable to move as those charred hands grabbed him and pulled him down into the cold darkness of the grave. As the coffin lid slammed shut behind him, he woke up screaming.

Neil lit another match and watched it burn.

O'Shea was the first to arrive. He was built like a bouncer and dressed in his usual attire: black button-up shirt, matching slacks, and a gold cross suspended by a chain around his thick neck, nearly lost in the underbrush of his chest hair. He looked more like a disco dancer than a gangster. O'Shea perused the restaurant, saw Neil sitting alone in the corner booth by the window, and nodded in his direction.

Shiva threw a new matchstick onto the blackened pile in the ashtray. "Mornin', O'Shea."

The wiseguy sat down across from Neil, grabbed a menu from behind the salt and pepper shakers. He gave it a quick once-over, his slight Irish accent a bit more noticeable this morning as he spoke, "You think I got time to order some sausage and eggs?"

Neil shrugged and took another sip from his coffee. "So what do *you* know about the job?"

"All I know is we gotta go clear up to fuckin' New Hampshire."

"New Hampshire?" Neil asked. "What's in New Hampshire?"

O'Shea put down the menu, evidently ready to order. "That's what I says to Ludwig. He tells me not to ask so many fuckin' questions."

A tap at the window beside them; Horror Show, beckoning them to come out. He stood with Carlo Tosti, somewhat of an elder statesman in the organization.

"Well," O'Shea sighed, "guess I don't get my eggs."

Neil nodded; he shoved the matchbook into his pocket, then followed O'Shea toward the door.

You could never have enough matches.

Horror Show's car, a light-blue Cadillac, sat parked in the alley, below the DELIVERIES IN REAR sign. He unlocked the trunk and threw it open, revealing its cargo. Neil Shiva's eyes grew wide as a child's on Christmas morning. Looking into the compartment was like looking into Heaven; guns of every size and caliber, incendiary fuses, and, best of all, several boxes labeled DANGER: EXPLOSIVES.

"What's all this?" O'Shea asked, unsettled. Horror Show had a knack for unsettling people.

"Our heat for this job," the hitman replied in his trademarked sandpaper whisper.

O'Shea was still shocked by the arsenal. "Who we goin' after? Osama bin Laden?"

"Hays' son was killed," Horror Show announced. "We're goin' after the pricks who did it."

"Who — ?"

Horror Show held up his hand. "Every question you got, you can ask Roger Hays when we get there."

This brought O'Shea's eyebrow to attention. He looked over to Carlo who offered a slow nod of confirmation.

Neil was sweating. Looking at the boxes, he saw a thousand fiery possibilities and wondered which would be at his command. He smiled. Whatever the explosives were, he would get a chance to study them, to *use* them soon enough. Why else would Hays have called upon him?

"We need to get goin'." Horror Show told them, then

slammed the trunk shut.

As they walked toward the car doors, O'Shea called, "Shotgun."

Carlo Tosti, who'd been strangely silent, laughed.

FORTY

"Why are you laughing?" Alan Everson asked.

He rested on their bed at the Sea Mist Inn, still telling himself that he hadn't just seen an evil spirit in the temple. Carol Miyagi sat on the floor beneath him, the ancient book in her lap. As she decoded its cryptic passages, she began to giggle, a sound that quickly grew to full-fledged laughter.

"This is wonderful!" Carol lifted her eyes from the yellowed parchment, tucked her raven hair behind her ears. "It's a history of...of *everything.*"

Before she could elaborate, a knock at the door gave both archeologists a start. In his mind, Alan saw the apparition from the temple standing in the hallway, its arms outstretched. He swallowed and looked at Carol. "Maid service?"

"I think the old man at the desk is the only staff this place has. Did you call Nielsen to tell him where we were?"

Alan nodded.

"Maybe the innkeeper has a message from him?"

"Let's see." Alan walked to the door, unprepared for the sight that greeted him when he opened it. Petty Officer Earl L. Preston, Jr. was in the hall. "What are you doing here?"

"Nice welcome. Can I come in?"

Alan stepped aside, allowed the guardsman entry. When Carol saw who it was, her mouth fell open.

"Hello again, Dr. Miyagi."

"How'd you find us?"

"There's only three hotels in Colonial Bay. This was the last one I checked." Preston's eyes fell upon the thick volume in Carol's lap. "A little light reading?"

"You still haven't said why you're here," Alan reminded him.

Earl looked at the floor, then to each of them in turn. "I'm in this town to solve a mystery, same as you. Colonial Bay's within spitting distance of two abductions, possible murders at sea. Your boss, Roger Hays, spends most summers on this island, and he had business dealings with at least one of the people that's gone missing."

"He's not our boss," Alan mumbled.

Earl went on as if he hadn't heard. "I'm here in this room because you're both respected and intelligent people. I was hoping we might forget about the...the nastiness back on the boat and look for answers together. Whoever did this knows something about what you found in Atlantis, like Hays."

Carol shook her head. "I don't think he has anything to do with this."

"You don't know that," Alan huffed. "I've said for over a year the guy's a crook."

Preston nodded. "He's been investigated by the IRS —"

"Just being wealthy is a crime to them," she remarked.

"— The FBI, *and* the State Department."

Carol frowned. "And I suppose you want to be known as the man who brought him down — to further your career?"

Earl shrugged. "If he's behind it, I want him put away. I'm not trying to make a name for myself here, and I happen to know that you didn't go after Atlantis because you wanted to make the cover of *Time* or be the next Lara Croft. You enjoy putting all the pieces together to see what the truth is. You're a detective, just like me."

She smiled hesitantly, unsure as to whether the man was being sincere or simply wanted to nudge her into helping him. "I just might have some answers for you. Pull up a section of floor. I was about to fill Alan in on what I've found."

The officer knelt down with a hint of trepidation. "Whatcha got?"

Her smile widened. "It's a kind of history book. We found it in a temple built under this town's church."

"A *what?*"

"An exact replica of one we discovered in Atlantis."

"That's pretty convenient, don't you think?"

She offered an uncomprehending glance. "I'm sorry?"

Earl explained, "You find a temple on an expedition funded by Hays, then another one here, on an island where he spends quite a bit of time. You still don't think he's somehow connected?"

Carol rolled her eyes. "This temple is beneath the town's only church. You think he moved it, carved a cavern out of solid rock, copied each and every pictograph, then put it back in a little over a week?"

"Okay." Earl frowned and pointed at the book. "So what's it all about?"

"It talks about gods that came in boats that sailed the sky." The enthusiastic grin returned to her lips. "In archeological circles, we call them ancient astronauts."

Earl looked mildly shocked. "You're serious."

She nodded excitedly.

Earl threw his head back and laughed. "Okay, see I'm with you on this whole Atlantis thing because it's there, you've found it...but we're talkin' aliens now? Brothers from Mars...'We are not alone'...anal probes? Tell me you don't believe that shit?"

"There are people on islands in southeast Asia who laugh at the idea of snow," she told him, then continued her translation, "The book says these beings, these 'creators,' took primitive animals from our land and sea, and from them made two races. One was to work the soil of the mountains and plains, the other would till the ocean floor. The riches they found there were to be given back to the gods as tribute."

Now Alan smiled as well. "Mining operations?"

"Hold the phone." Earl held up his hands. "Your boss owns a mine?"

Carol took a deep breath before speaking, knowing how her words would sound. "When you spend your whole life looking for lost civilizations, Atlantis or the Mu continent, you read everything you can on the subject along the way. One hypothesis has been that the city was a colony for visitors from another world." Earl snickered, but she went on, "And one of the theories as to why they came to Earth was to mine it."

Earl rubbed his eyes. "I take back what I said about you people being intelligent."

"Officer Preston..." Carol's face tightened. "No one invited you here. You came to us because you wanted our help."

"I need facts to believe this Sci-Fi Channel crap," he told her.

"Believe it or not, let's pretend for a moment that it's possible. The ocean floor has enough mineral wealth to rival a hundred California gold rushes. That's an undeniable fact. Human beings have only now created submersibles that can reach any kind of great depth without folding under the pressure, but marine life has thrived, even at the bottom of the deepest trenches, since the dawn of time. If you could create a worker, a *miner* who could survive underwater, under such great pressure, you'd have more wealth than Midas."

"I'm sorry," Earl said. "I just can't believe you'd think this shit has more to do with what's going on than Hays does. That could be some kid's storybook, an old school *Harry Potter* or something. Why would you believe any of it?"

"You haven't let me finish."

Preston regarded her with patience. "I'm listening."

"In time, these 'gods' lost interest in this world and left their creations behind."

"Does the book say why?" Alan glanced over her shoulder at the pictographs; the scientific side of him was interested in the book and what she'd deciphered from it, but the part of him that believed Roger Hays was a dangerous man was leaning heavily toward Earl's view.

"Not exactly, at least not that I can translate. This is written in quite a few different hands, and some of the passages have been covered over, painted out and then re-written...like they were in a big hurry. I'd say there were three possibilities: the visitors had what they needed, there was some kind of natural disaster, or an uprising took place, like the slave uprisings of the Roman Empire."

The guardsman flashed a quick grin. "I vote for the slave uprising."

Carol went on. "To make a long story short —"

"Please," Earl said, still impatient.

"After centuries of being hunted, the beings created to work the sea came to *this* island. They built a town, took human form."

Preston laughed again. "This shit just gets better and better. What, they're werefish?"

Alan spoke up in her defense. "Every society has a myth about shape-shifters, men becoming beasts and vice versa. In Asia, there are weretigers, in Europe, the werewolf, and so on. There are cultures on Earth that don't know what a kiss is, and yet we see these legends present in their mythos."

Carol nodded. "If this book is right, it's because we all spring from a common ancestry, and they're not just myths. The aliens have given these 'clans' the power to change shape the way a chameleon changes color."

"You're seriously telling me this town was founded by *mutant fish?*" Earl asked, clearly hoping they would hear just how crazy it sounded. "Even if this shit was for real, why would they start attackin' people now? They've been here for... what? ...hundreds of years, they set up a fuckin' tourist trade. What made 'em snap now?"

"The book refers to the settlers of Colonial Bay as the children of Poseidon."

"That's the Greek god of the sea, right? — the one with a trident?" Earl smiled. "Hot damn! That fits, doesn't it? Whoever's doing this read that book and drew that trident symbol at the crime scenes to try and —"

"Poseidon wasn't just the name of the Greek god," Carol informed him. "It was also the ancient name of Atlantis; children of *Atlantis*, *refugees* from Atlantis. When we discovered the city, it was worldwide news. Maybe it set these people off."

They looked at one another, the brief silence battered by a knock at the door. Alan was the only one standing; he moved to answer it, wondering who this new visitor might be. The knocking grew louder, more insistent.

"Hold on," Alan told them as he turned the knob.

The door opened and the wide barrel of a gun was pressed against his face.

•••

"Back up," Larry commanded. "Nice and slow."

The man backed slowly into the room, the flare gun from Brahm's yacht still glued to his cheek. The Asian woman sat on the floor with a black man, the yellowed book in her hands. When she saw what was happening, she leapt to her feet.

"*Alan!*"

With the speed of a gunslinger, the black man produced a pistol and took aim at Larry. "Let 'im go, motherfucker."

"Give me the book, and he's all yours."

"What are you doing, Preston?" the woman asked. "Put that away."

"It's a flare gun," Preston said.

"What?"

"The gun in your boyfriend's face. It's a flare gun."

Larry pressed the barrel deeper into his hostage's cheek and tried to speak forcefully, "But if I pull the trigger, it'll hurt."

The woman stepped forward, her arms outstretched to present the book to Brahm. "Here, take it."

"What the hell are you doin'?" Preston asked.

"I've learned all I can from it. You want it? Let him go."

Brahm took hold of the book's brittle binding, pulled it to him, but she gave an insistent tug on the opposite end.

"I said let him go."

Larry removed the gun from her boyfriend's face, leaving a ringed indentation in his cheek. She released her grip on the binding and went to him. The click of a weapon being cocked filled Larry's ears and he turned to look at Preston. Larry was dead in the man's sights.

Brahm chimed in, "Who are you people?"

"You come in here all *Reservoir Dogs*," Preston huffed. "Who the fuck are you?"

Larry's eyes went back to the woman; he pointed at the book. "We were down in the temple when you took that, and followed you here. Don't suppose you'd like to tell us what it is?"

She rubbed the circle in her friend's cheek. "It's a written history. I'm sure you'd find it very interesting. Shame you don't read Atlantean."

Larry snickered. "And you do."

"They discovered Atlantis," Preston informed him, his aim steady. "It's been in all the news."

"I've been on vacation." Larry swallowed; he shot a glance to the door and wondered just how fast he could run.

"Don't," Preston warned. "Who are you and why you trippin'?"

"There are amphibious sharks on this island," Brahm said, straight-faced. "They attacked Black Harbor Medical Center last night."

"They're after my fiancée," Larry added. "She got bit, and now she...she can change form."

The woman smiled, but thankfully didn't laugh. On the contrary, she looked as if she'd been validated by their claims, as if she'd just made some outlandish statements of her own. She moved to sever Preston's line of fire and slipped her hand over the flare pistol. Larry released the weapon to her, watching as Preston lowered his own gun.

"It seems we have a lot to talk about," she said.

•••

Carol brought them quickly up to speed. Earl glanced at his watch; he'd heard it all before. Larry's mouth had gone dry; he walked over to the bathroom sink, filled a plastic cup with water, and drank deeply. Brahm's face held a skeptical look; he thought for a bit, and they allowed him the time.

Finally, the doctor stroked the pouches beneath his tired eyes and said, "You *believe* this?"

"If the human race *had been* engineered," Alan offered, "it would explain why no paleontologist has been able to find a 'missing link' to show the steady progression of evolution. We should've been looking for ancient test tubes."

None of them laughed.

Earl was insistent. "I need proof...*facts*. Shark-men...aliens... Where's your evidence that any of it's real?"

"You want proof?" Larry lifted his shirt. Five cuts started at his left shoulder and trailed off at his right nipple; the blood had dried to crust, filling in the ruts. "When Peggy saw them take that book, she scratched me. I'd say her claws are a good six-inches long."

Earl studied the man's wrist and saw the scars. "You could've done that to yourself."

Brahm pointed to Larry, his voice rising. "His fiancée's DNA has been totally rewritten by engineered genetic information. That's a fact. I have blood samples and test results to prove it. This is some kind of advanced retro-virus using designer enzymes, probably the work of well-funded experimentation."

"Hays has pharmaceutical labs," Earl announced, further validated. "Maybe he's made himself some kind of biological —"

"Would you forget about Hays!" Carol cried, exasperated.

"Unless he's a very good shot, Hays is dead."

They turned to Larry.

The artist went on, his voice tense. "He didn't make them, if that's what you're thinking. These things are what killed his son. He hated them."

"I don't know who could have created these enzymes," Brahm confessed. "Neither do the experts I showed my findings to. But I'm certain it's *not* the work of alien prospectors."

"Actually," Carol began, "the idea of our creators running a mining operation makes a lot of sense, from an archeological perspective."

Earl flashed her a skeptical glare. "How's that?"

"Statues of deities are often given one golden hand, symbolizing that they're authorities on precious metals."

Alan joined in, "And megaliths are found in close proximity to mining sites."

"What's a 'megalith?'" Brahm asked.

Everson sectioned off a square of air with his hands. "Large stone markers covered in hieroglyphics."

"Plus, there are all the anachronistic artifacts." Carol's eyes were sparkling. "Two-thousand-year-old batteries found in Iraq. A sunken Greek merchant ship, dating back to 80 B.C., that had an object onboard with differential gears...but they weren't even invented for another thousand —"

Earl held up his hand. "Okay, I get that whatever that book says, you're buyin' it, but I can't accept this bullshit."

"I watched Peggy become this glowing, transparent...I-dunno-what," Larry told him. "Now that I've seen that, I guess I'd be willing to accept just about anything."

Carol nodded, a hint of her smile returning. "There's no light on the ocean floor. They must have engineered the workers to be bioluminescent. They have the ability to manufacture light within their own bodies."

"I saw her," Alan chimed in, relieved. "When we left the temple, I saw this glowing thing rise up from the rocks. I thought it was...I don't know what I thought it was."

"*It* was my fiancée," Larry snapped. His eyes darted from Alan to Brahm to Earl and then back again. "And *she* wasn't some laboratory test subject. She was attacked, viciously and violently attacked. She barely survived, and now...I watched her change. It was..." His face lightened at the memory. "It was the most incredible thing I've ever seen."

The physician offered him a look of disapproval, but Alan nodded his understanding.

"Look at the folklore," he said. "If you're bitten by a werewolf, you become a werewolf yourself."

Earl's eyes widened. "Whoa...now you're saying these things can...*infect* people, like some new strain of AIDS or Ebola?"

"Well...yes," the physician told him. "It appears they can pass it on through their bodily fluids, by mixing normal blood with their blood or saliva."

Carol stepped in once more. "If beings *could* develop a means to travel from one planet to the next, isn't it reasonable to assume that they would also have any number of advanced genetic manipulation skills like this? They could've been able to encode specific instincts and functions into organisms the way we program a computer. It would be like *growing* your own tools."

"I once had a microbiology professor with similar ideas," Brahm told her. "So much of our DNA seems to serve no function. It's indecipherable junk we call 'introns.' That's one of the reason's the Human Genome Project was started, to solve their purpose."

Carol pressed the physician, "Theoretically, isn't it possible to engineer a creature like the ones you've seen, using existing life forms as a starting block, adding elements of a foreign genetic structure to make them more humanoid, then guiding the growth of the resulting mutation?"

Brahm looked at her, silently impressed.

"Harvard," she said absently. "Theoretically?"

"As I said, they've only just completed the map. Just because you know where point A and point B are, doesn't mean you know the best route to get there. Designing an enzyme, sure, but an entire complex organism? It could take years before we have the skill to do it, if ever."

Carol was becoming increasingly frustrated. "But say there was a race that was older, more evolved, a race that had the map *sooner?*"

"Theoretically?"

"*Yes.*"

"Sure," Brahm conceded. "It's possible."

Earl shook his head. "I can't believe you can just —"

"I can't believe *any of you!*" Larry roared, pointing to the French doors and the sea beyond. "People are dying out there while you sit here and debate this crap! Who the fuck cares where these things come from, or how they got here? What matters is that they're real. Can we at least agree on that before they bust in here and bite us on the ass?"

The group looked wordlessly at him, belief and disbelief still at war within them.

Brahm was the first to speak, "He's right. Isolated boats at sea and lone women in alleys are one thing, but they're getting braver. We need to stop theorizing and get more information before their next attack."

"And we need to be careful." Carol ran her hand across the text in her lap. "If this is true, the townspeople *are* the creatures. But, even if it's just a storybook, they *believe* it's true, and that still makes them dangerous. The temple proves they still worship these things the way their ancestors did."

She turned to Earl. "You're a reasonable man. Surely you can at least consider the possibility that these creatures exist, no matter what their origins might be."

Earl thought of the Indian legends of sea monsters, of the species of whale that had remained undiscovered until the end of the last century. He remembered the bits and pieces of strange creatures that occasionally wash ashore, and the clawed mattress from the *FantaSea*'s cabin flashed across his eyes.

He walked to the phone by the bed.

"Who are you calling?" Alan wanted to know.

Wordlessly, the guardsman dialed and waited for someone to pick up.

"Black Harbor Medical Center," a young, female voice proclaimed. "How may I direct your call?"

"Yeah," Earl said. "My mama's in your hospital. She just had her hip replaced. Anyway, I heard about what happened there and I wanted to make sure she was all right."

"Yes sir. I'm sorry if you haven't been notified yet. As you can imagine, the phones have been ringing off the hook here, and with all the privacy laws, it does take time to confirm or deny a patient's status."

"I don't doubt it," Earl said, then offered up another lie, "One of the stations said it was a wild animal or something."

There was a pause.

"I'm afraid the matter is still being investigated by the police," she said at last. "Would you like me to connect you with your mother's room?"

"Tell ya what, let me speak to one of her doctors."

"I can have them paged," the girl offered. "Do you know the name of her attending physician?"

Earl covered the receiver with his hand and looked at Brahm. "What's your name?"

"Dr. Kyle Brahm."

Earl removed his palm and repeated, "Dr. Kyle Brahm."

"I...I'm sorry, but Dr. Brahm is one of the people still missing after the attack."

And there it was. *The attack.*

"I see."

"If you give me your mother's name I can —"

Earl hung up on her. "All right, I believe there's *something* out there." He turned to face Larry and Miyagi. "Now, I wanna meet your fiancée and see this temple for myself. Any idea who runs it?"

Larry swallowed. "Barbara."

FORTY ONE

Peggy Hern sat at the bottom of the temple's lagoon, the empty carapace of a lobster on a rock beside her. She'd been starving when it crawled to the edge of her light. Instinctively, she snatched it up in her glowing talons and bit down on its back like a nutcracker soldier, shattering the shell; its legs were still twitching as she tore away hunks of raw, tender meat. She devoured it so quickly that the horror of her actions did not strike her until she'd finished. Only then did she drop the animal's vacant husk and back away.

Oh...that was so disgusting! It tasted like...like...

Actually, it tasted quite good. The freshest sushi she'd ever had.

Laughter came as an explosion of bubbles; she relaxed back into her seated position, tried to put her thoughts in order. Back in New York, she would take hot baths to emotionally decompress, just lay in her tub, her head resting against an inflated vinyl pillow. Sometimes she would burn candles and enjoy a glass of wine. Sometimes she would read. Sometimes Larry would join her and the bath would become something else entirely. And sometimes she would just fall asleep, but, whenever she drifted off, there was always the fear, very faint but very clear, that she might slowly sink beneath the bubbles to drown in her slumber.

Peggy smiled a bit at that.

Drowning was now the least of her worries.

At these times, when she was totally relaxed, Peggy often found clarity. She'd agonize over the right wording for a passage in one of her stories, or sweat out the plot of a novel only to have the answers come to her in the dreamy twilight of consciousness. Now, however, it was not the path of a character she charted, but her own future.

She'd chosen to live.

That was a big step.

Peggy stared off into the depths of the tunnel and her eyelids grew heavy. She knew the open sea lay at the end of this rabbit hole, a whole new wonderland to explore. She also knew that there was no cookie or elixir that would reverse what had happened to her. Given the reality of her circumstances, it would be easy for her to give in to life as a mermaid, to unplug herself from the world and escape into that blue void where she could have all the lobster she could eat. But Larry was also part of her reality. He was the anchor that kept her on the more difficult road, a return to human life. There was no doubt now that he loved her, that he would always be there for her. When he held her, when he *kissed* her, all the questions about her new life seemed to burn off like morning fog. He would come back for her and together they would —

What time is it?

Her eyes sprang fully open. She ran her hands down her face, then looked at her fingers with an expression of mild surprise, amazed that they were still clawed and webbed.

Did you really think they'd just go away?

No, she didn't.

Peggy gave the looted shell beside her another glance, then shook her head. Larry had accepted her new condition. It was time she learned to deal with it as well.

With a push of her talons and a twist of her paddle-like tail, Peggy surfaced. The transition from gills to lungs went smoothly this time, and she climbed from the water to crawl across the grotto floor. Looking around the temple, she saw no sign of her lover; she was alone with the statue of Varuna.

Peggy gazed up at the Lord of the Water's etched face. Where she had once seen a threatening maw of fangs, she now saw a comforting smile. *Just wait here with me a while longer*, the grin said. *Larry will be here soon*.

She rested her chin on her laced talons and something odd caught her eye. A glow, like that of a blacklight; it shimmered around the trident emblem on the statue's base. She crawled over to the seal, traced the carved shape with her claw. The stone vibrated, sent tingling waves across her transparent flesh; it was as if she were touching a tuning fork.

"What the hell?"

The glow and accompanying vibrations ended as quickly as they began.

Peggy studied the rock more closely. The seal now appeared to be a cap, a stone cork. There was something hidden inside the statue.

Something powerful.

FORTY TWO

Karl Tellstrom joined the crowd, crossed a bridge, and moved toward a pyramid of gold and raven glass. The splendor of the buildings around him was truly glorious, as if all the world's monuments had been stolen from this place and scattered like seeds across the globe.

This was the way his people were meant to live.

As Karl neared the opposite side of the canal, darkness moved across the procession. Every member of the gathering looked to the sky, and he found himself doing the same. The sight that greeted his eyes was a mammoth black arrowhead hovering high above the city of Poseidon. It was Varuna. Varuna was calling for him.

Karl awoke from his slumber to find the pool chamber's tiled floor beneath him. Christine laid in his arms, still in her natural, nautical form; the human coloring that normally clouded her flesh had evaporated, leaving the skin gloriously sheer. He gazed at her anatomy, tried hard to see the child maturing amid the iridescent contours and shadowy ribbons of her inner physique.

His child.

His *heir*.

Karl gently stroked her abdomen, not wanting to wake her. The female body was a marvel. To be able to feel life grow and move within you, to give birth to it, to feed it from your own body...truly wondrous.

Tellstrom swallowed and his thoughts returned, as they so often did, to his own mother. When her ruined body had washed ashore, the only concern the adults had was to hide her, to drag her out of sight and throw her in the ground before anyone, any *human*, could see. Even his father had been concerned with what these murderers would think.

It was then that Karl saw the fear in their eyes; they were afraid of human beings, so afraid that they couldn't even seek justice for a murdered wife and mother.

Karl ran to the temple; he asked Varuna to bring his mother back to him, to seal her wounds and start her heart beating again. And, when those prayers went unanswered, he asked for more strength and cunning than the humans, powers that were not made weak by benevolent shackles. Karl Tellstrom asked his god to one day grant him revenge.

Tonight, *those* prayers would be fulfilled.

If the gods could share the power of creation with a mother, they could allow a father to wield their tool of destruction.

Karl thought he saw something move in the jaundiced gloom of Christine's belly, a small shadow, no larger than a finger. It jerked, no *kicked* and turned. His child was alive and moving in her womb.

"You," he whispered to her luminous naval, "will be born into a world where men will fear you. You will rule over humankind the way they rule over the ants and the slugs. *I* will make this possible for you. Tonight, we will all be free." His eyes drifted to Christine's sleeping face. "And they will never hurt your mother the way they did mine. I promise you."

Karl breathed deeply. On the tile around him, his followers rested; he slowly scanned their diverse shapes and textures, and his eyes came to rest on Jason. The boy's wounds had healed up nicely. They were an army now, ready for the task before them.

Karl smiled.

Tonight, there would be no more rallies, no more speeches. Tonight, the hand of the gods would be his.

FORTY THREE

Deputy Ray didn't report for work that morning. By itself, this was quite unusual. Ray had always been conscientious and dedicated. In fact, to John Cannon's memory, the boy had taken a total of only two sick days in the last three years. By all accounts, he'd been a model law enforcement officer. Cannon thought he might run by the boy's apartment to check on him when the office fax spit news.

People had been murdered at Black Harbor Medical Center the night before.

Canon took off his wide-rimmed hat and sank into his chair. A trio of thoughts danced in his mind. The first one told him that Ray was one of *them*, and that he wouldn't be reporting to work today or any other day. The second said that Barbara and Peggy Hern were probably among the dead. His final thought, and most frightening of all by far, was that Tellstrom had finally made a very public strike...and way too close to home.

Canon put down the State Police fax and made a phone call to Ed at the Sea Mist Inn. This alleviated some of his fears. There had been an attack, but Barbara was standing in Ed's living room and the other woman, the Callisto, waited in the temple.

"Relax, John," Ed assured him. "They're safe."

The chief then went about his business to the best of his ability; patrolling the streets, directing tourists, handling minor disputes here and there through the course of the day. His face was the most positive he could muster. It was hard to be pleasant when you knew your world was about to topple around your ears.

Now, as sundown approached and the tourists staged their nightly retreat, he parked his patrol car and sat silently with his keys in hand. He looked up to the false church on the hill. The evening breeze through his car's open window was both cooling and calming. After a few minutes of quiet fretting, he moved his bulk into the office.

You're wrong, Ed, he thought, staring at the fax that still laid upon his desk. *None of us are safe.*

FORTY FOUR

Barbara DeParle walked into Ed's kitchen to pour herself some tea, her face made bright orange by the setting sun. She picked up a glass, her hands so numb that they no longer seemed a part of her, and looked out the window. In summers past, the streets would be clogged with tourists anxiously running to each and every shop before the doors were closed and the last ferry left them stranded. But this was not the past.

This was the *now*.

The now was shop after shop unopened. She'd opened hers, feeling guilty for doing so, but also believing that it was important to make a show. The now was fewer tourists. Oh, first thing in the morning was still as busy as ever, but, once it was clear that Colonial Bay was a mere skeleton of its former self, they'd left in a hurry. And of course, the now was Karl Tellstrom.

Barbara was scared. No, it ran deeper than that. She was terrified, so terrified that she thought she might go mad if she spent too much time thinking about it.

She poured her tea, trying to remember any hint or clue that would've told her what Tellstrom was capable of, something that could've foretold this desperate state of affairs. She remembered his grief at the death of his mother, his polite tears at the funeral of his father, his easily coaxed temper. She wondered if insanity suddenly took hold of the boy, or if it had been growing steadily within him over the years, changing him so gradually as to have been imperceptible.

But, if it hadn't been Tellstrom, how long before someone else came along with the same war cries? The ruse of Colonial Bay was only meant to buy Poseidon's children time to rest, to regroup. It was never meant to be an eternity. All any of the elders could do was teach their own children, tell them about the devils they were forced to imitate, warn them what might happen if they showed their true natures to a world that did not want to understand, a world that thought they were monsters and aberrations, a world that might be angry that, given the choice of living a lie or revealing what they were, they had not chosen the lie.

As Barbara drank her sweet tea, Ed walked into the room. His face was grave, his eyes pale. She thought for a moment that he might have more bad news to deliver her. Another attack had taken place and ended badly. Somewhere, Christine was now tied to the hood of a redneck's car.

"John'll be here soon," was all he had to say.

She nodded, not really relieved by the announcement. There was little Canon could do to turn the tide. There was little any of them could do. Even if she knew Tellstrom's next move, they were now the minority, and a weak one at that. They were Paralichts, the most peaceful of the three clans. Sure, they were strong, they had to be to remove precious metals from the dark floor of the abyss and carry the loaded baskets up to the great pyramid of Poseidon, but they weren't warriors. The Charodon and the Kraken...they were the ones that had been bred to fight, to *kill*. The odds for any confrontation were clearly not stacked in her favor. Unless...

There was always the hand of the gods.

Barbara closed her eyes and the blue flicker from within Varuna's statue lit her darkness, set her nerves to tingle. It was there, waiting to be picked up, to be *used*. If she went to Karl with this power, could he stand against her? No. Nobody could stand against her. Nobody would dare...

Her eyes leapt open.

Is this what it's come to? Clansmen killing clansmen? Civil war?

Barbara shook her head. It was up to her to find a better way, a more civilized resolution. She was "The Teacher," as was her mother before her, and her mother before *her*. Until she received some sort of vision or divine guidance, she was still Varuna's voice here on Earth.

Peggy.

Yes. The Callisto was proof that Poseidon's children and the humans were all related, the same flesh, created by the same gods. If Barbara could convince Karl's followers, could convince her own daughter, then perhaps she could also persuade them that killing the humans was wrong. She would make them see this. She had to.

What if I don't?

Christine was under Karl's spell. How long before she told him about the power? How long before he tried it on for size? If that happened, it wouldn't be a matter of civil war, but full-blown Armageddon.

The bell rang at the front desk, giving her a start; Ed left to answer it, and Barbara walked over to the bay window. When it was dark, she would go to the temple. She would get Peggy and move the god's wrath to a new location. Barbara sipped her tea and watched the shadows grow longer on the vacant street.

•••

Larry rang the bell.

Carol Miyagi could hardly contain her excitement. For most of her career, she'd become grudgingly accustomed to the reality that the evidence and clues she excavated might never manifest into the lost city itself, but would instead remain pieces of a puzzle far too complex to ever really be solved. Over the last month, however, each new discovery seemed more spectacular than the last. First, to find Atlantis, then the trail of artifacts that led them to Colonial Bay, and now, knowing that there were actual descendants of the great city all around them, it made her want to dance. Carol needed to meet this DeParle woman, needed to see if she knew more about what happened to Atlantis, and their motley crew needed all the help they could get.

Ed DeParle finally appeared behind the check-in counter; by the look on his face, their group was not what he expected to see. "Help you folks?"

"We need to talk to Barbara," Larry told him.

The old man studied him, then looked cautiously over the other members of the group, trying to get a hint of their intentions. "What's this all about?"

Surprise burst onto Larry's face, then turned quickly to irritation. "You know damn well what this is about."

"It's important that we speak to her." Carol held up the ancient book she cradled in her arms. "And I think she's going to want to talk with us."

Ed's face nearly hit the floor; he reached for the text with surprising speed, his hand shaking. Carol snapped it back out of his reach.

"That don't belong to you," Ed told her.

"Then I'll gladly give it back to Barbara."

"Give it back to *me* and I won't call the Chief of Police. Stealing from..." His eyes danced uncomfortably. "...from a *church*. You people oughta be ashamed o' yourselves. What the hell were you lookin' for anyway?"

"The truth," Carol told him. "And by your interest in this book, I'd say we —"

"Who says I give a shit about that there book? I don't have any love for thieves is all. Just a bunch o' gibberish to me or anybody else still livin.'"

She offered him a level stare and quoted, "'Varuna brought forth three clans from the Great Abyss and called each by name: Charodon... Kraken...Paralicht.'"

DeParle could not hide his shock. "How did you — ?"

"We've been to —" Carol was about to say Atlantis, but quickly changed her wording for better effect. "— Poseidon."

The old man's eyes widened and locked with hers. "That's a damned lie!"

"I assure you, it's not."

Ed's face reddened. "Get out."

"No."

"I said get out!"

Earl spoke up, "Sir, I'm an officer in the United States Coast Guard. If you'd like, I can make a call and have the FBI or Homeland Security ringing your bell instead of us. I don't think you want that."

Ed smiled mirthlessly. "Son, you think they'd believe a word you said?"

"I don't have to cry 'fish-people.' This —" He pointed to Brahm. "— is a doctor from Black Harbor Hospital. I think you know what happened there last night, don't you?"

Ed said nothing, his eyes drifted across their faces and back down to the book.

The guardsman continued, "With or without that call, how long do you think it'll be before they show up at your door?"

"None of this is my doin'."

"But you know who's behind it," Larry said. "Who are you so scared of?"

"Son, I'd say I was scared o' you. How'd you feel last night when they came for your Peggy?"

"I was terrified."

"Then you know how I feel right now havin' you come for Barb."

"We're not here to *kill* Barbara."

Ed's face lightened. "No, I 'spose not."

Carol realized the old man's combativeness had actually been born of true fear.

Larry appeared to realize it, too. He shook his head and the corner of his lip crept up. "Even when they leave you, they never really go, do they?"

Ed offered him a questioning stare.

The artist elaborated, "Wives...girlfriends...they think that they can just slap a big 'ex' on the front and all the feelings will just go away. You might even play along, but there's always something there, some connection that won't ever let you totally forget that you used to love them. I know how it feels to want to protect someone, even when they don't want it. So does Barbara. She saved my life last night. Please, help us stop this, help us protect more people from being hurt."

DeParle ran a hand across his face, tugged at his lips; at last he motioned for Larry and the others to follow him. "Come on then. The way things are goin', guess we don't have much left to lose."

They moved past the front desk and down a hallway toward Ed's private quarters. Carol hid the book behind her back, not wanting yet another person to grab for it when they entered the room. When she saw the elderly woman standing by a window, she thought of her father. Carol would find him looking out the glass, but not seeing the scenery beyond; the expression on his face had been one of great sadness, of great loss. This woman looked the same way.

"Barb?" Ed called out. "We got company."

The old woman turned to look at them and her face changed, concern giving way to anger. "What the hell are you doin'? Who are all o' these — ?"

"It's all right," Ed told her. "I think they're batting for our team, not that we could even field a team, as few players as we got right now."

DeParle's nostrils flared, as if she noticed something was burning, and her eyes found Larry. "I can smell her on you," she told him. "You went to the temple?"

He nodded.

"I thought she was going to make you leave."

"She tried. Kind of backfired. After your grand entrance last night, I can't believe you just left Peggy alone in that cave. If those things found her up there —"

Barbara held up her hand to quiet him. "They'd never harm her there."

"They went on a rampage in a public hospital."

"What they did, they did because they believe in Varuna's will. They may be fanatics, but they wouldn't spill blood in his temple. They'd be too afraid of his wrath." DeParle scanned the group; she appeared very uncomfortable. "Look, I don't know any of you and I think you should all just get out of here before —"

"But I know *you*, what you are." Miyagi held up the book. "This is all quite an impressive act you've been able to keep up here. But it's falling apart. I think you understand that."

Barbara reached for the aged volume and Carol let her take it. The old woman leafed through it briefly, then held it tightly against her breast. It looked as if an incredible weight had been lifted from her shoulders.

"We were led to your temple," Carol told her. "There's a force there that pulled at our compass needle, drew us to the statue. What is it?"

Barbara's teary eyes shot to her. "You know so much. How could you read the book and not see the wrath of the gods?"

The wrath of the gods.

Zeus struck people down with lightning bolts. Odin's fits of rage caused the north winds to blow, the storms destroying everything in their path. Even modern Man referred to natural disasters as "acts of God." But this woman was not speaking of anything natural. Carol remembered the etchings on the temple wall, cities destroyed by holy fire, and her stomach sank.

"Okay," she said softly, "what is it?"

PART THREE
THE WRATH OF THE GODS

FORTY FIVE

From his balcony, Roger Hays watched the sun set on Colonial Bay. Given what he knew now, he expected the view to be somehow different, more sinister. But it wasn't. The town looked just as quiet and tranquil as ever.

It sickened him.

His wait ended just after nine o'clock with a loud, very insistent knock. Roger checked his clip, then ran across the room, handgun ready as he threw open the door.

A tall, brawny man stared calmly down the barrel of Roger's weapon with a stoic poker face. "Mr. Hays, Mr. Ludwig sends his condolences."

"You must be Horror Show." Roger holstered his .45. Behind the hitman stood three shorter henchmen; he waved them all inside and locked the door behind them. "Did Ludwig get you the weapons I asked for?"

"Yeah. He said you would fill us in on the wet work when we got here." Horror Show motioned to his men. "We're here."

"My son is dead."

"Yes, sir. We're sorry to hear that. Nobody should outlive their own child."

"He was killed by..." Roger searched for something they would believe. "...a crazy cult."

The man to Horror Show's right spoke up. "Christ Almighty! A cult?"

Roger noticed the slight hint of an Irish accent. *O'Shea, I presume.* "I want to get them. I want to get them for what they did to my boy."

"Did I hear you right?" Horror Show asked. "You wanna whack a bunch of hippies?"

"They attacked *me* last night. I want them dead, all of them *dead.*"

Horror Show held up his hand. "You want to calm down, sir. You're upset, letting your emotions fuck with your head. Hell, if my son was hit, I'd be kickin' ass and takin' names too. But, Mr. Hays, I want you to think about what you're askin' here. I take care of problems for you, usually one problem at a time. Sounds like you wanna start some kind of war."

"It's not a war. We find where they're hiding, blow them all to shit, then torch the place to cover our tracks. They'll think it was another Waco."

Horror Show frowned. "There were seventy people in that Branch Davidian compound. Most of 'em women and children. Is that what we're talkin' about here?"

"This is one man with no more than a handful of people helping him."

"Give me numbers, Mr. Hays. Is it five? Ten? Fifty?"

Roger grew annoyed. "Let's say ten. Does that help you?"

"They got shot guns, scud missiles, anthrax, pipe bombs?"

"They tore my son apart with their fucking hands and ate him!"

Horror Show was struck dumb. O'Shea crossed himself. The other two men looked at the marbled floor.

Roger quickly broke the silence, his tone forcibly made level. "Gentlemen...I killed one of these sick freaks already last night."

Horror Show's head made a surprised twitch.

"With or without you, I *will* go after the rest of them. I should point out, however, that I pay you all quite well for your talents, and if I can't get a return on my investment, I might just have to see that certain bits of evidence find the light of day, evidence that would help clear some cold cases from the NYPD books. I'm sure none of you want that to happen."

O'Shea was quick to speak up, "We're all loyal to you, Mr. Hays."

Roger nodded, his eyes still locked with Horror Show's.

"You're the boss," the hitman said at last.

"Good." Hays smiled. "Then we should get going."

•••

When Hays burst through the door, the look on John Canon's face was one of total surprise. Horror Show and Carlo rushed in and were on the chief in a flash; they lifted his bulk from the leather seat and slammed him against the paneling. The fat man struggled against their muscular grasps. "What the hell are you people doin'?"

"Shut your hole," Carlo ordered.

Hays strolled toward the chief's desk, his black trenchcoat lending him the look of a Gestapo agent. He glanced down at a photograph; Canon and his young deputy, the monster in man's clothing that tried to kill Roger the night before. Hays held the picture out for the chief's inspection, tapped the deputy's face with his forefinger. "This *man*...where are the others like him?"

Canon's eyes still floated in astonishment. "You lost your fuckin' mind, Hays?"

"No, I've lost my fucking son." Roger tapped the photo more insistently. "Where?"

The chief said nothing and Horror Show smacked him hard across the face. "The man asked you a fuckin' question, Lardo."

Canon remained silent.

With a flick of his wrist, Horror Show unfolded a straight razor and held it over the man's flabby hand, a guillotine ready to fall. "Answer the man's question or lose a fuckin' finger."

"*Screw all o' you!*"

The razor came down, severed Canon's index finger just below the knuckle, and the chief bit his lip until it bled, denying them the satisfaction of his pained screams.

"Jesus Christ," O'Shea exclaimed from the doorway where he and Neil Shiva acted as look-out. "He's a fuckin' cop."

"*He's one of them*," Hays roared back.

O'Shea looked at his shoes, his head wagging.

Carlo's eyes widened. "Santa Maria!"

On the desktop, Canon's severed digit writhed like a snake with its head removed; the skin bubbled, as if coming to a boil, and a long, bony talon poked out through the fingertip. The finger flipped over; tiny suction cups ran down its length, each rimmed with jagged teeth, lending them the appearance of hungry mouths.

His true nature revealed, Canon roared with rage; hair retreated into his scalp as the back of his head exploded into a vast pulsating mass. His nose grew into a long trunk, and tendrils of sinew shot away from his skull to form a squirming beard of tentacles.

"Where you goin'?" Neil called.

Hays turned to see that O'Shea had deserted his post. *Worthless bastard!*

"*Help me hold this fuck down,*" Horror Show cried.

Carlo nodded; he pushed down on Canon's chest, felt it undulate beneath the uniform.

Something moved in Canon's pants, as if the man had a tremendous cock that wanted to slither free of its master. The zipper gave way, allowed a long, maroon tentacle to slither from his fly and whip through the air.

Carlo released the aberration and backed away; he kissed his right thumb and crossed himself, his lips moving in silent prayer.

With his arm now free, Canon reached over and threw Horror Show across the desk. The hitman rolled to his feet and held up his straight razor, a move that was far more defensive than threatening.

Canon ripped off his shirt and threw it to the floor. His black-speckled skin changed color again, the fury of his emotions reflected by the chromatophores buried deep within his flesh; he was now blood red, his eyes black as India ink. Fluid, triggered instinctively by Canon's body chemistry, sprayed from his pores; in water, it formed a poisonous chemical cloud that cloaked his escape, but, in the air-conditioned office, it hid nothing.

Some of this poison rained onto Carlo's hand and he screamed as it burned into his skin.

The beast ripped its pants off, freed the nest of serpents that wriggled between its legs, then it roared at the hitmen, facial tentacles spreading like the petals of a red orchid, revealing the open beak at the center of the blossom.

O'Shea rushed back inside, an AK-47 in his hands. .30-caliber slugs ripped across the room, burrowed through the creature's body, and exploded from its back. The ruined monster fell to the floor in a heap; the entire room shook from the impact.

O'Shea kept his finger on the trigger, emptied all thirty slugs into the carcass. Smoke poured from the chamber, a ceiling fan twisting it into a funnel around his head. Spent shell casings blanketed his feet, each jacket the size of a Bic pen.

Roger ran over to him, wrapped his hand around his neck and screamed into his face, "*Nice shooting, Rambo!* We needed him to tell us where the others were hiding."

O'Shea pried the man's hand from his collar. "That motherfucker wasn't gonna give you shit. Coulda killed us all!"

Hays spun around and his face met Horror Show's fist; he fell to the floor, his lip split under the force of the punch. "What — ?"

Horror Show's face never changed, but his tone made it clear that he was pissed. "You knew exactly what the fuck we were dealin' with and didn't say dick."

Roger wiped his mouth, stared at the blood on his fingers. "And you would've believed me when I told you we were in a town full of monsters?"

"Maybe not," the hitman agreed, "but you don't pay me to have an opinion. I asked you what we were up against so I could have my crew prepared. Dealin' with..." He pointed toward the desk and the riddled corpse beyond. "...whatever the hell that was is a lot different than dealin' with a bunch of comet freaks waitin' for their mothership."

Roger wiped the last of the blood from his lips. "Point taken."

Horror Show extended a hand to help Hays up and the businessman took it.

O'Shea stood motionless in the center of the office, the AK-47 lowered but still clutched tightly in his hands; he stared at the desk and the blood-splattered wall behind it in disbelief.

Horror Show gave him a pat on the shoulder to get him moving again. "Good work."

O'Shea blinked. "What was that thing?"

Horror Show shrugged and turned to Roger. "Truth time, Mr. Hays. What the hell are we after here?"

"Sea monsters. The whole town is nothing but sea monsters." Hays ran a hand across his face. "The bastards...they...they *ate* my son. Who knows how many other people they've killed. They have to be destroyed."

"'Who knows how many other people they've killed.' Lookin' out for the good o' mankind." Horror Show stepped over to the thing's corpse. "How fuckin' noble."

He examined the chest, watched to make certain the beast wasn't breathing, then kicked the animal with the steel tip of his boot. "Well, at least we know they can be killed. It always pisses me off when the monster won't die."

The hitman reached into his pocket, felt the granite shard he kept there, thinking again of Dillinger and the movie theater; he found himself wondering, perhaps too late, if Hays had become his woman in red. After a moment of silent contemplation, he turned and walked across the room, kicking spent metal jackets from his path and coughing at the stench of ammonia and gun smoke that hung thick in the office air.

Neil studied the raw patch on Carlo's left hand.

"How is it?" Horror Show asked.

Carlo glared at him, then winced. "How do you think? Hurts like a son-of-a-bitch."

"He needs a doctor," Neil announced.

"Doctors can wait!" Carlo said, then looked to Horror Show. "I'll be fine if you got somethin' to take the edge offa this."

"Sure." Horror Show reached into his pocket, produced a prescription bottle filled with pills and popped the cap, flicking two white tablets into his palm. Neil examined the blue and green flecks that littered their chalky surfaces. "What are you giving him?"

"Vicodin." Horror Show handed the pills to his friend, then reached inside his jacket and produced a small metallic flask. "Wash 'em down with this."

"And what's that?" Shiva's voice was a shy whisper. "Vodka."

"Shit yeah!" Carlo took the flask, pushed the Vicodin onto his tongue, then washed it down with a healthy surge of alcohol.

"You think that's smart?"

"It's not your fuckin' hand, firebug!" Carlo whined through clinched teeth.

"I know. I only meant, if you're carrying a gun, I don't think you want to be fucked up with pain-killers and booze." Shiva lifted his shirt to reveal a large mass of scar tissue on his belly. "Fire and that shit don't mix."

"Kid, I was havin' buckshot pulled outta my ass when you was still in Juvi Hall. Hell, I'm probably so tolerant of this shit it won't even gimme a buzz. If you're worried I'll pop you, stay the fuck outta my way." Carlo splashed some Vodka on his open sore, then slammed his eyes shut and stomped the floor; if the man had a bullet between his teeth, Horror Show thought he might have bitten it cleanly in two.

Horror Show took back his flask, rubbed a hand through his friend's hair and assured him, "When this is over, we'll tell the hospital you spilled battery acid on it."

Carlo wiped his mouth. "Yippy."

Hays looked toward the office door. "I'm sure someone heard all the gunfire. We should go now."

The hitmen were more than happy to oblige; they followed Roger into the parking lot. Horror Show was about to ask if Hays had any ideas on how to proceed when they saw a rusty green Cordoba race by, headed up the hill and out of town. Roger recognized the car, or perhaps one of the passengers he saw through its windows.

"Miyagi," he said aloud, then his eyes shot back to Horror Show. "Wherever she's headed, we should follow."

•••

"This doesn't make any damned sense," Earl Preston told Barbara as he climbed into her Cordoba. "Your people were being slaughtered, you had this prehistoric Weapon of Mass Destruction, and nobody's thought of using it before now?"

She offered him a look of disapproval. "You say you were a soldier, Mr. Preston?"

He stiffened in the passenger's seat. "I'm an officer in the United States Coast Guard."

The old woman nodded, threw the car into reverse, and backed onto the street. "Somebody hands you a gun, shows you the enemy, and all you gotta do is pull the trigger. You don't have to stop and think about what might happen afterwards."

In the back seat, Carol frowned. "When Einstein saw the first atomic bomb, he wished he'd been a watchmaker."

"It's a doomsday bomb?" Brahm asked.

The car sped down darkened roads as Barbara shrugged. "The Book tells us the creators used it to punish the disobedient."

"A whip for their slaves," Earl said with contempt.

Barbara nodded. "Legend says it holds all the fires of Hell. The Paralichts thought it was magic. They knew the warrior clans wouldn't be smart with it, so they hid it away."

"In the place they go worship?" the guardsman asked.

She briefly took her eyes from the road to look at him. "*I* didn't hide it. Never seen it myself. Back then, Poseidon's children all lived in fear. To them, there was no safer place than under the watchful eye of a god. When the ones that hid it died, the only one to pass it on to the next generation was The Teacher. And so we've kept it secret and left well enough alone."

Alan chimed in, "So you're sure Tellstrom doesn't know where to find it — how to work it?"

"Like I said, my daughter Christine is the only one but me that knows about it." Barbara turned onto the winding street that led up to the church. "I don't think she'd tell him, but then, I never thought she'd run away. That's why I want to go and move it. If Karl ever found it, he wouldn't need to know how it works. It'll help him."

"You want to tell me what the hell that means?" Larry asked, worried more than ever for Peggy's safety.

"We're all the creators' tools, each of us made for a reason. Karl, the other Charodons, and the Krakens, they've all been itching to fight, so has the weapon."

"So," Alan began, "this gun *wants* to be fired?"

Barbara nodded. "If Tellstrom finds it, it'll show him how."

Earl looked out the windshield. A white-painted steeple stood out against the velvet backdrop of night. As they drew close, his hand moved to his service pistol.

223

FORTY six

Peggy Hern knelt at Varuna's feet, tracing the trident symbol with her claws. She dug at the seam, watched silt fly onto the temple floor in filthy showers, and the light reappeared; it pulsated, as if timed to the beat of her heart. The stone hummed, vibrations making her fingers and lower arms tingle. Then, as suddenly as they began, the light and the hum vanished in unison.

She had no idea why she felt so compelled to see what was hidden within this idol, just as she couldn't explain her need to attack the book thieves. It was almost...instinctual. She cleared away the last of the muck, and her talons found purchase in the rounded stone cap. She pulled, amazed at her new-found strength, and the cork fell forward, struck the floor with a loud *bang*. She stared down at the stone, watched it roll back and forth on the ground, then her eyes rose slowly to the gaping hole she'd created in the base of the statue; something reflected the flicker of candlelight.

Peggy reached in with cautious fingers, found metal, very cold metal, and brought it out into the light. A golden sculpture, nearly a foot in diameter, an orb held in the clutches of a bizarre, six-fingered hand — exposed muscle and corrugated tubing, with fingers that resembled spinal columns, elongated tailbones forming claws. Where the wrist should have been, a pair of lips pouted. While bizarre, Peggy had to admire the artisan; there were no seams, no flaws, not a single chisel scratch anywhere.

As she studied it, the orb glowed in her hands; its golden surface burned away, replaced by blue-white luminance, and the sculpted mouth opened, revealing a hollow within. Peggy had the strangest urge to slide her hand into that gap, to fill the empty alien digits with her own claws and wear the object as a glove. She held out her hand to do just that, tracing the opening with the sharpened talon of her index finger, and her mind filled with a sudden glut of imagery, like surfing a million frequencies in the blink of an eye.

One vision burned itself into her.

Fire. Instantaneous...intense...searing...

Tiger-striped fingers reached down and snatched the device from her grasp.

Peggy blinked and stared up into a hellish grin.

"I'll take that, Callisto," the creature told her, its voice a menacing gargle.

She crawled backward, pressed herself against the altar, wondering how this thing had snuck up on her. "Who — ?"

"Karl Tellstrom," it said. "I've been wanting to meet you...Peggy, isn't it? We've all looked so forward to it."

Panic forced the feeling from her body. This vicious looking monster was Karl, the one who sent the creatures to the hospital to find her, the one who wanted her dead. Her eyes shot to the lagoon at the far end of the temple, looking for a way to escape.

More animals crawled from the water. One of the faces in the crowd looked familiar: a glowing, transparent being with thickened lips like her own.

"Barbara?" Peggy asked, hopeful.

The woman shook her head; Tellstrom held out his hand for her and she took it.

"This is Christine, DeParle's daughter," Karl said. "You'll find she doesn't share her mother's misguided notions about you."

The sound of distant gunfire made all of them jump.

"Humans!" The voice came from the stone steps that led to the church above. "Humans are attacking!"

It was as if someone had yelled "fire!" Some of Tellstrom's brood ran, others cried out, filling the chamber with a horrid wailing. Karl scanned the frightened mob, then his mouth opened in an ear-splitting roar that made Peggy wince. The crowd stopped in its tracks, every eye rushing to meet Tellstrom's.

"*What's the matter with all of you?*" he demanded. "You hear the sounds of battle and run for cover like *minnows* caught by a light? *We are the children of Poseidon! We are the creators' chosen race!"*

Karl held up the golden sculpture Peggy had unearthed, held it high above his head for all to see; they stared at it agog. "I hold the power of the gods in my hand! *Nothing* is going to defeat us!"

Tellstrom stroked the sculpted lips with his tiger-striped talons; the relic opened, as if it longed for him to fill its vacant interior. Karl's hand reached into the device until its wanton mouth was sucking at his wrist. The brilliant, blue-white fire returned, and a square of video static materialized in the air above it, a television screen waiting for a signal. It did not wait long. The visual noise diminished, replaced by a pixelized view of the cavern.

Karl smiled with delight. He moved his newfound toy around the room, and Peggy noticed that objects were being highlighted on the floating screen, ominous red Xs projected over them.

It's a weapon.

She remembered the visions, fire...unimaginable fire, and shook her head as if to waggle the conclusion from her brain. "Oh my holy God."

The reverberation of a muffled explosion filled her ears in reply.

FORTY SEVEN

"Stop the car!" Roger Hays yelled.

Horror Show slammed on the breaks and O'Shea and Carlo jerked forward.

Neil Shiva wasn't with them. Roger had spoken to him in conspiratorial whispers. Horror Show hadn't been able to hear their conversation, but when they'd finished, Neil removed the explosives from the trunk, moved them into Hays' car, and drove off for ports unknown. Shiva was an expert at using fuses, chemicals, and other materials to make torch jobs look accidental, but he wasn't right in the head. For Neil, it was all a power trip. The larger the explosion, the more damage it could do, the stronger he felt. Add to that the fact that Hays wasn't thinking clearly either, and any possible result of their hushed conversation filled Horror Show with dread.

Off the road to the left sat an old wooden church, a Cordoba parked at its doorstep, doors opened, spilling passengers onto the lawn.

"That's them," Roger said, pointing. "Take us over there."

The Cadillac rolled across the grass; the strangers heard its approach and turned their faces into its headlights. Quite a gathering: a tall, beefy black man; a young Asian woman, a frail-looking old lady, a middle-aged man with graying temples, and two other men in their late twenties to early thirties. They all appeared to be human...for now at any rate.

Horror Show brought his car to a halt, its headlamps still blinding the other party.

"Shut off the lights," Hays commanded.

Horror Show did as he was told, brought darkness back to the scene, and the strangers unshielded their wondering eyes.

"Let me do the talking," Roger said. "When I say,'I'm full of surprises,' you all get out of the car with your guns."

Horror Show shook his head. *Motherfucker*.

Hays opened the door and rose from the car. "Good evening, Miyagi."

The Asian woman squinted. "Mr. Hays?"

One of the younger men appeared shocked. "I see you made it out of the hospital."

"And Neuhaus," Roger said, amused. "Yes, you'll find I'm full of surprises."

Christ, Horror Show thought, *there's the cue*.

They stepped from the car, weapons drawn.

The black man immediately brought a pistol into view.

"The nigger's got a gun," Carlo yelled.

Horror Show aimed his Beretta 9mm at the black man's feet and fired a slug into the ground; a dust cloud rose from the impact.

Miyagi screamed, "For God's sake, Preston, drop it!"

A split second of hesitation, then Preston tossed his pistol; it sank into the green sea of grass, leaving a shadowy dimple in the smoothness of the lawn.

"What the hell are you doin', Hays?" Neuhaus asked.

"What the hell am *I* doing? Justice, my friend. An eye for an eye, a tooth for a tooth, a life for a *fucking life*." He pulled the .45 from beneath his trenchcoat, then turned his attention to the chapel doors. "They're in there aren't they?"

"Who?"

"The creatures," Hays snarled. "The things from the hospital. That's why you've come up here."

"We've come for a prayer meeting," the old woman told them.

Hays laughed, still gazing at the wooden doorway. "I'm sure."

Neuhaus stepped forward. "Look...Hays, my fiancé is in there. You remember Peggy? She was attacked, just like your son. They've infected her with something." He pointed to the man with gray temples. "He's her doctor. We're here to get her, to help her."

Roger's eyes sparked. "They came after *her* last night."

"Yeah, they did."

Horror Show pointed to the group. "Whatcha want us to do with 'em?"

"With them? Nothing. I'll cover them." Hays pointed at the doors with his gun. "I want you to go in there. If you find the woman alone, I want you to bring her out —" His eyes went to Neuhaus. "— unharmed. Maybe they'll come for her again. If she's not alone, I want you bring me the head of the thing that looks like a shark."

Horror Show's eyes joined Roger's at the church. "And if there's more than one of 'em in there?"

Roger's sadistic grin widened. "Make me a pile."

Horror Show reached under his steering wheel and popped the trunk. "You heard the man."

The three hitmen moved to load themselves down with weaponry, each grabbing their share of grenades in addition to their chosen firearm. O'Shea still held onto the Kalishnikov as if it were a safety blanket. Carlo grabbed a 10-gauge Winchester — a sawed-off, lever-action shotgun — and strapped a flashlight around the muzzle with duct tape. Horror Show went for the big gun: a CAR 15 assault rifle with night-scope and laser sight. He also kept the Beretta 9mm automatic as back up.

In his head, Horror Show could almost hear music building. *This is the part of the flick just before the show down. The hero straps on all the weapons he or she can get their hands on and then goes off to kick some major ass.* He smiled, saw that his men were sufficiently armed, and closed the trunk.

Carlo glanced down at his scorched hand; it still looked quite raw. "Let's go erase these fucks."

They moved away from the car, looking as if they'd just stepped from the pages of *Soldier of Fortune.* Hays smiled in their direction. The old woman fell to her knees in the tall grass, her eyes closed, her mouth moving in prayer. The others stood by in silent amazement, Preston's eyes firmly on the gun in Roger's hand.

At the door, Horror Show grabbed the wrought iron handle. "Ready?"

O'Shea nodded and Carlo switched on his flashlight.

They hustled inside, their ammunition belts clanking as they moved down the center aisle, Carlo's flashlight illuminating their path. Slowly, as their eyes adjusted to the dark, shadowy pews became visible... and something else.

Glowing white, football-shaped blotches; cartoon eyes that blinked as they approached.

Carlo hit them with his flashlight, revealing their owner. The "eyes" were actually bioluminescent pouches on the creature's cheeks. Horror Show had seen something similar on the Discovery Channel: glowing pockets that helped schools of fish stay together through the darkness of the ocean depths. The beast itself looked harmless enough; it was tall, slender, and black. A succession of multi-colored ribbons extended from its bald scalp like the plume of a tropical bird. Its lips were huge, bloated. As the animal came closer, the pouches under its eyes rotated inward, creating the illusion of "blinking." Horror Show could've sworn he saw a pattern to this motion, a kind of Morse code, as if the animal was communicating something through the gloom.

"Is this the best they could do?" Carlo chuckled.

The beast, as if offended by the slight, opened its mouth to display a nasty set of fangs. It hissed in their direction, then lurched forward with outstretched claws.

Carlo squeezed the Winchester's trigger, opened a hole in the animal's midsection as large as a dinner plate.

The blast from the shotgun muzzle also served to light the interior. It revealed a room filled with hundreds of creatures, things that sat in the pews ready to pounce, things that didn't shed any light to give away their position, things covered with spots and stripes, things with claws and teeth, all looking right at them.

"*Fuck me!*" O'Shea had seen the hidden army as well; he sprayed the tabernacle with rapid fire. Shells ripped through the surrounding horde. Their bodies fell over the backs of pews and littered the aisle.

Carlo joined him, blasting away, ventilating benches and animals alike, filling the air with wood splinters and viscera.

The monstrosities kept coming.

Horror Show stood amazed at their speed and agility. Unlike most sea animals, these beasts were neither helpless nor clumsy on land. For every one they took down, two more seemed to appear.

"*Where the fuck are they comin' from?*" O'Shea yelled over the roar of weapons fire and attacking beasts.

Through the night scope of his rifle, Horror Show saw them

pouring in from around the altar. His view filled with a rising blur and he fired, blew a hole through the forehead of a golden chimera, a beast whose extensible jaw had opened wide enough to engulf him whole.

Their weapons' fire continued to strobe the interior in funhouse lighting, granting only brief glimpses of the monsters as they climbed and leapt over pews and the corpses of their fallen comrades.

In the darkness between these flashes, one of the beasts rushed up to O'Shea. The animal was beautiful, covered in alternating stripes of red and black. Long, flexible spikes extended from its back and the sides of its arms. Tiny eyes sat just above a gaping jaw, and, from its chin, white tendrils hung in a fleshy goatee, swaying gently, almost hypnotically.

The creature wrapped its muscular tail around O'Shea before he could fire off a shot, squeezing and constricting him in its coils. The air filled with a crackle of arcing electricity and the man convulsed; his hair rose, stood on end, smoke billowed from his ears, and his eyes suddenly burst, spilling their boiling contents down his smoldering cheeks. The delicate filaments that covered the creature's tail danced and swayed, rejoicing in the act of murder.

Horror Show could watch no more; he gave the beast a red nose with his laser sight and pulled the trigger.

The animal collapsed onto an ever-growing mound of corpses; O'Shea's fuming carcass fell with it, contorted for a moment, then became lifeless.

Horror Show fired blindly into the onslaught. "*Fuckers!*"

A rainbow-colored beast glided through the smoke-filled air; large veiny fins stretched from its sides like wings. It landed in front of Carlo, knocked the shotgun from his hands and pushed him back against a nearby pew. His spine snapped just above his waist with a loud *pop* as the creature buried its head in his breast and tore a section of glistening flesh from his ribs.

At that moment, it was over. Horror Show knew it, and, more importantly, the animals knew it. The lone hitman backed away toward the entrance, firing in all directions. He'd always sensed, no matter how often he denied it publicly, that one day he would die a violent death. But it wasn't going to be today, not at the hands of these freaks. The rifle suddenly jammed, betraying him to the horde. He flung it into the

darkness and sprinted for the doors, the ammunition belts draped over his shoulder battering his chest.

A neon clown surfaced from the shadows, blocking his path, its gaping maw lined with crystal incisors. Horror Show pulled the Beretta from his waistband, emptied its clip into the creature as he ran. He was still firing shells into the animal's skull at point blank range, reducing it to ragged blooms of calcium and tissue, christening the oak doors with its gray matter.

Horror Show opened the doors, plucked the pin from a grenade, then threw his entire ammo belt into the void behind him.

The grenades will explode...

"*Get down,*" he screamed to Hays as he ran from the entrance.

They'll ignite the ammo from my belt, from Carlo's belt, from O'Shea's belt...

"*Get your asses on the ground,*" he cried to the others as he sprinted across the lawn, trying to reach minimum safe distance.

The blast's turbulent roar was deafening, a dinosaur howling into his ear. A hot gust of wind, strong and unrelenting, like the palm of the Devil's hand, pushed against his back and forced him to the ground. His chin made a dimple in the soft earth and his mouth filled with grass.

•••

Brahm dove.

Daylight emanated from every seam in the building, as if the church could no longer hold the sun as its prisoner. The entire structure splintered; a ball of flame shot skyward.

The doctor covered his head with his hands. His body stiffened, prepared for the falling debris.

The concussion shattered Barbara's windshield. Boards, some blackened, some still burning, rained down upon the scene. Bricks, chunks of concrete, twisted sculptures of wrought iron, and shards of stained glass soon followed. Silence descended with a shower of dust and glowing embers, and slowly, as if none wanted to be the first to move, they rose to their feet and brushed themselves off.

"Everyone all right?" Brahm's eyes gave each of his comrades a hurried exam. Larry, Carol, Alan, and Earl all nodded in turn; outside of a few cuts and bruises, each appeared to be in good health.

The old woman was still on the ground, her eyes fixed on the blazing rubble.

Brahm walked over to her, his hand outstretched. "Barbara?"

She continued eyeing the ruins, seemingly catatonic, then one side of her mouth twitched into a half-grin.

"Are you okay?" the doctor asked.

"A three-hundred-year-old lie...gone." She sounded relieved; at last, she took Brahm's hand and climbed to her feet.

Roger Hays staggered toward the blaze, his forehead opened by shrapnel and streaked in blood. Instead of being pleased by the destruction, he looked pissed. When the man who ran from the church tottered up to stand beside him, handgun still drawn, Roger punched him square in the face.

The gunman's head snapped back; he stiffened and raised the barrel of his 9mm so that it was flush with Roger's ripped temple. "Hit me again...bitch."

Hays stared at the muzzle, then raised his .45 to the gunman's crotch. "Get that thing out of my face or you'll *be* a bitch."

The gunman withdrew his weapon and took a step back. "What's your problem?"

Hays turned his gun on the flames. "I wanted his head!"

"Carlo was my best friend in the fuckin' world. I got the bastards back for the both of us. Havin' one as a trophy for your den won't make it any more dead."

"Dirty sons o' bitches." Larry; he took a step toward them, and Brahm suddenly remembered that Peggy had been in the building.

Oh shit! He's gonna get us all killed.

The physician grabbed onto Larry's arm, pulled him back toward the smoldering Cordoba.

Larry's glare burned into his skull. "Take your hands off me!"

"Let it go for now! You want to get your ass blown off?"

"I don't give a shit."

"Well I do."

Larry did manage to free himself, but he turned and took out his frustration on the Cordoba, kicking its tire repeatedly.

"Time to go, Roger," the gunman instructed.

"Wait," Hays protested. "We need to make sure they're all dead."

Frustrated, the gunman looked to distant bonfires in the heavens, then returned his gaze to the one blazing where the church once stood. "That'll burn all night. Nothin' coulda lived through that blast. Now are you comin' or not?"

"You work for me, asshole."

"If you wanna fire me, sir, go right ahead." The gunman climbed into his car and started the engine.

Roger Hays picked up a smoking board and threw it onto the pyre; it landed in a fountain of sparks. He then stormed over to the car, took one last look at their group, and his eyes rested on Carol.

"Be seeing you, Miyagi," he said, then disappeared into the Cadillac.

The car's bright eyes ignited and it headed back down the road to town. When it was lost to the darkness, Barbara walked over to Larry.

"Okay." She placed a hand on his shoulder to comfort him. "Peggy's still all right."

Neuhaus looked at her, his eyes dancing. "Are you sure?"

Barbara nodded.

"Bullshit," Earl spat. He was back on the ground, searching for his service pistol. He found it, stood, and stared into the blaze. "Fuckin' goon had it pegged. Anything in there is fried."

Barbara shook her head. "The temple's carved out of solid rock, and its deep under the church. Should be fine. Besides, there's nine hundred of us on this island. Couldn't all be in there. There's another way into Varuna's chamber underwater. Wouldn't be hard for Tellstrom, or one of the others, to swim in and get the creators' weapon."

"Underwater?" Carol gave Alan a pat on the back.

FORTY EIGHT

A grinding bellow echoed through the stone temple, and the entire chamber shook; the staircase belched a thick cloud of dust, and rocks and wooden planks caved in from above, sealing off the passageway to the church. The sheer amount of rubble made it obvious that the building was gone.

Karl shook his head in denial. How many of his followers had been up there — a hundred, maybe more? They couldn't all dead. It wasn't possible.

As the dust settled, Jason ran up to him, his voice filled with angry sarcasm, "Is this your glorious war? Did you plan on 'em fighting back? Or'd you just expect 'em to lay down 'n' die for us?"

In that moment, the Charodon standing before Tellstrom wasn't Jason; it was Ed DeParle, telling him this path was a road to insanity; it was Principal Monroe, telling him his mother would hate what he was doing; and, most of all, it was Karl's own father, cowardly and afraid. In their minds' eyes, none of them could see the world as it should be, the way *he* would make it. They had no sense of the future. They had no —

"You can't win."

Karl whirled around to find Peggy Hern standing behind him; his thin lips wrinkled back, revealing the glistening, jagged fangs of a wild animal.

"They'll come," she told him. "They'll find the entrance to that lagoon, and they'll come in here and kill us all."

When Peggy uttered the word "us," Karl snapped; he became the angry boy who'd just lost his mother, the boy who'd seen what was left when the propeller finished having its way with her. He lunged at Peggy, pushed her back against the stone altar, and his clawed hand pressed in on her larynx. "You fucking half-breed! No matter how hard you try, you'll never be *us*! At your core, you're still nothing but a human! You're still a murdering shit, no different from all the others!"

"Karl," Christine cried from some distant reality, "Stop it!"

The rabid fury evaporated from Tellstrom's tiger-striped façade; his voice was the whimper of a lost child. "She killed my mother."

"*She* did?" Christine asked, unnerved.

Karl trembled; he removed his hand from Peggy's throat and she fell to her knees, coughing and sucking in air, her lungs aching. Slowly, Tellstrom backed away and stared into the questioning eyes of his audience. The chamber was a vacuum, void of all sound, but his head echoed with the noise of a hundred silent screams. His blood ran thickly to his brain as he fought to regain some semblance of control.

I almost threw it all away, he realized. *I almost pissed all over it.*

His roaming eyes found the gods' weapon on his own talon and a smile returned to his lips like the sun from an eclipse.

"Nothing's changed," he announced, more to himself than his followers.

Karl stepped down from the altar and the crowd cleared him a path to the lagoon. On the way, he called out several members of the gathering, commanded them to join him. They did as he asked, but there was more than a hint of trepidation in their steps. When they reached the water's edge, Tellstrom turned and addressed the whispering masses.

"Forgive my outburst," he told them. "I was...I was *outraged* by this new attack from the Landers, as you all must be. Do not mourn the building above. It was built for the humans, for *their* society, not ours. So I say, let the humans have their church back. *This* is our temple."

The correct buttons pressed, the crowd who doubted Karl now cheered him on.

Tellstrom raised his hands to silence them. "As for our fallen brothers and sisters...they will not be forgotten, and we will make sure that they did not die in vain. I tell you now that I will not return until the humans are gone from Colonial Bay, and we are all free."

They cheered all the louder.

Stay focused, he told himself. *Don't lose it now, not when you're so close.* He bared his teeth in an uneasy smile, then spun toward the lagoon.

•••

Still shaking, Peggy grabbed the altar for support and rose to her clawed feet. "He's fucking nuts!"

"You don't know what he's been through," Christine told her, then added, "He's a great leader."

"You saw the way he acted just now." Peggy rubbed her throat, watching as Tellstrom and his handpicked crew disappeared beneath the waters of the tidal pool. "You can't tell me he doesn't scare you."

Christine looked at her own webbed toes, her voice wavering. "I love him."

At that, Peggy turned her attention to the rubble of the stairs; she wondered where Larry was, and hoped he would stay out of harm's way.

FORTY NINE

Carol Miyagi climbed aboard the *Sea Wasp*; she found a duffel bag, unzipped it, and produced a one-piece chainmail suit — four hundred thousand individually welded stainless steel lengths. She stripped down to her underwear and slipped it on, her movements quick, her face serious.

Alan followed her aboard, but Larry and the others stayed at the edge of the dock.

"What are you doing?" Larry asked.

Carol fastened her suit. "I'm going to swim into the temple... bring out that weapon and your girlfriend."

Brahm blinked. "Those things could be down there."

"Probably." Carol jerked the chainmail hood over her head, then dragged a large trunk to the center of the boat. She looked to Alan. "Help me with the pod."

"No." He placed his hand on her shoulder to pull her aside. "I'll go."

Carol shook him off. "This anti-shark suit wasn't made for you."

"I don't need the suit. I'll strap on the pod and —"

Carol grabbed him by the sides of his head, her voice gentle but firm. "*Domo*, but I'm the more experienced diver. I have to do this. You know I do. Help me?"

Alan sighed heavily, then moved to the trunk, helping Carol hoist its contents: a bee-striped plastic bubble with several wires and canvas belts dangling from it.

Earl pointed at the device as Carol strapped it to her back. "What the hell is that?"

"A shark pod."

"A what?"

Carol grabbed one of the hanging wires, attached an electrode to her ankle. "It emits an electrical field in a twenty foot radius around a diver, in this case me, and frightens away sharks. We knew Roger's son was attacked. We wanted to be protected in case we had to make a dive in these waters."

"Ron and Valerie Taylor field tested it," Alan assured them, then, seeing that the names meant nothing, he elaborated, "They're the Australians who filmed great white footage for the *Jaws* movies. Using this pod, they've been able to swim in open water alongside white sharks, without cages of any kind."

Miyagi held up a small joystick; like the electrode, it too was wired to the pod. "If a shark comes near me, I press this button and *sayonara*."

Earl's eyes screamed at her before his mouth even opened. "Wait just a damn minute! We're all smart people here. Let's come up with a better plan than this."

"No time. If Tellstrom didn't have the weapon before, he'll want it more than ever now that he's been attacked." Carol looked to Barbara. "The underwater passage is the only way in or out of the temple now, right?"

"Ayuh," DeParle nodded. "Unless we want to go dig a new one."

Carol returned her attention to the guardsman. "Not much of a choice."

"Use some fuckin' logic!" Earl rubbed his unshaven chin. "These aren't *really* sharks. They've been livin' in houses...houses wired with electricity. Your gadget might not do a damn bit o' good."

"I've considered that. I have." Carol snatched up her dive mask and strapped it to her face. "But the only great white ever to live in captivity would swim just fine in its lighted tank. Only when it reached a certain spot — a concentrated, localized electronic field behind the concrete — did it go crazy and butt its snout against the walls."

"I repeat, these freakazoids aren't sharks."

"That's why I have this." Carol shoved her hand back into the duffel bag, brought out a heavy metal pistol; the closed chamber had been replaced with an open cylinder of tiny aluminum arrows.

The guardsman was impressed. "Wanna tell me where you got that?"

"Alan had it specially made for us." Carol removed the weapon's twin from the canvas bag and tossed it to him. "It holds six steel-tipped darts. If the shark pod doesn't send them running, these will make them think twice."

Earl studied the modified spear gun. "Nice. But, like the old lady said, there's nine hundred of these cock-suckers. Even if they can't all fit in the temple, even if some got fried when the church went up, you're still gonna come up short in the ammo department."

"Then, for all our sakes, you'd better wish me luck." Carol stabbed her feet into black flippers, the name Cressi rising from the rubber in white-painted letters, then drove her hands into chainmail gloves, rapidly flexing her fingers. "Barbara, I need you to lead the way."

When Miyagi glanced up, she froze.

The old woman's flesh moved in ways that should have been impossible; her gray hair receded, and her skin, wrinkled with a roadmap of lived years, smoothed itself into a thin transparency. Aged limbs lengthened, elderly hands morphing into webbed talons. When Barbara stripped off her dress, her sagging buttocks wove into a long, paddle-like tail. Pale blue eyes were devoured by black holes, her spine rose up to form a ribbed sail of dorsal fin; and, when Barbara opened her mouth toward the moon, Carol saw crystalline needles thrust from her gums.

Brahm saw it too; Carol watched the denial in his eyes try to find a voice, but words eluded him.

Earl did manage to speak, his tone uncharacteristically meek, "Great God almighty."

Barbara stepped down into the *Sea Wasp*. "Stay close and we'll be fine." Her large, black eyes fell to the joystick in Carol's hands. "Just not *too* close."

"Oh..." Miyagi broke free of her trance and nodded. "Sure."

Carol followed Barbara toward the speedboat's railing, and Alan rubbed his hand across her metal hood. "You be careful," he told her.

"I will."

Carol equalized her mask, shoved the rubber regulator between her lips, and breathed deeply. She gazed down upon the surface of the water, her hands wrapped tightly around the butt of her dart gun and the pod's control.

Here we go.

Miyagi gave Barbara a nod and they leapt over the railing together, splashing into the darkness below.

•••

"Even after seeing it, I still can't believe it's real." Earl tossed the second spear pistol to Alan and backed away from the edge of the dock.

"I told you." Larry did a double take. "Where are you going?"

Preston pointed toward a ferry moored nearby. "I'm gonna get the mainland cops up in here. I saw three gangsters with more guns than *The Terminator* go into that church, but only one bastard got out alive. If the old lady's right, and those things are still alive, we'll need help."

Brahm was still speechless.

Larry asked the question for him. "What are you gonna tell 'em?"

As he walked down the pier, Earl gave a shrug. "Shit if I know. I'm playin' this by ear."

Alan did not watch the guardsman walk away. He sat in the *Sea Wasp* and studied the ripples Carol left on the surface of the water.

•••

Barbara's incandescent form lit the way through a barnacle-infested grove of wooden pillars; she soared through the water, her arms and legs kept tightly at her side, her flat tail acting as a rudder. Every so often, she gave a powerful stroke with her webbed hands, moving the water past her and advancing.

Carol was so fascinated by the old woman's movements that she didn't see the Charodon until the last second; it propelled up at her like a torpedo, its maw a gaping pit rimmed in jagged death.

FIFTY

The Historical Society's boiler room was humid.

Neil Shiva unbuttoned his collar, wiped the sweat from his neck, then kneaded a pliable block of C-4 plastic explosive. He marveled at Roger Hays; that a man could love a son enough to avenge his death, to let loose the power of the flame to punish this town, this den of demons... it was the most wonderful thing Neil had ever seen.

His dewy fingers slimed the incendiary clay.

Hays had given him very specific instructions: leave the hotels, level everything else; make Colonial Bay look like the gates of Hell itself. Glorious. This was a holy mission, a chance for Neil to use his considerable skills in a truly righteous pursuit.

Sweat gathered on the tip of Neil's nose, formed a dangling teardrop; he wiped it away with the back of his hand.

The arsonist shoved his fuse into the explosive gray blob he'd made. Satisfied, he climbed off the rickety crate he'd been using as a ladder, then gave the wiring a final glance. The copper boiler sat on concrete blocks; Shiva had attached an olive-colored claymore mine to one of them, wiring it to the same radio-controlled relay switch as the C-4. There were a dozen switches just like it spread throughout the town, each wired to countless mines and molded blocks of destructive Play-Doh. He'd even duct-taped claymores to propane tanks behind several shops, creating tremendous bombs.

The *entire town* was now a bomb.

Neil smiled. He picked up the remote detonator; at first glance, it appeared to be the radio control for a miniature racecar or model plane. A closer inspection, however, would show an ominous red plunger where a joystick should've been. The relays were set and sequenced to go off in rapid succession, like a fiery dominos display. Push the plunger down and: *click...KABOOM!*

The arsonist grabbed up his toolbag on the way to the stairs, then glanced at his watch; he had a ferry to catch.

Breaking glass.

Neil froze in his tracks.

A piece of the window I smashed getting in here. It was loose, but it didn't fall until now.

That sounded reasonable, but the window was at the back of the building. This noise came from the front.

Neil crept down a narrow service hallway, looked in on the exhibition floor.

Monsters. They were gathered around a shattered display case, raking glass from an item of interest. One of the creatures had a hand made of gold; it pulled a white cloth from the smashed display and unfurled it. Centered on the cloth was a huge, red symbol: a three-pointed pitchfork. *Hays was right! These* are *demons, monsters sent from Hell!*

Neil's arms went limp and the toolbag slipped off his shoulder; it fell to the floor with the clatter of metal striking metal. He jumped at the sound.

So did the monsters.

The gold-handed animal pointed at Neil. "Kill him!"

Terrified, the arsonist ran back down the hallway; he reached the back room, leapt through the same broken window he'd used to enter, and struck the ground hard with his shoulder. Neil heard a pop and felt the bone give from the force of the impact. He cried out against the pain, then stumbled to his feet and ran again.

He still held the detonator, held it so tightly that his fist was numb.

Behind him, the demons broke free. Neil glanced back across his screaming shoulder and saw them charging with incredible velocity. In a moment, they would be on top of him.

Shiva looked at the transmitter in his grasp and pressed the red plunger.

FIFTY ONE

Carol Miyagi pressed the button on the shark pod's joystick, switched on the electronic field.

The beast's head jerked back as if someone had tugged on its reigns; it thrashed its pointed snout about in the water, then kicked with its powerful hind legs and swam off into the black nothingness, gone as quickly as it had appeared.

Miyagi lifted her thumb off the button; she swam faster now, concerned that she was churning too much water, creating vibrations that the animals would sense and descend upon, but she didn't know what else to do. Barbara could move much faster than she.

Another shadow sped toward her, from the opposite direction as its predecessor, its skull the unmistakable flattened "T" of a hammerhead. These chimeras had more in common with large crocodiles or marine iguanas than sharks; they swam with their arms at their sides, their legs trailing, muscular tails stirring the water to propel them forward.

Once again, Carol hit the button, and, once again, the creature veered off.

She floated there a moment, scanned the limited visibility around her, looking for signs that they were exhibiting a typical feeding pattern. Sharks circle. Always tightening, always watching. Then, one will suddenly turn toward its prey, shoot through the water like a bullet, eyes covered in a protective shield of flesh, teeth exposed, mouth open in a deadly yawn.

Carol froze.

They gathered in the distance, didn't circle, didn't move at all, just hovered there, watching her, planning.

Her body tensed.

What are you up to?

It came at her from below, a gaping mouth filled with steak knives, its body distended so that she could see right through its gills. Before she could even hit the button on the shark pod's joystick, the Charodon had her arm in its claws. She screamed into her regulator, brought her spear pistol up to its soulless eye; a metal shaft shot through the orb, drove deep into her attacker's skull, and a dark cloud of blood exploded into the water. The creature released Carol and tried to pull the arrow from its own eyesocket.

She didn't wait to see if it was successful.

They'd been toying with her, trying to find a vulnerability they could exploit. Now, Carol could hear them snarl into the water, could feel them plow through the depths toward her fleeing form, but she didn't dare look back. Her mouth was clamped so tightly around the mouthpiece, sucking in deep gasps from the regulator, that she thought she might actually bite through the rubber. With a single kick of her flipper blades, the archeologist propelled herself into the shadow of the pier.

She'd lost sight of Barbara.

She was alone in a forest of overgrown stilts.

Carol swam behind one of the encrusted poles, pressed her back against it, and flattened the button on her joystick. She cowered there a moment in the gloom, afraid to move, then she peered around the side of the column. They were gone. The electronic field had scattered them, sent them plunging back into the shadows.

Wait...behind that pole on the right.

Her eyes strained to find detail in this bruise-colored world. Then she saw it again: a blotch at the edge of a shadowy pillar, there and gone. Something peeked, snuck a look at her as she snuck a look at it. At the edge of her mask, another pole, another blotch appeared and disappeared. There, in the distance, a third dark mirror of her own curiosity, but free of her tell-tail regulator bubbles.

They were hiding, trying to make her think that they'd left, that she was free to continue her dive.

Carol felt the blood rush up her neck, felt the heart that pumped it jump wildly in her chest, begging her to bolt. She closed her eyes and pressed herself against the pole, wanting to become part of it. She was breathing too fast, but she couldn't help herself.

Earl had been right. These weren't sharks. By her own theory, they weren't even natural beings, but rather the end result of splicing and tinkering, experiments guided by extraterrestrial minds she could never hope to understand.

When Miyagi opened her eyes, she saw movement on the pillar above. One of the Kraken had been roosting there, camouflaged, its coloring, and the bumps it raised on its skin, designed to blend in with the barnacles and algae. The creature let go of the pole, fell toward her like a skydiver leaping from a plane, its arms and legs outstretched, its distorted roar echoing through the water.

Carol raised the spear pistol too late.

It fell upon her. Its facial tentacles wrapped around her head, and she heard a grating sound, like finishing nails being raked across her chainmail hood. These tentacles were lined in jagged fangs, like the rasping teeth of a hundred lampreys; they would grate and shred a victim's flesh, moving like cilia to push morsels toward the beak that formed its mouth. Now the only thing that prevented Carol's scalp from becoming a scratching post was the metal casing of her suit, which suddenly seemed far too thin.

Her thumb buried the red button in the shark pod's joystick, but it had no effect. The animal was too close, or the electrical field did nothing to this clan whatsoever.

She shook back and forth, trying to throw her captor, her facemask filled with the Kraken's gnashing beak. Then, she felt a change in the water; something else moved in.

Another creature.

The Kraken's tentacles were pulled from her head and its beak retreated from her facemask, lost in a thick cloud. Claws went limp, released her, and a strong kick pushed Carol clear of the blood fog.

Barbara; she'd clawed out the Kraken's throat.

Teeth erupted from the billowing gore. Carol raised her spear pistol, fired one of her five remaining arrows. It pierced the soft tissue at the roof of the Charodon's mouth and drove deep into its brain. The creature belched a torrent of bubbles and blood, then drifted limply into the shadows.

Carol pressed the button on her joystick again. The rest of the animals reached the field's perimeter and howled, like dogs attempting to breach their invisible fence. They backed away, floated in eddies of silt that drifted between the columns, angered that they could not reach their prey.

Carol glanced over to Barbara, hoping the field had not harmed her.

The woman held the Kraken's body as if mourning a son. Miyagi holstered her spear pistol and tapped her on the shoulder, motioning in the direction they'd been swimming before the attack. Barbara nodded and released her kill; she took the archeologist's hand so they wouldn't become separated again, and, together, they swam toward a wall of rock.

Carol stole a quick glance over her shoulder, but the Charodon were nowhere to be seen; either they'd abandoned their chase, or they were just beyond her visual range.

The women entered a cavern, followed its twists and turns until Carol saw candlelight. At least, she hoped it was candlelight. For all she knew, the flickering illumination could be burning debris.

When Miyagi's face broke through the water, her eyes grew wide with shock. The chamber was intact, but filled with countless Atlantean descendants. None of them seemed to have noticed their arrival.

"You all right," Barbara rasped softly.

Carol nodded and yanked the regulator from her mouth. Her jaw ached from biting down on the rubber. "Thank you."

DeParle didn't respond to her gratitude, instead she looked into the temple; her eyes seemed to be focused on the huge carving of Varuna, her face glowing with joyous recognition.

Carol followed the old woman's gaze, saw another luminous being standing at the base of the idol. "You know her?"

"She's my daughter."

"Your daughter?"

Barbara stiffened, sure of her purpose. "Let's go."

"Go where?" Carol drew her spear pistol and surveyed the crowd. "It looks like we're interrupting a town meeting."

"You wanna end this, don't you?"

"Of course, but —"

"Then I gotta talk to 'em."

Miyagi scratched her forehead with her chainmail glove. "What makes you think they'll listen to you?"

"They did once." DeParle climbed from the pool. "I have to believe they haven't forgot everything I taught 'em."

Barbara grabbed Carol by the hand and pulled her into the gathering of monstrosities. The surprised creatures backed away, cleared a path for them. Some in the crowd were the squid-like Kraken, others were shark-based creatures, the Charodon, still others were amalgams of various forms of sea life, and Carol could not tell which clan they belonged to. The beings closed in around the women as they made their way to the altar, their icy stares silently threatening.

"It's the teacher!" someone shouted from the horde.

At that, the menagerie fell to its knees. Barbara's daughter remained standing, however; she stood at the foot of the statue, stared hard at them as they approached.

"You're not welcome here, Mother," she proclaimed.

"This is Varuna's holy temple, Chrissy. *All* are welcome."

Christine pointed to Miyagi's spear pistol. "And does that include armed Landers?"

"Put that thing away," Barbara urged.

Carol shook her head. "How do I know they won't kill me as soon as I do?"

"I won't let them. Besides, you only got four arrows left. How far you think that'll getcha?"

Miyagi looked back. The creatures closed off their path of retreat, perhaps a hundred standing between them and the lagoon. With a resigned sigh, Carol holstered her spear gun.

FIFTY TWO

"Where's Neil?" Horror Show asked. He looked out his windshield, watched the lights of Colonial Bay from the ferry's deck; one of his hands sat firmly on the steering wheel, the other massaged the sliver of tombstone.

He didn't believe in telepathy or a "sixth sense." People who said they were psychic just knew how to use their five existing senses to their fullest. From the look of a situation, the smell of it, perhaps even the feel of the air, you could divine truths hidden to those less aware. And, at that moment, Horror Show's senses were feeding him some very sinister signals.

Something dark was about to happen.

"He'll be here," Hays answered, unconcerned.

The ferry blew its air horn, signaling its intent to raise anchor and leave dock.

Horror Show turned away from the shore, wondering how many tourists had come and gone from this island over the years, never knowing it was run by monsters. "Well, if he doesn't get his ass on this boat in about ten seconds, he'll be a resident."

Hays sighed. "I'm sure Shiva —"

A barber-pole striped creature leapt onto the Cadillac's hood, a ruffled dragon, still dripping from its bath in the harbor; it stared through the windshield at them, murder in its radiant, mirror-like eyes.

Horror Show drew his 9mm and fired through the glass, but the beast ducked with lightning speed. Unharmed, it thrust a claw through the cracked windshield, wrapped its talons around his brawny wrist.

Roger drew his .45 and emptied the chamber. The rounds blew the creature's cranium apart; it fell onto the hood, aspirating its own fluids.

Screams emanated from elsewhere on the ferry.

Horror Show freed himself from the dead heap's grip and looked at his wrist. He wasn't bleeding. He shoved a fresh clip into his Beretta, then hurriedly climbed from the car.

"Where are you going?" Roger asked.

"To finish the job. Get your ass out here an' help." The hitman watched Roger step from the car and move to the ferry's railing, looking out at Colonial Bay as if he expected to see something. "What the fuck are you lookin' for?"

The next moment brought his answer.

"America's Home By the Sea" erupted in a series of thunderous detonations, like a string of fireworks, turning the storefronts into balls of flame. Horror Show shielded his face with his hands, but not Roger. Hays just stood there, trenchcoat billowing in the concussion breeze like a Halloween cape, his face twisted into a stupid expression of rapture.

It was as if the man had just climaxed.

•••

Earl hurried to his newly customized Harley-Davidson and threw his leg over the seat. He stabbed the key into the waiting ignition, turned it quickly and revved the motor. Smoke coughed from the steel exhaust pipes as the engine roared to life, the frame vibrating madly between his legs. He lifted his foot from the cobblestone street, gave the Harley some gas, and it roared off toward the last ferryboat.

Shape-shifting monsters. He was still trying to wrap his mind around it. Until Earl saw the old woman transform with his own eyes, he could still hold onto the belief that Roger Hays was somehow behind these deaths at sea. He'd been trained to deal with situations involving men, but this...this was beyond the scope of his experience.

Earl heard the blast of the ferryboat's air horn over the thunder of his motorcycle.

It's pulling out.

At that moment, the whole world seemed to explode around him; an entire strip of shops, reduced to fiery splinters.

Jesus Christ!

Earl ducked and his Harley swerved, but he managed to keep it upright. The ferry left dock. There was a moment of indecision, then a nearby explosion convinced Earl to give the motorcycle more gas.

The edge of the pier grew closer and closer. Earl glanced at his gages, saw the RPMs climb, and hoped it would be enough. His front wheel hit the loading ramp; he leaned back and his Harley launched at the departing shuttle. His grip slipped from the handlebars, and the motorcycle sailed through the air without him.

Earl landed on the roof of a parked Oldsmobile.

He opened his eyes and coughed. His hands moved immediately to the back of his head, rubbing it briskly as he tried to sit up. He craned his neck, expecting pain, feeling none, and searched for Colonial Bay's shore. Instead, his eyes focused on a blue Cadillac with New York plates.

Hays?

He moved without thinking, his equilibrium still shaky, he drew his gun and made his way to the Cadillac as fast as his unsteady gait would permit. Nerves flared, ignited spots in his eyes like warning lights, chastising him for the quickness of his actions.

Earl saw Roger perched on the barge's railing, watching Colonial Bay burn; he leapt at him, pulled him back against the Cadillac, and pressed his service pistol to the man's cheek. "Don't you fuckin' move, Hays!"

"Do you know who I am?" Roger growled.

"I said your name, didn't I?"

"Let him go."

Earl looked up and saw a 9mm pointed at him across the roof of the car.

"Let him go," Horror Show repeated roughly.

"I'm an officer of the United States Coast Guard."

"We just blew up a city. Let him go, boy, or I'll blow your black ass clean off."

"Don't call me 'boy!'" Earl pressed his gun harder against Hays' cheek. "And you can kiss my black ass when I throw yours in a fuckin' cell."

The shrill echo of a dying scream made all of them jump.

Horror Show withdrew his Berretta and shoved it into the

waistband of his slacks. He reached into the Cadillac, popped the trunk, then moved to what was left of his war chest.

Earl lowered his own weapon, slowly backed away from Roger and scanned the surroundings, not liking what he saw. Shadows between parked cars came to life. Earl could actually see the darkness shift upon itself as alien profiles moved through the labyrinth of steel and rust, climbed over automobiles with the formidable names of Jaguar, Ram, Firebird, and, ironically, Tiburon. He could hear claws scratch metal, and his mind's eye showed him slime-lubricated tongues licking shadowy lips. The creak and moan of the boat in the surf was drowned by a cacophony of car alarms, each playing its own deafening composition. Earl's feet led him back to the weapons trove. "You really got these mothers pissed."

In the distance, a man opened his car door and turned to run. A pink and purple blob slit his throat, using the fan of its tailfin as a swinging pendulum blade. The motion threw the stranger backward, fountaining blood as he hit the deck.

Horror Show saw none of this; he worked feverishly in the confines of the truck, assembling something.

Earl backed up another step, saw six barrels bundled together in a rounded metal cylinder, and his mouth fell open. He'd seen something like it mounted to the side of Viet Nam-era hueys.

Where the hell did he get this shit?

Horror Show hefted the G.E. Mini-gun from the trunk and a string of chain-ammo trailed from its side. The hitman slung the ammo over his shoulder, then nodded at Earl's service pistol. "Grab a real fuckin' gun."

Earl surveyed the inside of the trunk; his eyes and hands quickly found an M-16. It felt comforting, reminding him of the controlled environment of the base's firing range. What he wouldn't give to be there now.

Earl surveyed his battleground, thinking of his father.

Is this what it was like at the end, Dad?

Earl shook it off; he needed his wits about him, and he hoped this little battle would have a much happier outcome than his father's.

Horror Show stepped away from the trunk and laid down an uninterrupted field of gunfire, destroying everything non-human, moving or otherwise. Advancing creatures exploded into gore. Car windows shattered. Alarms died. Jets of steam and flame erupted into the air to both illuminate and obscure their view of the horde. The deck now resembled a traffic jam in Pandemonium; the air filled with screams, wails, and the smell of death and burning.

Earl shivered.

Is this how it was, Dad?

An iridescent green mass leapt from the roof of a nearby Durango, stood between Preston and Hays; its face and body were trimmed in spiny frills and squirming tentacles. The creature's skin expanded in patches, as if it were inflating a multitude of balloons or bladders to appear more muscular.

Earl's pulled his trigger; bullets raked the air, filling the beast with hot shells. It screeched, instinctively releasing its dark chemicals in a burning rain.

Earl was out of range.

Roger Hays wasn't.

The caustic spray caught the man square in the face, ate away his cheeks, nose, and forehead. Hays covered his dissolving features with his hands and smoke poured through the cracks between his fingers; he fell screaming over the shuttle's railing, disappeared into the churning wake.

The squid-thing also fell, its swollen body deflating as it died.

Earl turned away and saw that strange eyes surrounded him.

FIFTY THREE

Burning embers fell like the Devil's rain.

Neil staggered to his feet, his eyes drinking in the view that was once Colonial Bay — a vast inferno of his making, the summit of his accomplishments. His quivering lips curled into a proud smile, and joyous tears cleared tracks in the grime on his cheeks. It was the most incredible sight he'd ever seen.

Several of the creatures lay dead at his feet, impaled by flying debris. A pane of flying glass had decapitated one nasty-looking animal; its head was now an island in a sea of its own blood, its tongue dangling out between long, needle-like teeth. The others slowly rose to their feet, cut and bruised, but still living.

Their leader looked at Neil, its eyes burning with reflected firelight. "What have you done?"

Neil stiffened; he puffed out his chest in a display of pride. "I've sent you demons back to hell!"

The creature raised its gold-jacketed hand; the orb glowed brightly, became a small sun at the end of its arm. "You're the only demon here!"

Neil Shiva knew he was dead; he felt the explosion ignite within him, as if his veins were filled with kerosene and he'd just swallowed a lit match. He closed his eyes as every hydrogen molecule in his body released its energy in one intense burst.

I am fire!

And then his mind burned.

Neil exploded, an intense ball of flame that faded as quickly as it appeared, leaving a scorch mark on the asphalt and the stench of ozone in the air.

•••

Karl lowered the creators' weapon; he moved to the blackened residue, scratched at it with his clawed foot.

Every human I see will become a skid mark.

He smiled, liking the way that sounded.

"Tellstrom!"

At the call of his name, Karl's head jerked up. Through a wavy veil of heat, he saw a stranger walk from the flames, a man, a Lander. The fool strutted toward Karl as if to declare a challenge.

FIFTY FOUR

Every eye in the crowd fixed on Carol, and, for an instant, she felt as if she might fold beneath the weight of their stares. In their faces, she saw quiet restraint, but those eyes betrayed sanguine dreams of ripping and tearing at her flesh.

Her suit had been designed to block tooth penetration and spread bite pressure across her entire body. It would be strong enough to protect her from some of these beasts, but others might have powerful, crushing jaws that would shatter her bones even through the chainmail. The shark-pod was dry-docked. The spear gun would not defend her long. Her book of magic tricks had reached its final page, and she had no time to scribe another.

Barbara glanced at the altar. A glowing she-creature sat with her tail wrapped around her legs; she was not a member of this mob, in fact, she looked quite relieved to see them.

Peggy?

Not that she could do anything to help them. They were hopelessly outnumbered, their lives now firmly in Barbara's shaking hands.

The old woman locked eyes with her daughter. "This is over, Chrissy."

"No, mother," Christine countered, a coy bloodthirst dancing in her raven eyes. "The fun's just getting started."

"Slaughtering innocent people is your idea o' fun? I raised you better than that. 'Least, I thought I did."

"I don't need to justify any of this to you." Christine shifted her gaze to Carol. "Who's your puppy?"

Miyagi cocked her head, but said nothing; she merely continued to watch Christine's translucent face.

"This is my friend." Surprised objections erupted from the crowd, but Barbara continued to speak and the noise from the audience slowly yielded to her words. "We're all the creators' children. The Callisto's proof o' this."

Christine shook her head. "The Callisto's an abomination! We're the gods' chosen people. The humans don't even believe in the creators anymore. They've denied them, *forgotten* them." She glared down at Miyagi. "Haven't you?"

"Your gods were pirates," Carol replied. Barbara started to protest, but Miyagi cut her off with a glance. "They abandoned you because you weren't profitable for them anymore. This...this *thing*," she indicated the sculpture of Varuna, "left you and moved on to bigger and better treasures."

"You blasphemous bitch!" Christine spat.

Barbara stepped in. "The fact that a Callisto can happen at all proves that we all spring from the same flesh and blood."

"Have you ever tasted human flesh, Mother?"

Barbara looked away.

"It's sweeter than lobster." The tone her daughter was using, it was breathy, *seductive*. "And the blood...the blood is so *hot*."

Carol watched as the old woman closed her eyes and clenched her jaw. Was that sweat beading on her forehead, or was she still wet from their swim? When Carol saw Barbara's hands curl into fists, however, she knew.

Poseidon's children must have sensed her swelling fear. They began to whisper. Some even applauded. Instinctively, Carol's hand went to the butt of her spear pistol, gripped it tightly as she searched the grotto for any possible escape route.

A webbed hand reached out to blanket her white knuckles, Barbara's hand — soft, cool, and comforting. The old woman gave a reassuring squeeze and Miyagi reluctantly released her grip on the weapon.

Barbara's head snapped up. "Fighting humans, *killing* humans, is as wrong as killing another clan. Can't you see that, Chrissy?"

"Humans have murdered us for centuries!"

"And what will spilling more human blood do for us now?"

"'If it will feed nothing else, it will feed my revenge,'" Christine told her mother, her tone as dark and cold as the ocean depths. "'If you prick us, do we not bleed? If you poison us, do we not die? And if you wrong us, shall we not *revenge*?'"

Barbara shook her head. "You're missing the point o' that particular play, child. When he gets a chance to take his pound of flesh, Shylock refuses."

Christine scowled. "We don't have any choice in this."

"No, Chrissy, you've got —" Barbara took a few steps toward her daughter, then came to an abrupt halt. Her nostrils flared, sampling the damp air. There was a look of utter surprise on her gleaming face. Carol watched as the old woman's eyes fell to Christine's abdomen and remained there. "You're..."

Christine's hand rushed up to cover her navel; she appeared to blush, as if embarrassed or ashamed, but it was only for an instant. Beneath her skin, glowing ribbons flared and the girl struck a defiant pose. Her tail stiffened and her black eyes narrowed to slits. "You came here to scold your little girl, didn't you? Well, I'm not your little girl anymore, Mother. I'm a woman now, a woman with her own life and her own ideas. I decide what's right for me, for my family...not you or any of the elders...*I* decide."

Barbara nodded, then blinked. "We all have to make our own choices in this life," she said at last. "We try to do what we think is right, what's best for everyone. But sometimes...sometimes we're too weak to do what's right. We do what everyone else *thinks* is right, or what's always been done before. We don't stop and think what our decisions might do to others...to the ones we love."

As she spoke, Barbara's hand moved to the small of her back, to the trident tattooed just above the stalk of her own tail.

"Fighting a war we can't win's not the right decision. And it's not the decision a grown woman, a *mother* would make. Do you love this child?"

"Of course I do."

Barbara's eyes rose to meet her daughter's cold glare. "One day, he or she is gonna look at you the way you're looking at me right now."

"My daughter will look at me, will look at her father, and know that we did everything to make certain she would never be ashamed of who she was." Then, the boldness drained from Christine's stance and the defiance washed from her face; after too long a silence, she said, "You want us to keep pretending to be something we're not. I can't live like that anymore, and I won't damn my child to that prison either."

Barbara looked at her daughter's belly, at her grandchild within. "Colonial Bay was created to keep us safe, to keep the hunters away and allow us to live peacefully...in secret. Thanks to Karl, that peace is gone. For the first time in centuries, humans have come to our shores not to walk through our shops, or to stay at our inns, but to hunt us, to *kill* us again."

Christine thought for a moment, then shook her head abruptly. "Just because we're different from the Landers doesn't give them the right to —"

Carol broke in, "My father's entire family died in a Japanese internment camp during World War II."

She mounted the stairs. The Charodon to her right snarled, stepped in like a guard dog perceiving a threat to its master.

Christine gestured for him to stand down.

He did so without hesitation.

Miyagi continued, "They died for no other reason than the fact that they were different. They were *Americans*, had been since they were born, but that's not what people saw. They saw...they saw the enemy."

"*Why?*"

Barbara answered, "Pearl Harbor, Chrissy."

Carol flinched at the words. Her voice began to tremble, but not from fear. She hoped they did not mistake it for fear. "My father...he... he could never get close to anyone again after that camp. He may have survived it, but his spirit died there."

"I'm sorry," Barbara said.

Miyagi nodded but did not take her eyes off Christine. "Karl might be ready to die, *you* might be ready to die, but are you ready to kill your child? Are you ready to deprive it of its dignity?"

"I was in Black Harbor, Chrissy," Barbara told her. "If someone walked into my house and pointed a gun at you, I'd rip their throat out, I don't care how righteous their cause. Karl sent The Enforcers to slaughter people who didn't even know we existed, people who'd probably find us fascinating. Varuna only knows why he wants The Wrath. Do you really think they'll just go away and let us be after this?"

For a moment, they stared at one another, then Christine turned away; she looked at the floor, at Varuna's face high above her, and then her eyes finally locked with Miyagi's. With all the defiance left in her, she said, "*Your* family should've fought back. They shouldn't have let the other humans lock them away. If they had they'd —"

"Have you done the math?" Carol asked. "Have you really thought this rebellion through? Three thugs managed to destroy the town church and everyone Karl sent there. Imagine what will happen when what's left of your little army goes up against the millions on the mainland. No matter how hard you fight, or how just your passions, it's a battle you won't win."

An uneasy quiet descended on the temple.

After a moment, Peggy found her voice, "She's right, Christine."

"I don't need *your* opinion."

"I thought you said you had your own ideas?" Peggy stood and her paddle-like tail uncoiled. "Sounds like you only have *his*."

Christine's eyes bore into Peggy and a low growl rose from her throat; she took a step forward and drew back her talon, her claws clicking. "Do you know how easy it would be for me to kill you right now?"

"Go ahead," Peggy dared. "Do something else that *he* wants you to do. Kill me and then go kill all the Landers until none are left alive. Do it and prove your mother right. Human and Poseidon, we *are* the same."

Christine closed her claw and lowered it to her own abdomen, caressing her belly and the life that grew within, then her eyes found Barbara once more. "You want us to run."

Carol could see questions churn in the shadowy mass behind Christine's eyes.

"We shouldn't have to run away and hide. Not again. Even if we did, how long before their civilization grows to a point where there's nowhere left to run?"

Barbara shrugged. "Hon, Colonial Bay's not home anymore. After today...it can't be."

Christine's face fell; she looked up and said, "Karl will never leave Colonial Bay."

The Charodon to her right moved closer, placed a reassuring hand on Christine's arm. "If he loved you, he'd go *wherever* you go."

Christine turned to him, her voice and face cracking beneath the strain. "Jason..." She looked as if she needed him, and he looked as if he'd never seen that before. "Does he?"

Jason put his hands on her shoulders. "Chrissy, he loves your tattoo."

Christine's shoulders quaked, and her tail went limp; she rested her head on Jason's wide, scaly chest and wept.

Barbara rushed them; she took her daughter's webbed claw in her own and smiled. Christine left Jason's side, threw her elongated arms around her mother, and nearly knocked the old woman down.

"We'll make things right," Barbara assured her. "We'll end this."

"No." Christine shook her head, tears of hopelessness still streaming down her transparent cheeks. "Karl already has The Wrath."

Barbara's eyes widened, her mind showing her what a lunatic might do with such power. "Varuna help us. How long ago did he leave?"

"Long enough." Christine looked down at her webbed toes. "If I hadn't helped him —"

Barbara gently stroked Christine's dorsal fringe. "I pushed you to him with that damned ceremony."

"It wasn't just that."

"I know. Pardon me for saying this, but you need to get past it. Right now, there's something I need you to do for me, for all of us."

Christine wiped away the last of her tears. "Name it."

Barbara held Christine's chin, lifted it up. "The mark and your blood give you power, but respect...that has to be earned. And you can start right now." She looked out at the crowd. "I think they're waitin' for some direction."

"But, mother...aren't you — ?"

The old woman shook her head.

Christine trembled. "But...I can't —"

"You've always been able to handle me. Yes, you can."

With more than a little apprehension, Christine stepped

away from her mother; every eye in the chamber focused on her with anticipation as she spoke, "Children of Poseidon, I...I'm sorry. We can't...we *won't* leave any more wives without husbands, children without parents." She didn't have Karl's gift for speechmaking, but they were listening. "There can't be a war."

The masses roared with conflicting responses.

Jason moved once more to Christine's side; he took her talon in his own and his mouth formed an odd, non-threatening grin.

Christine squeezed his hand, drew strength from it; she hardened and tried to give her words authority. "Shut up and listen to me!"

Her audience slowly fell silent.

Christine waited thirty more seconds before speaking; she looked into as many faces as she could in that time, and she didn't blink. "We're leaving Colonial Bay."

"No!" a distant voice roared back at her.

"We're not cowards!" another snarled.

Christine shouted at the crowd, "Does anyone else have the mark of Poseidon on their back? Raise your goddamn hand now and you can take over!"

Her anger silenced them.

"Shut the hell up and listen to what I have to say!" Fresh tears formed in Christine's eyes. "This is my home. I wanted to follow Karl as badly as you did, but he's so full of hate that he can't see things. These women are right. Right now, because of what he's done, what he's *doing*... the only way to actually be free, to be who and what we are, is to leave Colonial Bay."

A murmur ran through the audience, but no one yelled out their dissent.

"Okay. Spread the word," Christine ordered. "We'll meet on the reef. Take what you can carry."

"Where will we go?" The voice came from a beautiful, golden creature in the front row.

Christine thought for a moment, then simply stated, "I'll find a place where the Landers never go." She ran her gaze across their shocked faces; they stood frozen before her, as if waiting for an order to move. She gave it, "Go on."

The clansmen looked at one another, still astonished at the turn of events they'd just witnessed; slowly, they moved toward the temple's watery exit.

With cautious steps, Peggy made her way to Barbara. "Did Larry leave?"

The old woman shook her head. "He's waiting for you."

Carol could see the surge of excitement well up within Peggy; the woman knew that she would soon be back in her lover's arms. Miyagi thought of Alan and felt the same way. It felt good.

The archeologist offered Barbara a relieved glance, then bowed slightly to demonstrate her respect. Before she could apologize for doubting the old woman, Colonial Bay's fiery demise rocked the temple.

FIFTY FIVE

To Larry, it appeared that Colonial Bay died in a single blast, but that wasn't true. It took a series of powerful detonations, all timed and choreographed like an exquisite ballet; the far side of town, by the remains of the church, had been first to go, followed by the main strip. The force of each blast shook the Sea Mist Inn's façade. Glass blew inward. Doors flew open, pushed by a gust of burning wind, the same gust that pressed Larry against the side of his rented Grand Am and sent Brahm and Alan to the pavement. The roar of the cataclysm died, replaced by human screams from within the hotel, and high-pitched whalesong from creatures lost to the flames.

They'd come back to finish packing their things, prepared to leave the island as soon as Carol and Peggy returned. As he staggered to his feet, Larry was grateful for that decision. The docks were now ablaze.

While the rest of the street was now fully engulfed, the hotel had remained virtually unscathed; other guests emerged, coughing and conversing in a stunned manner.

"Terrorists," Brahm coughed as he rose from the asphalt.

Prior to September 11th, Larry would've thought such a feat impossible, a Hollywood gimmick only Michael Bay would employ. Now, however, it was easy to believe. In fact, Larry often had nightmares about just such a scenario.

Alan shook his head. "It's that bastard Hays. He blew up a whole freakin' town."

As Larry scanned the devastation, he saw shadowy forms, distorted by heat and flame; he shielded his eyes with his hand, tried to make out some detail. One was unmistakably human, the rest mutant contours, and then Larry saw an object that glowed brighter than the surrounding blaze.

"The weapon."

Alan heard him. "What?"

"Right over there." Larry pointed to the shadow puppet theater in the distance. "There's a whole group of creatures. One has the weapon on his hand."

The archeologist squinted, tried to share Larry's vision. "How do you know?"

It was a good question. After all, Larry hadn't seen a picture, and Barbara never really described it to them. Something inside, however, told him that was exactly what he saw, just as it told him Karl Tellstrom was the one wielding it.

Larry took a step toward the flames.

Alan reached out and grabbed a handful of his shirt. "What are you doing?"

"I'm going in there."

"The hell you are!"

Larry glared at him. "What if it wasn't Hays? What if Tellstrom has the weapon and *this* is what it does?"

The archeologist's eyes skated across the blaze. These creatures could swim into the temple just as easily as Carol. If an alien weapon did exist, and, if they found it, God only knew what devastation it was capable of. And if these things were bent on the destruction of Man, it surely wouldn't stop with Colonial Bay. Alan gave voice to none of this, his look conveyed it all.

Brahm started to put his objections on record, then shook his head; he drew his flare gun, ready for action. "I can't believe we're doin' this."

The Sea Mist Inn's dry, wooden siding provided the perfect fuel for the advancing flames. Fire crawled up its walls as guests bolted, screaming shrilly. Without hesitation, the physician moved toward the stampede.

Wary of being trampled, Larry took a step back. "Doc, where the hell — ?"

"There might be injured people here. You two go on. I'll make sure everyone gets out and meet up with you if I can."

Brahm fought his way through the frightened crowd, moved diagonally toward the open door.

Larry watched the Inn swallow him, hoped it would not be the last time they would meet, then turned to Alan. "You ready?"

"How many ways can I say no?" Alan looked through the curtains of flame; still unable to see anything, he shook his head. "What's the plan? Run up to the wereshark and wrestle the doomsday weapon from his razor-sharp claws?"

Larry shrugged. "It doesn't sound so cool when you say it like that."

Alan snickered in spite of himself; he breathed deeply, his hand wrapped tightly around the handle of his spear pistol. "Let's go if we're going."

Together, they ran through the flames.

FIFTY SIX

Officer Eads yawned and looked at his watch. He and Bowker had been in the Photolab's video room for hours, watching grainy surveillance tapes of the various hallways and entrances to Black Harbor Medical Center. Anne King, their video technician, did her best to artificially light the darkened passages. The other guys liked to call her Miss Wizard. Eads just called her Anne.

Eads glanced at the stack of tapes yet to be viewed, then rubbed his eyes; he brought his coffee cup to his lips, upset that it was empty. "More coffee?"

Bowker nodded absently, absorbed by the black and white images on the monitor.

"Anne?"

"No, thanks." She didn't even look at him as she spoke, too enthralled by her equipment.

As Eads rose from his chair, something came into the camera's sights. A dark blob, no more than a blur really; it shot past the camera, in a hell of a hurry to get somewhere. "What was that?"

Bowker shook his head, amazed. "Can we slow that down? Clean it up?"

"I'll see what I can do," Anne told them. "You realize this is the crappiest tape you've ever brought me."

Eads smiled; he knew she loved the challenge. "Then your next two rentals are free."

Anne shook her head, her face lit by a spreading grin. She ran the footage through her computer. Enhanced photos weren't admissible as evidence in court, something to do with the fact that "pixels" were lost and then added back by the machine, creating a picture that wasn't a "true" image in the eyes of the law, but they were a better way for police to ID a suspect. Once caught, witnesses could then pull the perp from a lineup.

Lineups were almost always admissible.

When the computer finished tinkering, an enhanced image rolled by on the monitor: first, an empty section of floor, then a face; an inhuman, impossible face.

Bowker's eyes drank in the grainy horror. "Sweet Jesus."

"Can we get a printout of that?" Eads cocked his head and found that he'd lost Anne to the monster on the screen, its face reflected in her glasses, hiding her radiant eyes behind jagged teeth. "Anne?"

She snapped out of her paralysis. "Yeah?"

"Can we get a printout?"

Anne nodded.

Eads stared at the thing on the screen. It couldn't possibly be real. It was a man in a costume from the Halloween Outlet, a very detailed, very lifelike, but very fake costume. It had to be.

"Here she comes," Anne told them.

A mechanical whir, and the Kodak printer spit out a glossy. Anne took the photo, paused a moment to look into its black doll eyes, then gave it to Eads; her hand was clammy.

"You guys hear?"

They turned toward the doorway. Needleman, the office administrator; he'd been a beat cop until last year when he shot himself in the foot. Now, he sat behind a desk and walked with a limp.

"Hear what?" Bowker asked.

Needleman's voice was as pale as his face. "Colonial Bay's on fire."

"What...*the whole town?*"

"The whole town."

It was then that MacIsaac hurried by their door, trying to find the left armhole of his brown sheriff's jacket as he ran.

"Where's the fire, Chief?" Eads asked, then realized how stupid it sounded after Needleman's news.

MacIsaac finally found an opening and filled the sleeve with his arm. "The dock over on Shore Road called in some explosions on Colonial Bay."

"How bad?"

"You can see the glow from here."

"That's ten miles."

MacIsaac nodded, then his eyes found the image on the monitor. He froze. "Shit on me. What the fuck is that?"

Eads regarded him evenly for a moment before answering. "That, sir, is our fish-man."

FIFTY SEVEN

Black smoke clouded Brahm's vision of the Sea Mist Inn; he fought his way across the lobby, panic-blinded eyes paying him no mind.

"Everyone stay calm," Brahm yelled into the crowd, trying to slow this exodus, to keep someone from being trampled.

A creature smashed through the wall of flame and beveled glass on Brahm's left. Fully engulfed, it rolled toward the evacuating guests and seized a man's ankle in its burning talon. The man fell to his knees, screaming, his cries lost to the widespread hysteria.

Brahm fired his flare gun; a yellow streak collided with what should've been the animal's head, exploded it to cinders.

The tourist pulled his leg free of the dead thing's grasp; he fell onto an oriental rug at the doctor's feet, clawing at his wound.

Brahm knelt down to examine it.

The man's ankle was an ulcerated handprint, a blistering scorch mark. Brahm had seen this type of wound before; nematocysts: poisonous stingers, like the tendrils of a jellyfish, some toxic enough to cause death upon contact. The creature's hand must have been covered with them.

The man on the floor stopped screaming and his body spasmed violently. Brahm cradled him, tried to calm him, but the ultimate outcome was clear. The most venomous animals in the world lived in the sea, and these symptoms were coming in rapid succession; in a moment, the man's heart would be paralyzed by toxin, or tire and stop of its own accord. The stranger reached up blindly toward Brahm's face and the doctor took his hand until his grip faded.

After a moment, Brahm backed away from the dead man's body, checked his pockets for more flares and found none. He dropped the useless weapon, felt his way behind the front desk, then bolted toward the innkeeper's living area. With luck, there was something he could still do for the old man.

"Hello?" Brahm coughed; the hallway was a chimney, filling his nostrils with the pungent smell of blazing tar. What the hell was the old man's name? Fred? No, Ed. "You in here, Ed?"

He sat in a chair, holding a picture frame.

Brahm approached him, saw that the photo was of Barbara and a teenage girl. "Can't you see there's a fire?"

"I saw the blast. Everything's gone...they're all dead."

"*You're* alive."

"Get outta here!"

Brahm ignored him, took a step closer. "Can you walk, or do I need to carry you?"

"I didn't ask for your help."

"Fine. When I see Barbara again, I'll tell her you died sitting on your ass."

Ed frowned and rose to his feet, the picture clutched tightly to his chest as he led Brahm out. Thick smoke made it difficult for them to navigate their way down the corridor. Intense heat broiled their exposed skin; floral wallpaper smoked, then bubbled and burst into flame; a burning river of fire rushed across the ceiling, chasing them into the lobby. Windows shattered around them, giving in to the heat; Brahm hoped their bodies wouldn't do the same. A gush of flame incinerated the desk behind them, and a hot gale pushed them out the main entrance.

Asphalt stung Brahm's face and hands; he staggered to his feet, his knees screaming. The innkeeper lay next to him, rocked by a fit of coughing, his picture frame shattered on the pavement; Brahm touched the old man's shoulder. "You alright?"

"All the damned smoke," Ed told him between coughs. Brahm helped him up, saw fire in every direction, then motioned to the crowd. "We need to get these people out of here."

Ed gave another cough and pointed out to sea. "The reef."

"The reef? We can't have all these people in the water with those creatures. It'd be a smorgasbord."

"You think their odds'll be any better here?"

Brahm scanned the encroaching inferno; in the water there was at least a chance. He walked toward the crowd, suddenly reminded of the lifeguard days of his youth. The job had provided him with his first C.P.R. training, his first opportunity to save a life. Now, he was back in that role.

"Listen up everybody," he shouted over the confusion. "We can't stay here. We all need to get into the water and swim out to the reef in the —"

"I can't swim!" An overweight man huddled next to a smoldering BMW; he had his hands on the door handle as if he were trying to open it. The tires had all gone flat, and its windshield lay in pieces on the dash. How and where he thought he would drive it remained a mystery.

Brahm turned his attention to the rest of the assembly; every eye locked on his. "Okay, I'm a doctor, so believe me when I say that we're all going to get through this if you listen to me."

Some members of his audience nodded, others stared at him.

He went on, "We need to swim out to the reef. We can wait there for help. Pretend you're back in summer camp. Everybody grab a buddy. If your buddy can't swim, you pull them. If your buddy's hurt, you help them. If your buddy's tired, you keep them awake. Understand?"

Some nodded; most continued to stare.

"Okay," he told them, "let's go."

As the group made its way toward the beach, weaving through burning cars and debris with the slow, dreamy gait of people in shock, Brahm and Ed turned to bring up the rear. Behind them, as if on cue, the Sea Mist Inn collapsed like a dollhouse tossed on a bonfire.

They waded into the surf; some held hands, some had their arms wrapped around their buddy's waist, others were separated but mindful of their partner. Brahm hung back a bit, plucked the iPhone from his pocket and dialed. Salt water would fry the phone's circuits, and, if he survived his swim out to the reef, he didn't want to be stranded there for long.

A voice was in his ear. "Black Harbor Police, Becky speaking, can you hold, please?"

"No, ma'am, I can't hold. I'm a doctor here in Colonial Bay. The town's on fire and about fifty people are swimming out to the reef in the harbor."

"Some kind of explosion?"

"Yes, the whole town's just been bombed!" Brahm hated the harsh tone of his voice, but he couldn't help it; he didn't have time. "I need medical assistance, maybe even the Coast Guard, I need it out at the reef to help with survivors, and I need it now."

"Yes, sir," the operator said, shaken. "Sheriff MacIsaac is on his way there now. I'll tell him what's going on an' get the Coast Guard on the line."

"Thank you." Brahm dropped the phone into the surf and turned to Ed. "You're my buddy. Now let's get moving."

They headed for the safety of the reef.

FIFTY EIGHT

You can't save everyone.

Peggy's words still rang in Larry's ears as he hurried through the heat and flame, but it was too late now for second thoughts. Fire severed their path of retreat. He focused on the shadows ahead and ran.

Adrenaline must have heightened his senses; he saw the glowing orb through this firestorm, and swore he could almost smell the beasts in the clearing ahead. He watched the creatures close in on the human figure, watched the monster he knew was Karl Tellstrom raise the weapon. It burned brighter than it had before, as if building up a charge.

"God almighty."

"What is it?" Alan called from behind.

"The bastard's gonna fire it."

Alan shielded his eyes with his hand, squinted; smoke clotted the air, ash and embers forming a hot snowfall. "How can you see — ?"

A piercing howl filled their ears, followed by a thunderclap; whoever the human shape had been, it exploded in a ball of flame.

"Holy Christ!" The archeologist held up his spear pistol, his nervous finger on the trigger.

Larry suddenly realized he was unarmed, but he felt no fear. No. On the contrary, he was excited.

They bolted onto a clear patch of street. Walls of flame on every side made it appear as if an arena had been cleared for an impending battle. Larry's gaze shot to four hulking beasts at the far end of the oasis, halting on the tiger-striped animal in the center; its right hand was a shining globe.

Larry roared his challenge. "Tellstrom!"

Karl's head jerked up, his dark eyes aglow with mirrored firelight;

he found Larry through the haze and focused intently upon him.

Alan fired a spear at Tellstrom.

Karl's naked claw blurred out, pulled one of his shocked minions into the arrow's path. This beast towered over Tellstrom, and the metal shaft drilled into its chest. It dropped to its knees, mewling as it tried to pull the dart free.

The shark-man roared at his two remaining followers. "Kill them!"

They charged like tameless stallions.

Larry rushed forward, but the creatures did not engage him. They streaked by him as if he were off limits, as if they sensed something in him that kept them at bay. Larry saw none of this; his eyes were focused on the thing with the golden claw, remembering what Carol Miyagi had said: statues of gods were sculpted with a hand of gold.

Of course, you revere what you fear. They feared their overseers...their masters...*beings who could incinerate them if they stepped out of line, beings with a golden orb on one hand.*

Tellstrom bared his teeth, but stood frozen, sniffing at the air. He appeared confused. In this moment of hesitation, Larry sprinted to within a foot of the shark-man's snout; if Karl used the creators' weapon at this range, he would incinerate himself as well.

•••

A walking cuttlefish lunged at Alan, fleshy frills billowing like a skirt in the wind. He pulled his trigger in rapid succession, buried four aluminum arrows deep in its chest. The creature vomited blood as it fell to asphalt, turning every color of the spectrum before it died.

Alan turned to face his next opponent. The creature's eyes rotated inward, its devilish underbite gleaming as it lunged for his face. He fired; his final spear hammered into the animal's throat and punched through the back of its skull.

Alan heard a growl and turned in time to see Larry grab Tellstrom's scaly arm. The artist's shirt looked as if it were bulging, stretching; Alan thought it was a trick of the rising heat, but then the fabric split. Larry's back swelled, the skin shifting and folding, melting and thickening into a spiny dorsal ridge; his throat spontaneously slit open, as if an invisible claw had swiped his neck, leaving rows of bloodless lacerations.

Gills.

"My God," Alan muttered; his hand went limp and the empty spear gun fell to the pavement.

•••

Larry's face leapt forward to form a snout, and, when he blinked, his eyes turned a cold black.

Tellstrom did not fight against Larry's grip; he watched the change overtake him, then uttered a single word of gibberish. "Callisto?"

Larry said nothing, didn't even take time to wonder about his new condition. Instead, he took advantage of Karl's shock and grabbed the relic; it came free of Tellstrom's hand with an obscenely wet noise, audible even above the roaring blaze.

Alan stood in the distance, staring at Larry with wide, stupefied eyes.

Larry hurled the orb at him. "Catch!"

Alan snapped out of his trance, plucked the artifact from the air and pulled it to his chest like a football.

"Get out of here," the artist told him. "*Go.*"

•••

Alan stood frozen for a moment, as if more time with the vision might help him believe what he was seeing. Then smoke and flame swirled all around him, rose up to devour his visibility, and he finally turned to run. A succession of smoky veils parted before him, the final one revealing a field of black glass.

He hesitated at the water's edge, afraid a swim might be just as deadly as the blaze.

An explosion rocked the ground.

Alan whirled to see a jet of flame streaking toward him. He dove into the tide, the orb still clutched in his hand, and a burning arm reached out across the surf, angry he'd escaped its grasp.

He held his breath and kicked through the murky depths. Below, the water bled quickly from purple to black; if something nasty waited down there, he couldn't see it. Alan's lungs cried out for air, and, when he surfaced, he saw the reef.

People.

At least, Alan thought they were people. He didn't know anymore. He looked over his shoulder at the inferno, realized he had little choice, and swam for the shoal.

•••

The weapon was gone.

Karl Tellstrom lashed out at Larry with his armored tail, his spread tailfin slicing the Callisto's side wide open.

Larry roared in pain; his grip loosened for a moment, allowing Karl to twist away.

Tellstrom whirled around, stalked after Alan with open jaws.

Larry's powerful legs propelled him into Karl's back and knocked the large Charodon onto the pavement. They scrambled to their feet once more, circling each other.

"Who made you?" Tellstrom demanded; reflected fires burned in his raven eyes, growing in intensity like the madness that fueled him.

He charged.

Larry darted out of the way; he reached out with his newborn talons and tore bands of flesh from Karl's ribs.

Tellstrom roared with rage and pain, then whirled around, foam dripping from his jaws; his hand rose to find his side covered in blood.

"Now we're even," Larry told him through sprouting fangs.

Karl's nostrils flared, taking in a familiar aroma; his dark eyes rolled in their sockets, and he offered up a look of utter disgust. "You're *hers*, aren't you? That half-breed bitch turned you. I'll kill you both!"

Larry saw that Alan was now out of sight; he turned to face

Tellstrom, unimpressed. "With what? Your weapon's gone. Your followers are dead. You've got nothing"

Karl rushed forward and Larry sidestepped him again. Tellstrom's feet skid on the pavement, nearly tripping over the body of the creature he'd used as a shield; he regained his footing and faced Larry once more.

Larry shook his massive head. "Don't you get it? Your home's been blown to shit. It's over."

Karl reached out for his comrade's corpse, found the spear buried in its chest; in a single motion, he pulled the shaft free and plunged it into Larry's shoulder.

Larry howled; he stumbled back and yanked the arrow out. The open wound belched blood, then slowly closed as his body completed its transformation.

The blacktop shuddered beneath them; gas pumps ignited at the docks, erupting into burning geysers. Tendrils of flame rushed toward Karl and Larry from the firestorm. They forgot one another and dove for the ground, feeling broiling heat across their backs as they pressed themselves flat against the pavement. The sound of the blast was the bellow of an angry beast, building, lowering in pitch, then transforming into a whoosh as the flares receded back into the burning wall that surrounded them.

•••

Tellstrom staggered to his feet and stared at the encroaching hell. This was not how his war, his *vengeance* was going to end; he had to get away from this new Callisto, had to *think*. When his eyes drifted skyward, he found man-made light on distant cliffs.

The lighthouse!

It remained standing, the only structure left in Colonial Bay.

It's a sign from Varuna! He's still with me!

Karl sprinted for the cliffs.

FIFTY NINE

Carol Miyagi saw the blaze through her fogged divemask; she pulled off her hood, yanked the regulator from her lips, and stared in disbelief.

Barbara stood beside her on the sandy shoal, gave voice to her thoughts. "Tellstrom?"

"The ones that destroyed the false church."

Miyagi pivoted toward the husky voice and found Jason's toothy snout.

"They done this," he said.

Carol's eyes shot back to the flaming shore; she tried to find the docks, tried to slow to beat of her heart and the freefall of her stomach. *Alan's fine. He has to be.*

Peggy moved by them and her face and tail drooped; she fell to her knees, her glow dimming as the tears spilled from her eyes.

Miyagi took a step toward her and noticed bobbing shapes in the water. At first, she thought it was flotsam and jetsam from Colonial Bay, but no, these were people. Survivors were swimming out to join them on the reef.

"People are alive," Carol said, directing Peggy's attention to the wading figures. "I'm sure Alan and Larry are with them."

When the swimmers reached the shoal, they stood waist deep in the tide, not wanting to come ashore, their faces bathed in an odd mix of awe and horror. Miyagi scanned the menagerie behind her, then moved to the water's edge, allowing these refugees to see a non-threatening, human face. "It's all right. They're...they won't hurt you."

"What are they?" a wading girl asked; soot muddied her complexion even after the long swim. "Are they real?"

"We're real." Christine DeParle came forward. Her voice was a far cry from the catty, combative tone it possessed when Miyagi first met her; it almost passed for reassuring. "We're survivors, just like you."

Slowly, with steps that betrayed their mistrust and trepidation, the humans moved onto the reef and stood at a distance from their Poseidon counterparts; they shivered in the night breeze, looking back at the blaze they'd left behind.

Carol searched their faces, saw one she recognized. "Brahm!"

At the sound of her doctor's name, Peggy was on her feet; she looked over, saw him come ashore with Ed. He offered Miyagi an acknowledging wave and both women inquired excitedly about their lovers.

Brahm stared at Peggy with child-like wonder; he took a moment to catch his breath, then answered them, "Larry thought he saw Tellstrom...thought he had the weapon. He and Alan went to get it."

"Daddy?" When Christine saw Ed, her eyes lit up; she took a step toward him, then hesitated, unsure of her reception.

The innkeeper bolted across the reef and threw his arms around his daughter. "I thought I'd lost you, baby."

"I'm sorry," Christine sobbed. "I'm...I'm so sorry."

Barbara moved to join her family. "Thank Varuna you're all right."

Ed let go of Christine, flung his arms around his wife, and held her to him. When Barbara wrapped her tail around her husband's back, he pushed her to arm's length, looked her up and down. "What's goin' on?"

"We're...we're leaving Colonial Bay."

Ed glanced across his shoulder at the flames, then nodded helplessly.

Another man crawled from the tide.

Peggy tapped Miyagi on the shoulder and pointed. "He has the weapon."

Carol's eyes ignited with joy and she waved her arms wildly in the air. "Alan!"

He smiled, returned her wave.

"He was with Larry?" Peggy asked, hopeful.

Carol nodded; she removed herself from the group, anxious to wrap her arms around Alan, to tell him at last that she loved him.

"Where's Larry?"

Alan shook his head and held the golden orb aloft; he looked completely spent. "Larry was still fighting Tellstrom when he tossed me this."

Peggy's smile faltered; her eyes flew back to the inferno, scanning the flames for signs of life. "There...on the lighthouse. I can see two people on the catwalk."

Brahm followed her gaze, squinted, but saw nothing. "What would they be doing up there?"

Christine wiped the joyful tears from her face and moved away from her parents. "Karl goes there to think."

The sound of a gunshot filled the air.

Alan arched forward and a flower of blood bloomed from his shoulder.

Miyagi's eyes widened; her mouth moved speechlessly, unable to find words to express her shock. Alan dropped the alien weapon, fell forward into her arms. Carol eased him to the ground; she saw the alien relic sink beneath the waves, then looked off into the darkness, trying to glimpse her lover's assailant.

Something shambled toward them from the gloom, a glistening .45 pistol hunkered in its hand; it appeared rotted, the living corpse from a horror film. A jagged pit gaped where its nose should have been, and its cheekbones sat exposed, white boulders rising from scarlet mud. One of its eyes had gone white, scalded and unseeing, while the other searched the crowd. It wore black; a suit, burned and stained, and what had been a trenchcoat billowed in the wind, tattered and torn into a shabby cape.

The melted thing opened its mouth with great effort, and its newly fused lips snapped apart. "Where is he?"

Brahm was at Alan's side in a flash; he ripped open the man's shirt, gave the wounds a quick examination. Carol saw blood run down her lover's chest and back, and felt her insides churn. Brahm wadded Alan's torn shirt and pressed it firmly against the archeologist's shoulder.

After a moment, the doctor looked up at Miyagi. "The bullet passed through."

He said it as if it were a good thing, but as Miyagi watched the fabric turn red, she didn't feel good at all. She gave her attention back to the gunman.

"Where is he?" it roared again.

Roger Hays; even agitated, Carol knew the sound of his voice. Slowly, stone faced, she took a step toward him, anger boiling within her as she stared into his single, unrepentant eye.

Hays turned his pistol on her; water still ran from its metallic surface. "That's far enough, Carol."

She took another defiant step and the smell of burnt flesh assaulted her nostrils.

"I'm warning you —" Hays roared.

Carol whirled around, kicked out with her leg, and her foot struck Roger's hand. The gun flew into the gloom and disappeared. She brought her other leg up, drove her heel into Hays' chin, and propelled him backward.

He regained his footing and lunged at her, a mixture of saliva and gore trailing from his bony chin.

Carol feinted a jab, caused Hays to halt his charge and blunder back a step. Then, she whirled around again, thrust her foot up into his chest, and sent him tottering back, fighting to maintain his balance.

He couldn't.

Hays fell to the ground and his head rolled listlessly at the end of his neck.

At that moment, Miyagi could've stopped and turned away, but fury and fear conspired within her, pushed her to stand above Roger, ready to bring her fist down, to smash his skull like a moldy pumpkin.

"Stop it," Barbara snapped.

Carol's head jerked up and her eyes locked with the old woman's. "Just...stop."

Miyagi glared down at Hays. His eyes rolled in their sockets, blood bubbled up between his tattered lips. She'd hurt him badly. Slowly, Carol's rage dissolved and she backed away, unwilling to believe what she was almost capable of.

Half buried in moist sediment, the golden orb, the Wrath of the Gods, sensed rage. Somewhere nearby, there was a hand that longed for a weapon as badly as this weapon longed for a hand. The sphere stirred; it rolled out of the water and across the shoal. When it found Roger's palm, it opened, its vacant interior swallowing each of his digits, quenching its gnawing hunger to be filled.

The relic rejuvenated him.

He sprang to his feet, stared at the golden glove that glowed ominously on his right hand. Barbara had said the weapon would teach its owner, would explain itself and its power to him. And, as she looked at Roger, Carol could tell he knew; his lips curled into a hideous, tattered grin, and his working eye shot to her.

Miyagi took another step back, horrified.

Hays' well-mannered, educated voice was now a manic screech. *"Where's the animal that butchered my son!"*

When Carol looked into his eye, she saw nothing human; it had all been burned away. She never wanted to believe Alan's accusation, but there was no denying it now. Roger Hays was a monster, a heartless, soulless monster. It was all he'd ever really been.

Carol pointed to the blazing shore, careful not to take her eyes off Roger's new weapon. "He's at the lighthouse, now leave us alone!"

What remained of Hays' face jerked toward the cliffs, and his lips twitched into a snarl. When he raised his arm, the dimly glowing relic sparked. The orb was a sponge; it soaked up the man's desire for vengeance, stored it until it could hold it no longer, then projected it toward the lighthouse.

SIXTY

Larry chased Karl through the fire with newfound speed and grace. His legs pumped like pistons; they now resembled the hind legs of a dog, his clawed toes clicking against the pavement as he ran. Amazing and strangely invigorating sensations flooded him; he felt new muscles flex, felt hot winds blow against expanses of alien skin on his back, arms, and head; oddest of all, he felt the pull of his thick tail as it swung to and fro behind him.

There were other senses as well.

He could smell Tellstrom's scent, even through the smoke-infested air, could hear the beat of the creature's racing heart and could even see him running through distant curtains of flame. It was as if Larry's consciousness had been transported, and he had to keep reminding himself that this body was in fact his own.

His mind shouted questions, demanded answers; *how* had this happened to him? Brahm and Alan argued genetics in his head, telling him that it was the work of enzymes, enzymes that could be passed from one creature to another. Peggy had scratched him. Did that do it? Had that been enough to — ?

Larry remembered coupling with Peggy in the temple.

Didn't Preston compare the infection to AIDS? Yes. He did.

Larry banished all the queries from his mind and tried to focus. How this happened didn't matter, at least, not now. What mattered was that the strength and power of this new form gave him a fighting chance against Tellstrom, a chance to end this, to protect Peggy and everyone else. The consequences to his everyday life could be fretted over later.

He leapt from the flames and found himself at the base of a rock wall; Tellstrom clung to it, scaling the stone face toward the lighthouse that loomed overhead. Larry's talons dug into the bluff like metal cleats and he pulled himself up, flames nipping at the thickened skin of his heels and tail as he did so. Larry clawed at the stone outcroppings, dug himself a new hold, then repeated the process; his confidence grew, and soon he ascended the cliff-side as swiftly as a cat might climb a tree trunk.

Tellstrom glanced over his shoulder, saw that Larry had gained ground on him; he growled and smacked his pursuer in the face with his armor-plated tail.

The force of the impact caused Larry to lose his grip; he slid down the cliff, madly scratched for purchase, and finally dug himself in.

Karl clawed his way to the summit, scrambled for the lighthouse.

Larry resumed his climb; he crawled into tall, dry grass that lined the cliff and saw that a windblown spark had already ignited it. Soon, the sea of fire that drowned the rest of Colonial Bay would come lapping at the lighthouse door. Larry ran, remembering the night Susan's animated corpse stalked him along this same path. Then, from a place in his brain where he kept nightmares locked away, Larry heard her gargled voice:

You should've left Colonial Bay when you had the chance.

Tellstrom had smashed his way inside, left the door rocking in the hot wind.

Larry entered cautiously, used his new senses; thick smoke masked other scents, made it hard to see clearly, but he heard the rhythm of a pulse other than his own...distant...above him. He lunged up the metal staircase, took two or three steps at a time. Beyond the spinning beacon, a glass doorway stood open and waiting; Larry took a step toward it.

A clawed foot struck from nowhere.

Karl's roundhouse kick sent Larry flying into the window-wall; it shattered on impact, and he stumbled backward through the jagged frost. The narrow catwalk's railing kept him from traveling over the edge.

Tellstrom lunged through the opening, seized Larry's snout and forced it down hard against the railing.

Blood splashed from Larry's nostrils; he lifted his knee into Karl's crotch, hoping it would have the desired effect.

It did.

Tellstrom released Larry's skull to cover his own throbbing groin; he bit his thin lip against the pain, then took a serious step forward.

Larry retreated; he ducked, then thrust and scratched at Tellstrom. There wasn't much room to maneuver on the catwalk, and Karl tracked his every move.

"Murderer!" Tellstrom bared his ravenous teeth as they danced about on the ledge. "You killed my mother!"

Murderer!

Natalie's final word, the raving of a disturbed individual. Larry saw that so clearly now.

His eyes locked with Tellstrom's. "I've never killed anyone in my life. But you're hurting everyone I love, so I'll start with you."

Karl lunged at Larry with single-minded ferocity, pinned him against the curved glass; his mouth opened wide, revealed jagged, bone-white triangles ready to rip out Larry's throat. Suddenly, Tellstrom halted his killing stroke, his gaze focused on something beyond his intended prey.

Although he couldn't turn his head, Larry saw something reflected in the pitch-black mirrors of Tellstrom's eyes; a skeletal face with a permanent grin, rancid flesh sliding off the bone in great wet clumps. It took Larry a moment to realize the apparition was Susan.

Karl's eyes bulged until they gained the appearance of cannonballs; his jaw opened and closed to mouth a denial, and the cold, confident manner was bleached from his striped face. For the first time in his life, Tellstrom was terrified.

Larry took advantage of the moment; he kicked Karl hard in the abdomen. Tellstrom flew back against the wrought iron railing, teetered there a moment, then overbalanced and careened across the bar. Larry instinctively rushed forward, grabbed hold of Karl's ankle and halted his descent.

Tellstrom craned his head toward the newest of Poseidon's children; he snickered, then his face clouded over once more. "Am I supposed to thank you, Callisto? Am I supposed to say I was wrong about you humans now?"

"I'm not as human as I used to be." Larry's mouth formed a crooked smile, his serrated teeth gleaming with the glow of flames below. "And I can't save everyone."

Larry let go.

As Karl fell, his tail lashed out, slithered around Larry's wrist and pulled him forward. The artist wrapped his free arm around the railing to keep from going over the side, wondering how long he could support the animal's squirming weight.

"Feel like dying with me?" Karl called up, laughing like a madman.

Larry gave his answer; he bent down, clamped his teeth around the muscular tail like a sprung bear trap, and severed it.

Tellstrom screamed, blood spewing from the ragged stump where his tailfin had been; a long tongue of fire licked him, converted his body into a boiling, burning mass.

Larry spit the length of tail into the blaze, then pulled himself up, feeling the burn of his injuries and strained muscles. He remembered his ghostly helper and turned to face the glass.

"Thank you," he said aloud.

Susan, if she'd been there at all, was gone.

The air changed, swirled around Larry like a maelstrom. He felt something warm against his back, an expanding bubble of hot air; when it suddenly burst, fire shot through the metal mesh at his feet.

SIXTY ONE

The lighthouse exploded in spectacular fashion; a jet of flame snuffed its revolving light, shot the glass-walled chamber into the night sky like a bullet from a gun. Metal, glass, and rubble rained down upon the waves at the base of the cliff, then sank beneath the tide. There was nothing left of Colonial Bay now, just an island of flame in a cool New England sea.

"*I got you!*" Hays shrieked triumphantly, waving the orb like an Independence Day sparkler. "*You fucking paid for what you did to me!*"

Peggy ran for the burning shore; Barbara reached out for her, but she broke free of the old woman's grasp.

Christine intercepted her at the water's edge, pushed her back and held her tight. "You can't help them. They're gone."

Peggy's tail wilted; her shoulders trembled as she wept.

Christine closed her eyes, felt tears trace scalding lines down her cheeks.

*The father of my child...gone...*dead.

A loud hum filled Christine's ears. Her eyes snapped open, and she saw Roger Hays; he'd turned the creators' weapon on her.

•••

Ed DeParle dove at Hays, and his human guise melted away in an instant; he grabbed Roger's arm, tried to yank it from the sculpted sphere, tried to save his little girl.

Raving passions flooded Hays; this creature, this *freak*, wasn't going to steal his newfound power. It was his! *His!* Roger growled savagely and brought the orb crashing into the old man's chin.

Ed lost his grip and was flung backward. Hays didn't wait for him to regain his balance; he swung once more at the innkeeper's face, used the relic like the ball of a mace. Ed deflected the blow with the ribbed fin that lined his arm; he spun rapidly, slapped Roger with his paddle-like tail.

Hays fell on his back, rage burning through his veins like acid. Several Charodon rushed to join the fight, but, when Roger leapt to his feet, the orb glowed like a dwarf star, arcing blue electricity in all directions, turning what was left of his hair into a crazed mane. An angry roar exploded from Hays' ragged lips, and Poseidon's children backed away, fear of their gods' wrath ingrained within their collective mind.

Roger's eyes fixed on Ed DeParle, and the weapon moved with them.

•••

Ed felt a desert wind pelt his face. He looked away, found his wife and daughter standing nearby; he sensed their panic, smelled it on their skin and saw it in their eyes. He'd devoted his life to the masquerade of humanity, to the protection of Colonial Bay, sacrificing everything, even his family.

Only one sacrifice left to make.

Ed lunged at Hays, deliberately grabbed the sculpted sphere. Heat swirled around the combatants, and Roger's tattered black clothing rose and twirled in the forming cyclone; before Hays realized something was wrong, the orb exploded, discharged its full power. They became burning apparitions, bright specters that faded with Roger's furious, dying scream.

SIXTY TWO

Earl Preston looked up, found the ferryboat's wheelhouse; its windows were too dark for him to see within. They would have to have a radio up there, a way to call for help. He tossed a glance at Horror Show; the hitman's mini-gun still fired, still kept the monsters at bay, but for how long?

The guardsman bolted, tore through a space between two wrecked cars, and Horror Show's tracer fire split the air around him. Earl ducked; he stumbled and fell, then rolled back onto his feet to resume a staggering run. A red Dodge Caravan smoldered in his path; he hid behind it, pressed himself flat against the metal as bullets shattered its remaining windows.

That sonofabitch is shooting at me! I should have known I —

The Caravan shook violently behind him.

Earl looked up, saw shadows coalesce into an unimaginable form; before he could bring his gun into firing position, powerful talons reached down through the smoke and grabbed him by the shoulders. The Kraken rose up on dog-like haunches, lifted him off the deck toward its open beak. One of its facial tentacles brushed Earl's cheek, ragged thorns coaxing blood from his skin.

Hot shells burst through the creature's body; it screeched in Earl's ear, pulled him down to the deck, then released its hold. Earl pushed the dead hulk off him and crawled away, watching as its skin color faded from red, to pink, to gray; finally becoming a bleached, transparent white as the pigment factories of its chromatophores shut down.

Horror Show moved toward Earl from the whirling, heated smoke, the mini-gun still smoldering in his hands. The hitman's stern expression was the same one Preston had seen in his father's Gulf War photographs; it was the face of a man who'd seen enough death to become numb to it.

Earl held up his M-16. "That's close enough."

"What's your fuckin' problem?"

"You were tryin' to shoot my ass off!"

"I was trying to shoot *its* ass off. Where the fuck were you goin'?"

Preston lowered his gun a bit, uncertain if he believed Horror Show or not. "The bridge. I need to radio for —"

Something dove at them from the roof of a black Infinity; talons outstretched, the bloody gristle of previous kills dangling between its gleaming fangs.

The hitman reacted instantly with his mini-gun, and his shells all but obliterated the monstrosity before it could even shriek. He continued firing until the last empty casing flew from the rotating chamber, until the roar of its discharge became the whine of empty friction. Horror Show tossed the exhausted weapon down, barely missing his own foot, then grabbed the Berretta from his waistband.

Flashes from the hitman's anti-personnel weapon illuminated other nightmarish contours waiting in the wings.

Earl opened fire with his M-16, blew holes in the creatures' unfamiliar anatomies, his mind consumed once more with his father's death. Had the man been afraid, as Earl was now? Had he been thinking of his family? And then, Earl Sr.'s voice was angry in his brain: *Don't worry what the fuck I did to get killed, Junior. Just calm your ass down and think this through. The man who goes ahead stumbles so the man who follows may have his wits about him.*

He saw a metal staircase to the upper deck and called for Horror Show to follow him.

The hatchway to the ferryboat's cabin stood ajar.

A dead man lay at the foot of the controls, scratched and mauled. The wheel stood unbridled, lazily moving from side to side as if denying the carnage.

"Guess that's our captain," Earl muttered from the doorway.

Horror Show pushed past him, stared out the broken window at the front of the cabin; thick smoke from the deck below hid their destination. The hitman pulled a granite shard from his pocket, one side glassy, the other rough; it appeared to have been chipped off a monument of some kind. Horror Show rubbed it, as if he were trying to summon some genie to save them.

Earl entered the room; drops of fluid fell from the ceiling, struck his shoulder. His eyes shot upward, saw something alive in the shadows; its black coloring had camouflaged it, made it appear one with the darkness. It hung there like a spider, silently watching and waiting for someone to wander beneath it.

Horror Show was that someone.

"Look out!" Earl cried.

The hitman's gun rose toward the roof of the cabin. Shrieking, the animal instantly inflated, became a spiked balloon; it reached out for him with clawed, tree frog hands. Horror Show fired, parted the thing's skull; it fell from its roost, leaking fluids and gasses, filling the chamber with its stench.

Earl coughed, then took the ship's wheel; sluggish, like driving an eighteen-wheeler when he was used to driving a compact car. He studied the instrument panel, looked for anything that made sense. Much of the glass was either shattered or covered in clotting gore, making the information beneath impossible to read.

Horror Show smiled. "You can drive this piece o' shit?"

"Naw, not this fucked up."

As Earl looked out the window, a sudden breeze fanned smoke from his view, allowed him a glimpse of red and blue strobes.

Police cars?

He saw a striped guardrail, saw the concrete barricade of a boat landing, and realized they were seconds away from collision.

"Get down!" he shouted, then pushed on Horror Show's back.

The barge struck shore at full throttle.

•••

Officers ran from the boat landing as fast as their feet could move them. Sheriff MacIsaac dared a glance over his shoulder, saw the hull loom after him as the ferry beached itself like a huge metal whale;

he slid across the hood of his cruiser, hit the ground at the same instant as the barge.

The dock's concrete ramp exploded on impact; huge chunks of debris flew into parked police cars, shattered lightbars and windshields, dented hoods, and caved in hardtops. A rusted "loading and unloading" drawbridge toppled with the shriek of rending metal, smashed the red-and-white-striped barricade before it exploded into airborne splinters.

What remained of the ramp kept the ferry from coming entirely ashore, but inertia sent its cargo sailing forward. Cars flew twenty to forty yards; a Rav 4 crashed into the dock's control booth, a Honda Civic flattened one of the nearby cruisers — a woman dangled from one of its broken windows, her head hanging by a thread of tissue; a church bus struck pavement and skidded, its windows glazed in blood and filled with a jumble of arms and legs. Scattered fireballs lit the smoke-filled sky, and then it was over; the screaming roar of chaos faded to a gentle crackle of flames.

MacIsaac's head rose from between the safety of his legs. He'd lived more than half a century, but nothing he'd seen, neither real nor imagined, could ever match the site that greeted him. It was the Apocalypse, dropped smack dab at his feet.

Officer Eads moved toward the beached ship, but the Sheriff grabbed his shoulder to snap him back.

"Hold it, son," MacIsaac said, distressed.

"There could be survivors."

The sheriff nodded; he reached into his cruiser, grabbed the receiver from his police radio, and spoke into it. "Becky, you there?"

Her voice came through a curtain of static. "That you, Sheriff?"

"Yeah, Becky. I need you to —"

She went on anxiously, "My switchboard's got more lights flashing than one o' Walter Ferguson's Christmas displays. I got somebody says they're a doctor out there on the reef, and people calling in that it's some kinda terrorist attack on —"

"Becky, right now I need you to get the fire department and some ambulances out here to the docks. We've got a three alarm, shit, four alarm blaze out here and Christ only knows what on the island."

"Right away, Sheriff. Already called the Coast Guard."

"Fine, Becky." MacIsaac shoved his hand back into the cruiser; when it reappeared, the radio receiver had become a black flashlight. His eyes shifted from Eads to the wreck. "Let's go."

•••

The collision had thrown Earl against the ferryboat's control panel. His left shoulder now swarmed with bees, but he was grateful for the pain; pain meant he was alive. He stood slowly and looked out the hole that had once been a window, his eyes sucking in the devastation. An angry child had thrown fireworks onto a Matchbox playset; amid the carnage, Earl saw policemen, their flashlight beams searching for survivors.

He felt a slap on his back and spun to see Horror Show standing behind him, holding out his hand. "Come on, Coast Guard boy."

Earl looked at the hand, not wanting to shake it. "Call me 'Coast Guard boy' again."

"Hey, I saved your fuckin' life down there." The hitman withdrew his hand, used it to give Earl a pat on the cheek. "Show some appreciation, huh?"

"I warned you about that thing on the ceiling. As far as I'm concerned, I don't owe you shit."

Earl left the wheelhouse, made his way down blood-soaked steps to the main level, and Horror Show followed; spotlights crossed them, and Earl shielded his eyes against the brightness. "Over here!"

The lights grew closer, accompanied by a voice. "You two all right?"

"Fine," Earl told them

"What the hell happened here?" The man wore the golden star of a sheriff on his jacket.

Earl's mother had often told him, "Truth tellers make no mistakes." He stepped forward and cleared his throat. "Sheriff, my name's Preston. I'm a Coast Guard Officer. A man named Roger Hays is responsible for all this —"

"Roger Hays...the millionaire?"

"Billionaire, actually." Earl pointed to Horror Show and noticed the hitman's jaw tighten. "He hired this man and others to blow up Colonial Bay and some...some rare animals that have been attacking ships off shore."

"Rare animals? Like this?" The sheriff pulled a photo from his pocket.

Preston stared at the grainy picture of a monster; he paused for a moment before answering, wondering where the image came from. "I haven't seen one like that yet, but...yeah."

"Where's Hays?"

"Dead."

The sheriff rubbed the corner of his eye.

"You'll find dead creatures all over this barge to back me up on that much," Earl said, then he turned and sent his fist flying into Horror Show's unexpectant face.

The hitman's head jerked back, then nodded forward again; blood oozed from his split lip, and a stunned look glazed his eyes.

"*Now* you're under arrest," Earl told him.

SIXTY THREE

Sirens called from unseen ships in the distance, police, Coast Guard, or both. Time was short.

Christine wiped at her eyes and moved away from her mother, turned to face the clans that had gathered on the ridge; she cleared her throat loudly, and what followed was an impromptu eulogy, "When the fire dies, it'll be as if Colonial Bay never existed...but for every ending there has to be a new beginning, for every...every death, there has to be new life. We'll find a new home. My father just spared us the wrath of the gods to live as Varuna intended. That's what Kar — what Karl wanted too. We have run, to get away if we can." She surveyed the crowd, then added, "We have to live."

There was no applause, no war cries. Poseidon's children turned and moved wordlessly toward the tide and sank into darkness; they were the masters of that watery domain, and they had a long journey, a long search ahead of them.

Christine hoped the worst was now over.

A claw reached out to squeeze her talon, and her head jerked to the side. Jason. No matter what happened, he was always there for her. She was lucky to have his friendship.

"Ready to go?" he asked.

She nodded.

"Let's find someplace warm. I'm sick of New England winters."

•••

Barbara ran across the shoal, took Peggy's webbed claw in her own, pulled emphatically. "Come with us."

Peggy took a step forward, her mind crawling with questions and feelings. She remembered her dream, being a dolphin, the freedom she felt, and the thoughts she'd had after eating the lobster came once more to the surface, thoughts of swimming off into the void and deserting her old life.

Larry was gone.

The realization brought a tingling chill to the back of her skull, a chill that traveled to her shoulders and down the bumpy road of her spine, leaving her hollow and cold. If she returned to New York, if she had to look at his vacant chair, his blank canvases and paints gathering dust, his empty side of their bed... Going off with Barbara meant not having to deal with any of that; it meant there would be no danger of coming in contact with people they knew, having to tell them of Larry's death over and over, having to relive this night again and again. She could just...go away.

She froze, reconsidering.

Wasn't running away from your problems what brought you to Colonial Bay in the first place?

"We don't have much time," Barbara urged.

"I can't." Peggy swiped at her tears. "I need to go home."

"Your home is with us."

"No."

"If you're left behind, you'll be alone, afraid."

Peggy watched Poseidon's children enter the surf. To them, she was a freak, an anomaly, a *mistake*. Her eyes shot across the reef to the human survivors, thinking the same. Either way, she would be alone, but in the company of men she could at least feel superior.

"I'm not afraid. I'm strong. Isn't that what you told me? That wasn't bullshit, was it?"

Barbara looked shocked. "N-no. But you're young, and your abilities are still so new to you. You need someone to —"

"My mother died a long time ago. Don't take her place." Barbara shrank from the words like a dog struck by a rolled up newspaper; Peggy hadn't meant for it to sound so cruel, but she needed to convince the old woman she would be fine on her own. "I won't just automatically turn when the moon is full, right? I have control?"

"Well...yes, but —"

"Then I have control."

The old woman's smooth forehead furrowed, and Peggy could tell she was searching for more convincing words.

"Mother!" Christine waited impatiently at the water's edge. "We need to leave...*now!*"

"You should go," Peggy urged.

Barbara looked out to sea; when she spoke again, there was great sadness in her voice. "You'll grow tired of playing human."

"I was human for twenty-eight years. You never were. It might not be a problem for me."

"Perhaps. But, if it does become a problem, come to us." Barbara squeezed Peggy's hands gently, then released them; she joined her daughter, and, together with Jason, they approached the waves.

"How will I find you?" Peggy called after them. "Where will you be?"

The old woman didn't look back. "When the time comes, you'll know."

They dove beneath the surf and were gone.

Alone among the humans, Peggy watched as her long, powerful arms and legs turned stubby; her deadly hooked talons became flat, impotent nails. An itch spread across her scalp and crotch, replaced just as quickly by the tickle of sprouting hair. Finally, her skin thickened, grew opaque, obscuring the beautiful light within her body.

Peggy's eyes moved from her own breasts to the gathering of refugees across the reef. Some of the men saw her and stared at her figure. Before the attack, Peggy would have felt a flood of mortified heat and tried to conceal her nudity; now, such thoughts did not occur to her.

•••

Carol chewed on her knuckle, watched as Brahm continue his work with Alan. "Will he be all right?"

"I've done all I can do out here," the doctor told her. "I called for help from shore. They'll be here soon."

"What can I do?"

The physician grabbed her hand and pulled it to the wadded fabric. "Keep applying direct pressure. I need to check on the other survivors."

She nodded, not looking at him, staring at the blood; wet strands of hair hung like black icicles to hide her face.

Brahm reached out and brushed them aside. "Hey, this could have been a lot worse."

Carol cradled Alan's head in the crook of her arm as her frantic eyes surveyed his injury. She pressed down hard on the wound to stop the bleeding, felt warmth between her fingers as the rag soaked up his life. How much blood could he loose? How long did he really have?

"He's stable now," Brahm assured her.

"Is he?"

"Yeah, he is. But I'll come running back here if you need me."

Carol looked up and tried to smile. "*Domo.*"

The physician returned her grin before moving away.

"Alan?" she whispered, rocking him back and forth. "Alan, can you hear me?"

His eyelids slowly slid open and he offered her the pitiful ghost of a smile; his words sounded as though they were rising through gravel. "I hear you."

"You hang on. Help will be here soon. You hear me? You're not going to die. You–"

"I love you," he croaked.

She shook her head; her lip trembled violently. "Don't you do this! Don't you dare! You can't just tell me you love me and then leave me here all alone! You have to stay with me! You have to–"

"I wasn't saying good-bye."

Carol's body ached to cry; she bent down and pressed her mouth to his, desperately wishing her kiss held fairytale powers that would restore his health in a magical instant.

"*Ai shite imasu,*" she told him when they parted, then repeated it in English. "I love you. You understand? I love you. You were right about Hays. I'm so sorry I didn't–"

Alan's hand rose up to touch her check. "It feels really good, doesn't it?"

Carol's face sank into his palm, her tears ran over his fingers and down his arm. It *did* feel wonderful to finally tell him how she felt. Why had it been so hard to bring three simple words to her lips? She told him again and again, sometimes in English, sometimes in Japanese. She told him until the sound of far-off sirens silenced her and brought her eyes up to meet the horizon.

Carol saw no ships, but noticed that Poseidon's children were gone. Only Peggy remained, her faint light illuminating the far end of the shoal. Miyagi watched as the creature shifted back into its human guise, then noticed something move in the water behind her. At first, Carol thought she was seeing the other creatures depart. When a shadow rose from the waves, however, she realized it was something else entirely.

•••

"Peggy!"

At the sound of her own name, she turned to see a large creature rise from the tide; it staggered forward and looked at her, its voice unmistakable.

Peggy stared back at it in disbelief. "Rembrandt?"

The beast nodded.

She broke into a run, pounded the surf. When Peggy reached Larry's new form, she threw her arms around it, kissed the sides of his face, kissed the tip of his snout, then lingered on his toothy mouth.

"How do I look?" he asked when their lips parted.

"Incredible."

"Liar. I must look like shit."

Peggy ran her hand across the rough, alien terrain of his head. "How–?"

Larry's elongated finger rose to her lips. "Does it matter?"

She shook her head and held him close to her, rested her cheek on his shoulder, whispered in his ear. "I love you."

Larry held her tightly in his arms, never wanting to let her go.

•••

Red and blue lights lit the smoky horizon, boats, police or Coast Guard, maybe both.

Brahm moved toward Larry and Peggy. They would all need to convey the same story, and a damn good one at that. "Here's what happened here tonight," he said. "It's total shit, but I think they'll buy it, at least I hope they will. Even if they've got some doubts, it should keep us out of an asylum." He ran his eyes across Larry's animalistic form. "And if you can follow Peggy's example and...change back, it'll keep you out of the zoo. All right?"

Larry nodded. "Tell us what we know, Doc."

"Nothing."

They looked at each other a moment.

"Spend hours thinking that one up?"

Brahm elaborated, "We were at the Inn, the town blew up, and we swam out here." He motioned to the crowd of survivors on the reef. "They can corroborate that."

Peggy offered him a skeptical gaze. "And what happens when they start talking about fish people and ray guns?"

"We'll say that we ran into the arsonist here on the reef. He'd wired himself to a bomb. Carol fought to disarm him, but he shot Alan and blew himself up."

At the words "shot Alan," Larry's eyes flew to Miyagi, watching as she rocked the man in her arms. "Jesus. Is he — ?"

Brahm shook his head. "He'll be fine."

Peggy looked out at the approaching rescue strobes. "But will they believe all that?"

Brahm nodded with hopeful certainty. "It'll make a lot more sense to them then werefish and alien weapons. The audience over there saw our archeologist friend fight Hays, saw him *blow up*. They can see Alan's been shot. They'll buy it."

"I think we can remember the gist of it," Larry said.

EPILOGUE

Sounds of thunder seeped through the walls of Black Harbor Medical Center, signaling the onset of yet another late summer storm. As Dr. Kyle Brahm walked toward the nurses' station, he read the invitation in his hand. He didn't want to read the card, but he couldn't take his eyes from it.

You are cordially invited to an exhibition of fantasy art

by

Larry Neuhaus

Brahm wanted to get the experience of Colonial Bay behind him and move on, but, as the days since the fire became weeks, and the weeks months, he wondered if that were even possible, if he could ever forget what he'd seen and go back to pleasant dreams.

"Dr. Brahm?"

He turned and saw a nurse, Emily Hunter, standing behind him in the hallway. "Hi, Emily. What can I do for you?"

She started toward him, paused, then moved forward again. "Are they dead?"

Brahm stared at her blankly, wondering to which patients she was referring.

"You know," she looked around, checked to make certain no one would hear, then whispered, "the fishpeople."

Brahm looked at her in shocked wonder; when he opened his mouth, his voice was as meek and child-like as his answer, "The bad ones are, yes."

Emily closed her eyes and exhaled as if she'd been holding her breath forever; she moved down the hall, patted Brahm on the back as she passed. "Thank God," she muttered.

Brahm watched her disappear into a patient's room.

What a strange new world.

•••

Dozens of paintings lined the gallery walls. All bore Larry's distinctive signature. He strode through the swarm of critics and bidders with a confidence Peggy hadn't seen in years. Everyone wanted to talk with him, to touch him, as if his talent could be absorbed through contact.

Peggy removed herself from the crowd, a sensuous sway to her step. She passed several canvases for which she'd modeled, locking eyes with her nautical reflections, then strolled on. A waiter passed and she took a glass of champagne from his serving tray, winking at him as she did so. The young man smiled, and Peggy felt his stare upon her as she slinked away.

She stopped in front of a large canvas, sipped from her glass as her eyes drank it in. A glorious beast held a paintbrush in its clawed hand; the brass title plate read, "Portrait of the Artist." Peggy smiled, her admiration shifting to the sparkling diamond teardrop on her own left hand. The engagement ring was loose, but that was how she needed it; her fingers swelled when she changed, and she never wanted to take it off.

Her nostrils filled with her lover's scent long before she felt his arms around her waist, his mere touch igniting a passionate blaze in her racing blood. Peggy let loose a muffled, guttural growl, too low for anyone but Larry to hear.

He pressed his lips against her ear and whispered, his breath a tickling breeze. "You know...the hotel has a pool."

She licked her lips seductively. "Really."

Larry nodded. "How 'bout a late-night swim?"

"What if someone sees?" she asked coyly, not really caring if it happened.

Larry shrugged. "We wind up on the cover of the *Weekly World*

News. 'Fishpeople Found in Hotel Pool.'"

"Well...I guess we should give the Bat Boy a break."

He kissed the nape of her neck. "Then it's a date?"

"It's a date," she answered dreamily.

As she stood in Larry's embrace, her eyes wandered to one of his nearby seascapes and found the veneer waves; they looked very inviting.

•••

Carol Miyagi laid her head on Alan Everson's good shoulder; they stood on the deck of the research vessel *Ambrosia*, studying the waves as they rose and fell, passing their secrets. The water that witnessed the dawn of time was still with them, changing forms, becoming and then disintegrating, but always returning here to the sea. Her mind's eye probed beneath these waves and into the vast depths.

Wondering.

Below the ship, beyond the reach of light, Atlantis lay hidden as it had for centuries. Before, it seemed empty and desolate, but now the ruins felt different, somehow haunted. On each dive, Carol found herself looking over her shoulder, expecting Barbara or one of the others to swim up to her, to protest what she was doing. Archeology was, and had always been, a kind of grave robbing.

"You're thinking about them," Alan said softly.

She breathed heavily. How long they'd been standing there, silently staring at the water, she couldn't say; the sea was an endless blue void that paid no attention to the passing of time. "Aren't you?"

He nodded at his slung arm. "I was wondering how long until I can get back in the water."

"The doctor said it would be another week of so, didn't he?"

"You could be finished down there by then."

"It will never be finished," she told him, her eyes still on the waves, transfixed. "And the money Hays gave us will be gone in another year."

"What then?"

Carol opened her mouth to speak, then stopped herself, realizing she hadn't given the matter any thought. "Then," she said at last, "we go live with my grandmother in Tokyo and get some nice *Yakuza* to bankroll another expedition."

"A nice who?"

"*Yakuza*," Carol smiled slyly, holding back laughter; the *Yakuza* were the Japanese Mafia. "You'll like 'em."

Alan gave his head a resigned shake. "I've got to learn Japanese."

Carol looked away from the ocean, her eyes moving to the handsome features of his face; his eyes, his nose, his lips. He was incredible. She found herself wondering if her father ever looked at her mother this way, if he'd ever found this completeness standing next to her; if he had, the man never let on.

A stray lock of Alan's hair blew in the ocean breeze. She reached up and ran it between her fingers.

"I'll never make that mistake again."

"What mistake?" Alan asked.

Carol blushed, realizing she'd muttered her thoughts aloud. "Not telling you how I feel about you."

Alan kissed her forehead, held her close to him. In the serenity of that moment, Carol Miyagi realized she'd finally found what she'd been searching for her entire life, and, next to that, the majesty of Atlantis paled.

•••

Colonial Bay had been a poor substitute for Poseidon, and, while this sandy atoll provided only modest shelter, it was, for the moment, unknown to the world of Man. Christine DeParle glanced up at the stars, amazed by their vast numbers. It was beautiful, awe-inspiring, and she felt closer to her gods than ever before.

She laid on the beach, listened to the gentle music of the surf. From time to time, she would look around at her fellow exiles, would wonder fleetingly what thoughts crossed their minds. Christine wished she possessed Karl's gift for words, wished she could make some grand pronouncement that the coming dawn would bring with it a new day for them all, but she would let the view speak for itself.

Jason held her close; she welcomed his arms around her, welcomed their comfort against the loneliness of the night. Two youngsters crawled along the water's edge, their tails drawing long lines in the wet silt. She rubbed the crest of her swollen stomach, felt the child stir within, and smiled at the sky.

"Beautiful," Jason said, stroking Christine's dorsal fin with an awkward tenderness, and it took her a moment to realize he wasn't speaking of the stars.

"Am I?"

"You certainly are."

Christine shook her head. She didn't believe it, just as she didn't believe they were really safe. They'd bought themselves some time, that was all. How long before humankind reached out across the open sea, before Zeus met Poseidon and began the slaughter anew? Would it be within her daughter's lifetime, her grandchildren's lifetime? She looked over at her own mother, wondering if Barbara and Ed DeParle had the same fears back in Colonial Bay.

Karl was right, a war was inevitable.

Christine snuggled closer to Jason, her eyes scanning the heavens, imagining a time when Man would be as numerous as the stars above.

It will happen, she warned herself, *just not today*.

•••

Days crawled into weeks, and weeks dragged into months. The FBI put Earl up in a ritzy Concord hotel — every morning, a fully stocked mini-fridge, every night, chocolates on his pillow. They let him workout in the gym, swim in the pool, and eat the finest carryout, but he couldn't make a single phone call, nor could he leave without armed escort. Those fieldtrips were few and far between, reserved solely for his testimony.

He'd told the story so many times now that he could recite it in a dead slumber; who knows, as often as he had the nightmares, maybe he did. But it was always just that: a story. Even when his hand was pressed against the Bible, his words never told the whole and complete truth. But his answers were consistent, and that was all anyone seemed to care about.

The door opened and Earl sat bolt upright on his bed, his hand reaching for a holster that wasn't there.

A white man in a black business suit entered, but different from the other business-suited men before him; he was older, silver-haired, an American flag pinned to his lapel. Under his arm, he carried a thick manila envelope.

"My name is Patrick Tate," the man said. "I'm with Homeland Security, and I served with your father in the Gulf."

Earl said nothing; he didn't know if it was true or not, but he'd grown tired of these suits trying to be his buddy.

Tate slid a chair over and sat down. "To get right to the point, Officer Preston, we're concerned about a possible threat to our national security."

Earl snickered. "Aren't you always?"

Tate frowned. "Let me be blunt. These creatures you fought... they were quite extraordinary, but there's more, isn't there? Something you're unwilling to put on record? Afraid the truth might make you sound crazy, am I right?"

They locked eyes for a moment; Earl said nothing.

"Let's just say that we might have the same concerns." Tate opened the folder in his hands; he pulled out an 8x10 glossy and passed it to Earl. "This is one of the drawings you found."

Earl gave the photo a cursory glance, it was the bloody wall of the *FantaSea*.

"I'm sure you've heard of crop circles?"

Earl frowned, remembering Miyagi's alien theories. "What about 'em?"

Tate pulled out a second photo. "This shape appeared near a British military instillation one week before the Colonial Bay incident."

Earl took this new picture, compared it to the first; the symbols

— one scrawled in blood, the other grain — were identical.

Tate took another 8x10 from his folder. "Now *this* shape appeared in an Indiana cornfield, not far from where the Hays boy attended college."

Earl studied it. Stalks had been twisted, flattened, creating the negative shape of a lightning bolt in the green field; like the tridents, it was imprisoned by a thin hoop.

"The local media thought that one was the work of high school kids, there's a football team called 'The Flashes.'" Tate brought out yet another photo. "But, one week later, the same design appeared in a Kansas wheatfield, ten miles from one of our nuclear silos, identical in size and shape."

Earl returned the photos to Tate. "You think these are signals? To who? For what?"

Tate slid the materials back into his folder. "We don't know. But, given their proximity to military targets, not knowing is...troublesome."

"So what do you want from me?"

"You followed the trident symbol to Colonial Bay and Roger Hays." Tate stood and tucked the folder back under his arm. "Now, I'd like you to put those detective skills to work for me."

Earl sighed; he glanced around his hotel room, the same four walls he'd stared at for months, then returned his eyes to Tate. "If it means getting out of this cell, you got yourself a deal."

•••

Some said the "D" in D Block stood for Damnation. The guards led Dante "The Horror Show" Vianello toward his new home; a hole that New Hampshire had dug for its worst offenders. One of the officers unlocked his manacles, and the other gave him a forceful push into the cell.

"Here's your new roomy, Preacher," said the guard with the keys.

The bars slid closed with a loud metallic clang.

Horror Show rubbed his wrists, then turned and blew his jailers a kiss. The guard who pushed him flipped the bird as they walked away, leaving the hitman to his dimly lit accommodations. He took a step toward the bunks, his eyes never leaving the cinder-block walls and the artwork that covered them.

There were drawings of mountains, of pyramids, of people marching toward the bright light of dawn. Writing framed each sketch, volumes of it, as if an author were composing a novel upon the brick, then illustrating it. Horror Show moved closer to the mural, tried to read what had been etched there; he didn't recognize the language.

"Gibberish," he told the wall.

"*Sanskrit*," a voice corrected.

Horror Show turned. A silhouette stood in the gloom; the man had been so silent, so still, that he hadn't even registered. "Preacher?"

"That's what they call me," the man murmured. "And you must be the one they call The Horror Show."

"You draw this crap?"

"That 'crap' is The Return, The Second Coming."

Great! I'm trapped in here with a born again wacko.

"You blew up a town," Preacher said. "You killed thousands of people."

"Save your sermon, padre. I've killed plenty, but there were no *people* in that town."

"No." The man was still in shadow, but there was a smile in his voice. "They were sea monsters, am I right?"

"Is that how I got this cell assignment? Bunk the crazies together?"

"It's fate that brought you here to me."

"Don't flatter yourself, Reverend. It was a nigger, the damn Patriot Act, and a federal judge that got me here. There was nothing miraculous about it."

"Lights out," guards trumpeted from somewhere down the cellblock.

The hitman walked over to the metal gate and gave it a shake. "Anybody ever bust outta here?"

"Have faith." Preacher reached out to clutch his shoulder, offering consolation. "When the time comes, we'll leave together."

Horror Show moved his eyes to the man's hand and found the

hairy claw of an animal; he spun around, flattened himself against the bars, his eyes wide with shock and revulsion.

"The gods brought you to me." Preacher came into the light, a snarling beast that was neither wolf nor man. "And when the time comes, you will help me do their work."

The lights went out on D Block.

For the first time in his life, Horror Show screamed.

NOTES AND ACKNOWLEDGMENTS

I believe that even Fantasy and Horror need a foundation in reality. To bring as much realism as possible to this project, I drew on the education and talents of many marine scientists and biologists — particularly the writings of Jeffrey S. Levinton, Menico Torchio, and Charles Darwin; as well as conversations with Bruce Robinson, of the Monterey Bay Aquarium Research Institute in California; A. Peter Klimley, of the University of California at Davis; Dr. John Music and Ken Goldman, of the Virginia Institute of Marine Science; and the staff of the Waters Pavilion at the Indianapolis Zoo. It was through my discussions with them that I was able to breathe life into Poseidon's children.

•••

And thanks to: my family, especially my wife, Stephanie, and my sons, fellow Horror movie fans Kyle and Ryan, for their never-ending love and support; Susan Christophersen, for editing my first draft; Amanda DeBord, for whipping the final version into shape; Stephen Zimmer and the entire staff at Seventh Star Press, for making this series a reality; Matthew Perry for his always amazing cover art and illustrations; the United States Coast Guard, the New Hampshire Fish and Game Department, and the Indianapolis Fire and Police Departments (particularly Video Technician Doug Baker), for their vital knowledge, advice, and input; my pre-readers: Dione Ashwill, Maurice Broaddus, Rodney Carlstrom, Nikki Howard, Sara Larson, David Lichty, Marlys Pearson, Natalie Phillips, Glenn Sheldon, Melinda Thielbar, and Chris Vygmont, for putting up with all my emails and for giving me their honest opinions; all the Indiana Horror Writers; and, of course, my faithful readers everywhere.

ABOUT THE AUTHOR

Michael West is the critically-acclaimed author of *Cinema of Shadows*, *Skull Full of Kisses*, and *The Wide Game*. He lives and works in the Indianapolis area with his wife, their two children, their bird, Rodan, and turtle, Gamera.

He loves to walk on the beach, but he still doesn't think it's safe to go back in the water.

Check out the following pages to see more from

All Seventh Star Press titles available in print and an array of
specially priced eBook formats.

Visit www.seventhstarpress.com for further information.

Connect with Seventh Star Press at:
www.seventhstarpress.com
seventhstarpress.blogspot.com
www.facebook.com/seventhstarpress

Now Available from Seventh Star Press, Michael West's newest Harmony, Indiana novel, featuring illustrations and cover art by acclaimed artist Matthew Perry!

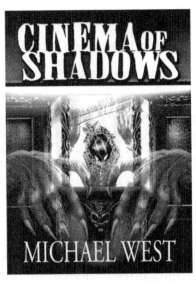

Trade Paperback ISBN: 9780983740209
eBook ISBN: 9780983740216

Welcome to the Woodfield Movie Palace.

The night the Titanic sank, it opened for business... and its builder died in his chair. In the 1950s, there was a fire; a balcony full of people burned to death. And years later, when it became the scene of one of Harmony, Indiana's most notorious murders, it closed for good. Abandoned, sealed, locked up tight...until now.

Tonight, Professor Geoffrey Burke and his Parapsychology students have come to the Woodfield in search of evidence, hoping to find irrefutable proof of a haunting. Instead, they will discover that, in this theater, the terrors are not confined to the screen.

Now Available from Seventh Star Press, H. David Blalock's newest urban fantasy, featuring illustrations and cover art by fantasy artist Matthew Perry!

Trade Paperback ISBN: 9780983740230
eBook ISBN: 9780983740285

Why do bad things happen to good people? Simple. In the ancient war between the Angels of Light and Darkness, the Dark won. Now it is the job of an undercover force simply known as The Army to rectify that.

Using every tool available, The Army has worked to liberate our world from The Enemy for thousands of years, slowly and painfully lifting Mankind out of the dark. On the front of the great Conflict are the Angelkillers, veterans of the fight with centuries of experience.

Jonah Mason is an Angelkiller, and his cell is targeted as part of plot to unseat a very powerful Minion of The Enemy. Mason and his troop are drawn into a battle that stretches from real-time to virtual reality and back. The Conflict is about to expand into cyberspace, and if Mason is unable to stop it, The Enemy will have gained dominion over yet another realm.

Epic Urban Fantasy-The Rising Dawn Saga

A shadow falls across the world, and realms beyond, as a war that has raged since the dawn of time itself draws closer to a decisive clash. As groups aligned with a movement called The Convergence speed up their efforts to bring about a global economic and legal order, resistance mounts after the host of a syndicated radio show, Benedict Darwin, discovers the true nature of a virtual reality device that has come into his possession. The Rising Dawn Saga will take you into mythical, supernatural realms as it unfolds, as the most unlikely of individuals rise to confront powers that have existed since before the world began.

Book One: The Exodus Gate
ISBN: 978-0615267470

"With The Exodus Gate author Stephen Zimmer sets the stage for an adventurous new science fiction fantasy series that is sure to entertain the reader from beginning to end. Zimmer has weaved a tale of fantastic realms populated with exotic creatures. Keep a sharp eye out for this new series."
                                                    -Mark Randell, Yellow30 Sci-Fi

"…a book that Fantasy Book Review recommends for lovers of thoughtful-fantasy. It is also a book with an ending that is near-prophetic, written as it was before the world's economic meltdown."
                                                    -Fantasy Book Review

Book Two: The Storm Guardians
ISBN: 978-0982565636

"This novel transports me from my bedroom to the edge of an upcoming storm — a battle to be fought by incredible villains and noble heroes of all forms. I love Zimmer's imagination, as each of his creatures play a pivotal role in the bigger picture. Unfortunately, for every auspicious being there is an ominous beast lurking in the shadows. Zimmer's weave of fantasy and religious fables leaves the reader sated"
                                                    -Bitten By Books

"The scope of The Storm Guardians is massive, opening up and expanding on the conflict only hinted at in The Exodus Gate. The intrigue and action promised in the first book is fully developed and mercilessly exhibited. The Storm Guardians is a non-stop thriller that lives up to the promise of The Exodus Gate and points at an even more amazing denouement in the final book of the series. Once again, Zimmer has used his command of cinematic imagery to give us a spectacular vision of war both heavenly and hellish. Two thumbs up on this one."
                                                    -Pure Reason Book Review

Book Three: The Seventh Throne
ISBN: 978-0983740247

NOW AVAILABLE!